Lay Siege to Heaven

Lay Siege To Heaven

A Novel about
Saint Catherine of Siena

by
Louis de Wohl

IGNATIUS PRESS   SAN FRANCISCO

First edition published by
J. B. Lippincott Company
Philadelphia and New York

Cover by Christopher J. Pelicano

Reprinted with permission of Curtis Brown, Ltd.
ISBN 978–0–89870–381–8
Library of Congress catalogue number 91–72758
Printed in the United States of America

"I saw how the Bride of Christ can give life, having in herself such vital force that no one can stay her; I saw that she shed forth strength and light, and that no one can deprive her of it; and I saw that her fruit never diminishes, ever increases."

"What then is my nature? Fire is my nature."
Saint Catherine of Siena

Book One

Chapter One

VESPERS WERE OVER, and a thin stream of worshippers came trickling out of the cool twilight of Saint Dominic's into the afternoon sun.

"Now then," Mona Lapa Benincasa said energetically, "come along, my girl, keep your head up and your eyes down, watch your movements and don't slouch."

The girl at her side was very young, and her mother's strong-boned frame made her appear even thinner than she was. Gathering up their long robes, they descended the stairs to the street.

"*Bella*", said a youth in a yellow doublet with hose to match, just loud enough to be heard. "Pretty one". He grinned admiringly and laid his hand on his heart.

The girl pressed her lips together. Her mother gave the youth a withering look. "Some people's parents are to be pitied", she said. "Such manners!"

"It's that horrid stuff you put on my cheeks, Mother", the girl murmured when they were out of earshot.

Mona Lapa sniffed. "It wasn't done in my time, but now that they're all doing it, why shouldn't you?"

"That boy was just having his little joke, anyway", the girl said with a shrug. "I shall never be pretty."

"I've seen worse looking girls who got good husbands", her mother retorted. "You're small, but that's better than being too tall. A man hates having to look up to a girl. *Good* evening, Messer Nanni . . . "

The large man dressed in brown velvet, with a magnificent golden chain around his sturdy neck, gave a rather perfunctory salute and waddled on, deep in thought.

"A scoundrel," Mona Lapa said, "but how rich he is; a

banking house, silk, jewelery—ah, well, may the good God be as patient with him as he is with his debtors. Two of them were put into the tower last week. But he was looking at your hair, Catherine, did you notice?"

"No, Mother."

"I'm glad I made you take those sunbaths on the roof. The sun has done your hair good."

They had to press their backs to the wall to let a few heavily laden donkeys pass by.

"Father Montucci preached the other day against women who don't mind roasting their brains on the roof as long as the sun will bleach their hair", Catherine said with a half smile.

"*He* doesn't have to marry off any daughters", her mother said acidly. "It isn't brains that makes a girl desirable. And your hair is nice."

They reached the Campo, Siena's pride and the place where the three *tèrzos* of the town converged, the Tèrzo di Città, San Martino, and Camollia. In the form of a wide-open fan, a rose-colored fan, the biggest in the world, its handle was the town hall, rose-colored too and shimmery and gilded, with many portals and gracefully rounded windows, with deep dungeons below and proud battlements on top. But the pride of the town hall was the Mangia tower, with its slender, rose-colored stem blossoming forth into a white flower so high up that it could be seen from afar long before the town itself came into view.

This was the center of the world. Here, on six days of the week, was the great market where could be found meat and poultry and fish, vegetables, fruit and cheese, wine, flowers and even rare spices worth their weight in gold. Here also was the assembly place for political meetings.

In the town hall laws were thought up, debated, and proclaimed, the laws of a free city, owing filial obedience to the Pope (who was far away in Avignon), respect to the Emperor (who was far away in Prague), but allegiance to nobody.

And here in the Campo the *Pálio* took place, the great race on Assumption Day, when all the *contradas,* the districts of the three *tèrzos,* sent their best runners to compete for the great banner of the Blessed Virgin, and all Siena perched on specially built seats to watch with bets running up to thousands of golden florins and the air full of screams of triumph and defeat.

But at present the Campo was almost empty. The two municipal guards at the main entrance of the town hall were chatting with each other drowsily as the two women crossed over to the maze of narrow streets.

"Where are we going, Mother?" Catherine asked. "This isn't the way home. We should have—"

"*Ahimè!*" Mona Lapa interrupted impatiently. "Why is it that the chick always wants to know better than the hen! You come along. I knew Siena like my own kitchen twenty years before you were born."

The street of the leather-workers had its own peculiar smell, and Catherine wrinkled her nose.

"That large shop on the right belongs to the Morini family", Mona Lapa said casually. "Very respectable people. Your father has a high opinion of them. If somebody should be in the doorway, I want you to bow a little and smile, do you hear?"

"Yes, Mother."

As they approached they saw two people in the doorway. A woman in her forties, well dressed and with an air of cheerful indifference, was talking to a young man with his back to them. He was wearing a doublet of green cloth, trimmed with squirrel fur.

"Mona Favolina Morini", Mona Lapa muttered, "and her only boy, Sandro. He used to come and play with your brothers when they were children. Don't you remember him?"

"No, Mother."

The young man turned round. He was dark-eyed, dark-haired, and as handsome as a prince.

"Good evening, Mona Favolina", Mona Lapa said. "Good evening, Messer Sandro."

There were greetings and smiles, all curiously artificial. Catherine remembered just in time to smile too when her mother presented her.

"Oh, but what a lovely girl", Mona Favolina said in a high-pitched voice. "Quite lovely. A little on the slim side, perhaps . . . "

"She's strong, though", Mona Lapa retorted. "Many a time she's gone up those stairs of our house with a full donkey's load of cloth on her back; isn't that so, Catherine?"

"Yes, Mother."

The two mothers began to exchange the courtesies prescribed by custom. "Won't you come in, Mona Lapa?"

"Oh, no, thank you, you're most kind, but . . . "

"Surely a little wine and cake . . . "

"No, really, we mustn't, Mona Favolina. Your husband is well, I hope?"

"In excellent health, thank you so much for enquiring. And Ser Giacomo is well, too?"

"Always the same, thank the Madonna for that, and more work to do than ever. . . . "

Sandro Morini said pleasantly, "You have grown up."

Catherine said, "It is the fate of many children", and they both laughed, but only a little and guardedly.

"Now we really must go", Mona Lapa said. "My respects to your husband, Mona Favolina. Good-bye, Messer Sandro. What a charming young man, Mona Favolina! Come, Catherine, we mustn't be late."

All along the street of the leather-workers Mona Lapa remained silent. Only when they had passed the little fountain at the end, she said, "You did quite well, my little one."

"What do you mean, Mother?"

Mona Lapa patted her on the shoulder. "You'll see, my girl. He's a good boy and handsome. I can't say I approve of the fur on his doublet, one shouldn't try to ape the nobles, it was punishable not so long ago, but nowadays the young bloods will do that kind of thing, and the nobles are no longer what they used to be, so I suppose it doesn't matter much. Anyway, he'll have other things to think about once you're married."

"Mother! You don't think . . . you don't mean . . . "

"Come on girl, and keep your voice down; there are two old hags watching us."

Catherine's cheeks were glowing under her makeup. "You were jesting, Mother, weren't you? Why, Ser Sandro wouldn't dream of marrying me . . . "

"Never mind his dreams", her mother said placidly. "The Morinis are sound people and not given to dreaming. Neither are the Benincasas. This was a First Visit, and one can't be quite sure, but your father has agreed with me that it would be a suitable match, and there have been talks between him and Ser Angelo Morini. Mona Favolina is still giving herself airs; she's always been a great one for that, but it should be all right. And why not? You're both the right age and—"

"Mother, you can't mean it. I . . . I don't want to . . . "

"Be quiet." Mona Lapa looked over her shoulder. The two old women had disappeared. No one was in sight, except for a few urchins playing in the mud. She stopped. "Now listen," she said, "you wouldn't marry Francesco Naldi, and your father and I didn't insist on it, because he was thirty years older than you and that mightn't have been good for your children. We didn't encourage Ser Giovanni Barola because he has no standing and no money; we didn't even tell you about it. But there is nothing at all wrong with Sandro Morini, and I hope he will marry you and so does your father. Now then!" It was the tone of voice that usually settled all arguments in the Benincasa family, and no further word was spoken on the way home.

The house of the Benincasa family in the Via dei Tintori, the street of the dyers, was a little world by itself. On the ground floor Ser Giacomo Benincasa ruled supreme in his workshop, with his three sons Bartolomeo, Orlando and Stefano, two journeymen and two apprentices. Here all was barrels, vats, and mortars of many sizes, with drying lines crisscrossing the fairly low ceiling. A staircase, steep and broad, led to the upper floor, Mona Lapa's realm, with the bedrooms and the kitchen, bright with copper pans and casseroles, with pewter pots, earthen

13

vessels, and jars stacked up on triple ledges, and with the long table, at which everybody in the house assembled for meals.

It was a large house, and it needed to be. At present only eleven people were living there, but there had been times when it held almost double that number. Mona Lapa had given birth to twenty-four children in twenty years, of whom thirteen had survived, an unusually high number as the family physician, Ser Girolamo Vespetti justly declared, and due, next to his skill, to the care Mona Lapa had given them, despite her continuous pregnancies. But now all of the surviving daughters except Catherine, the youngest, and some of the sons were married and had set up houses of their own. Many of them had children of their own. Not yet fifteen, Catherine was an aunt a dozen times over.

In the workshop the journeymen and apprentices were busy stacking up piles of cloth of a brilliant sea-green color. Ser Giacomo Benincasa watched them. He was a small man, with greying hair and the sallow complexion of a man who does not get enough fresh air, but his features were finely cut, the features of an artist rather than an artisan. "Stop", he ordered suddenly. "Let me see the next one."

Both Bartolomeo and Orlando stiffened. The father alone prepared the exact color shade for all the more important orders, but it sometimes happened that he was dissatisfied with his own work when he saw it finished, and in such a case he was quite capable of starting all over again, a waste of days of work, as no one but he himself could see the difference.

Giacomo Benincasa took the cloth an apprentice handed him, inspected it closely, and rubbed it with expert fingers. "Just right", he said, and his sons grinned with relief. He looked at them sternly. "I know what you're thinking", he went on, returning the cloth to the apprentice. "But this is for the new liveries of the Salimbeni servants, and nothing but the best is good enough for the Salimbeni. They gave me my first big order when business was as bad as it could be. I won't forget that, and I won't have you forget it either."

Bartolomeo nodded. "You've told us that before, Father. It was just after the year of the great—"

"Yes, yes", Giacomo Benincasa interrupted hastily. "Better not say the word, Son. It isn't lucky. Yes, that was when they helped me, and may God bless them for the great noblemen they are. Most of the people nowadays will offer you help only when you don't need it. I don't mean the government people, of course", he added with a glance at the bench where the journeymen were still folding and piling up the green cloth.

Siena had a government of commoners; the nobility was excluded from holding office of any kind, and it was not advisable to say anything that could be regarded as criticism of the powerful men in the town hall on the Campo.

A youth of sixteen entered, clear-eyed, with a shock of unruly brown hair. "Mother and Catherine are back, Father."

"Thank you, Stefano. I'll go and see your mother. Tomorrow morning at nine o'clock you will take the cart and deliver the cloth to the Palazzo Salimbeni. With my humble respects. Don't wait for payment; they always send their own clerk."

"Yes, Father."

"Now, you can help Orlando mix the blues for the tunics of the municipal guards. I'll be back soon."

When the door had closed behind Ser Giacomo, Stefano turned to Bartolomeo. "I think it's been a success", he whispered.

"What?"

"The First Visit. Catherine. Sandro Morini."

"I'll believe that when it happens", Bartolomeo muttered. He was a slow, meticulous young man, strong-boned like his mother, but quiet and given to fits of brooding. "The Morinis are a haughty bunch."

The three brothers were huddling together. This kind of thing must not be overheard by the journeymen and apprentices.

"It's about time the girl marries", Orlando said. "She's moping a bit, I think. Don't know why."

"Girls often do at her age", Stefano stated owlishly.

Bartolomeo smiled a little. Orlando laughed outright. "Bartolomeo is right, you know", he said. "A First Visit is a First Visit and no more. The Morinis may respond, and then maybe they won't. That's exactly why First Visits are kept so casual—so it's no insult if the matter goes no further. Still, if I know anything about Mother, she wouldn't go even that far unless she had the ground well prepared."

"You'd better start mixing those blues", Bartolomeo warned. "Father will be back soon. Leave the marrying business to Mother. She knows all about it. After all, she's already married off five daughters."

Chapter Two

THE MULE CART was laden with the cloth, and Stefano had taken his place in the driver's seat, when Catherine came racing out of the door. "Take me with you, please", she said breathlessly.

"What? To the Palazzo Salimbeni?"

"Of course not. Drop me at Saint Dominic's. It's on your way. And when you come back, you can pick me up again."

"All right, climb in." He grinned at her mischievously, as she settled down beside him. "Going to confession, eh?"

"That's not your business."

He smacked his lips, and the mule began to move and fell into a trot. "What have you got to confess, I wonder", he said. "You only went last week, didn't you? What have you done, little one? You don't look at boys the way I look at girls . . . when they're worth it. As for Sandro Morini, you can't have seen enough of him for any need to . . . "

"I don't want to listen to such talk."

"Oh, come, there's nothing to it. We're all human. Sandro is a handsome enough fellow, of course, so it would be quite understandable if you . . . what are you doing?"

Catherine leaped to her feet. Without a moment's hesitation she jumped off the moving cart.

Stefano tugged at the reins, bringing the mule to a standstill. "Come back, little one", he cried. "Don't be a fool. You can't run around in the streets alone. You're no longer a child. What will people think?"

"I don't care. I told you I wouldn't listen to such talk." She walked on grimly, her eyes burning, her hands clenched into fists.

"All right, all right, I'll be good as gold", Stefano said

hastily. If Mother were to hear about this, there would be hell to pay. "Come back, Catherine. I didn't mean it. . . . "

She turned, walked back, and climbed up to her seat again.

Stefano gave a slight snap of the whip, and the cart moved on with a jerk. "Peace?" he asked.

"Peace."

"Then suppose you tell me what you want to do at Saint Dominic's at this time of the day?"

"I'm going to see Fra Tommaso."

"Your confessor! There you are . . . "

" . . . but I'm not going to confession."

"Oh, well, if it's a secret, I won't ask any more questions", he said with a touch of sulkiness. "Anyway, I don't understand how you could ever have him as a confessor. Why, he lived at our house for years and years until they sent him to the Dominican college. I have the bedroom he used to have! I couldn't go and confess my sins to somebody who knows me that well."

"I wish he knew me better", Catherine said tersely. "I wish he knew me as well as God does. Then he could . . . " She broke off. They had reached the church. "Thank you for the ride", she said and once more jumped off the cart. Stefano saw her race up the stairs as quickly as a squirrel. Crazy, he thought. But in some respects she really was almost as good as a boy. He touched the mule with his whip and drove on toward the Palazzo Salimbeni.

Pugino, the sacristan, listened to Catherine with his head cocked. Then he hunched up his massive shoulders. "Fra Tommaso della Fonte is leaving for Florence", he began ponderously. When he saw the girl's crestfallen expression, he added quickly, "I don't think he has gone yet. I'll see whether I can find him." He waddled off, leaving her alone in the atmosphere of beeswax and stale incense.

After a while Fra Tommaso entered, a young man of twenty-five, with humorous eyes and an obstinate chin. "You caught me just in time, child", he said. "They're saddling my mule this very moment. I've got to go to Florence. You look worried. What's happened?"

"Nothing yet", she said. "And it mustn't happen. It can't."

"What do you mean?"

"Mother wants me to marry."

The young Dominican nodded. "That's understandable. You're a grown-up girl."

"But I can't marry."

"Why not? Who is the boy, anyway?"

"Sandro Morini."

"The son of the leather merchant?"

"Yes."

"And you don't like him?"

"I . . . something in me wants to like him, but I won't let it."

"Why not?"

"Because I *am* married."

There was a pause. "Say that again", Fra Tommaso said. "You are . . . what?"

"I'm . . . I'm a bride."

"My dear child, you don't seem to know what you're talking about. How can you possibly —"

She stamped her foot. "I'm a bride, Fra Tommaso."

The young Dominican was nonplussed. Less than a week ago she had been to confession to him; the sins of a mere child. It was inconceivable that she had started a love affair behind her parents' back. She would not. And she could not even if she tried. Not with Mona Lapa ruling the household of the Benincasa family. "Very well, then", he said dryly. "Whose bride are you?"

"I'm a bride of Christ."

I must not smile, he told himself sternly. If I do, I'll lose her confidence. I must not smile.

He did not smile. He said quite evenly, "Nuns are brides of Christ, Catherine. But you are not a nun."

"No. But I made a vow to our Lord that I would belong to him alone as long as I live."

He frowned. "You never told me that."

She gave him a look of surprise. "Why should I? It's not a sin."

He shook his head. "I didn't mean that you should have told me in confession."

"I haven't told anybody."

"It would have been much better if you had discussed such an idea with me beforehand."

"But you were only a boy."

He stared at her. "I was a boy?" he repeated. "My dear child, when did you take that vow?"

"When I was seven."

He turned away quickly. He managed to master the urge to laugh. He reminded himself that a child of seven was after all a rational being. And she was so serious, so desperately serious. "It was a very rash thing to do, I'm afraid", he said and turned again to face her. "But such a vow is by no means irrevocable. The Church can release you."

"But I don't want to be released", Catherine blurted out.

He looked at her sharply. "Do you want to become a nun, then?"

"I don't know", she replied gravely. "That's just it, don't you see? I don't know whether he wants me to. He hasn't told me yet."

"I see", Fra Tommaso said, amazed.

The sacristan appeared in the door to the *clausura*. "The Reverend Prior says the documents are ready", he said. "And the mule is ready, too."

"I'm coming", Fra Tommaso said. "I'm afraid I must go now, Catherine. But what are we going to do about you?" He smiled good-naturedly. "Perhaps I should have said: What are we going to do about Sandro Morini? Has there been an exchange of visits?"

"Mother and I have passed by their house and . . . "

"Only a First Visit, eh?" Fra Tommaso looked relieved. "Nothing definite yet. For all you know the matter won't go any further."

"Mother thinks it will."

"Does she? Well, well . . . that's awkward, isn't it? And even if she should prove to be wrong, there will always be other young men, so the problem will arise again. We must talk it over when I come back from Florence."

"Perhaps I must elope", Catherine said somberly.

"Elope!"

"Yes. Like Saint Euphrosyne in the book."

Fra Tommaso grinned. He had read the legends of the saints to the Benincasa family on many a winter evening, and Saint Euphrosyne had been Catherine's special favorite: an enterprising girl who left her parents' home, disguised herself as a young man, and joined an order of monks.

"I don't think you could pass for a monk," he said, "and I certainly couldn't advise you to try to join our community here. We'd recognize you at once. Besides, you would have to cut off your nice hair. You wouldn't like *that,* would you?"

The sacristan appeared again in the door. He coughed audibly.

"I must go", Fra Tommaso said hastily. "Well, I hope it won't come to the worst—whatever the worst may be. I'll be back in a few weeks' time. Perhaps we can talk it over again then. Give my respects to your parents. God bless you, child."

Hurrying off, he dodged the sacristan's reproachful look and disappeared in the *clausura.*

Catherine left by the door to the church nave. Kneeling before the tabernacle, she told the Lord as usual exactly how she felt. "I really don't know what to do. Fra Tommaso has been no help at all, as you can see, but it's not his fault, he was in a great hurry. You can stop it all quite easily, really, if only you'd make Sandro Morini feel that I am too small or that he doesn't like the shape of my nose. *His* parents wouldn't force him to marry me because he is a boy and not a wretched girl as I am. Amen", she concluded almost grimly and rose and left the church by the main portal, just in time to see Stefano driving up in his mule cart.

On the way home he told her, starry-eyed, about the splendor of the Palazzo Salimbeni, the tapestries and carpets, the gorgeous attire of the servants. "Nobles aren't what they used to be, they say, and we citizens are in power, but all the same . . . " He was so full of impressions that she did not have to contribute anything to the conversation, which was just as well.

At home, Mona Lapa was waiting for her. "Where have you been?"

"At Saint Dominic's, Mother. Stefano drove me there and came back to fetch me, so don't be angry."

Mona Lapa was flushed with excitement. "You just missed them", she said enigmatically. "But it doesn't matter, this time. What matters is that they were here, both of them. And we are invited to their house next Sunday."

"The . . . the Morinis?"

"Who else? And the very day after the First Visit! We're very pleased, your father and I. Sunday, that's the day after tomorrow. There's no time to get you a new dress, but I had a look at your blue one and it'll do. This afternoon I shall freshen it up nicely, with silver braid. You'll look like a princess. Now I must go and prepare the meal." She walked off to the kitchen.

Stefano grinned at Catherine. "Congratulations", he said. "Now I know why you wanted to see Fra Tommaso. You told him, of course. Well, I thought it would happen. Orlando and Bartolomeo were not so sure."

She fled to her room.

Sitting down on her bed, she tried to think. The thing was no longer a danger on the horizon; it was upon her. Fra Tommaso could not help her; he was on the road to Florence. And the Lord himself had left her prayer unanswered, or rather, he refused to intervene on her behalf. What did that mean? It could *not* mean that he did not want her to belong to him alone. He always responded to love. So it could mean only that she was left to her own devices. Perhaps she would have to elope after all.

Sunday! The day after tomorrow. She must act quickly. On Sunday evening they would proclaim the official engagement, and then there would no longer be a way out, not for a girl from a respectable family. Three things only could follow an official engagement: marriage, death, or scandal. Therefore she would have to act before Sunday.

She began to think how to set about eloping. Where to? It could not possibly be any place in Siena—she would promptly be taken back to her parents. But she had never been anywhere else. And the roads were full of robbers and other dangerous men. It must have been easier, somehow, in Saint Euphrosyne's time. For the life of her she could not remember where the saint had got male clothing from. The story did not seem to have mentioned it at all. Saint Euphrosyne just "put on male clothes".

Stefano was the youngest of her brothers, but even he was taller than she by at least a head, and the idea of trying to wear his clothes was downright ludicrous.

She could try to make them fit, of course, but she was not much of a needlewoman, and besides it would take hours and could not be done in secret. With almost a dozen people in the house someone was bound to find out, and the someone was Mother, more likely than not, Mother who was going to freshen up her blue dress for Sunday evening. Silver braid. Look like a princess . . .

Mother was not given to procrastination, Catherine thought, when she saw the blue dress carefully laid out on her clothes chest, with a small bundle of braid beside it. There was something final about the sight; this was what she would put on, and nothing else. And once she had put it on, all would go as Mother had planned.

She stared at the dress and the braid as if they were enemies. Then she saw something else lying beside the braid, something long and thin and metallic: her mother's large scissors.

Chapter Three

THE SCREAM WAS SO LOUD and piercing that everybody in the house heard it. Down in the workshop the apprentices stopped stirring the vats; the journeymen dropped the freshly mixed bags of blue dye. Bartolomeo, Orlando, and Stefano stared at each other; even their father was sufficiently shaken out of his usual serenity to bang the pestle against the brass mortar and look up, frowning, at the cracked ceiling.

There was another scream, followed by staccato noises, wild and inarticulate, and now the men began to move, as if on command, toward the source of the trouble.

They knew it was Mona Lapa who was screaming. All of them, down to the youngest apprentice, had heard her scream before and more than once, for unlike her husband she believed that an argument was more effective when it was proclaimed as loudly as possible, and she rarely lacked matters to argue about. But this time there was no doubt that the trouble was serious. Perhaps she or somebody else had broken a leg. Or she was being attacked, though it was difficult to imagine anyone in Siena with courage enough to do so.

As they raced up the rickety stairs, the staccato noise began to condense into words.

" . . . punished", Mona Lapa shrieked. "Punished, that's what I am, for having you as a daughter, you brat, you ill-favored goose, you graceless little bit of calamity . . . "

Giacomo Benincasa turned on the stairs. "Go back to work", he told the journeymen and apprentices crowding up behind him. "This is a family matter."

The journeymen shooed the apprentices down the stairs and then followed, not without regret.

"... the only one to bring shame and dishonor on us. Look at you! Just look at you!"

Giacomo Benincasa opened the door to the living room, entered, and stopped short, while his sons peered over his shoulder.

"Madonna!" Stefano ejaculated, horrified. "Have you ever seen anything like it?"

"Giaco", Mona Lapa yelled. "Look what she's done, the crazy one, the mad animal ... *she's cut off all her hair!*"

Benincasa stood quite still, gazing at his daughter. "What a pity", he said sadly. "How could you do such a terrible thing, *figlia mia?*"

"How, indeed!" Lapa howled. Her bony arms akimbo, she thrust forward a belligerent chin. "But I know why she's done it, the miserable wretch. She doesn't want to be like other girls, decent girls who know that the good Lord has made them to be wives and mothers and that they won't be either unless they find a man first who thinks they are attractive. She prefers to stay at home and eat our bread and shirk her duty...."

The pale girl with the closely cropped hair looked up. "I did it because I do *not* want to shirk my duty", she said. Her voice was calm, but her chin was up like her mother's.

"And her hair was her best feature", Mona Lapa groaned. "Saints above, the trouble I had to make it really pretty. For weeks on end I made her lie on the roof to get the sun to bleach it. Every morning I rubbed it with the ointment Mona Rosa gave me — two florins I paid; and *she* cuts it all off. Good Lord in heaven, what have I done to be punished with such a child? Haven't I always done my duty? All my daughters are married except this one, and she must go and mutilate herself. Giaco, don't stand there like a sheepdog; tell her what you think of her!"

"You have done a great wrong, Catherine", Giacomo Benincasa said, and he sighed deeply.

"The Morinis", Mona Lapa cried, flinging up her arms. "Mona Favolina! Sandro! We're supposed to dine with them on Sunday. What are we going to *do*, Giaco? What are we going to tell them? We can't take *that* thing with us, can we? How could we explain this madness? They were as good as engaged. We're going to be the laughingstock of the whole *contrada*. Sandro Morini! Such a fine, good-looking young man . . . "

"I won't marry him, Mother."

"It's he who won't marry you, my girl, not while you look like a scarecrow, and that's exactly what you do now."

"I shall never marry, Mother."

Lapa stamped her foot. "I refuse to listen to such nonsense. It's . . . it's heretical. It's sinful."

The merest hint of a smile appeared and vanished on the pale little face, like summer lightning, very far away. "It was my confessor who suggested to me that I might cut off my hair", Catherine said.

"What?" Mona Lapa made a step forward. "Fra Tommaso? You're lying."

The girl's curiously slanting eyes opened a little wider. "I never lie, Mother."

Mona Lapa opened her mouth to contradict, found that she could not, and said instead, "I shall certainly speak to Fra Tommaso. I'm sure you put him up to it in some way."

"He said it in jest, I think", Catherine said. "He didn't believe I would do it."

"I should say not. Who would, but a demented creature! You're so ugly, I'm ashamed of you. Go away, out of my sight. Go to your room, lest I forget myself and lay my hands on you."

Obediently, the girl turned and began to walk away.

Mona Lapa said between her teeth, "Giaco, what am I going to do with her?" Before her husband could think of an answer, she swung round toward her daughter. "Don't think you've got the better of me", she shouted. "Your hair will grow again, and then we shall get you married, if it's the death of you."

Silently Catherine passed through the door, closing it behind her.

Mona Lapa burst into tears. "Her hair," she sobbed, "her one beauty, masses of it and the color of honey. Oh, it's too much, Giaco. This time I demand that something be done. I demand it, do you hear? You have been much too lenient with her. . . . ”

“Perhaps you’re right”, her husband admitted. “But she is at an age when girls can be difficult. . . . ”

“Nonsense, she passed that long ago. Mother of God, the girl is fifteen! But the trouble I had to make her put on a new dress and to put some makeup on her cheeks . . . ” Her eye fell on the three young men who were still standing in the doorway. “What are *you* doing here?” she snapped. “Have you no work to do, you lazy oafs?”

“Sorry, Mother,” Bartolomeo said with elaborate courtesy, “but you screamed so loud, we were afraid something dreadful had happened to you.”

“Something dreadful will happen to *you* if you don’t disappear this minute”, Mona Lapa retorted.

“So now it’s war”, Orlando said, as they went down the steep stairs. “Mother against Catherine, with poor Father in the middle. Who’s going to win?”

“Mother, of course”, Stefano declared. “She always does. Can you imagine her letting someone else have the last word?”

“Well, I don’t know”, Bartolomeo said thoughtfully. “Catherine can be awfully stubborn.”

“Mother will break her”, Stefano insisted. “But I would like to know what’s come over the girl.”

“Nothing. She’s always been a bit touched, if you ask me”, Orlando said. “It’s a shame, but there it is.”

“I’ve sometimes thought so too,” Bartolomeo admitted, “but most girls are a *little* touched. Occasionally, at least.”

“But why is all this? Why doesn’t she want to marry?” Orlando asked. “Do you have any idea, Stefano?”

But they had reached the workshop where Stefano saw a dozen pairs of ears greedy for gossip. He gave no answer. Father was right—this was a family matter.

Up in the living room Mona Lapa was still in a rage. “The Morinis will never forgive us for this. We can make excuses about Sunday, of course, say Catherine is ill or something like that, but sooner or later they’ll find out. You have no idea how

28

difficult it's been to get the whole matter going. Months and months of effort, all spoiled by a few snips of the scissors."

"But why, Lapa?"

"God knows! Moods. Fancies. What else could it be?"

"She's a very devout girl. Fra Tommaso says—"

"Fra Tommaso is a very young man, Giaco, much younger at twenty-five than Catherine at fifteen. You know him as well as I do. He's lived with us ever since the . . . you know what, when his parents died."

Giacomo Benincasa nodded. He shivered a little. No one in Siena would mention the name of the horrible monster that had come to town in 1348, fourteen years ago, breathing poison and putrefaction. Two-thirds of the population had died, none more than a week after the first symptoms appeared and many within two or three days. Even those whom the monster held in its claws would not utter its name. "*Ahimè, sento il grosso*", they cried, when the first swellings appeared under their armpits and in their groins. When the black vomiting started, they could not speak at all. During that time the Benincasas had taken orphaned little Tommaso della Fonte into their house; one small mouth more didn't matter. And the boy proved to be a blessing: he was good and eager to learn, and later the Dominicans accepted him with joy, so now the Benincasa family had an adopted son who prayed for them at every Mass. But perhaps he really was a little too young for hearing Catherine's confession. Would he know the difference between what a girl thought she had done and the world of real things? Might he not be deceived by a show of piety?

"The girl is brooding," Mona Lapa declared, "and I'm going to cure her of it. There's a very good remedy. Work."

"But she isn't lazy", Benincasa protested. "Whatever she's asked to do, she . . . "

"I know that, and I never said she was lazy. But she's spent far too much time alone, all the time a healthy girl would use for . . . "

" . . . standing in the doorway, making eyes at the boys, and singing little love songs, primping herself for this occasion and that."

She glared at him. "And what's wrong with that, Giaco? It's what all normal girls do; it's the beginning of courtship, and it ends at the altar of the cathedral. It's what I did, and if it hadn't been for that, Giacomo Benincasa wouldn't have paid a First Visit to my parents and in due course asked for their permission to marry their daughter Lapa. The way Catherine is behaving is not normal, it's all wrong, and I am going to cure her, if it's the last thing I do."

"What are you planning?" he asked with a sigh.

"I'm not satisfied with the work of Carmela."

"What has Carmela to do with it?"

"She is not a good servant. Untidy and lazy. Also she eats for three."

"She is a big girl."

"I shall dismiss her. Catherine will do her work."

"Lapa!"

"She'll help me cook the meals for the family, the journeymen, and the apprentices. She'll do all the beds. She'll do all the cleaning. She'll wait on the family and the journeymen and the apprentices at table. She will mend doublets and skirts and clean shoes and stoke the oven, and there will be precious little time left for brooding. What's more, she will have to give up her room."

"But why? Surely—"

"Because that's where she spends hours, building up some silly little world of her own. I first thought of making her sleep in Carmela's little room, but that's no good; it wouldn't change anything. She mustn't be alone, don't you see? So she'll have to put her bed up in Stefano's room."

"He won't like that, Mother, and she—"

"I don't care whether he likes it or not, and I am quite sure she won't like it at all, but that's what I want and they will obey me."

"You are too hard on her, Mother."

"Oh, am I? She's cut off her lovely hair. Why? So that no man will be interested in her. She doesn't want to marry. She wants to stay here, in her parents' house. Well, if she insists on being fed and housed and clothed, she will have to take what she gets, and she will have to make herself useful. Today, after the evening meal, you will tell her and the boys what you have decided."

"What *I* have decided?"

"Of course. You don't want them to think *I* am the head of the family, do you? Come, Giaco, you know I'm right."

"Where are you going, Mother?"

"To tell Carmela she must leave."

"Mother . . . must we do this to Catherine?"

Lapa turned. Her face, dark and taut with anger, softened a little when she saw his anguish. "Dear Papa," she said with good-natured contempt, "don't worry too much. In a month or two she'll give in, I promise you."

Sighing, he went back to the workshop. His thoughts were heavy and would not let him go, and thus the doublets for the municipal guards became at least two shades darker than they should have been. There would be another argument about *that,* with Ser Talani at the town hall. Giacomo Benincasa hated arguments.

Chapter Four

WHEN FRA TOMMASO DELLA FONTE came to see the family about a month later, the young men greeted him with shouts of welcome and dragged him off to Bartolomeo's room. "They're busy in the workshop and in the kitchen", Bartolomeo said. "Here we can talk. Sit down there . . ." He pointed to the only chair. "We have all the room we need on the bed. Where have you been all this time?"

The young Dominican sat down and smoothed the folds of his white robe. "In Florence," he said, "and it's good to be back."

"Florence?" Orlando exclaimed almost with horror. "*Per Bacco!* I'm glad they let you get away alive."

"If they did," Fra Tommaso said, "it had nothing to do with a heathen god. Anyway, we're at peace with Florence again."

"Because we trounced them soundly when they attacked us a year ago", Stefano declared. "The lying, fickle, treacherous braggards . . ."

"Such admirable charity", Fra Tommaso said. "I hope you won't forget to mention it when you go to your next confession. It is shameful for Italian cities to war against each other. *O tempora, O Mores,* as Cicero used to say. Italy was pagan in his day, and many frightful things happened, but at least there were no wars between Italian towns."

"But what were you doing in Florence?" Bartolomeo enquired.

"Don't be so curious, Son," Giacomo Benincasa said, entering. He shook the young friar's hands. "I'm glad to see you back, Father." It always gave him a thrill to address his adopted son as Father. "Mother! Mother! Fra Tommaso is here."

"It's about time, too", Lapa shouted. A moment later she

33

appeared, wiping her hands on a dishcloth. "Welcome, Fra Tommaso. I want to talk to you."

The young Dominican laughed. "I feel as if I were ten again and had been at your honey pots. What have I done now?"

Lapa told him, for the better part of a quarter of an hour.

"Unbelievable", he said, when at last she fell silent. "She cut it all off?"

"There's nothing left on her head but short bristles", Mona Lapa told him grimly. "And she had the impudence to say that you advised her to do it."

Fra Tommaso looked startled. "*Ahimè*", he said. "I remember now that I did suggest it to her, but I wasn't serious, of course. I thought it might distract her from . . . from some fanciful ideas. She had nice hair. It never occurred to me that she would really cut it off."

"You should have known her better", Mona Lapa declared with some vehemence. "Whenever she gets an idea into her silly head, she acts on it."

"And since then you've been treating her as a servant?" Fra Tommaso asked, frowning a little.

"Certainly. And we shall go on doing so till she has come to her senses, *and* until her hair has grown again."

"It doesn't look as if either will happen soon", Stefano said, not without bitterness. "Mother's made her share my room with me, and it's a thorough nuisance."

Fra Tommaso did not look pleased. "Is it? Why?"

"Well, one wants to have one place for oneself", the boy said sullenly. "Besides, she prays all the time."

"How do you know?" the Dominican asked curtly. "Don't you sleep at night?"

"Oh, I sleep all right," Stefano replied, "but whenever I do wake, there she is, kneeling in her corner of the room. One can't sleep kneeling, can one?"

"It has been tried", Fra Tommaso said dryly, and he thought of a few friars he knew.

"Anyway, it's no fun having to spend one's nights in a kind of church or chapel," Stefano complained, "and that's what she's made out of my room. Sometimes I even imagine I can smell incense."

"Now that you're here," Mona Lapa said, "you must stay and have the noon meal with us."

The Dominican seemed to awaken from a reverie. "I'm sorry, Mother dear, but I have no permission to have a meal outside the monastery. I'll keep you company, though. Where is Catherine, by the way?"

"Preparing the table", Mona Lapa said. "You'll see her soon enough, and she isn't a pleasant sight either."

"In the meantime do tell us what you've been doing in Florence", Bartolomeo pleaded.

Fra Tommaso laughed. "The Master General is there," he said, "and we have to report to him from time to time like every other priory."

"Surely it's a great honor that you were chosen to do that", Giacomo Benincasa said. "We are fortunate in our adopted son."

"I was little more than a messenger", Fra Tommaso protested.

From afar came the booming of the Sovrana, the great bell of the dome, the oldest bell in Italy and perhaps in Christendom, announcing the noon hour, and Catherine appeared at the door.

"The meal is ready", she announced.

"Never a minute late", Orlando whispered to his brothers, and Mona Lapa gave him an angry look.

Catherine smiled and bowed to Fra Tommaso, but she disappeared before the Dominican could address her.

The journeymen and apprentices came up noisily from the workshop, and they all trooped to the large room, at once living room, dining room, and kitchen, where the long table was ready for them.

Mona Lapa saw that the girl had quickly set an extra chair for the priest. There were a plate, a spoon, and a goblet for him, too.

Fra Tommaso said a short prayer, and they all sat down.

"Is it true, Bartolomeo, that you are thinking of entering

35

politics?" he asked. The girl was wearing a white kerchief. She had lost weight. There were shadows under her eyes. Not enough food and not enough sleep. She was busy, filling the goblets with coarse, red wine.

"I'm interested in it, Father", Bartolomeo said. "The nobles are trying to regain some of the power they lost. One's got to be careful, or we shall find ourselves back where we were a hundred years ago." He went on talking about the new Council of Twelve, his heavy, melancholy face taut with interest.

The girl moved quickly, her long, slim fingers were deft, and she did not bang the plates on the table, as Carmela used to do. The dishes were nicely arranged, too.

"Not all the nobles are like the Salimbeni," Bartolomeo said, "decent as well as powerful."

"More bread, Catherine", Mona Lapa ordered gruffly.

The girl rushed to bring it. She knelt to pick up her father's napkin and gave it back to him, still kneeling. She rose and began to refill empty goblets all along the table.

"Decent and powerful", Giacomo Benincasa repeated. "It seems to be very difficult to be both."

"I could name some who don't even try", Bartolomeo said hotly.

"No doubt you could," Fra Tommaso said, "but it might be wiser if you didn't." He was watching Catherine out of the corner of his eyes. "Hatred doesn't make for sound sleep", he added. "Neither in private life nor in politics."

"I hate no one", Bartolomeo protested. "Nevertheless . . . " He rambled on about the new Captain of the people who did not seem to be energetic enough, about the insecurity of the roads, due to some minor nobles who had turned highwaymen. "You can't call them anything better, Father."

She serves the apprentices as if they were nobles, the Dominican thought. The boys did not seem to enjoy so much courtesy. The same was true of the journeymen, and even her brothers. They were all embarrassed yet did not want to show it.

"More beans for your father", Mona Lapa demanded. "And my goblet's empty." Her voice was sharp.

A moment ago Benincasa had refused a second helping of beans. Now he refused again. Mother Lapa was deliberately harrying the girl, and the girl was taking it like a lamb. Or was she?

Fra Tommaso was glad when the meal ended. He said another short prayer, and then the men trooped back to the workshop.

"It's always the same thing", Stefano whispered to him. "Exasperating."

"What do you mean?" the Dominican asked in a low voice.

"Catherine, of course. Mother thinks she'll give in. I used to think so myself, but no longer."

Giacomo Benincasa passed by. "Must go down to the shop", he murmured. "So, if you'll excuse me, Father . . . " His eyes were downcast.

"But of course."

Catherine was clearing the table.

"When you've finished this," Mona Lapa said, "go and do the laundry. I want it ready by tomorrow morning. All of it."

"Yes, Mother."

Mona Lapa looked at the Dominican. "Tell her to come to her senses", she said. "The sooner the better." She walked away. Catherine went on clearing the table.

After a while Fra Tommaso said, "How do you stand it, child?"

She stopped, turned and smiled. "It's easy", she said. "I tell myself that they are the Holy Family."

"What?"

"Father is our Lord. Mother is the Blessed Mother of God . . . "

Fra Tommaso bit his lip. Once again he knew that this was not the moment for laughter.

"My brothers are the apostles," Catherine went on, "and the journeymen and the apprentices are the disciples. There is nothing wrong about that, is there, Father? Our Lord did say, 'What you have done to the least of my brethren, you have done unto me.'"

The Dominican nodded. "It is a good idea", he said. "The

Benedictines have a rule that every guest must be received as if he were Christ."

"The Benedictines", Catherine repeated dreamily. "There are so many holy orders, Father. I wonder . . . " She began to stack up the dishes, ready to be washed. "I wish I knew what to do, Father. I always want to make up my mind at once, but in this matter I must wait till I am shown what God wants of me."

"I shouldn't have teased you about cutting off your hair", Fra Tommaso said.

"I am so glad you did. But I'm sure I would have done it in any case. Like Saint Euphrosyne. I couldn't elope, though. She knew where to go, but I didn't."

As he had many a time before, Fra Tommaso felt that he knew less about the way her mind worked than about almost any other mind he knew. There were moments when he thought that Mother Lapa was right and that the girl was merely full of fancies of all kinds. At others . . . He braced himself. "I must go," he said, "and you must do the laundry. Pray that God will show you what he wants of you . . . but then, you'll do that in any case. But I'll add this: I think you don't eat enough. You have served at table, but you haven't eaten anything yourself."

"Neither have you, Father", she said, smiling.

"I must wait for my meal in the monastery. It's the rule."

"My rule", she said, "is still in the making. But I am not very fond of food. Don't worry about me, dear Father, but give me a blessing before you go."

She knelt, and he blessed her and left.

Giacomo Benincasa felt upset. He had a very strong sense of justice, and he felt that Lapa's treatment of the girl was not right. Something must be done about it, but what? No use in talking to Lapa; she was so sure of herself and would only start ranting. Perhaps if he talked it over with the girl herself . . .

He left the workshop and walked up the stairs. Lapa, fortunately, was not in sight.

The door to Stefano's and Catherine's room was closed. He opened it gently.

She was kneeling in her corner of the room, her back to him, and the white dove that was hovering over her head circled and flew out of the window.

For a moment or two he stood immobile. Then he closed the door and slowly walked back.

There were many doves in the Via dei Tintori, Lapa would say. White ones, too, no doubt. Lapa was a very sensible woman.

That same night Catherine fell asleep and had a dream. The venerable figure of an old abbot appeared to her, and she knew with the strange certitude of dreams that he was Saint Benedict. Behind him approached a number of other figures. She recognized Saint Francis of Assisi in his tattered, grey-brown habit, smiling at her, Saint Romuald, Saint Bernardo Tolomei, and finally a magnificent, austere figure, bearded, with deep-set, luminous eyes, and there was no doubt who he was: the father of all Dominicans, the great Spaniard, Saint Dominic. As he approached, she saw him holding out a black-and-white habit to her, and she could hear his voice, clear as a silver bell: "Be of good heart, my daughter; assuredly you will wear this habit." She felt an upsurge of happiness so intense that the delicate web of her dream was torn, and she awoke and knew at once that she had been given the answer she had been waiting for.

It was still dark. She could hear Stefano's regular breathing. Outside, the street of the dyers was as quiet as a tomb. No citizen was allowed to leave the house so early, unless for an important reason, and if carrying a candle of prescribed length . . . not before the great voice of the Sovrana bell had announced that it pleased God to give the town of Siena a new day, just as it had pleased him to give his handmaid Catherine a new life.

She began her thanksgiving.

Chapter Five

BARTOLOMEO CAME DOWN into the workshop. "Family council", he announced to his brothers. He was grinning sheepishly.

"Really?" Stefano asked. "I wonder what Mother wants this time."

"It isn't Mother who asked for it", Bartolomeo told him, and his grin broadened.

"Don't be silly. I know as well as you do that Father always convokes it and Mother really wants it."

"It isn't so this time."

"Stop being so mysterious. What is it all about?"

"Catherine demands it. She's just told me. She's told Father and Mother too. And she's asked me to tell you."

"She *is* crazy", Orlando declared. "I told you so before, didn't I?"

"Crazy or not, I'm going to see the fun. Aren't you?"

"Wouldn't miss it for anything. When is it supposed to be?"

"Now."

"My, the girl is in a hurry."

"I can't help feeling sorry for her", Stefano said. "Whatever it is she wants, Mother's going to crush her."

The process of crushing seemed to be in progress when they entered the living room.

"And let me tell you this", Mona Lapa said vehemently. "It isn't up to you to ask for a family council at all. You are only a girl. You are the youngest of the family. And you are the least useful—"

"Please forgive me, Mother," Catherine interrupted, "but I am well aware of all that. Even so I must speak, and I don't want you to say anything you may well feel sorry about later."

"Is that the respect you owe to your parents?" Mona Lapa asked angrily.

"Because of respect for my parents I have never spoken out before," Catherine replied, "but now it is necessary." She was very pale, but perfectly calm.

Mona Lapa walked over to the ledges on the wall, took down a large copper pan, and threw it clattering on the stove. "I'm not going to listen to such rubbish", she declared. "I've got work to do. Get out of here, all of you."

The men looked at each other.

Catherine stood immobile. "You have thought right to punish me because I would not accept a man to be my husband", she went on. "Now I can tell you that I could not do so because I made a vow to our Lord and to his Blessed Mother that I would never marry, and that vow is binding to me, although I made it when I was only a child. I am no longer a child, and I am telling you that I shall never obey you in this matter."

"We shall see about that", Mona Lapa snapped, looking over her shoulder.

"You should know by now that you cannot persuade me or force me", Catherine said tersely. "It would be easier for you to melt a stone on that stove than to make me change my heart and mind."

No one said anything. Mona Lapa was still staring over her shoulder at Catherine.

"If you wish to keep me here as your servant," Catherine went on, "I will gladly do any work you order me to do. If you want to send me away, so be it. It will alter nothing. For I have a Bridegroom so rich and powerful, he won't let me suffer want. He will provide me with all I need."

At long last Mona Lapa turned round, drawing a deep breath. But before she could say anything, Giacomo Benincasa spoke out with such firmness that mother and sons stared at him in utter surprise.

"My dearest daughter," he said, "may God forbid that we should try to hinder his Will. And there is no doubt to me that this is his Will and not a fancy of yours."

"Giaco . . . "

"Quiet, Lapa", Benincasa said, without raising his voice and without taking his eyes off his daughter. "Keep your vow, Catherine," he went on, "and live as God moves you. None of us will put obstacles in your way again."

Mona Lapa broke into harsh sobs. "Giaco . . . Giaco . . . what are you doing?"

"There is only one thing I want to ask from you," Benincasa continued, "which is that you pray for us that we may be made worthy of the promises of . . . your Bridegroom."

Catherine walked up to him, bent low, and kissed his hand. Then she faced her mother. "Don't cry because of me, Mother", she said gently.

Lapa stood erect, a rigid and formidable figure. She wiped her eyes with the back of her hand. "Come with me", she said in a strangled voice. "You must have your old room back."

It was a small room, with a few stone steps leading up to a single window, and there was no furniture in it, except for a wooden bedstead, a rickety table, a chair, and an old oil lamp.

"Carmela is on her parents' farm near Lecceto", Mona Lapa said. "I shall send for her. Stefano will carry your chest back and your bedding."

"I won't need the bedding, Mother."

Lapa looked at the rough boards. "You can't sleep on that", she said, horrified.

"Oh, yes, Mother, easily. I did in Stefano's room, too. That's why he was always so surprised that my bed was made, no matter when he woke up. It never occurred to him that I always slept on the floor."

"You'll need a pillow for your head, surely. . . . "

"A log of wood will do, Mother."

"But why, why? This is terrible."

"Please, Mother, I must have it my own way."

Lapa was wringing her hands. "What will become of you?" she muttered. "You'll kill yourself. Even nuns have more comfort." Her eyes widened. "Are you . . . are you going to be a nun?"

"I want to join the Dominican Sisters of Penance."

Lapa gasped. "A Mantellata? You? At fifteen?"

"I shall be sixteen on Annunciation Day."

"Child, the youngest of them is twenty years older than you are. They're all old spinsters or widows like your aunt Agnes."

"I shall be a Mantellata, Mother."

"They won't accept you."

"It is God's will", Catherine said evenly. "Will you ask them for me, Mother?"

"What did you answer?" Giacomo Benincasa asked, when his wife told him about it later in the day. They were sitting very close to each other at the long table. The room seemed strangely empty and quiet.

"Nothing", Lapa said. "I ran away. It was the only way I could prevent myself from saying yes, and I couldn't say yes, could I? Now could I? You know what kind of life they lead, poor things. They not only fast on the usual days, but every day in Advent and in Lent and every ordinary Friday as well, meat only on Sundays, Tuesdays, and Thursdays, and they get up twice at night for prayers. . . . "

Benincasa smiled. "Hasn't it occurred to you that she has already been living like that?"

"N-no, it hasn't."

"Do you remember a single day within the last six months when she has eaten meat? And have you seen her eat anything at all, except bread and vegetables and salad these last weeks?"

"That's why she looks so thin and pale. Giaco, we cannot permit it; we mustn't. We have a responsibility."

"I have yet to hear of any Mantellata who died of starvation", Benincasa said. "And, as you said yourself, most of them are old, so it doesn't seem to shorten their lives."

"I don't know what's happened to you, Giaco; you have an answer to everything."

"I often have, Mother. But usually you supply the answers to your own questions before I can give you mine", he said serenely.

"I did so want her to have a good husband and children", Lapa lamented. "Why can't she be like other girls?"

"I wonder whether she ever was like other girls", he mused. "At least since . . . that day . . . "

"What do you mean? What day?"

"Don't you remember? She was only six and on her way home with Stefano . . . "

"Oh, Giaco, I can't even listen to such nonsense. Seeing things . . . and on the Via de Vallepiatta, too."

"Above the church of the Dominicans", Benincasa said in a low voice. "Our Lord on the throne, dressed like a pope, and the apostles Peter, Paul, and John with him. And he blessed her."

"Giaco, you don't believe that! She has always had a lively imagination."

"But she has never lied to us. She is the only one of our children who never lied to us." He rubbed his chin. "She didn't talk about it at first," he said, "but I knew there was something on her mind the moment I saw her. I took her aside and set her on my knee and asked her why she had no confidence in me. Then she told me. I shall never forget her voice, so full of awe."

"I'm sure she believed it herself, Giaco, but what if she did? Do you remember little Rosa Pellicori who thought she saw wild animals in her bedroom and had convulsions . . . "

"I know, Mother, but this was different — or so I think."

"Why should it be different?"

"Because Catherine only saw it once. And because that one experience was strong enough to change her. It was from then on that she began to think and to be serious, yes, and devout."

"Trouble", Lapa said bitterly. "That's what she is. That's what she always has been. No, no, I don't mean it's her fault. It's just a fact. Don't you remember what happened when she was born?"

He shivered. "As if I could ever forget it." Lapa had given birth to twins, two tiny little girls. But Giovanna died a few hours later, and for a while it seemed that Catherine would follow her. And Lapa never had another child.

"I'm an unfortunate woman, Giaco, that's what I am. First little Giovanna died, and now Catherine too wants to die to the world. I might as well not have gone through it all...."

"Mother!" He crossed himself. "You mustn't say such things."

"I can't help it", Lapa said miserably.

"The girl doesn't even have to leave our home", Benincasa reminded her. "The Mantellate aren't nuns, only tertiaries. They don't have convents and either stay alone or with relatives...."

"I know all about them, thank you very much", she snapped. "Now don't say anything, Giaco, let me think. I have an idea..."

Benincasa sighed. He said nothing.

"The girl has had a very dull time", Lapa said after a while. "And she's frail. I'll take her to the hot springs in Vignone. The baths there will help her."

"They are good", Benincasa had to admit. "There's iron in the water and copper and even a little gold and silver, I'm told. But—"

"She needs more strength," Lapa went on quickly, "and who knows, perhaps the springs will flush all that nonsense out of her."

"There is none in her," he said, "but the springs are good, and you may take her there if you wish—and if she agrees."

To his surprise Catherine agreed.

They set out the next day. A week later they returned— Catherine with bandaged arms and shoulders and Lapa strangely subdued. "It's hopeless", she told her husband, when the girl had gone to her room. "I should have known."

"What happened?"

"When she saw the spring... oh, Giaco, it was terrible."

He waited patiently until she controlled herself.

"They have a pool there, where everybody takes the baths; it is very large and the water is cooled. But at one end the

46

spring comes in, boiling and foaming, and she saw it. I think it frightened her. . . . "

"That I do not believe", Benincasa said quietly.

"Well, her eyes went all big and round. Then she waded toward it. The men who are in charge shouted, don't go nearer, stop, stop, but she went nearer till the fumes were all around her. They got her out. She was frightfully scalded all over. How I scolded her! But she simply said, 'It's bound to be much worse in purgatory and in hell. But now I've had a taste of it, and it may be acceptable to God for my sins, so I may be spared worse things.' "

Benincasa nodded silently.

"She's been ill ever since, of course", Lapa went on. "What can one do with such a girl? It is a form of madness, no doubt. I tell you, Giaco, there are moments when I can't believe she's my child. She's mad. How can I ask the Mantellate to take a mad girl? It's hopeless."

"This happened on the first day?"

"Yes. She couldn't bathe again, of course, not with all those burns. She is better now, though this morning she had a headache and her hands and face were hot again. It may be a touch of fever."

It was. Moreover, the fever mounted and a rash broke out.

"I think it's chicken pox", Lapa sighed. "She's the only one of the children who never had it. And they say it's much worse when they get it later. Nothing but trouble with that girl."

Ser Girolamo Vespetti, the physician, was called in and confirmed Lapa's diagnosis. "The patient ought to have a mattress", he said reproachfully, "and some cushions."

Lapa bit her lip. It had taken her the better part of an hour to persuade Catherine that she must have at least a rug and one thin pillow as long as she was ill.

The physician prescribed cold compresses against the fever and a special medication, which he prepared himself. He insisted that a curtain should be drawn across the one window, as sunlight would be bad for the patient's eyes. He did not seem too happy about the girl. "Call me again if the fever gets worse", he said and departed with the boy who was carrying his medicine chest.

The fever seemed to grow neither worse nor better. Lapa stayed with her daughter day and night, changing compresses, fetching drinks of lemon and orange juice and all sorts of tidbits. But Catherine would eat nothing.

"Surely there must be something you would like", Lapa cajoled. "Just tell me what it is, and I'll get it for you, little one."

The girl's cracked lips parted, and she said, almost inaudibly, "I want to be a Mantellata."

"I'll go and see the Prioress", Lapa promised. "I'll go as soon as you're well enough."

The girl made a tremendous effort. "I'm . . . well enough . . . now", she managed to croak.

"No, no, you aren't, but please God you will be soon."

From that hour the fever went down. Even Ser Girolamo Vespetti nodded with satisfaction when he came again. "We're over the worst," he stated, "thanks above all to that medication of mine. It is a little expensive, perhaps, but most effective, as you can see. The pustules will soon begin to dry up, and they will itch."

"I know", Lapa told him.

"Very well. Then don't forget to make it clear to your daughter that she must not scratch, however irritating the itch may be. For if she does, her face will be permanently pitted, and this would greatly diminish her chances of finding a good husband."

To his astonishment the patient's mother threw up her arms, wailing aloud.

"She behaved as if I had told her that her daughter was dying", the physician told his wife afterward.

Lapa went to see the Prioress of the Mantellate of Siena at the large, somber house only a stone's throw from Saint Dominic's, where the Prioress lived with some of the Sisters who had not a home of their own and no relatives who could give them shelter. The Reverend Mother Nera di Gano was a tall, dignified woman with an aquiline profile. Although little more than sixty years old, she walked with a slight stoop. The room in which she received her visitor was furnished with only two chairs. On the wall behind the guest chair—unlike the other chair it was covered with a thin cushion—was a large crucifix.

"A girl of sixteen, you say?" the Prioress asked with a frosty smile. "Out of the question. It is unheard of."

"I have told my daughter that, but she won't believe me."

"Tell her so again, from me, Mona Lapa."

Lapa raced home with the news, steeling herself for a stream of tears and laments. But Catherine smiled. "She will change her mind", she said. "So much that is now a matter of course was unheard of at *some* time. And there is nothing against it in the Rule of the Mantellate. Please, go back to her and tell her so."

"What? I can't go back there again. I don't want her to think that I am crazy too."

"I shall be a Mantellata", Catherine said. "If the Prioress here will not accept me, I must go elsewhere until I find one who will."

Mona Lapa battled on valiantly for a few more hours. Then she went back to the Prioress.

"It is quite true that there is nothing against it in our Rule", the stern lady said with a glint of amusement. "But a girl of sixteen . . . she will change her mind in a few weeks or months."

"I thought so, too," Lapa said, "even when she cut off her hair because she didn't want to marry. . . . "

"Did she do that?" the Prioress asked with interest.

Lapa told her about it at length, and about her daughter's behavior as a servant and at the baths of Vignone. "There", she said breathlessly. "Now I've told you everything. Now tell me that I'm a fool to have come to you about this girl of mine."

After a pause the Prioress asked blandly, "Is she pretty? We had a great deal of trouble over a pretty young widow, nine years ago. It was not her fault at all, poor dear, but I am quite re-solved not to go through all that again. Is your daughter pretty?"

It took Lapa a few moments to recover. Then she said with unusual modesty, "It's not for her mother to say. Perhaps the Reverend Mother would like to see her?"

After a slight hesitation, the Prioress nodded.

Three days later she and two of the Sisters came to the house in the Via dei Tintori. She could hear old Sister Angelina whisper to Sister Palmerina, "This certainly is the first time that we have considered the acceptance of a Sister while she is recovering from chicken pox. One wonders whether our next visit will be to a prospective member of our order while she is cutting her first tooth."

"That prospect", Sister Palmerina replied, "would resemble some of our dear Sisters at least as far as the number of teeth is concerned."

The Prioress wisely pretended to have heard nothing. A few minutes later the three Mantellate entered Catherine's room. They found a slim girl with short-cropped hair, her face still disfigured by a few dried-up pustules, her lips covered with fever scabs. No one could have called her pretty. In fact there seemed little likelihood that she would be pretty under the most favorable circumstances.

Mona Lapa brought chairs for the visitors.

The Prioress began to ask questions.

"Black for humility", Sandro Morini said. "White for purity." His beautifully chiselled lips curled a little, but his eyes were full of warmth and compassion. "So these are your colors now, my poor Catherine. It is hard to believe."

Catherine stared at him, aghast. "What are you doing here?" she asked in a trembling voice. "Who permitted you to enter my room?"

He bowed courteously. "I asked for permission first, of course", he said. "I am a friend of the family, am I not? I asked your parents and my own, too. After all, you're not a nun and you are not a Mantellata . . . yet."

"I shall be, tomorrow. The Prioress—"

"Oh, yes, I know all about that. My poor Catherine, what a life for you! Can you do nothing better with your youth than spend it either alone or in the company of those holy scarecrows?"

"I forbid you to use such language."

"What will you mean to them anyway? They tell me the Prioress accepted you because you gave a few nice humble answers to a few nice but less humble questions . . . "

"They accepted me and . . . "

"Of course they did. Why not? One more victim to share their lives of boredom and monotony. And what do you get in exchange? A beggar's dress. Black for humility, white for purity. You will never be able to stand their kind of life. You're the most vivacious girl I ever met; you're full of fire. I know! That's why I fell in love with you. That's why I wanted to marry you. And you? You made people laugh at me by your refusal."

"I didn't want anyone to laugh at you", Catherine protested.

"Ah, but they did", Sandro Morini said bitterly. "Look at him, they said, he's so unattractive that a girl cuts off her hair rather than marry him. Can it be a good thing you are planning, when it means pain for someone else? And you caused much pain not only to me, but to all your family—especially your poor mother, who gave you life and looked after you. You have constantly offended her, yet when you were ill she nursed you day and night. You are cruel, cruel to those who love you and cruel to yourself."

"I'm not cruel."

"I know it's not your real nature", he said warmly. "I know you so much better than you think, Catherine. Forget all those dreadful illusions; come to your senses. Don't waste your youth and beauty on pale old frumps who will only envy you for them. Forget the beggar's dress. Look what I have brought you."

Only now she saw the parcel with its cover of yellow silk. He unwrapped it eagerly. It contained a robe of gold cloth, set with tiny pearls, a robe for a queen, the most beautiful thing she had ever seen.

"This is the right dress for you", he said, beaming. He swung it before her eyes as the banner of a *contrada* is waved on a feast day. He too was dressed magnificently, with a doublet of green silk, trimmed with squirrel fur and a golden chain around his neck. He was very handsome.

"Why do you think all this beauty exists, if not for us to enjoy it?" he asked gently. "Come, let me see how you look in a robe worthy of you. . . . "

It was the wrong word. Worthy of me, she thought. "Lord, I am not worthy that you should come under my roof, but say the word and my soul shall be healed."

"Take it away", she said, stepping back. "I don't want it, and you can't make me want it."

Sandro Morini stared at her, his handsome face distorted with pain, frustration, and rage.

"In the name of Christ and of his Blessed Mother, *go!*" she cried wildly.

He turned without another word and was gone.

Suddenly she began to wonder whether he had really been there at all and whether he really was Sandro Morini.

But now that he had gone she felt that there was something, there was perhaps even a great deal in what he said. She would have to give up much. Good things . . . blessed things. The life of a healthy young woman, the love and companionship of a husband. Children, to be conceived and born and reared, fresh young souls to be molded and formed for the service of God. And God did not, he could not, hate beauty in whatever form it was expressed. Beautiful things like that robe . . . a beautiful creature like Sandro.

O God, the tempter had not left at all. He was still there, invisible, within her. . . .

With a great cry she threw herself on her knees before the little crucifix on the wall.

Help came at once.

The next day Catherine Benincasa was led into the Chapel

delle Volte in the great church of Saint Dominic's, where Father Montucci clothed her in the white habit, the belt, the white coif, and the black mantle, in the presence of the Prioress and of all the Sisters of Penance.

She looked radiantly beautiful.

Chapter Six

S T. DOMINIC'S NEEDED new sets of altar cloths, and a number of Mantellate volunteered to provide them. They met at the house of the Prioress for the purpose, and Mother Nera di Gano put a room at their disposal. It was winter and grew dark early, so the Prioress put an oil lamp in the middle of a table, and they sat around it like so many large black-and-white moths.

"Seven of us to do all the work", Sister Palmerina said with some bitterness. "I don't know what the Sisters are coming to these days."

"The Reverend Mother is writing", Sister Angelina said.

"I didn't mean her, of course", Sister Palmerina said hastily. "But there are twenty-nine of us, aren't there?"

"Not all are good needlewomen", Sister Angelina reminded her. "Not that I'm very good myself", she added modestly. When no one contradicted she added rather sharply, "One should think that some of the younger Sisters might show a little more interest, though. Sister Mathilda for instance — or Sister Catherine. By the way, is it true that Sister Catherine eats nothing but salad?"

"I wouldn't be surprised", Sister Palmerina declared. "She is very thin, isn't she? She looks consumptive to me."

"She has lost weight", Sister Marcella assented. "Not that she was very robust when she first came to us . . . when was it? Two years ago?"

"Two years and five months." Sister Angelina sniffed a little. "I should know. I had the honor of paying her a visit to see whether or not she was suitable for our order."

"You?"

"Yes. And the Reverend Mother Prioress, of course."

"And I, in case you have forgotten", Sister Palmerina said.

"Oh, yes. Yes, of course. Well, I did tell the Reverend Mother that in my opinion she was much too young and might give us a great deal of trouble, but my advice, as usual, did not prevail."

Sister Alessia's pleasant round face looked up from a piece of intricate embroidery. "I'm so glad", she said gently, and both Sister Giovanna and Sister Francesca giggled over their sewing.

"Oh, I know *you* always think that everything she does is right", Sister Angelina said, sweetly patient. "Perhaps, when you're as old as I am, you'll know better."

"Better in what way?" Sister Alessia asked, working away on the flower pattern of the altar cloth.

"Ambition is both wrong and dangerous", Sister Palmerina said darkly.

The Sisters Alessia, Francesca, and Giovanna exchanged a little smile. They all knew that Sister Palmerina felt she should have been the Prioress instead of Mother Nera di Gano and would have been were it not for the malice of some of the Sisters and the sad lack of recognition she received from those in authority.

"In any case our dear Sister Catherine is overdoing everything", Sister Palmerina said. "There can be no doubt about that. Not only her fasting. The absentmindedness! Kneeling at the altar rail and simply forgetting to get up. I don't wish to imply that she is playacting", she added quickly. "Heaven forbid that I should seem to sit in judgment over her. She may well be quite, quite sincere. . . . "

"She is", Sister Alessia said crisply, sticking her needle into the cloth with some vehemence. "I'll vouch for that."

"I felicitate you, Sister Alessia", Sister Angelina said. "The reading of hearts is not given to many."

Sister Alessia bit her lip. She said nothing.

"Well, she *is* absentminded", Sister Palmerina went on. "Even you must admit that. Many a time I've asked her something and got no answer. She just stares ahead with those huge eyes of hers. But then, perhaps she is a little deaf like our dear Sister

Agnes. Deafness can be a family trait. My nephew, a physician, told me so."

"What did you say about me?" asked Sister Agnes, cupping a gnarled hand to her ear.

"Nothing, dear Sister. I said Sister Catherine might be a little hard of hearing."

"What?" asked Sister Agnes, frowning.

"Hard of hearing", Sister Palmerina repeated with a trace of exasperation.

"You don't have to shout at me", Sister Agnes said.

"I am sorry."

"What?"

"I regret."

"Sister Catherine can hear well enough", Sister Francesca said, lifting her soft little snub nose. "Unless, of course, you insist on addressing her while she's praying."

"The trouble with Sister Catherine", Alessia said, "is that she is as we all ought to be and aren't."

"May I remind you, Sister Alessia, that the idea of our order is Saint Dominic and not Sister Catherine Benincasa", Sister Angelina said stiffly.

"Saint Dominic would be the first to agree with me", Sister Alessia said cheerfully.

"I'm afraid our spiritual father would not agree that the sewing hour should be the occasion for his daughters to chat away like magpies—" The Prioress had a knack of appearing from nowhere. "Especially when such chattering is devoid of charity."

For the rest of the hour silence prevailed.

At the end of it, when the other Mantellate were leaving, Mother Nera di Gano gave Sister Alessia a sign to stay. She waited for a minute or two, till she felt sure there was no one within earshot. Then she said, "You are teaching Sister Catherine to read, I hear. How is she getting on?"

"Not very quickly. These things are much easier to learn when one is a child."

"Why does she wish to learn it? Many of the Sisters cannot read or write."

"She wants to read the Office. They're jealous of her, Reverend Mother."

"I know. It is both natural and sinful. In some ways she is setting up a standard impossible for others to meet."

"They should be glad to have a saint in their midst", Sister Alessia said hotly.

"Hush, child. Only the Church can decide about sanctity and never does before a person's entire life is open to the closest examination. Sister Catherine is nineteen years old and may live to be a very old woman. It is remarks like yours that may give rise to envy and to gossip."

"I am sorry, Reverend Mother."

"You like her, don't you?"

"I'd gladly give my life for her," Sister Alessia said quietly, "and so, I think, would Sister Francesca and Sister Giovanna and perhaps some others."

The Prioress smiled incredulously. "Sister Francesca Gori comes from peasant stock", she said. "Sister Giovanna di Capo's father is a little town official. You are a Saracini; your family's title goes back five hundred years. What is it that attracts you so much to the dyer's daughter?"

"I used to wonder myself," Alessia said, "but not because she comes from a burgher family. One does get accustomed to mixing with them rather freely here in Siena, and in some respects things seem to be topsy-turvy these days, with the burghers enjoying more rights than the nobility. . . . "

"True enough", Mother Nera di Gano said, looking down her nose.

"But Sister Catherine is thirteen years younger than I am", Alessia went on. "When I was nineteen, a woman of thirty-three seemed old to me. With Catherine it's different. She . . . she doesn't seem to be of any age at all."

"Yet you are her teacher."

"Oh, no, no, Reverend Mother. I am trying to show her how to read, and I must be doing very badly or she would make better progress. But it is she who is teaching me . . . and Francesca and Giovanna and the others."

"Is she indeed?" The Prioress' eyes narrowed a little. "And what is she teaching you?"

"Everything she learns from . . ."

"Well? From whom?"

The Saracinis never lacked courage. Sister Alessia looked up. "From our Lord", she said firmly.

After a grim silence, the Prioress asked, "You mean to say, Sister Catherine claims to receive private revelations?"

"She makes no claims," Alessia replied, "but she does receive revelations."

The Prioress sighed deeply. This could be very troublesome. "You know that you're not bound by someone else's private revelations, I take it, Sister Alessia?"

"Yes, Reverend Mother."

"How long have you known about this?"

"I found out a year ago, when you sent me to tell her that Mass was to be an hour earlier, because of the *Pálio.*"

The Prioress nodded. Last year the government had advanced the hour for the start of the race on the Campo, which meant that some of the Sisters could not cross it on their way to church. "Tell me what happened", she ordered.

"Yes, Reverend Mother. She was staying at the house of her parents in the street of the dyers—"

"And she still is. I know that, of course. Come to the point, please. What *happened?*"

"Her mother told me I would find her either in her cell—that's what they call her room—or on the roof. The Benincasas have a little garden on the roof. Well, she was up there, and she was singing away, looking so happy! When she saw me she said, 'We've been singing for a long, long time!' so I asked her, 'Who is we?' and she said, 'Listen! Don't you hear them? They are singing in heaven.' I told her I couldn't hear anything, and she said, 'They don't all sing alike . . . those who have loved God most here on earth have the clearest and loveliest voices, and Mary Magdalen has the most beautiful voice of them all.' "

"And after that surfeit of music", the Prioress said dryly, "she told you about other revelations, I suppose?"

"No, Reverend Mother. But I first saw then that she was . . . that there were things going on around her of which I had known nothing. It was months later she told me about the most important thing of all, the foundation stone."

"I see. And what is that?"

"Self-knowledge. And the three stones into which it is divided: the contemplation of the Creator; the contemplation of our sins, and of the goodness of God in sparing us immediate punishment. Together, these three stones will do away with the root of all evil that is self-love."

"Sister Catherine will be interpreting Sacred Scripture to the Sisters next, I presume", the Prioress said.

"Is there anything wrong in what I have said? In what Sister Catherine said, I mean?" Alessia asked softly.

"N-no, I couldn't say that. Who taught it to her, though?"

"Our Lord himself."

The Prioress stood rigid. "Did she say *that?*" she asked.

"Yes, Reverend Mother."

The Prioress began to walk up and down the room, slowly, controlled even in her agitation. "She is without any experience in such matters", she said. "She may not know that such revelations more often than not have a very different source. The enemy knows better than to teach us falsehood only—if he did, we would recognize him at once for what he is."

"Oh, she knows that quite well", Alessia said. "She says one can always learn how to discern spirits."

"Really? How?"

"She says a vision that comes from our Lord begins by inspiring fear but ends in a feeling of safety. It begins with bitterness but ends in sweetness. But a vision coming from the enemy starts with sweetness and safety and ends in bitterness and terror. She says there is still another sign. A true vision makes one humble, whereas a false vision makes one proud and boastful."

After a pause, the Prioress said, "Father della Fonte may have told her that."

"Oh, no, Reverend Mother. She told Father della Fonte."

"So now we're giving spiritual advice and instruction to priests", the Prioress said. "Better and better. And who instructed Sister Catherine? No, don't tell me. Our Lord, of course." She added, in a casual manner, "Her parents and brothers must be very proud of her."

"I am sure they are," Alessia said, "but not because of these things. They know nothing about them."

"How do you know that?" the Prioress asked quickly.

"Because she told me so. She asked me never to talk to her family about it. 'They would think I've gone crazy', she said. 'At least my mother would, and my brothers. Father would believe me, but he would be very worried. Much better to say nothing at all.' "

"We must be thankful for the smallest mercies, I suppose", the Prioress said. She sat down. "I will hear no more about it, at present", she decided. "And I can only hope Sister Catherine's way of receiving wisdom won't prove to be infectious. I can't think of anything worse than a band of wild-eyed Sisters, each believing in her own knowledge, infused from on high."

"There is little danger of that with me", Sister Alessia said, smiling, "or with any other of the Sisters that I know."

"There is one thing I find most curious, however", the Prioress said, and now she too was smiling — at least, the corners of her mouth rose a little.

"Yes, Reverend Mother?"

"You told me how difficult you find it to teach her to read. Well, if our Blessed Lord can teach her so much spiritual wisdom, why doesn't she ask him to teach her how to read as well?"

Surprisingly, disconcertingly, Sister Alessia beamed. "That's a wonderful idea, Reverend Mother. I shall tell her at once."

The way to the church of Saint Dominic was the way to heaven, and every step was joy, although some of the Sisters worried because she went there with her eyes closed — surely the simplest way to shut off anything that might distract her mind.

Catherine smiled contentedly. Her feet knew the way so well, there was no need to supervise them. *They* were getting nearer with every step, but mind and soul too must get nearer and could do so best when there was no sight to divert their attention. She much preferred to go alone. Some of the Sisters would always try to "help" her by leading her by the arm, and there was no need for that at all. Besides, she had never forgotten what happened when he granted her the first vision. She was only six at the time. The wondrous beauty of it had transfixed her. But little Stefano who had been with her, came running up and shook her arm, and she looked at him and at once heaven was gone. She had cried for hours, afterward. It was then she had first grasped the necessity of being alone with the Lord, alone as often and for as long as possible. The best of all—to be alone with him forever. What else would a girl in love wish for?

She talked to him all the way, until her feet touched the stairs of the church and carried her into his house, and there she opened her eyes, took her place with the Sisters on the left side of the nave, and looked at him, still hidden in the tabernacle and yet not quite hidden to her. Soon now she would see him and receive him.

Father Montucci was saying the Mass.

"*. . . quia peccavi cogitatione, verbo, opere et omissione . . .*"

They did not seem to think of that enough: that God was sinned against not only in thought, word, and action but also by omission, nonaction, by not saying or doing what was right and meet and just, the praise or reproach not given, the help not rendered. What was the sin of the priest and the Levite on the road from Jericho to Jerusalem but a sin of omission, the Samaritan doing what either of them should have done?

Let me never omit anything you want said or done, Lord, never . . .

The Mass rolled on majestically, and the great moment of silence approached, heralding the coming of the King who gave himself to the least, the poorest, the most wretched of his subjects. Less than slaves we are, for after all a master bought his slaves; he did not create them. His things we are, his creatures, yet of his incomprehensible, overwhelming goodness he made us his brothers and sisters, in one wild, terrifying, glorious act of adoption, and here the priest's hands raised him up and he shone, white and radiant, my Lord, my God, my own, all I have and all there is, enough and brimming over. A few moments more and she would rise and go forward to receive him; he was coming down to her, down the altar steps, the newborn babe, the boy in the temple, the crucified One, the risen Lord who had defeated death and ascended to heaven, and he was smiling at her as he entered her whole being, her nothingness that became being only through him, he who is came to her—her who was not, and heaven surrounded her like the waves of the sea and yet not like that at all, and the earth was no more. . . .

"It's that woman again", said the Brother Sacristan irritably. "Go and get her up quickly."

The communion rail was empty but for the small, forlorn figure in black and white. The Mantellate, deep in their prayers, did not see the sturdy lay brother approaching.

Brother Sebaldo touched Catherine's shoulder. There was no response. He bent down to her ear. "Please, get up, Sister", he said, not unkindly. She made no move. But now he saw that her face was as white as snow, and he drew himself up and signed to the Brother Sacristan, who murmured something not very charitable and came over, slowly and ponderously.

"Fainted", Brother Sebaldo whispered.

"Fresh air", the Brother Sacristan murmured. Between them they picked her up and carried her away, a lifeless little bundle.

Outside the church they set her down and hurried back to their duties, too quickly to see the body of the little Mantellata crumple up and fall in an inert heap, head forward.

A couple of street urchins stared and stopped.

"Think she's drunk, Pietro?"

"Don't be a fool. That sort don't drink. Drink costs money. She's dead, more likely."

"How do you know?"

Pietro kicked the inert figure. There was no response. He kicked her again and a third time. "See?" he said. "Quite dead. Just like father's mule."

"What the devil are you doing?" roared an indignant voice. The urchins gave one look and fled as fast as they could.

"Now what have we here?" said the elegantly dressed young man. "My God . . . do they let their nuns die in the streets these days?"

He bent down, his arms outstretched, ready to lift her up. But he did not. He saw the white face, the wide-open eyes looking right through him into space, fixed on something, far away or near, something so immense that he was nothing, not even an obstacle. He could not bring himself to touch her. He could not even bear to look at her. No man had the right to see this unbridled, terrifying happiness.

He stepped back. And when he saw a group of Mantellate leaving the church he gestured to them weakly and fled, as the urchins had fled before him, the folds of his silk cloak fluttering behind him like a yellow flag.

Chapter Seven

AFTER THAT INCIDENT the Prioress had a heart-to-heart talk with Father Montucci, the tall grey-haired spiritual director of the Mantellate. Whereupon Father Montucci went to see Fra Tommaso della Fonte at the monastery of Saint Dominic's. He found him in his cell, dictating something to his cell neighbor, plump little Fra Bartolomeo de'Domenici.

"It's about Sister Catherine Benincasa", Father Montucci said. "Can you spare me a few minutes?"

The other two looked surprised.

"She seems to disturb the mental peace of our good Prioress very considerably", Father Montucci went on.

"That I can well believe", Fra Tommaso della Fonte said dryly.

"Yes? Well, you must admit, she isn't exactly the . . . shall we say, the usual type of Mantellata?"

"I quite agree."

Father Montucci began to feel a little impatient. "Frankly, I understand the Reverend Mother's worry. The good Sister can't leave the communion rail after Holy Communion, faints there and has to be carried out; she believes in all kinds of private revelations. . . . "

"Does she boast of them?"

"N-no, not exactly. No, she doesn't. But she has mentioned them to some of the Sisters, and there are about three or four of them, perhaps more, who believe in her. There always are, in such cases, of course."

"What cases?" Fra della Fonte asked innocently.

"Come now, you know about that kind of thing as well as I do."

"If by any chance you are referring to overwrought females,

babbling nonsense and pretending it's wisdom infused by the Holy Spirit, posing as saints and . . . "

"Well, from the indications we have . . . "

"Sister Catherine Benincasa", Fra della Fonte interrupted firmly, "is not overwrought, she never talks nonsense, and she isn't posing as anything."

Father Montucci raised his eyebrows. "Do you mean to say that in your opinion she is . . . she is . . . "

"She might be", Fra della Fonte said. "I wish I knew for certain."

There was a pause.

"You have known her a long time, of course", Father Montucci said. "But on the other hand — "

"On the other hand I am young and impressionable and not very experienced and may yearn to be the discoverer of a saint", Fra della Fonte said. "Well, I don't. On the contrary, I'm a bit afraid of it. I'm a pedestrian sort of fellow, Father. But I have taken to writing down certain observations about her, and I was in the process of doing so when you came in. Moreover, I didn't trust my own judgment, although I have known the girl practically all my life. So I asked Fra Bartolomeo here to assist me."

The dark-eyed, bushy-browed, plump little friar spoke up for the first time. "Four eyes see more than two," he said in a surprisingly high voice, "and two intellects are better than one."

Father Montucci looked at him keenly. "You are not usually given to snap judgments, Fra Bartolomeo — or too easily impressed."

"That is why I wanted him", Fra della Fonte said.

"And your opinion?" Father Montucci asked. "But I suppose I need not ask."

"No, you needn't", Fra Bartolomeo said gravely.

"You are her pater confessor, Fra Tommaso", Montucci said slowly. "And I admit I haven't seen very much of her. But I must say, it isn't exactly an easy thing for me to swallow the notion that one of our Mantellate should be that rare thing . . . so much rarer than anything else in the world . . . that Catherine Benincasa should be . . . "

" . . . what all of us ought to be", Fra della Fonte said.

Father Montucci gave a little laugh. "But why this particular one?" he asked. "Why Catherine, of all people?"

"She asked the same thing, once", Fra della Fonte said.

"Of whom? You or Fra Bartolomeo?"

"Our Lord."

Father Montucci drew in his breath sharply. "And . . . did she get an answer?"

"She always gets an answer, as we all do, when we ask in earnest *and* listen humbly enough and long enough", Fra della Fonte replied. "She told our Lord, 'I'm only a woman and ignorant. What can I do?' And he answered, 'In my sight there is neither man nor woman, neither learned nor unlearned. But I know that in these last times the pride of those who call themselves learned and wise has risen to such heights that I have resolved to humble them. I will therefore send unlearned men, yes, and women, who will put to shame the learning the men think they have.' I learned that one by heart", Fra della Fonte concluded with a grin. "It might be just as well not to forget it."

Father Montucci fingered his sleeve. "Nothing is impossible, of course", he murmured bleakly. "One tends to forget that, sometimes. Everyday life . . . ah, well, I suppose I'd better leave it to you what to do about Sister Catherine. There is just one thing: I would suggest that she not go to Holy Communion too frequently. It does seem to put her into a state of . . . exaltation, and it does make people talk. I still feel . . . "

"No one can keep our Lord away from her in any case", Fra della Fonte said stonily.

"Exactly, exactly. Well, I must be going." In the doorway Father Montucci turned. "There is one thing I do feel that our good Prioress is right about nevertheless", he said sweetly. "Apparently Sister Catherine has great difficulty in learning how to read. For a . . . for a person destined to great tasks one should think that our Lord might come to her aid there." He vanished before he could get an answer.

Fra della Fonte took Fra Bartolomeo with him to see Catherine. The plump little friar saw the tears well up in her eyes when she was told that she must not go to Holy Communion more often than once a month, but he noted with satisfaction that there was not the slightest attempt on her part to remonstrate against what was bound to be to her a much harder punishment than a month of complete fasting to a glutton. She merely bowed obediently.

"And I do wish you'd eat a little more, Sister Catherine", Fra della Fonte said kindly. "You will need your strength."

"I wish I could comply", she said in a low voice. "I often feel I would like to be like everyone else in that respect. I assure you it is not my will that opposes it but my nature. I cannot keep food down, Father."

"You are ill, then."

"I don't feel ill . . . as long as I do not have to eat. And I am quite strong."

"What about sleep? When did you sleep last?"

She hesitated for a moment. "I always sleep when I know that the friars of Saint Dominic are awake."

"You mean you want to hold the castle while the soldiers are sleeping?" Bartolomeo asked quickly.

She nodded, and for a heartbeat or two Fra Bartolomeo experienced something akin to a vision: the pale little Mantellata growing to a towering height, higher than the dome of Siena, armed with shield and spear, protecting the great monastery and church of Saint Dominic, alone while the friars slept soundly in their cells, warding off the enemy who was always ready to pounce.

Fra Bartolomeo laughed, cheerfully, without a trace of mockery. "We Dominicans are soldiers", he said. "And the Mantellate are Dominicans." He could always get himself out of an overexalted mood. "Maybe one day you'll be a general, Sister Catherine."

Sister Catherine smiled like a happy, mischievous child. "Father," she said to Fra della Fonte, "what exactly were you doing yesterday at the third hour?"

He looked at her, fidgeting a little. "Why . . . yesterday . . . "

"I can see you don't want to tell me", she said, and her smile broadened. "So I'll tell you. You were writing."

After a moment's hesitation he said cautiously, "No, I wasn't."

She chuckled. "You're right, Father. You weren't writing. You were dictating something to somebody else . . . to Fra Bartolomeo here."

The two priests froze.

"That is correct", Fra della Fonte said a little hoarsely. "But what was I dictating?"

Catherine looked down. "It was about the marks of grace which God has given his handmaid", she murmured, suddenly very serious.

There was a long silence.

Fra Bartolomeo said, "Sister Catherine . . . Father Montucci and the Prioress . . . " He broke off.

Fra della Fonte took over. "Reading doesn't come easily to you, Sister Catherine, does it? Your progress is slow."

"That is true", Catherine said. "Or rather it was true. But then I asked our Lord to teach me, and he did."

Another silence.

"You mean . . . you can read now?" asked Fra della Fonte.

"Oh, yes."

The Dominican produced his breviary, opened it at random. "Here", he said. "Read this."

" 'Domine exaudi orationem meam; auribus percipe obsecrationem meam in veritate tua: exaudi me in tua justitia' ", Catherine read. " 'Et non intres in iudicium cum servo tuo, quia non iustificabitur in conspectu tuo omnis vivens—' "

"Stop", Fra della Fonte ordered. She had read the beginning of the great psalm fluently, almost a little too quickly, and she did not really want to stop, for she sighed a little; but she obeyed.

"Do you understand what you have read?" he asked.

"Oh, yes."

"Translate it for me, will you?"

"Lord, hear my prayer", Catherine said. "Listen to my pleading in your truth and answer me in your justice. And enter not into judgment with your servant . . . "

"Enough", Fra della Fonte said, and she fell silent. "Now here . . . this word: spell it for me."

"Spell it?"

"Yes. Tell me the single letters of which it consists."

She looked at it and shook her head. "I can't", she said, "I don't know letters."

"But good heavens, girl . . . Sister Catherine," Fra Bartolomeo exclaimed, "how can you possibly read when you don't know the letters?"

"I don't know", Catherine said calmly. "But that's how it is."

"What is it you see when you read?" Fra Bartolomeo asked, breathless with excitement.

"Words, of course", Catherine replied, astonished.

"But every word consists of letters", Fra Bartolomeo shouted.

Again she shook her head. "They are sounds, living sounds, and they give birth to meaning."

Fra Bartolomeo nodded. "That will do for me", he said and wiped his forehead. When they had left her to go back to Saint Dominic's, neither of them spoke for some time. At last Fra Bartolomeo said, "I suppose that is what would happen . . . "

"What do you mean?"

"That is what would happen when one is taught to read by the Word himself."

Chapter Eight

THE TIME OF MADNESS came again to Siena, the break-down of all restraint, the days of folly, of unbridled merriment that preceded Lent, and the blood of the ancient town turned hot. The very stones seemed to rock with convulsive laughter.

Bands of music played in every street, and their wild strains mated in an unholy cacophony. Thousands of the Sienese lost their identity behind the weird screen of masks and paint; there was dancing on the Campo and dancing in the streets, and all the *contradas* became one as the pagan gods rose up from Hades to take over once more and rule supreme: Venus and Bacchus, Silenus and Cupid, glittering ghosts, ruling in the stark light of the sun as well as throughout the nights.

There was beauty in the vibrant energy of the dancers, the riot of color of banners and costumes. Siena's loveliest girls paraded through the streets on carts so piled with flowers that they looked like moving flowerbeds, while crowds of young men shouted their admiration and ran alongside to urge the girls to secret meetings at nighttime. For all the stern civic laws were suspended for the days of the carnival, and thus no one had to stay at home after the Sovrana bell struck the hour of curfew.

The young poet Neri di Landoccio and his friend Malavolti pranced through the streets, dressed as fauns, with pointed ears, short horns, and breeches of fur, ending in goats' hooves, searching for nymphs and finding so many that they had to enlist the help of a Roman centurion and two three-quarter-drunk Moors to cope with them.

Orlando, young Stefano, and even the grave-faced Bartolomeo Benincasa, wearing masks of red, green, and blue velvet, chased a swarm of maenads, but the swarm split apart in flight, and the brothers lost sight of each other, to meet again only in the morning at their father's barrels and vats, where they exchanged the stories of their adventures in a whisper.

On the Campo, the wealthy banker Ser Nanni di Vanni, disguised as a prince from Cathay, with a silk turban and long earrings, a curved and jewelled sword dangling across his mighty stomach, bribed a bevy of tipsy fruit sellers and their women to seize Nina Pacci, the largest fishwife in town, and to cover her with black paint. The crowd roared with laughter as the victim struggled and cursed. For a while it looked as if she might escape her tormentors, but they subdued her in the end and painted her with joyful thoroughness from head to foot.

"Give us a dance, Nina", Ser Nanni shouted gleefully. "Ten gold florins for a dance, my black beauty."

The fishwife took the florins. Grinning sheepishly, she began to flop about like a stranded whale, with the paint spraying from her huge body, amid screeches and applause from hundreds of onlookers.

Three young nobles searched the town for their sixteen-year-old sister, who had secretly joined the wild tide. They discovered her in a tavern in the arms of a burly masker, ran their swords through the man, and escaped with the shrieking girl before the municipal guards arrived on the scene.

Five other murders were committed during the carnival, always the most convenient time to settle old feuds: among the victims a member of the government, knifed by a jealous husband who promptly fled from town.

Shrove Tuesday was the climax. All Siena went mad in a frenzy to compensate, in one night, for the propriety and soberness of the time to come, greedy for all the pleasures of the senses.

Couples united, quarrelled, and united again. Love affairs started and ended by the thousand, and danger stalked through the streets behind masks of velvet and silk.

Into Catherine's solitude the carnival intruded under the guise of noise. Her room was at the back of the Benincasa house, where the street, the Vicolo del Tiratoio, led uphill so steeply that room and street were at equal height.

The noise went on, day after day, and there seemed to be no end to it. Sometimes it was no more than the humming of a swarm of insects somewhere outside, and that was when they were parading through the streets or marching to assemble on the Campo. Sometimes, in plain daylight as well as at dusk and at night, there were shrill giggles, rising to shrieks, and the hurried running of women's feet with masculine feet pounding in hot pursuit, ending with louder shrieks, with cries for help, and gusts of rough male laughter.

There was the twanging of mandolins, the distant music of a band, and quite near, the breathless love talk of a young couple, demand and refusal, and a sudden yielding.

All along the Vicolo del Tiratoio the chase was on; then, just below her window, there was ardent kissing and embracing and whispering, "I love you, *carissima,* you alone, the most beautiful girl in the world."

Catherine could not help hearing. The strong, young voice was so near; the man might have been here in her room, her cell. But the words were not for her. No one would ever say them to her, or anything like them. Men would give her the right of way in the street, at best with a glance of respect, mingled with compassion or even a kind of tolerant contempt for a woman who was not allowed to be a woman, for a young living corpse, carrying her black-and-white coffin wherever she went. Male arms would never encircle her. No man would burn her lips with his kisses. . . .

Then she knew that these thoughts were not born of her own will, that the enemy was trying to stir up the fire of her senses, and she fought back fiercely. But for one thought she killed, two others sprang up, alive like animals, alive like humans; the cell was full of them. They mocked her and laughed; they danced in pairs, male and female, some with wild abandon, others gesturing and posturing shamelessly, winking at her, beckoning her to come and join them.

"You are a girl of flesh and blood, aren't you? Aren't you?"

They were naked and beautiful, full of strength and rhythm; they were merry and gay and stretched out their hands to her, come dance with us. . . .

This could end in only one way. She must yield, as the girl out in the street had yielded, surrendering and embracing, burning with passion. There was nothing left but that, it was inevitable, she was drawn, drawn irresistibly, sucked down into the whirlpool of beauty and joy. Why did she still hesitate still hold back? There was a time for everything, and surely now was the time for this, now, at once.

"Jesus!" she ejaculated. "Give me more faith. Give me more faith!"

The dancers shivered; the hellish rhythm faltered.

"Jesus! Jesus!"

Pale shadows vibrated weakly, dissolved—and were gone. The cell was empty. The noise outside abated to a faraway humming as of a swarm of insects, and then that too died away. She had won through invoking, with the last, ebbing force of her innermost will, the Name which is above all others and at which all knees must bend.

The cell that was a battlefield rocked as he of the Five Wounds appeared, and she fell at his feet.

"O Lord, O Lord," she sobbed, "where were you when they tormented me?"

"In thy heart."

When her friends, Sister Alessia and Sister Francesca, came to see her a week later, she told them. "At first I couldn't grasp what the Lord said. How could it be that he was in my heart and I be unaware of it? And I was, you know, utterly unaware. All I could feel were horror and disgust and bitterness that I was to be carried away into the world of the foul fiend. And I told him so. But he answered me: and I could see at once that he was right, as he always is right, even when we do not understand him. For it was because he was in my heart that I felt the horror of the evil tempting me and had the strength to go on resisting it. The will was mine, but the strength was his and it was there for the asking."

"But why did he allow you to be tempted at all?" Sister Alessia asked uneasily.

"He was testing me."

"You mean he wanted to know what you would do?" Sister Francesca asked.

Catherine smiled. "The Omniscient has no curiosity", she said. "God did not want to find out what Abraham would do when he asked him to sacrifice his son Isaac. He knew. But it made Abraham a new man and a better one, because he had shown readiness, up to the last moment, to sacrifice the dearest thing he had on earth to God. After that Abraham was a *real* man, you might say."

"But what was he before?" Alessia asked.

"What a creature is. Nothing. By himself—nothing. Creatures come from nothing and go toward nothing. And in sin they become nothing. That is why Saint Paul said that the wages of sin are death. That is why our Lord said that without him we can do nothing. We do not exist, not really. We exist only through him and in him."

Sister Francesca rubbed her little snub nose. "*Tròppo cecca*", she decided. "I'm too silly to understand such things. I just love him, so I try to do what he wants."

"Dear Cecca," Catherine said, thereby giving Francesca her nickname for life, "no one can do more. None of us can understand God. Nothingness cannot understand Being."

Many of the younger Mantellate had nicknames for each other. Thus Giovanna di Capo was "mad Joan" and Alessia Saracini, "Chubby", although she was no more than pleasingly rounded.

It was Catherine who had started that game, and she was quite prepared to defend it, when the Prioress objected.

"I don't think our dear Lord minds it", she said. "He rather likes nicknames."

The Reverend Mother Nera di Gano would have liked to ask how Sister Catherine could possibly know that, but she dreaded the answer "He told me so", and so she said nothing.

Catherine smiled at her. "He gave people nicknames himself", she said. "He called Simon 'Peter'—and James and John the 'Sons of Thunder'—and Judas Iscariot 'the Son of Perdition'."

The Prioress abstained from further comment. She tried to tell herself that a person who was fond of giving people nicknames must have a sense of humor and that this was a good sign. Mystic-minded fanatics never had any. Nevertheless she still worried. The Mantellate were an order and they had their vows, but they neither lived a community life nor were recluses. They had their meetings and they went to Mass together, but most of the time they were on their own, and their only really constant supervisor was their consciences. This made it all the more important that they should draw as little attention to themselves as possible and do nothing that might give cause for gossip or scandal. And Sister Catherine seemed to have a knack for getting herself talked about. Not that she was seen often, except in church; on the contrary, she stayed at her parents' house and even there kept entirely to herself. According to what her confessor had told Father Montucci, she took no part in the family meals or family discussions, but remained in her room, which was respected by all the members of her family as her cell, her *clausura*. No one visited her there, except occasionally some other Sisters. There was nothing one could reproach her for. And yet, the Reverend Mother Nera di Gano felt, there was danger. Danger for Sister Catherine—and danger for the order. When it came to private revelations, the accent had to be on "private". There could be nothing worse than a member of a religious order who insisted on receiving her instructions not from her prioress, her confessor, spiritual director, or even the Master General, but directly from on high.

Catherine was happy. They had forbidden her to go to Holy Communion more than once a month, but he came to her every day. When she read the Office, he read it with her. So, at every *Gloria* she said, "Glory be to the Father and to *thee* and to the Holy Ghost." The beauties of the Office, the ancient and hallowed words leaped to her lips, edible pearls, drinkable jewels. It was like living in the anteroom of paradise, with the great doors opening every day wide enough for a glimpse and more than a glimpse, and what mattered was not to move from here, until the moment came when she would be allowed to enter and stay for all time.

But when he left her, one day, he said, "Love of me and love of one's neighbor are one and the same thing." And when he came back the next day, his first words were, "You cannot do anything for me, but you can serve and help your neighbor."

Suddenly she knew why he had said it. She would not be allowed to stay. A new time, a new life loomed up before her. She had been living like a recluse, a hermit, alone with him. Now she was going to lose her daily happiness. She tried to remonstrate, to plead. She had given up all worldly cares . . . was she then to take them on again? But immediately she heard his answer in her heart: "Did I not give mankind two commandments: to love God and to love thy neighbor?"

She had learned the first lesson; now she would have to learn the second.

"Have you forgotten that I want you to go out and bring souls to me? To help the needy and to humble the proud?"

Terrified, she asked for strength, for grace, for help and was told that she would have them all and have them abundantly. The rest was prayer, the kind of prayer when time stood still. Sometimes, on awakening from it, she found the day was gone or the night; sometimes it would carry her through ages of rapture and ecstasy, yet when she awoke from it, only a few minutes had passed.

One day she heard, as so often before, the sound of a clock striking, the clock hidden in the white flower on top of the long, red stalk, the clock of the Mangia tower, striking noon.

Now her parents and all the household would sit down for their midday meal.

Why was she thinking of that? Did he . . . did he want her to go so quickly? Was there to be no time for preparation? Would it have to be at once? Now?

77

"Yes, my daughter, now."

They were arguing at table, which often happened especially since Bartolomeo had become a member of the Great Council, a great honor, naturally, although the fickle nature of the Sienese brought about governmental changes so often that few men held a position in the Great Council for more than a few months.

The news was that Pope Urban V had left Avignon for Rome, and Giacomo Benincasa was very pleased about it, because Rome was where a pope ought to be. He had no high opinion of the Romans—after all, they had murdered the first pope and the apostle Paul as well. But the tombs of the two great apostles were in Rome, and anyway, Avignon was in France.

Bartolomeo shrugged his shoulders. "Whether he is in Avignon or in Rome, Father, the Pope is still a Frenchman, his predecessor was a Frenchman, and his successor will be a Frenchman."

"You can't know that for certain, Son."

"What else could he be? The great majority of the cardinals are French, and *they* will never give their vote to an Italian. And has anything good ever come from France? Look at the papal legates they sent us! One worse than the other. Even so, I hope the Pope will hire Ser Aguto."

"Aguto? The English commander? What makes you think of him? I thought he was in the service of the Duke of Milan?"

"He was, yes, but no longer. And we've had reports that his men are looting the countryside again, just as they did three years ago."

"Aguto is the devil incarnate", Mona Lapa said. "Everybody knows that. Pass the wine, Stefano."

"It's bad enough when he is in the service of some prince", Bartolomeo said. "But it's far worse when he isn't. When there is no one to pay him and his band of brigands, he will take everything he can lay his hands on. He would take the last coin from a beggar and rob the poor boxes of every church."

"Duke Bernabò of Milan was the right master for him", Stefano said. "I don't think any better of French papal legates than you do, Bartolo, but you can't treat them as Bernabò did. When they brought him the bull of excommunication, he made them eat it, didn't he?"

A few of the journeymen broke into laughter, and Giacomo Benincasa looked at them reproachfully. "It's sad enough that such things are possible", he said. "It makes one wonder how long God will permit them to happen. Bad rulers everywhere ... "

He broke off, and there was a sudden hush, as the frail little figure in black and white came in and sat down among them. That had not happened for years. Some of the journeymen and most of the apprentices had never set eyes on the Mantellata daughter of the Benincasas, and now they stared at her curiously. But even to the family it was as if Catherine had come back to them from the dead.

Lapa gasped.

Giacomo Benincasa, lifting his goblet of wine, was the first to smile happily. "Welcome, Daughter", he said. He was the first also to feel that Catherine's visit signified the beginning of something new, but he could not make out what it was.

Even Catherine herself was not sure. She was twenty-one. Five years of prayer, fasting, and penitence, of secret scourgings and endless vigils had trained her for battle. Now it was about to begin.

Two days later Fra Tommaso della Fonte rushed into Fra Bartolomeo de'Domenici's cell. "Would you believe it?" he said. "She's out and about."

"What do you mean? Who? Sister Catherine?"

"She's paying daily visits to the Misericordia hospital. She has washed all the soiled linen at her parents' house. There are more than twenty people living there now, what with all those nephews and nieces, so she must have been at it all night. And now she is baking bread. What's come over her, all of a sudden? What does it mean?"

Fra Bartolomeo de'Domenici blew out his plump cheeks. "It means that he has let her loose", he said. "Now watch . . . I think we're going to see things happen."

Book Two

Chapter Nine

Fra lazzarino of the Order of the Friars Minor was a very good-looking man with a pronounced sense of beauty, and he managed to wear the grey-brown habit of Saint Francis of Assisi with elegance. He was also an erudite and eloquent orator, and the great Franciscan monastery of Siena was glad to have him as a lecturer on theology, especially sturdy, red-haired Fra Marco, who had come to visit him in his cell—if one could call the charmingly furnished room a cell.

The two Franciscans were sipping wine from silver goblets, the gift of a noble family in appreciation of the sermon Fra Lazzarino had preached at the occasion of their daughter's wedding feast.

"I want to talk to you about that Mantellata", Fra Marco said. "The thing's preposterous. Something should be done about it, and I think you're the man to do it."

"Sister Catherine, you mean, of course." Fra Lazzarino's long, well-kept fingers were playing with a beautifully illuminated book. "Dear Lord, if there is anything in the world I can't stomach it's a female of that sort. Where does she hail from? Is she a Sienese? Don't tell me she's from Pisa; I couldn't bear it."

"You don't have to worry about the honor of your town. She was born in Siena and has never been anywhere else. Fontebranda. *Contrada dell'Oca.* Not exactly a fashionable district, as you may gather from its name."

"The District of the Geese." Fra Lazzarino laughed. "How very, very appropriate. It shouldn't be so difficult to deal with this particular goose. Do have some more wine."

"I'm not so sure", warned Fra Marco, holding up his goblet with obvious pleasure. "Real nectar, this wine of yours. What is it? Orvieto?"

"Dear me, you old barbarian. It's Greek, rather a choice vintage from the island of Samos. But to come back to that wretched little woman. I'll tell you what I'll do. I'll preach a sermon against her, a good one. The dear Dominicans won't like it, but they brought it on themselves. They should have been the first to silence her. It's just as we were told, back in Pisa: the Sienese Dominicans have come down a bit in the world. They must have."

"They have no major lights at all", Fra Marco assented. "Lost touch with the people, too, I think. Or maybe they have never had any."

"Hold themselves aloof, eh? Well, humility has never been their strong suit."

"If they had more knowledge of the people," Fra Marco went on, grinning, "they might have remembered the proverb: *'Dio ti guarda da nobil poverino—O di dònna che sa latino.'* "

"Not bad", Fra Lazzarino said, smiling. "The impoverished noble, always borrowing money, of course; and the Latin-speaking woman who has always been an abomination. Saint Paul spoke against her clearly enough."

"What do you mean? Everybody spoke Latin in his time."

"Don't tell me you've forgotten: *mulier taceat . . .* "

" *. . . in ecclesia.* " Fra Marco shook his head. "Sorry, but that shoe doesn't fit. She doesn't speak in church, or at least she hasn't tried that yet. She only faints and playacts. From what I'm told she must be a consummate actress. Even some of the other Mantellate are convinced by her."

"Ah, but you're quite wrong about Saint Paul," Fra Lazzarino said gravely, lifting a warning finger, a gesture he used with much effect in his sermons. "*Ecclesia* does not simply mean the church as a building; it means the community as a whole. And how right Paul was and what a blessing it would be if he were obeyed to the letter. A whole stream of bickering and nagging, of voluble and volatile chattering would instantly dry up. We would have a better world at once. I think I ought to write a thesis about this interpretation. Wonderful material."

84

"That's all very well." Fra Marco took a long sip of the Samos wine. "It won't help us much here, though. You ought to have something far more substantial than mere generalities. We are concerned with one particular person, the Benincasa woman, not with women in general. And so far no one seems to have been able to get at her. It's all so vague. Faintings in church, tears, making herself talked about, a lot of silly women and, I'm sorry to say, a few silly Dominican friars as well, dancing around her and lapping up everything she says. Some of them saying quite openly that she's a saint. . . . "

"Good Lord. Whatever next?"

"But if there's no proof of that, as of course there isn't, there is also no proof—or not enough proof—against it. For all we know she is living even more austerely than the Rule of her order demands. She has come out lately to visit two hospitals, the della Scala and the Misericordia, and she is working there regularly. The patients like her; in fact, they eat out of her hand, both actually and figuratively. There is no moral accusation against her that I know of. So what can we do?"

Fra Lazzarino listened attentively. "What *is* this woman, in your opinion, Fra Marco?" he asked softly.

Fra Marco shrugged his shoulders. "She may be a hysteric who really believes that she has visions and hears voices. When such a belief is held strongly enough, it can be infectious. Or she may be a downright impostor, posing as a saint, probably not for the sake of material gain—at least I have never heard of anybody giving her money or presents of value—but for the sake of vanity and of the power over weaker souls. I don't know which."

"In other words, you want me to find out more about her", Fra Lazzarino said slowly. "Very well, I will. After all, she talks to quite a number of people, doesn't she? And quotes from Scripture? And tells them what she thinks or says she has been told by her wonderful heavenly visions? That means she is *teaching* people. And whatever she may be, she's not a learned theologian. If she dares to interpret Sacred Scripture, well, then . . . "

85

"That's it", Fra Marco nodded. "And she will dare it. Her vanity will be the spur."

"And that may prove her to be a heretic as well as an impostor", Fra Lazzarino said quietly.

"We shall give the Master General of the Dominicans some work to do." Fra Marco rubbed his hands. "A stern man, Friar Elias of Toulouse. He won't like it if one of his precious Mantellate turns out to be a heretic, and he'll like it even less if she is found out by mere Franciscans. Too bad, isn't it? And we shall be rid of the woman. The church of Saint Dominic is packed whenever she goes to Mass."

"You shouldn't say such things, you know", Fra Lazzarino said, his hands fluttering a little. "People might think we want to get rid of her because she is a . . . an attraction, an asset to her order. They might think we're against her out of some kind of professional jealousy."

"Now that's absurd", Fra Marco flushed deeply. "You can't seriously think . . . "

"Not I. But some people will believe anything."

"True enough. That inner circle of hers is so besotted and infatuated with her that they're called the Caterinati."

"Caterinato, Caterinato", Fra Lazzarino laughed. "Not bad."

"I think one of the Mantellate thought it up. They aren't *all* happy about her."

"I shall have to think about the right approach", Fra Lazzarino said thoughtfully. "I can't go and see her alone, obviously. And I must have the permission of the Dominicans."

Fra Marco wrinkled his nose. "They won't give it to you."

Fra Lazzarino smiled. "Something tells me they will", he said. "Don't worry. I have an idea."

Ten days later Fra Lazzarino of Pisa paid a visit to Fra Bartolomeo de'Domenici. "I would like your permission to visit Sister Catherine Benincasa of the Mantellate", he said courteously.

The plump little Dominican frowned. "I heard that you preached about her last Sunday in the church of San Francesco", he said acidly. "Or rather, against her. And against all those poor, benighted people who think well of her, including myself."

"I did", Fra Lazzarino admitted with beautiful frankness. "But now I am no longer so sure that I was right. Too many people speak of her with genuine respect, and I felt it might be best if I could have the opportunity of meeting her. A personal impression may set things right."

The Dominican hesitated. "I shall have to ask Fra Tommaso della Fonte for his permission first", he said, rather stiffly.

"Of course. May I wait here for you?"

"Please do." Fra Bartolomeo de'Domenici rushed over to Fra Tommaso della Fonte's cell and returned after five minutes. "I shall take you there myself", he said.

Sister Catherine received her two visitors with friendly respect, offering Fra Lazzarino a seat on her clothes chest and Fra Bartolomeo the wooden contraption that served as her bed. Then she sat down on the bare floor, at Fra Lazzarino's feet.

After a while the Franciscan said, "I have heard so much of your holiness, and that the Lord has granted you insight to understand and interpret the Scriptures. Therefore I have come to you in the hope of finding both comfort and uplift."

"I am very happy that you are here, Father", Catherine said. "I know you are daily interpreting the Holy Scriptures. Surely you have come to enlighten me and to build up my poor soul."

Fra Bartolomeo de'Domenici's eyes widened a little. Could it be that there was a trace of irony in the girl's voice? Why, she knew what a powerful man the Franciscan was. It was most unlikely.

Fra Lazzarino in any case did not seem to notice it. He said with a little bow of his well-groomed head that he had come to learn and not to teach, and Catherine asked almost timidly how an erudite man of great renown could possibly hope to learn anything from an ignorant woman, and that kind of talk went on for quite a while. Then Fra Lazzarino began to bring up theological problems. Catherine listened with great attention, but when he asked her direct questions about them, she said submissively, "I would love to hear your answer to it, Father", and as he could not very well plead ignorance, he was forced to comply. Thus he was speaking most of the time, holding forth about a number of knotty problems as if he were teaching the nuns of Saint Francis' convent, with the little Mantellata sitting at his feet and looking up to him.

No pretension of erudition, he thought. Modesty? Stupidity? It was difficult to say. There was nothing in the least extraordinary about the woman; she was a little nun like a thousand others. Why on earth were people making such a fuss about her?

Then the bell of the Mangia tower struck, reminding him that he had to return home for his supper. He rose. "I'll explain that passage to you at another time", he said graciously. She too rose, walked with him to the door, knelt down, and asked for his blessing and his prayers. He made the sign of the Cross over her, murmured the blessing, added somewhat airily, "Pray for me too, Sister", and left, with a somewhat bewildered Fra Bartolomeo at his heels. "Thank you for bringing me here", he said. "I really think we may have been unduly worried about the good Sister. Just a nice, simple soul, isn't she?"

"I am glad you think so", Fra Bartolomeo said, still bewildered. He was not exactly satisfied with the way Catherine had behaved. The Franciscan would go home and tell everybody that the Dominicans . . . some of them . . . made a great deal of fuss about a nonentity.

Fra Lazzarino went home. Tomorrow he would have to tell Fra Marco that the campaign against that little Sister was scarcely worthwhile. Dear Lord, it was like sending an army against a small child. She wasn't even intelligent, just a naïve little nun, humble enough, and quite willing to learn from her betters. He went to bed early. Tomorrow he was scheduled for a lecture on the nature of Christ, and he still had to prepare his notes.

But he slept badly. Several times he woke up with a start, his heart beating madly. Was he going to be ill? When he rose in the morning he felt no better. Perhaps the game pie at supper?

No, it could not be that; he would have had physical pain, and he had none. But what else could it be? Outside, the sun was shining, but there seemed to be something menacing about its brutal light, and its rays showed myriads of tiny particles of dust or dirt dancing and whirling about. He washed, and the water seemed to hurt his body rather than to refresh it. He dressed. His morning prayer was flat and stale, and he could not concentrate on it. The words were dancing around like those little particles of dust in the sunlight.

This won't do, he thought angrily. He hated emotionalism of any kind, and he was not going to tolerate it in himself. There was nothing wrong with him, nothing. He had no pain. He really had not.

Somebody was passing by in the corridor. Steps. They were coming to bring him bad news. That was it . . . he was having some kind of premonition. The steps passed, and there was silence. A premonition of what? Could it mean that his mother was ill? Dying, maybe? Or his brother? He had a distinct feeling of danger. Why should he? What was there to be afraid of?

Suddenly, to his surprise and disgust, he found himself crying. He tried to stop and could not. There must be something wrong with him after all; there must be. He set his will against his tears as hard as he could, but after less than a minute's pause he was crying again. This was absurd, ridiculous. Why, he was behaving like a stupid female. He was due to say Mass in half an hour. How could he, with the tears streaming down his face? He would have to send a message to the sacristan that he was ill. He would not even go to the refectory. The very thought of food disgusted him.

But what did all this mean? It was not anything physical — except for the tears, of course. It was not of the mind either — he could think clearly and logically. The best thing to do was to sit down at his desk and get those notes together.

A few minutes later he knew it was impossible. He could not concentrate. Long shudders of fear kept shaking him. He would be unable to give his lecture. He was made powerless, useless. Could he have offended God in some way?

But unlike some priests and friars he might have named, he was a clean-living man. He had always attended to his duties. Certainly none of the grosser sins was weighing on his conscience. Little sarcastic remarks, barbed replies to stupid questions, impatience with fools—nothing worse than that. Imperfections, assuredly, but nothing really, nothing that would endanger him spiritually.

Then he cried again. In a turmoil of anger, fear, and exhaustion he sank into his favorite chair with its comfortable leather cushion, only to find that he could not endure it because it was too soft. He wanted something hard and angular, like the wooden bed of that little Mantellata. What a wretched little cell she had for a room, no carpet, not a thing of value. She was living like those first Dominicans whose austerity and purity of life outshone the heretical purists of their time and—

He started up. He could see her eyes again, looking at him as he held forth about his theological intricacies, her large, luminous eyes. She had been listening to him, but all the time there was a question in those eyes, a hidden question. He had not realized it then; he had been so busy showing off his knowledge and erudition. But the question had been there and had stayed with him, and even now he did not dare try to formulate it. She had asked him to bless her, and he had murmured the ancient words unthinkingly and without any real wish that his words might reach the throne of God. She had asked him to pray for her, and he had forgotten; no, worse, he had never intended to. From mere habit he had tossed her an airy, condescending "Pray for me too, Sister." And with a shock he realized that she had done so and that he was in the iron grip of her prayer, mounting to God and holding him with a terrifying force. She was tearing his little world to pieces, showing it for what it was, a cocoon of luxury. . . .

He had a broad bed, filled with a soft mattress and even softer cushions. This chair of his might have graced the study of an archbishop, a cardinal. He collected illuminated manuscripts, enjoyed the taste of rare wines. He was clever at analyzing theological niceties. And when it came to themes of real importance—how much did he care for them, and how much for what his audience would say about him?

In the glare of that sudden self-cognition, the examination of his conscience only a short while ago was exposed for what it really was: pharisaical hypocrisy, vanity, sham. And that little woman had revealed what he was, not by anything she said but by the way she lived. And he had gone to expose her—he who had casually, completely broken the Franciscan vow of poverty. . . .

Suddenly he realized that he was no longer crying. That terrible, irresistible urge had gone. He felt weak, exhausted, but rather happy. For now he knew what he must do.

The next day, very early in the morning he stood at the door of Catherine's cell. When she opened it, he fell at her feet. She led him inside. He refused to sit on either bed or clothes chest but sat down on the floor with her. Once more he spoke and she listened, but this time he spoke against himself. He told her everything. When he had finished she nodded gently. "The cell of self-cognition is the first step", she said. "You must go back to your great father Saint Francis. He is waiting for you with open arms, he and the great lady he loved: the Lady Poverty. That is your way to salvation."

"You have prayed for me", he said hoarsely. "Go on praying, I beg of you, so that I may persevere."

"I will", she said simply. "You have had the shell of the Faith. Now you will have the kernel."

On his way back Fra Lazzarino felt what he had not felt in many years: a huge, overwhelming joy. He laughed aloud. He felt like dancing. That same day he gave away all his possessions to the poor, keeping only his breviary and his missal.

"What on earth has happened to you?" Fra Marco asked, when he came in. "All your things are gone. Are you leaving us?"

"No."

"I don't understand. Why didn't you come to see me? You told me you were going to pay that woman a visit. . . . "

"I did."

A light began to dawn on Fra Marco. "Don't tell me . . . it isn't possible. She didn't . . . this isn't her work, is it?"

"Yes."

Fra Marco gasped. Then he turned and walked away. In the door he turned again. "Caterinato", he jeered.

"I consider that a most honorable name", Fra Lazzarino said.

Fra Marco threw up his arms and stamped out of the room.

Chapter Ten

"THIS ONE A FRESH DRESSING, Sister", said the man with the brown robe and the black cap.

"You mean Ser Vogliani", Catherine said with a hint of reproach, and the patient drew himself up a little and smiled. "I'll see to it straight away." She unwound the bandages, stained with blood and pus, gave a keen look at the huge bluish-red ulcer. "A little better, I think", she said. "How do you feel, Ser Vogliani?"

"Good when I see you, Sister Catherine. You treat a man as a man and not just as an ulcer."

"Oh, you're a man all right," Catherine said, "and a proud and cantankerous one at that. Have you ever taken the trouble to think how much work the regular nurses here have to do? Pray that they have all the strength they need instead of complaining about them. There . . . this will keep it clean and dry. I'll have another look tomorrow." She gave him a nod and a wide smile and marched on to the next case, a man who had managed to cut off half his leg with his scythe and needed a drink of poppyseed to dull his pains.

Sister Francesca came up. "Ser Matteo wants to see you", she said. "He's in his office."

"I'm coming, Cecca."

Matteo Cenni, the Rector of the Misericordia hospital, was a giant of a man with the strength of a bear and the eyes of a dreamer. "Nice things I hear about you, Sister Catherine", he boomed. "Giving away your cloak and to a common street woman too."

"She needed it more than I did."

"That may well be so, but it isn't seemly that a Mantellata should walk about without her cloak."

"I'd rather be without a cloak than without charity", Catherine said, and her chin went up.

Ser Matteo's huge frame shook with laughter. "Nicely answered, Sister Catherine. However, one of my male nurses saw you from the window and told me and I got the cloak back for you. Here it is."

"Messer Matteo! Now the poor woman—"

"The poor woman accepted three florins for it and was delighted. But you mustn't do that again, Sister Catherine. Not only because I can't redeem your cloak for you six times a day, but your Prioress would be extremely angry if she knew. That cloak is part of your regular dress. It should be worn only by a Mantellata, not by an ordinary laywoman, and least of all by the kind of person to whom you gave it. We must be prudent, Sister Catherine. Some of the older Mantellate are not too happy that you and your little brigade do hospital work. There isn't anything against it in the Rule, but it's highly unconventional, and therefore it will be better to give them no further cause for complaint."

She said nothing, and he grinned broadly. "I needn't tell you how grateful I am for having you and your Sisters to help us", he went on. "So are my nurses and indeed my patients. I don't know what I'll do if the Prioress forbids your work here."

"Ser Carlucci in Ward Two will die tonight", she said. "It will be well to have the priest here before dusk."

The Rector looked at her sharply. After a pause he said, "He will be called."

"I think the physician is wrong about Mona Ricarda", Catherine said. "She is worse than he thinks, and we ought to keep her here for some time."

"I shall have a look at her myself", Ser Matteo said. "Anything else?"

"Not at present, Messer Matteo."

"Thank you, Sister Catherine."

Outside the office Alessia Saracini was waiting for her. "It's time to go home", she said wearily. "I've had ten hours of this and you've had sixteen."

94

"I'm not a bit tired, Chubby."

"You never are, but one day you'll break down completely."

"There is so much to do, so much useful work . . . "

"The hospital isn't the only place where you're needed, *mamma*." They all called her that: Alessia, Cecca, Lisa, Colombini, Giovanna di Capo, even Fra Tommaso and Fra Bartolomeo de'Domenici, although she was the youngest of them all.

"You promised to spend a few days in our house", Alessia reminded her. "Father is worse than ever. I've never seen such hatred, and I have no influence on him; on the contrary. I can't bear his constant cursing and ranting against the Church any longer. He hates all the priests and most of all poor Father Montucci."

"What has he got against him?"

Alessia gave a bitter smile. "He'll tell you, *mamma*. He regards him as his worst enemy. But then he seems to think that the whole world is his enemy. All he is fond of is his horses and his falcons. He's an old soldier, and there is still some soldiering left in him, but no enemy to make war against. So he's declared war on everybody, but his pet hates are the priests and among them first and foremost Father Montucci."

Ser Francesco di Saracini was a man of seventy, but vigorous enough, despite a lame leg. With his thin lips, beak of a nose, big round eyes under shaggy grey eyebrows, and an obstinate little tuft of white hair over his forehead, he curiously resembled the falcon that perched on his gloved hand. "That's Caesar", he told Catherine. "Best falcon I ever had and worth more than a lot of people I could name." He smoothed the bird's plumage. "You're a friend of my daughter's, she tells me. She's a fool, but at least she's not dishonest. Most people are both."

"She too is a soldier", Catherine said quietly.

The old man threw back his head, laughing. "Alessia a soldier", he jeered. "With a Rosary as a sword, eh? I may as well tell you that I never approved of her joining those part-time nuns, or whatever you are. But it's sad for a girl to lose her husband. No children around either, worse luck. So I

95

thought, let her, if it gives her some kind of comfort. The thing that upsets me is that you have that archfool, that cheat and humbug of a Montucci as . . . what d'ye call it? Spiritual mentor?"

"Father Montucci is the spiritual director of the Mantellate, Father", Alessia murmured. "And he has become Prior of the Dominicans, too. Doesn't that go to prove that he—"

"It proves what I have always thought and said: that all priests are fools, cheats, and humbugs. Prior, eh! They elect them, I believe. So either he is the best of them, which would mean that the rest of them are still worse, though I find that hard to imagine. Or they have chosen him because he's imposed himself on them, just as he tried to do with me, the insolent fellow."

"Father, really, you mustn't—"

"You be quiet, Daughter. Comes here and has the effrontery to ask me why I didn't go to Mass. Who does he think I am, the stupid, oily rascal? And who does he think he is?"

"Father—"

"Quiet, I say. Well, I told him why and what for, and he won't forget it so easily. 'Because you priests are humbugs', I told him. 'Because all you can ever think of is your own advantage. Bobbing up and down in front of the altar, all dressed up in silk and finery, eating the fat of the land. The land, ho-ho! And how did you get the land? Threatening old people with hellfire unless they leave their money to the Church, most likely.' He didn't like it much, but it's the truth, and I always speak the truth, never mind who hears it. I'd tell it to the Bishop, too, *and* the Pope, if I had the chance, but I haven't. *He* sits in Avignon with his cardinals covered with jewels and his court of pretty ladies . . . "

"Father, I beg of you . . . *And* the Holy Father is in Rome now. . . . "

"Very pretty they are, I hear, all ribbons and frills and face paint. Not much better here either, I should think. Wouldn't surprise me in the least if that Montucci and his black-and-white mice had visitors at night. Told him that, too! What about that miserable priest in the *Contrada* of the Tortoise, with his housekeeper? All Siena knew what was going on. Well, he couldn't take any more after that and he fled, the Father Montucci, I mean, and good riddance, I thought. *He* won't come back. But what did he do? Went and preached a sermon against blasphemous nobles who did not want to do their duty toward God and his Church and therefore maligned the priesthood to give themselves an excuse to stay away from it and not to give alms. The wretched calumniator!"

"Father is the most generous of men when it comes to almsgiving", Alessia said. She was near tears.

Catherine said nothing. She was looking at the irate old man with a kind of attentive serenity, as if he were quoting a passage from an edifying book.

"I suppose one can't expect anything from a priest but a pack of lies", Francesco di Saracini went on grimly. "But heaven help your precious Father Montucci if I ever set eyes on him again. I'll kill him with my bare hands. They'll put me on the rack for it, I suppose, but at least I shall have rid the world of one of those pests, and one of the worst at that."

Catherine said evenly, "You are a soldier, Ser Francesco. That means you have respect for soldierly deeds."

"Indeed I have", growled the old man.

"And when you know a great captain and hero who has been fighting a mighty battle against the most ferocious foe and in the course of it saved your life as well as that of many others, you will bear him both respect and love."

"Certainly. But what are you talking about?"

"And if you happened to be an officer in that captain's army and the battle, though won, was still raging, you would not desert him. You would go on fighting under him. Am I right?"

"Of course, but what has all that to do with Montucci? He certainly isn't —"

"Our Blessed Lord is the greatest Captain of all", Catherine said. "His charger is the Cross. He has shed his blood for every one of his soldiers, and the one thing that matters is to go on fighting on his side against the common enemy of God and man."

"I have no quarrel with that", the old man said gruffly.

"That enemy is not only strong; he is subtle, too", Catherine continued. "He is spreading the idea that the men fighting on your right and on your left are all traitors and felons, that they are humbugs and cheats and liars. He sometimes succeeds in undermining part of the great Captain's forces. But only the weaker part. The strong and loyal will not lose confidence."

"But they *are* humbugs and jackanapes", bellowed the old soldier. "I know they are. Take that Montucci creature . . . "

"And if it is so," Catherine interrupted firmly, "if they all are what you say they are, that would still be no reason for a real soldier to leave the army."

"Why can't I be loyal to the Captain without paying attention to the priests?" Ser Francesco stormed.

"Because he said to his apostles, 'He who despises you, despises me' ", Catherine replied. "And the apostles passed their ordination on to their successors, and so did they in turn. However bad they may be, it is given to them and to them alone to call our Blessed Lord down to the altar in the form of bread and wine. It is the Lord, the great Captain himself, who comes to you through their hands. Their unworthiness makes no difference in that. And for that reason, for the sake of their office, we must honor them all, good or bad."

"By thunder," the old man said, "they've got themselves a good advocate in you, girl. If it weren't for that rascal of a Montucci and his impertinent sermon — what is this din? Have those people all gone mad?"

Alessia went to the window. "The street is black with people", she said. "There is a cart coming . . . oh, that must be the robbers they seized the other day. They'll pass by quite near."

Ser Francesco, the falcon still firmly on his gloved hand, rose and had a look. "That's right", he said. "They're getting the red tongs all the way to San Stefano à Pecorile. There they'll die, and they deserve every bit of what they get. These robbers are the plague of our time."

Slowly Catherine too walked to the window, just in time to see the tumbril pass. The two criminals, chained and roped so that they could not move an inch, screamed curses and blasphemies as the executioner's aides touched their bodies again and again with iron tongs, made red-hot over a small brazier. She could see the faces of the two men clearly, one middle-aged, bearded and in such a rage that he looked like a devil; the other young and pale with wild despair in his bloodshot eyes; and both screaming, screaming. . . .

She stepped back and fell on her knees.

"Deserve every bit of what they get", Ser Francesco repeated grimly, but Alessia closed her eyes and covered her ears.

Catherine did not hear him. Her body had become an empty shell. Her spirit was no longer in the room; it was down in the street, on the tumbril with the two men who were in a danger so great that the excruciating pain of their bodies was nothing in comparison. Here the enemy of mankind had no need for subtlety. Here he was in open attack. Hatred and despair, the demons guarding the gateway of hell, were tearing at the men's souls.

The smoke of the brazier flickered and twisted. The people on both sides of the street shouted abuse. The executioner's aides went on with the task they were paid for by the stern administration of the town, trying to deter other robbers as well as to punish the crimes of the two men caught, and the criminals went on screaming curses. None of them knew of the bitter struggle going on around them, the stream of prayer rolling on, trying to pass through menacing fog, trying to rise despite the most terrible pressure of threats of violence, of threats of possession, of lunacy, of disintegration of mind and soul.

Catherine was uniting her lot with theirs, creating and recreating a tie of love that would not and could not hold, that slipped away, fell off, broke again and again. She knew that help could come, would come if only she held out; she was holding a pass against an army; she was doing the one thing that could be done. The stench of sin and horror was suffocating; she was going down into dark depths of filth and slime, and still she struggled.

She was torn to pieces, drawn and quartered; there was nothing left but to shout the Name, the one Name; and here he was, at the very gate of justice, hands and feet pierced and bleeding, the gaping wound in his side, the crown of thorns on his head, and the two thieves crucified to the right and left of him.

She saw him, and through her the two men saw him too and his look of infinite sadness and pity, and their curses ceased and they wept.

"What's happened to her?" asked Ser Francesco, startled. "Has she fainted, or is it the falling sickness?"

But Alessia put her finger to her lips.

The old man stood dumfounded. Catherine's eyes showed only the whites. There were no pupils. And her face was like one not of this world.

There was a deep, shuddering sigh.... Did it come from her? Color came back into her face; her eyes returned to normal. She smiled. But Alessia had to help her to get back on her feet again.

"Alessia . . . "

"Yes, *mamma* . . . dearest *mamma* . . . "

"Thank God with me . . . they have repented."

Alessia held her up. "I must take her to bed at once", she said and led her away to the guest room.

The old man, the falcon still on his hand, stood speechless.

In the morning, when Catherine left her room, she found Ser Francesco waiting for her.

"I have made enquiries", he said. Then cleared his throat.

"Enquiries, Messer Francesco?"

"Yes. About those two men. They did repent. They were allowed to confess before they died. How did you know?"

Catherine said nothing.

Ser Francesco had to clear his throat again. "All right", he said. "I don't quite know what you have shown me, but you have shown me something. Now what do I do? I'll do anything you say. Anything." The old soldier mopped his brow.

"Go to Father Montucci", she told him briskly. "Tell him you have forgiven him for what he has done to you. Ask him to forgive you for the things you said to him. And the great Captain will forgive you as well. Go to confession to Fra Bartolomeo de'Domenici."

Ser Francesco bit his lip. "I promised to do anything", he said. "I'll do it. Now." He turned sharply, left the room and shouted for his hat and stick.

The servant who brought them announced mechanically, "The falcons have been fed."

Ser Francesco stared past him. "What's that you said?"

The man repeated it.

Ser Francesco gave a sigh. Then he walked over to the aviary. "Give me Caesar", he ordered.

Luigi, the falconer, brought the bird to him, and Ser Francesco pulled on a thick leather glove and let him sit on it. "I wish it didn't have to be you", he murmured sadly. "But then it wouldn't be worth anything, would it?" The falcon stared back at him, clear-eyed. "Hood him, Luigi. I'm going out with him."

The falconer obeyed, and Ser Francesco smoothed the little hood over the noble bird's head, gave Luigi a nod and stalked away.

Outside the servant was still waiting with hat and stick.

"You come with me", Ser Francesco told him, and they marched off to Saint Dominic's church, where the old man waited patiently in one of the pews, utterly unaware of the amazement of a number of worshippers at the sight of a fierce-looking old noble with a large falcon perched on his fist.

"Why, it's Ser Francesco di Saracini", a woman whispered. "He hasn't been here for years."

"Perhaps he wants to have that bird of his blessed?"

"He needs it more than the bird, I should say."

"Going to let it loose on the priests, more likely. He hates 'em."

"How do you know?"

"Everybody knows that."

An outraged sacristan came up, but before he could say anything Ser Francesco snapped, "Get the Reverend Prior here." It was the voice of a man accustomed to instant obedience, a man who had shouted orders to six hundred horsemen in battle.

The sacristan ran. Prior Montucci listened to his report, shook his head, and decided to have a look at the mysterious intruder. When he entered the nave, Ser Francesco rose and walked toward him.

The Prior gasped. From a dozen sources he knew that the old soldier had threatened to murder him on sight, and now here he was, with a great bird of prey, ready to pounce on him. Prior Montucci gave a shout of terror, jumped back, and fled as fast as he could.

Ser Francesco beckoned his servant. "Follow him", he ordered. "Tell him I have come in peace."

The man obeyed, but the better part of a quarter of an hour had passed before the Prior reappeared, very gingerly, and flanked on both sides by no less than eight of his sturdiest friars.

"Reverend Prior," Ser Francesco said, "I have wronged you and your priests, and you have wronged me too, I think. But seeing that you are a priest of God, it is up to me to come to you and ask for your forgiveness."

Pale and trembling, Prior Montucci was unable to reply.

"As a sign of contrition I give you Caesar here", Ser Francesco went on. "Of all my falcons he's the one most dear to me, so he's the one you should have. But get yourself a stout glove, or better still come up here and pull off this one while I hold the bird, lest he scratch your hand with his talons and I add to my sins by shedding the blood of a priest, and in his own church, too."

Unlike many another ecclesiastic dignitary, Prior Montucci was not in the least interested in falconry, but he had recovered sufficiently to realize that the old soldier meant exactly what he was saying. His spirits rose, his mind began to work again, and he would have liked to tell his former enemy that giving

Caesar to God's Church was definitely a faulty interpretation of a famous passage of Scripture. But from what he saw in the old man's eyes he knew that this was no time for irony, and he accepted the bird with suitable dignity.

Ser Francesco sighed deeply. "Now then," he said, "never do anything by halves. Where is your Fra Bartolomeo de'Domenici? I have to make my confession to him."

Chapter Eleven

GIACOMO BENINCASA'S STROKE came quite suddenly, without warning. His entire left side was paralyzed, his breathing irregular and labored, and Messer Girolamo Vespetti, the physician, confined himself to elaborate shrugs, raised eyebrows, and murmurings about the regrettable limitations of the medical art. The entire family was assembled around the large four-poster, the same bed in which Mona Lapa had given birth to twenty-three children, half of whom were still alive and present. Mona Lapa, herself dissolved in tears, sat next to the dying man.

Catherine, hurriedly called back from the Misericordia hospital, was kneeling at the foot of the bed, praying for a grace so great that only a very few could hope to receive it: that the soul of her father would be allowed to go straight to heaven, without going to purgatory first. "If there are any pains he would have had to suffer, Lord, let me suffer them for him here and now."

Was it true that a dying man could sense things hidden from all others? Giacomo Benincasa's right eyelid fluttered; it opened, and he looked at her with the ghost of a smile. A few minutes later it was all over. The room echoed with cries and lamenting.

Only Orlando saw, bewildered, that Catherine was beaming with joy, her hand pressed to her side. For days he could not bring himself to mention it at all. At last he did, and she told him what she had been praying for. "The moment he died, I felt the pain. It was unlike any other, stinging and yet sweet. So I knew Father was in heaven. Can there be a better reason for joy?"

But the death of the head of the family proved to be a great loss materially. Many a time Mona Lapa had stormed against his good-naturedness and wailed that he always let others take advantage of him. But Giacomo Benincasa knew his Siena, where nothing was better liked than generosity and nothing more hated than meanness. Generous by nature, he felt he would always have what he needed, and as he was conscientious as well, his customers always came back to him.

None of his sons could compare with him, and none tried. Old Giacomo alone negotiated with his customers.

Now that he was gone, Orlando and Stefano must try to win the favor of their father's customers, and that did not prove to be easy, especially as their older brother Bartolomeo had gone into politics and was in favor with the Salimbeni, most powerful of the noble families, and for that very reason suspect to many citizens who feared Salimbeni ambition. Why give work to a family who openly supported the Salimbeni?

Then Stefano too began to find politics more interesting than mere business, and Orlando was angry when he found that he had to do most of the work.

"Somebody must be interested in the welfare of this town of ours", Bartolomeo told him gruffly. He was in a bad mood, too. There had been another change of government, and he had had to resign his office.

"Consuls, they call themselves", he told his family with a twisted smile. "And there are thirteen of them. Rome, during her finest period, was content with two. And all because they are afraid of the Emperor."

Emperor Charles IV was passing through Siena on his way to Rome, and to the freedom-loving Sienese his visit, however brief, spelled danger. There was a rumor—no one seemed to know who started it—that the Emperor intended to sell Siena to the Pope. Siena, their Siena was to be part of the papal states, with a French legate to rule over it! Excitement ran high, not only in taverns and inns but also in the town hall.

Turbulent scenes took place when the Emperor arrived, and worse followed when he passed through again on his way back. The commander of his escort—a mere twelve hundred men—treated the dignitaries of the town hall in a very offhand manner. Bitter quarrels ensued. The crowd on the Campo assumed a threatening attitude. The imperial commander ordered his horsemen to disperse the mob, and fighting broke out.

The bell on the Mangia tower gave the great alarm, the call to arms; the citizens streamed out of their houses, and a series of street battles followed. The imperial troops were routed. The Emperor was forced to take refuge in the Palazzo Salimbeni and to open humiliating negotiations with the irate citizens who demanded his immediate departure. He left in a hurry, glad to escape with his life.

But the fury both of the government and the people of Siena now turned against the nobles and first and foremost the Salimbeni.

All the hospitals were filled with wounded men. The prisons were crowded. Constant executions served to make room for fresh arrests.

Most of the nobles fled to their country estates.

At the Misericordia hospital Matteo Cenni and his staff were working day and night.

"All this because of some stupid, poisonous rumors", Alessia said bitterly. "Not a shred of truth in them, either. But at least they're leaving Father in peace. I begged him to stay at home till things had quieted down again, but he insists on going to Saint Dominic's every day."

Catherine did not seem to listen. She made a strangely anxious gesture, as if trying to prevent somebody from doing something dangerous. Then suddenly she hurried away, and Alessia became worried. "She's been working eighteen hours a day, Cecca," she told Sister Francesca Gori, "and sometimes even twenty. I've warned her many a time she'll break down, and now I think she's near that point."

"I know, Chubby. She won't listen to me either."

Catherine was going home, where she found Mona Lapa in a state of great excitement. "This is a terrible time, Daughter, a terrible time. No one's safe any longer anywhere. I'm only glad that your poor father didn't live to see it. What are we coming to, when a family like ours—"

"Where is Bartolomeo, Mother?" Catherine interrupted. "Where is Stefano?"

"They left the house for asylum in some church. We've had warning that the government is going to have them arrested. My sons, arrested! Of all the wicked—"

"Where have they gone, Mother?"

"But they wouldn't listen to me. If I told them once, I told them a hundred times they should stop meddling in politics; nothing but trouble would come from it. Their father never did, did he? And business is going badly and getting worse all he time. Now this. We shall all die in the poorhouse."

"What church have they gone to, Mother?"

"What does that matter? One church is as good as another, isn't it? Asylum! Sons of mine must seek asylum, like brigands. The fine Lords of Salimbeni, of course, are quite safe. They have left town, I hear, so no one can do anything to them. That's justice for you!"

"Please, Mother, what church have they gone to? I *must* know."

"It's Sant'Antonio. Why? Do you want to go there yourself? They haven't sunk so low that they'd do anything to a woman, have they? And you a Mantellata . . . "

"Forgive me, Mother, but I must go to them at once."

Catherine hurried off. The beating of her heart had told her that her brothers were in danger, and now it beat even faster. There was no time to lose. The church of Sant'Antonio was the obvious choice, really, as it was the parish church of Fontebranda. It was where they would go. But they must not stay there, they must not stay there. . . .

In front of the church a crowd was waiting, sullen faced and expectant. An agitator was ranting against the nobles and what he called the lickspittle toadies of the nobles.

Inside the church she found her brothers sitting dejectedly in a pew. There were fifty or sixty people sitting and kneeling around them; impossible to say whether they also were taking asylum or whether they were worshippers.

"Come with me at once", Catherine told her brothers.

"We can't", Bartolomeo whispered back. "There are some men outside who know who we are."

"Government officials?"

"Worse. They want to kill us."

"If they do," Stefano said wearily, "the government will probably do nothing about it. Why should they? It only saves them the work of doing it themselves. That's what one gets for loving Siena."

"Calling us Salimbeni slaves", Bartolomeo muttered. "Aren't the Salimbeni just as good Sienese as those wretches, and better?"

"You are not safe here", Catherine urged.

"It's the only place where we *are* safe", Bartolomeo insisted.

Catherine took his hand and drew him up and out of the pew. "Come with me", she said almost roughly. "You too, Stefano."

Stefano rose sulkily.

She made them walk on either side of her. When they appeared in the portal of the church someone shouted, "That's one of them, the fellow on the left. He's a Salimbeni spy", and Bartolomeo stopped, his face contorted with fear.

"Death to the Salimbeni and their creatures", the man shrieked.

Catherine stared at him, at the sullen, menacing crowd, and again at the speaker, a scruffy-looking individual with the face of a ferret. In two swift movements she threw the folds of her black mantle first over Bartolomeo, then over Stefano. Another sharp stare at the crowd and she walked on with measured steps, leading her brothers as if they were children.

And the crowd, in silent stupefaction, let them pass.

After a while they were stopped by a patrol of five armed men.

"You're Bartolomeo Benincasa, aren't you?" asked the leader, a sturdy man with a shock of reddish hair protruding from his beret. "You're one of the Salimbeni dogs. And so is your brother. You'll come with us."

"They will stay with me", Catherine told the man. "Go on your way."

"They're wanted", the man snapped. "And I've got them. Why should I let them go?"

"Because it is God's Will and mine."

The man stared at the little Mantellata with the pale face and the large, luminous eyes. He opened his mouth to say something, thought better of it, shrugged, and walked on, giving his men a sign to follow him.

Soon afterward Catherine led her brothers into the Misericordia hospital. "You are safe now", she told them. "No one will look for you here. But you must stay inside until I tell you."

That same day two hundred city soldiers broke into the church of Sant'Antonio, killed a number of people who were resisting arrest or trying to escape, and dragged all the others away to prison.

Catherine managed to slip over once more to the Via dei Tintori to let Mona Lapa know that her sons were really safe now. "I won't tell you where they are," she said, "so you won't have to lie if you should be asked about it."

A few days later the government announced that there would be no more arrests on political grounds; Bartolomeo and Stefano could return to their home. However, the government had not forgotten them. They were fined one hundred florins for "having given support to the enemies of the people"— a name any Sienese faction in power always liked to give to those factions who were not in power.

The fact even more than the amount of money was embittering, and both Bartolomeo and Stefano decided to emigrate to Florence.

"She no longer eats anything at all", said Fra Tommaso della Fonte.

Fra Bartolomeo de'Domenici did not have to ask whom he meant. "Nothing, you say?"

"Only the Host at Holy Communion. I tried to make her

eat, using my authority as her spiritual director, but she suffered so much that she had to stop. And her sleep is down to an hour a day and often enough only half an hour."

The chubby little friar nodded. "I know that. Matteo Cenni told me she worked at the hospital for three days and three nights, almost without a pause, last week. He and his men watched her and counted the very minutes when she was asleep—dozed off, rather—in some corner of the Misericordia. Two hours and a half altogether, in three days."

Fra Tommaso made a note. "She has raptures now every time she receives Holy Communion," he said, "but it seems there has never been any like the one on the Feast of Saint Alexis, the eighteenth of July."

"She told you about it?"

"She did. She couldn't describe it, of course. They never can, as you know. One would have to create a new language. All earthly joys and beauties were like dirt, dull and grey, even spiritual things, like the consolation she used to pray for. And she asked our Lord to take away her will from her and give her his Will instead."

"We all pray for that, surely, when we say the Our Father. 'Thy Will be done . . . ' "

"Yes, but do we really mean it? She did . . . literally. She was answered, too. The Lord told her he would give her his Will, and it would make her so strong that nothing could change her, whatever happened."

Fra Bartolomeo de'Domenici mopped his forehead. "I've never dared pray to be allowed a vision", he muttered. "Praying is such a very dangerous thing. Before you know where you are, you're heard."

"There is more", Fra Tommaso said. "She believes the Lord has taken away her heart and given her his instead."

"She didn't mean it literally, of course. This is lovers' language."

"Of course it is. But what is charming generosity and delightful allegory on the plane of earthly love . . . think what it must be on the plane of ultimate Reality. And that's where she is, or was during her vision. With her, everything is real, not symbolical. And since then she has been abstaining from food altogether."

Fra Bartolomeo groaned. "One can't tell anyone about this. No one would believe a word of it."

"I believe it all", Fra Tommaso della Fonte said quietly. "And you? What do you say?"

Fra Bartolomeo gave him an owlish look. "I'd say that you're either as credulous as seven old women or that you're the most fantastic liar I ever met . . . if I didn't know Catherine."

On the next Sunday at nine o'clock in the morning, when Fra Bartolomeo was preaching in Saint Dominic's, he became aware of a certain unrest down in the audience. He was a good preacher in an order famous for its preaching, and he did not know what to make of it. People kept whispering to each other, and it seemed that some kind of message was being passed from one to the other, causing consternation and sorrow. Then he heard steps coming up the stairs behind him, and he turned his head. It was Fra Giovanni da Siena, a lanky young friar with the red patches on his thin cheeks that spoke of lung trouble. They all knew he was not likely to live long, and they knew also that he did not want to die, having done so little yet for the cause of the Lord.

"I'm sorry to disturb you," the young man stammered, "but they say Sister Catherine Benincasa is dying." He turned and slowly, shakily, climbed down again.

Fra Bartolomeo finished his sermon as well as he could. Then he went to find Fra Giovanni. "Where is she?" he asked hastily. "At home or at the hospital?"

"At home, they said. Are you . . . are you going there?"

"Of course."

"Please, may I come with you? I tried to get Father Prior's permission, but I couldn't find him. I . . . I've seen her so often in church. May I come?"

Fra Bartolomeo nodded without speaking, and they set off at once.

The Via dei Tintori was so crowded with people that the two friars had to shoulder their way through.

"You're too late", an old man told them. "The saint is dead."

Of a sudden the world seemed poorer, greyer. Fra Bartolomeo bit his lip and clenched his fists. "It mustn't be", he thought. "God can't want it." But then, of course, God could want it. He could want her for heaven, where she belonged. Only, what a pity for Siena. If ever there was a time when she was needed . . .

Fra Giovanni beside him was crying quietly. Yet he had never even met her; he had only seen her in church.

"I don't believe it", Fra Bartolomeo said obstinately. "I just don't believe it."

Slowly they pushed their way into the house and up the stairs, which were crammed with people, most of them praying.

"Is she really dead?" Fra Giovanni asked in a strangled voice.

"She died some hours ago", a woman told him. Her eyes were red from crying.

At long last the two friars reached Catherine's cell, now her death chamber. Mona Lapa was there, shaking with convulsive sobs; Alessia Saracini, Francesca Gori, Lisa Colombini, all on their knees crying their hearts out. Prior Montucci was there, Fra Tommaso Caffarini and Fra Tommaso della Fonte. They made room so that the two newcomers could have a last glimpse at the dead young woman.

She was lying on her wooden couch. Her face had the grey pallor of death; the nose seemed more pointed; the lips were bloodless. They had closed her eyes and crossed her hands over her bosom. There was a strange, majestic serenity about the frail little body on the wooden couch.

Her eyes, Fra Giovanni thought in bitter pain, I shall never see her eyes again. He had had doubts, very terrible doubts about the Faith, about God who would not let him live long enough to serve him well. Yet Sister Catherine Benincasa's eyes, shining like faith itself, had dissolved his doubts as if they had never existed. And now they would never again look on anything on earth; they lay dead and broken and glassy under those closed lids, with those deep, violet shadows all around them, violet, the color of penitence. Wild sobs shook his body, and suddenly blood shot up into his mouth, filling it so fast that he could not contain it; it went cascading down his white robe, and still it thrust up with a savage, uncontrollable force, great gushes of it.

"A hemorrhage", Fra Bartolomeo thought, horrified. "Good Lord, the poor boy is dying too."

Fra Tommaso della Fonte, immediately, almost without thinking, did a strange thing. He reached over, gently seized Catherine's right hand, and laid it on Fra Giovanni's breast. The young friar gave an inarticulate shriek. A thin stream of blood trickled down from the corners of his mouth and ... stopped. The hemorrhage ceased.

I knew it, Fra Tommaso della Fonte thought in an upheaval of triumph and grief. I knew it. . . .

Fra Bartolomeo crossed himself. This was the proof, the elementary and essential proof, the very hallmark of sanctity . . . if Fra Giovanni da Siena was cured, really cured. One would have to wait, of course, wait for many months, for years. But if he was really cured . . .

The one who did not think of that at all was Fra Giovanni himself. He stared at the deathbed, his eyes protruding from their sockets. His thin forefinger pointed. He tried to speak and could not. But the others looked and saw, and a cry went up from half a dozen throats at a time.

A thin red was creeping into Catherine's cheeks, and her white robe was moving just a little.

She's breathing, Fra Tommaso della Fonte thought, beside himself. "O my Lord and God, she's alive."

For the first time in her life Mona Lapa fainted.

Her eyes, Fra Giovanni thought, trembling with happiness. Her eyes are open again.

Catherine looked around. The serenity of her face vanished, changed into a sadness, a grief so deep and terrible that the joy of her friends froze. She turned to the wall and wept.

She wept continuously for days. In vain they tried to comfort her, to find out if she was in physical pain and what they could do. Her only response was that she was unhappy, desperately unhappy. At long last Fra Tommaso della Fonte exerted his authority. "What is it, Catherine? You must tell me."

Her voice seemed to come from far away. "*Vidi arcana Dei*", she said.

He understood then. She had been on the other side. She had seen the great secrets of God, of which ordinary mortal man could know very little more than that they existed. Always, in such a case, it meant that in some ways one was no longer the same person as before. A child could not go back to its mother's womb; an adult could not return to childhood. The seal of eternity was upon her. When it happened to Saint Thomas Aquinas, he could no longer write. "All I have written is like straw", he told his friend Reginald of Piperno. Earthly joy must be impossible for those who had seen the joy of heaven. There could be no earthly fear, either, for those who had seen the terror of hell and the pain of purgatory. They were new men and new women, and for the first time Fra Tommaso della Fonte felt clearly that however hard he might try, he could no longer consider himself an adequate spiritual director for a being whose spiritual experience was infinitely wider than his own. He tried to think of someone who could qualify, not an easy task, as it demanded an almost brutal integrity of thought. In the end he had to give up. There was no one in Siena whom he felt he could wholeheartedly entrust with that task.

The Lord himself would have to sort out that problem. Meanwhile his servant Tommaso della Fonte would continue as best he could.

Chapter Twelve

THE VEILED LADY crossed the narrow street in the *Contrada della Civetta* and disappeared into a house whose entrance was topped by the wooden figure of an owl or owlet. Cautiously, she descended the steep stairs leading to the cellar and, after some hesitation, pulled the bell string. The door opened and a servant, sleek and with knowing eyes, bowed to her and let her pass. There was a short, dimly lit corridor, with another door at the end and another servant to open it. The room to which it led was that of a very wealthy noble. There were carpets from Persia, velvet draperies, and beautifully carved tables and chairs; the light came from half a dozen heavy silver candlesticks holding three candles.

Handsome young Ser Francesco Malavolti rose with alacrity. "You have come", he said, delighted. "What a happy devil I am." He tried to embrace her, but she stiffened and looked about her. "Are we safe here?" she asked.

"Safer than anywhere else in Siena. I realized it might be imprudent for you to come to the Palazzo Malavolti . . . "

"Madness! The whole town would talk about it tomorrow."

" . . . or for me to come to your house when your husband happens to be away."

"*Ahimè!* He never is. Besides, the servants are unreliable."

"But here we are quite, quite safe, *bellissima.*"

"How so? This is an inn, a tavern. Anybody could come here at any moment."

"Come here, yes. Come in, no. At least, not without my permission. And this is not a tavern."

"Why, the Golden Owlet . . . "

"Was a tavern before I bought it. The place is mine, Mona Giulia. I bought it so that some of my friends could meet, at a time when any kind of assembly other than one called together by a government of worthy cutthroats was forbidden. Now that some kind of peace seems to be established, my friends and I meet here for less dangerous purposes."

"Women friends, of course. All the women who are stupid enough to believe you when you swear that you love them." Mona Giulia pulled off her veil, smiling.

"Ah, but you wrong me", Malavolti protested. "And now I shall be quite unable to defend myself. Your beauty is enough to drive out all reason from the heads of Plato and Aristotle. Upon my word, you look like Queen Cleopatra, whom even old Julius could not resist . . . "

"And who had to die because the men in her life proved to be worthless." Laughing, the lovely lady showed teeth that Malavolti promptly compared to pearls surrounded by rubies.

"Hey, Pastrano!" he shouted. "Where is the fellow? Pastrano! A pitcher of Mavrodaphne for Queen Cleopatra. Sit down, *bellissima,* and tell me how you managed to escape from that horrible man who thinks he owns you merely because he is your husband."

"Let's not mention him", the lady said with a slight and very becoming shudder. "If he ever finds out, he will kill me."

"Never", Malavolti said. "Venus is a goddess and therefore immortal. Besides, if he so much as tries to harm you, I shall run him through, even if they banish me or kill me for it in some disgusting manner. I swear it."

The wine came, golden brown and sweet, a woman's wine, and he filled the goblets.

"By what are you going to swear?" Mona Giulia asked, watching him carefully.

"By your love for me," the young man said, "and don't tell me it can't stand the test. I couldn't survive such news."

She laughed again. "You are an attractive rogue, Messer Francesco. I wouldn't trust you any farther than I can see. I wonder how many women you have received in this very unusual love nest of yours."

"None worthy to serve as your bathmaid, Mona Giulia."

"My vanity and your reputation tell me that this means most of the women in Siena", she said dryly.

"Really, you're making me out worse than I am", he protested.

"Most of the time my visitors are men. Gabriele di Davino Piccolomini, for instance; Paolo di Guccio, Niccolo di Bindo Ghelli, and Neri di Landoccio dei Pagliaresi, the poet, you know. He used to be the very best and finest of my friends."

"Oh, I am sorry he died."

"He didn't. Or yes, perhaps, in a way he did." Malavolti gave an uneasy laugh. "He has become mad or pious or both; I can't quite decide. Joined a group of people all dancing around some nun whom they believe to be a saint, though they all call her *mamma*. She's adopted him too, it seems . . . "

"Is he good-looking?"

"Very."

"What a pity. It's all wasted on a nun, isn't it? Unless, of course, she's only posing at being saintly."

"My dear, you don't know Neri. He loves to put people on some sort of pedestal, and then they have to live up to it. If they don't, he is so bitterly disappointed, he won't even look at them. So that nun will do well to behave."

"Is *she* good-looking? I'm sure she is."

"*Bellissima,* how do I know? I've never set eyes on the creature, although Neri tried very hard to get me to go and see her."

"Oh, he did . . . "

"Yes, but I laughed it off. What have I to do with nuns? She would bore me to distraction. Come now, enough of Neri and nuns. What are your commands for supper? Whatever it is, Pastrano will produce it in no time at all. He's an excellent man—if one pays him well enough."

"Which no doubt you're doing", Mona Giulia said lightly. "All the world knows that Ser Francesco di Vanni Malavolti is as generous as he is rich." Her eyes were greedily appraising the rings on his fingers.

"Ah well, we get by", he said cheerfully. "My father and my grandfather had excellent business sense, which means that they busily piled up florins, guilders, zechine, and bezants so that I can spend them on those things that make life worth living. I would have bought the Golden Owlet gladly for a single opportunity to meet you here, if it hadn't already been mine."

"To hear you talk one might think you're really in love with me", she smiled.

"Love", Malavolti said, taking her hand and studying her pretty fingers. "I've often wondered what it is that makes a man ready to make a fool of himself for the sake of a woman. Why he should be inconsolable if he doesn't succeed, as indeed I should have been if you hadn't come to me today, Mona Giulia. What is it about you? That promise of hidden passion in your eyes? The sweep of your delightful little nose? Your lips?"

She wriggled prettily. "May I have my hand back now?" she asked.

"Why? You have it all the time . . . grant it to me a few more minutes."

"I very much fear that like the devil you may not be content with a mere hand but will take the whole arm."

"How little you know me, *bellissima.* I am far less modest than the devil."

She giggled. "You seem to know him very well. I really am the most courageous woman!"

There was a sharp, metallic sound, and she looked around, startled.

"That wasn't the devil, *bellissima*", Malavolti said, grinning. "Only someone tugging at the bell string outside."

She jumped to her feet. "Ascanio", she whispered. "I'm sure it's Ascanio. He's laid a trap for me. It's just like him. Oh, what shall I do?"

"But you said he has left town for a day . . . "

"So he told me, and I saw him leave the house, but . . . oh, I wish I hadn't come here. He'll kill me."

"No, he won't", Malavolti said. He drew his sword, beautiful blue Damascene steel, thin and deadly. "I'm a very good swordsman", he told her, smiling. "Bad luck for Ascanio . . . if it is Ascanio. We shall soon see. Here's Pastrano."

"Ser Neri di Landoccio dei Pagliaresi to see Messer Francesco", Pastrano announced.

Mona Giulia gave a gasp of relief. Malavolti grinned and put his sword back into its velvet scabbard. "Didn't you tell him that I am not to be disturbed?"

"Oh, yes, Messer Francesco, but he says it is important, and he would never forgive himself if he did not tell you at once. He is quite excited, Messer Francesco."

"Maybe his nun has thrown him out", Malavolti said. "*Bellissima,* will you excuse me for a few minutes until I have got rid of my impulsive poet? It won't be long."

She pouted prettily. "I don't want to be left alone", she complained. "Why don't you ask him to come in? He doesn't know me, and I'll put my veil on again so he won't recognize me if I should meet him by accident." She readjusted her veil. "See? Am I not right?"

Malavolti laughed. "Why not? Tell Ser Neri to come in, Pastrano."

He really is good-looking, Mona Giulia thought, when the young poet entered. Slim, elegant, with large, dark eyes. Well dressed, too. But poets were so unreliable.

"This is Neri di Landoccio dei Pagliaresi," Malavolti announced, "a poet second only to Dante and my very good friend. Neri, *carissimo,* this is the most beautiful lady in the whole of Italy, and I am sorry to say you will never see her face or hear her name."

Mona Giulia giggled.

Obviously ill at ease, Neri said, "I am sorry to have intruded on you like this, Francesco. I didn't know, of course . . . "

"The lady forgives you," Malavolti said, "so I can only do likewise. Sit down."

"The only excuse I have", Neri said, "is that we are old friends, which means that I feel like coming and telling you at once when things happen, whether they are terrible or wonderful."

"Have some wine", Malavolti said, "and tell us all about it. No one has died, I hope? I mean, no one particularly dear to you, of course. No? Good. Has your father lost his fortune? Has he married again? Have you been . . . I scarcely dare hope for it . . . have you been thrown out of that holy and extremely annoying group that has attracted you lately?"

Neri shook his head. "What makes you so sure that my news is bad?"

"Well, isn't it?"

"Not at all. But I have just witnessed one of the most remarkable battles ever fought, so exciting and with an end so unexpected and overwhelming that I couldn't wait to tell you about it."

"A battle?" Malavolti exclaimed. "Surely the Salimbeni haven't started all over again?"

Neri smiled; he looked like a small boy. "Not that kind of battle", he said. "The battlefield was a small room; you might call it a cell. The opposing armies were on one side the Reverend Friar Giovanni Terzo Tantucci of Siena, Master of Theology, of the Order of Saint Augustine, and the Reverend Friar Gabriele of Volterra, also Master of Theology, of the Order of the Friars Minor, the greatest scholar and preacher the Franciscans have at the present time, and the Superior of the whole of Tuscany; on the other side one very small Mantellata, aged twenty-five. Present as witnesses: Fra Tommaso della Fonte of the Order of Preachers, Matteo Tolomeo, Niccolo de'Mini, old Tommaso Guelfacci, five assorted Mantellate, and a certain Neri di Landoccio, a scribbler of no importance at all."

Malavolti looked at the veiled lady and back to Neri. "Do you mean to say that you have come here and insisted on seeing me, never mind what I was doing, because you wanted to tell me about some theological discussion? Because, if so—"

"Wait a moment", Neri interrupted. "Have you no sense of proportion? Has there ever been a battle more exciting than that between David and Goliath? And here it was a battle between a David who was a young woman and two Goliaths, bent on her destruction."

"Arguments", Malavolti said, shrugging his shoulders. "Who cares? Who but hairsplitting dialecticians, miserable strainers of gnats—"

"Ah, but you don't know what happened, Francesco."

"Now if you have nothing more interesting—"

"But why don't you let him tell his story", Mona Giulia said. "One young woman and two men . . . that could be quite amusing."

For some reason Malavolti disliked the remark.

Neri did not seem to have heard it at all. "It did start with arguments", he admitted. "The two ponderous and learned men chose the most difficult and captious themes to ask questions about. For a while Sister Catherine answered very simply and humbly. So they asked questions to which there was no answer at all to make her appear ignorant or worse, and when she would not be drawn into saying anything wrong, they suggested that an ignorant person and a woman to boot should remain quiet about things quite beyond her understanding. She said that it was now her turn to ask a question. They nodded with condescension, and she asked, 'How is it possible for you to understand anything of that which pertains to the Kingdom of God, when you live only for the world, and to be honored and esteemed by men? Your learning is of little use to others and only of harm to yourselves, for you seek the shell, not the core, of the Faith. For the sake of Jesus Christ crucified, do not live in this way any longer.' The silence, Francesco, the unforgettable silence! We all knew in what style these two men were living . . . a cardinal would be satisfied with it. I saw Volterra's face. How he struggled to keep up his superior attitude, how he sought for some word to beat her with and yet couldn't find one. At last he looked at Tantucci for help, but Tantucci had hunched up his shoulders and was quite pale around the gills, so no help could be expected from him. I'm sure Volterra would have liked to get up and fly, but he was nailed to his seat by an accusation that demanded a reply. There was only one reply and he knew it, and that's why he wanted to avoid it so desperately. At long last he took the keys from his belt and said in a broken voice, 'Is there anyone here who will go to my cell and take everything he finds there and give it all to the poor?' I suppose he didn't trust his courage sufficiently to do it himself."

"I suppose so, too", Malavolti said dryly.

"And he wanted it done at once, before he could talk himself out of it. Well, old Tommaso Guelfacci took the keys, and he and de'Minni went and cleaned out the most sumptuous stable of Augeas—I mean to say the most elegant cell in Siena. Tantucci said he would do the same, but for himself."

" . . . and escaped?"

"And went and did it, too."

"Quite remarkable, that nun of yours", Malavolti said. "She did a similar thing before, to some other Franciscan friar, if I remember it rightly. Well, if she wants to reform the clergy, I for one have no objection. Heaven knows, it needs reforming. But when she steals away my friends, that is quite another proposition."

"I'm a happy man for having met her", Neri said. "Can you blame me if I want to see those I am fond of happy too?"

"I once knew a man who loved eating a certain curious herb they grow in Araby", Malavolti said. "It's some sort of hemp. They call it hashish, and he who eats it has extremely pleasant and exciting dreams; in fact, he believes that he is in a paradise full of joys . . . all the joys. Unfortunately he then wakes up with a splitting headache and vomits his heart out. Even so, he will always try it again. Hashish eaters also invariably urge others to join them."

"Do I look as if I had a headache?" Neri asked.

"You look very handsome", the veiled lady said.

"You may not have a headache," Malavolti said, "but far from having the joys I mentioned by chewing your particular kind of herb, I very much fear you've had to give up whatever pleasure you had before. I have no intention of doing that, I assure you. Not before I am ninety, anyway."

"Just as you like," Neri said, "but why can't you come with me and meet Sister Catherine just once?"

"No, thanks", Malavolti said. "It would be a waste of time."

"It may well be . . . for her", Neri said angrily.

"Exactly. So let's drop the idea."

" . . . but I'll take that risk."

"Look, Neri, we've been through all this before. If you wish to play the fool, sitting at the feet of a young nun instead of . . . of behaving like a normal man, it's sad enough, but I don't seem able to stop you. Me, I want to live the way I like, and I'd thank you not to interfere. You won't succeed in changing me. Neither will your nun or any nun or all the nuns in Christendom. And you can throw in the Hope for good measure."

Neri sighed. "Can't you do one small thing for me and simply meet her? For our friendship's sake?"

"Neri, what's the use—"

"Francesco dear, you must be terribly afraid of that poor woman", Mona Giulia chimed in surprisingly.

Malavolti stared at her. "Afraid? I? You're joking, *bellissima.*"

"Well, if you're not, why can't you have a look at her and be done with it?"

"By God, I will", Malavolti said. "Now, are you satisfied, Neri?"

"Indeed I am", Neri said, beaming. "Shall we say tomorrow morning at eight? Oh no, I forgot, you never rise before ten. At eleven, then? Excellent. I shall come fetch you. And thank you for having been so patient with me." He smiled at Malavolti, bowed to the veiled lady, and withdrew.

"Now what have you got me in for?" Malavolti said irritably.

Mona Giulia laughed. "It was the only way to get rid of him. These fanatics are all the same. Tomorrow you can always find an excuse not to go, can't you?"

"No", Malavolti said firmly. "A promise is a promise."

"Just as you like, of course." Mona Giulia took off her veil. "I don't think I have much to fear from that nun as a rival", she added, smiling.

He jumped up, took her into his arms. "You have no rival," he said, "and I wish we hadn't lost so much of our precious time on Neri and his nonsense. To Hades with him and his nun. I want life. I want you."

"Eleven o'clock", Neri said.

Malavolti yawned. "I don't believe it. It can't be that late."

"It is", Neri told him. "And the twelfth hour is beginning."

"Don't say that in such an ominous voice, I beg of you. I promised to come with you, so I'll come." Malavolti groaned. "Half an hour ago I was still in bed. Ye gods, I don't feel up to this at all."

"A little fresh air will do you good."

"I've never cared much for it. Hey, Pietro! My hat and cloak. But I tell you here and now, Neri: if that nun of yours starts talking at me about penitence, about having to begin a new life and all that kind of rot, I shall be damnably rude to her. Also I shall be out of her cell before you can count five."

"That's all right, Francesco; no one will force you to stay. And if you're rude to her, I shall open the door for you myself."

"She may get theologians and monks and some such to crawl before her, but I have broken no vows, and I will not be sent to confession like a naughty little boy."

"Of course not. You're a *big* boy, my Francesco."

Malavolti eyed him suspiciously. "And don't be sarcastic", he snapped. "Come on, let's get this over with."

When they ascended the stairs in the house on the Via dei Tintori, Malavolti chuckled. "A dyer's daughter, eh? No wonder she's so good at whitewashing people."

In the cell they found Fra Tommaso della Fonte, an old man neither of them knew, and several Mantellate standing in front of Sister Catherine's couch. The Dominican looked at Neri and at once began to shepherd the others out. He too left, and Malavolti saw the tiny figure in her black-and-white habit sitting on the wooden couch. Her face was bloodless. The wide-open eyes were looking right through him into space, fixed on something so immense that he was nothing, not even an obstacle.

In a flash he knew he had seen her before, lying on the steps of Saint Dominic's; some urchins kicked her and fled at his approach. He too had fled a moment later because he could not bear the sight. No man had the right to see such unbridled, terrifying happiness.

He wanted to flee now, but that was impossible. Neri would laugh at him and rightly so. No, that was not the reason at all. He did not know what the real reason was and he could not think it out, but there was a reason, and a good one. Besides, she had said nothing. Perhaps one could not speak at all in the state in which she was . . . whatever that state might be. Or, if she could, she would not speak to him. She was not here. She was as far away as her eyes. To run away was impossible. He did not really want to. He was going to face this; oh, yes, he was. One does not run away when one is a Malavolti. It had been different that day, on the steps of Saint Dominic's. That was not a challenge, and help was coming for her anyway.

A shudder went through the little body. She smiled and her eyes came back from eternity. They gazed on the visitor and held him. Was it the eyes or the smile? Neither. Or both. One thing was certain: she *knew*. She knew him, better than his mother had known him, better than he knew himself. She knew him as God knew him, and yet she smiled at the fool he was, the silly, insipid little skirt chaser, the idiotic pleasure seeker, pretending to himself that the world owed him a continuous and immediate fulfillment of every whim, warding off what he knew to be true by arrogance and rudeness.

She knew, and yet she smiled. He had kicked her and everything she stood for, just as truly as the urchins had kicked her on the steps of Saint Dominic's. An urchin, that's all he was. And what he had done to her was on the same level as what they had done to her Master and were still doing to him. In fact, she was a symbol of him. Was that what was meant by sanctity?

Oh, God, he thought, the whole terrible thing is true. Why didn't they tell me? But of course they did tell me, and I wouldn't listen, and now here she is, and she is smiling.

Then she said something. One single word. "Welcome."

How could he be welcome? How could he face this woman in the state he was in, a bag of dirt, stinking dirt?

He cried out, turned, and ran.

"I am sorry, *mamma*", said Neri, shocked and disappointed. "I thought . . . I hoped he would at least listen to you. Perhaps I shouldn't have brought him here after all."

"Don't worry about him", Catherine said placidly. "He'll be back soon. He's only gone to confession."

Chapter Thirteen

I MUST TALK to you, Ascanio."

Ser Ascanio Robaldi disliked being disturbed when he was studying his ledger, and Giulia had a knack of coming into his sanctum when he was doing just that. More than once he suspected that she knew when the great ledger was out of its habitual hiding place, and that she wanted to check up on the figures and then make more demands on him for things she said she needed, although her chests were full to overflowing with everything the most luxury-loving lady could think of. Giulia was an expensive wife.

"I am very busy at the moment, my dearest. Can't it wait until later in the afternoon?" He noted with some relief that she was standing at a distance which made it impossible for her to see the figures in the ledger.

"No, it cannot, Ascanio. It is an important matter."

He sighed. "Very well then, my dearest, what is it?" Velvet of all colors, part striped, part plain, sixty thousand florins. Belts, silk, golden ornaments after the Syrian mode, seven thousand two hundred florins.

"Ascanio, it is up to the women of standing to watch over the morals and manners of the community, isn't that so?"

"Oh, quite so, my dearest, quite so." Bags for brides, gold and silver embroidery, of the size of twelve inches, five thousand four hundred florins. Bags of the same make, same purpose, half size, two thousand seven hundred florins. Fillets, silk, all colors, six thousand florins.

"Ascanio, you're not listening to me. . . . "

"But of course I am, dearest. There is no one else to listen to, is there?"

"Close that book, Ascanio."

With a sigh he obeyed.

"We have a duty to watch over the morals of Siena," she repeated, "and when we hear of somebody behaving in a particularly wicked and shameless way, we cannot close our eyes, can we?"

"I hope no one has dared to behave in such a manner toward you, Giulia", Ser Ascanio Robaldi said, frowning.

"Oh, no, no, no, the matter has nothing to do with me personally, nothing at all. I am talking of a so-called Mantellata by the name of Sister Catherine Benincasa."

"A Mantellata! They're all elderly widows and the like, surely. One of your own aunts is one, isn't she?"

"Sister Palmerina, yes. Such a good and devout woman! She gave all her possessions to the order."

"She had no business to do so as long as relatives of hers were alive", Ser Ascanio Robaldi stated severely.

"Nevertheless, she is a good and most reliable woman, and the things she has told me about that Sister Catherine are most upsetting."

His fingers drummed nervously on the closed ledger in front of him. "Really, my dearest," he said, "this has nothing to do with either of us, has it? If that good Sister behaves badly, there is her Prioress to deal with her."

"Indeed there is, and if Aunt Palmerina were the Prioress, as she ought to be, she would have done so long ago. But the present Prioress, Nera di Gano, is one of those vacillating women who never do anything, and in the meantime the matter has become an open scandal."

"In that case it is for the ecclesiastic authorities to take the necessary steps."

"Exactly," Giulia said triumphantly, "but they will do so only when there are complaints. Many people are *quite* upset about it all, but they always say, oh, the ecclesiastic authorities will deal with it, and so no complaint is ever made. And poor Aunt Palmerina can't do anything. Mother Nera di Gano doesn't like her because she knows that my aunt would be a much better Prioress than she is. And Sister Catherine has managed to exercise some kind of domination over a group of other Mantellate. Aunt Palmerina says the complaint must come from outside the order, from some leading citizen or citizens of Siena."

"But why should that involve us?" Ser Ascanio asked. He felt out of his depth and longed to go back to his ledger.

"Duty", Mona Giulia said with great dignity. "Civic duty. You are one of the leading citizens of Siena. You are one of the biggest taxpayers. . . . "

"That", Ser Ascanio said with some bitterness, "is only too true. Not that one ever gets any thanks for it."

"There you are, Ascanio. It's up to you to do something about it."

"My dearest child . . . about what? I know nothing of the whole thing."

"If you would only listen to me, you'd know more than enough. Sister Catherine is most probably a witch."

"Good Lord in heaven, whatever next . . . ? How could a Mantellata be a witch?"

"A witch", Mona Giulia repeated emphatically. "There is no other explanation. She pretends to be a saint, of course. But she behaves so queerly in church that the priests won't give her Holy Communion! She is collecting a group of men around her, young men, mind you, good-looking young men. . . . "

"I see."

"Exactly. And they adore her and worship her and sit at her feet. Fine, upstanding young nobles like Neri di Landoccio and Francesco Malavolti . . . "

"Malavolti too, eh? Well, he's got a pretty bad reputation with women."

"Exactly", Mona Giulia repeated acidly. "It's common gossip that he likes seducing attractive women and then leaving them. And such a man goes to see a Mantellata every day! Every day, Ascanio, and that has been going on for weeks. And he completely forgets his obligations toward . . . toward his family."

"What I don't understand is why the Dominicans aren't

keeping an eye on that woman. Surely . . . what are you laughing about?"

"My dear Ascanio, how naïve you are! They *are* keeping an eye on her . . . only too much so. She spends *hours* every day with some of the friars. Young, nice-looking friars, Ascanio. Three, four, half a dozen of them. Aunt Palmerina gave me the names. She meets them in her cell. She meets them at Saint Dominic's. For what, do you think? To talk about religion, eh?"

"This sounds serious." Ser Ascanio was genuinely shocked. "Well, well, I must say, it came as a bit of surprise to me at first that you should be taking such an interest in . . . civic duties. But from what you tell me, one should seriously consider—"

"Don't consider", Giulia said hotly. "Act! *Do* something!"

"I might tell Ser Bruno di Dorsano. He's one of the leading members of the government, and I flatter myself he always listens rather carefully to anything I have to say."

"When are you going to see him?" Mona Giulia asked eagerly.

"I must go to the town hall tomorrow morning anyway. I shall talk to him then."

Mona Giulia embraced him. "You are the best of men", she exclaimed, kissed his sallow cheek, and rustled silkily out of the room.

One never knows with women, Ser Ascanio thought. Who would have thought that Giulia would take an interest in matters of public morals in general and the morals of a nun, a Mantellata in particular? Dresses, ribbons, and pleasurable gossip, yes, and money, of course. How fortunate that she herself had asked him to close the ledger. When she kissed him, she would have seen all the profits of the last year, very substantial profits, and she would certainly have insisted on another visit to Giambeni, the jeweller. With a smile of satisfaction he opened the ledger again. Silk kerchiefs, ornate with gold leaf, showing pomegranates, stars, rays and moons, eight thousand five hundred florins . . .

"We have the saddest news", Fra Tommaso della Fonte told Catherine. "The Holy Father has left Rome again. He is going back to Avignon."

Catherine paled. "He has left us", she stammered. "Oh, it can't be. I will not believe it."

"It is true", Fra Bartolomeo de'Domenici confirmed.

"But why, why? He's such a good and saintly man. How can he prefer—"

"Urban V is not a very strong man, *mamma,* and things in Italy have proved too much for him. Ever since the death of Cardinal Albornoz he has had no one to lean on, and they have besieged him like the bulls of Bashan. The impious Duke of Milan ... "

"Bernabò ... "

"Yes, the same man who was excommunicated by Innocent VI and then forced the prelates who came to present him with the document of excommunication, to eat it, leaden seal, silk strings, and all. He is an intriguer as well as a brute. And the papal legates ... well, you know how worried we always were about their ways. The many factions, all ruled by greed, all out for their own advantage ... it proved too much for a mild and gentle man like the Holy Father."

"The French cardinals had their hand in it, I think", Fra Bartolomeo said with feeling. "They always have."

"But the crusade he planned?" Catherine asked in a trembling voice.

"There has been precious little talk about that lately", Fra Tommaso della Fonte said with a shrug. "It seems to be impossible to persuade our princes to take any action that does not mean an immediate increase of their power and wealth. Advantage! Selfish advantage seems to be the only idea of our age."

"It has always been the idea of all ages," Catherine said, "and it's there to be overcome daily."

"That's what Princess Birgitta of Sweden told the Holy Father", Fra Tommaso said sadly. "She tried hard to make him change his mind, but even she did not succeed. And she is very likely a saint."

Catherine was pressing her nails into her palms. "If only I could ... " she murmured and then broke off. "What a wretched woman I am", she whispered. "I can do nothing, nothing at all." Her face took on that strange expression the two Dominicans knew so well, as if she were listening to her own heartbeat. "He should not have done it", she said. "Oh, he should not have done it. He too was thinking of himself, and that is how he lost courage and will lose . . . more." She seemed to wake up. "We are orphaned again", she said in deep distress. "And this is a day of sorrow."

Sister Andrea was very ill. There was an ugly swelling on her left breast, emitting pus and other foul matter, and such was the odor of it that many people were glad when Rector Matteo Cenni gave the order to have her carried back to her home. "There is nothing we can do for her", he told Sister Catherine, "except change her bandages every day. Once this kind of thing has started . . . " he shrugged his shoulders. "There will be other such swellings in a month or two or perhaps later, and after a while her whole body will be poisoned, and she will die. I won't keep her here. It isn't only because of the odor, although that too will get worse and would cause suffering to other patients. It isn't because of her nasty temper . . . yes, yes, I know about that, too, Sister Catherine. We could deal with all that and would if we had to, but fortunately she has a good bed at home which is more than some of our other patients have. It wouldn't be right to refuse somebody else a bed in order to keep her here."

"Somebody must look after her. It isn't only the changing of bandages. The sore must be pressed out; she must be washed and otherwise looked after."

"Well, yes, I know. But . . . "

"I will do it, Matteo."

"I am glad, *mamma.*"

Less glad was Mona Lapa. "*Maladetta figlia*", she shrieked, when Catherine came home, tired from hours of nursing. "You accursed girl! Is it not enough that you insist on destroying yourself with your insane fastings and vigils? Must you fill the whole house with the stench of putrefaction as well?"

When she herself fell ill, a few days later, she maintained that Catherine had brought in some horrible infection.

Ever since Bartolomeo and Stefano had gone to Florence she had been in a bad temper, and now it became worse than ever. Catherine had no right to look after other people when her own mother was ill. Let her stop her visits to the hospital and to that stinking old crone....

"Of course I shall look after you first, Mother."

Messer Girolamo Vespetti, the physician, did not think it was more than a mild attack of the ague, but after a few days he had to admit that he did not really know what it was. Lapa's fever mounted steadily, and she seemed to grow weaker. On the fifth day Vespetti had to tell the family that there was not much hope left.

"You're an old humbug", Mona Lapa told him venomously. "If I die, it'll be because of your poisonous medications."

"Mona Lapa," the physician said, outraged, "there are limitations, unfortunately, to the medical art, and ultimately all mortals must be prepared to—"

"Will you go and leave me alone, bird of ill omen?"

Catherine had been constantly at her mother's bedside, leaving Alessia, Lisa, and Francesca to look after Sister Andrea and the patients at the hospital. Now she saw what she had seen there so often before: the deepening of the shadows around the eyes, the nose getting longer and more pointed, the restless twitching of the hands. She sent word to Fra Tommaso della Fonte, but when the priest came in, Mona Lapa said sharply, "What do *you* want? Don't think I'm going to play the poor black sheep and confess my sins. I wouldn't dream of it."

"The sacraments wouldn't do you any harm, Mona Lapa", the Dominican said gently.

"Go away. I have as little use for you as I have for that windbag of a Vespetti. I am as I am and that's that."

"Mother, I have seen people get better so often, once they had received the sacraments...."

"You be quiet. I won't hear of it."

Catherine hung her head. She knew her mother had not

135

been to confession for a long time, and now she deliberately refused to receive the Lord; she was pushing him away. There was no way of influencing her. To her mother she was still a child, an erratic, incomprehensible child.

Mona Lapa gave a grim chuckle. "If you're so holy as they're always telling me, go and pray that I'll get well. Yes, go away, do you hear? And leave me in peace."

Obediently, Catherine left, but she sent Lisa Colombini, Lapa's relative by marriage, and two other Mantellate to look after her mother for a few hours. She herself went back to the hospital. There she first prayed for a while in the tiny, windowless chapel and then tended the sick.

In the evening Lisa Colombini came rushing in, her eyes red with tears. "Oh Catherine . . . my poor Catherine . . . "

"Mother? She is worse? She . . . she isn't dead, she can't be."

Lisa embraced her. "She died half an hour ago", she sobbed.

Catherine freed herself. "She died . . . without the sacraments?"

"You know how she was. She wouldn't change her mind."

Wordless, Catherine turned away, walked back to the chapel, crossed herself, knelt, and on her knees began her assault on God in heaven. "Lord, you promised", she stormed. "You promised me that none of mine shall be lost. You put your seal on that, and I wear it in the constant pain of my body. Is this how you keep your word?" She did what Hiob did and the widow in the Lord's parable of the wicked judge whom she plagued with her petition so constantly that he finally capitulated as the only way to get rid of her. "You implied that we too should be insistent," she told him, "and insistent I will be. You implied that if even that wicked judge had to give in to the widow, how much more surely would you who are Justice and Mercy. You promised, Lord, you promised. . . . " She did not let go; she wrestled with him as Jacob did with the angel, hurling up her prayers like lightnings thrown by a Titan, offering herself up for any pain her mother would have to bear, cajoling, begging, insisting.

Then she felt the touch of a hand, and she turned. Behind

her stood Rector Matteo Cenni. "I just heard about your mother", he said. "I'm so glad, *mamma.*"

"Glad?"

"Yes, of course. She's come round and old Vespetti says she is out of danger."

"But Lisa told me mother died. . . . "

"They all thought she was dead, I know. Her breathing stopped, and her pulse. I . . . I don't know how or why she recovered after that, but she did, that is certain. Sister Lisa told me herself."

"But . . . I don't understand," Catherine stammered. "Lisa was here only a few moments ago to tell me that Mother was dead. How . . . "

"That was last night, *mamma.* It is morning now. The sun has been up for some time. It's a good, cool morning. . . . "

Chapter Fourteen

WILLIAM FLETE, B.A., of the University of Cambridge was sitting on the lush grass of the forest clearing near Lecceto. He was in his favorite position, with his long, lean legs drawn up so high that he could rest his chin on his knees, and with his long, lean arms folded around them as if they needed protection. He was staring up at the luminously green foilage of the holm oaks, with eyes as blue as the sky, set in a long, lean bony face, topped by an unruly mop of hair so fair that it looked white. He was meditating and thus did not see the four figures, one dressed in white and three in black and white, approaching from the shore of the lake.

"Hey, holy William, visitors coming", shouted a voice in excellent English, and the hermit's eyes deserted the sky, and his head turned in the direction of the call. "Tantucci", he muttered irritably. "Aye, and three birds of Saint Dominic's, jabber, jabber, jabber." But when the visitors approached he rose politely enough. "Welcome to Lecceto", he said eying them sharply. "And if one of these Sisters is Sister Catherine Benincasa I will forgive you all for disturbing me."

Master of Theology, Giovanni "Terzo" Tantucci, thickset, swarthy, and moon faced, smiled broadly. "Venerable Sisters," he said, this time in Italian, "permit me to introduce to you the holy hermit William Flete, Bachelor of Arts of the great University of Cambridge in foggy England, where I first met him during my studies. William, this is Sister Catherine Benincasa, Sister Alessia Saracini, and Sister Francesca Gori."

"Ah," said William Flete, "so it's you who saved my learned friend from being drowned in luxury. I wish I had been there when it happened." His Italian was atrocious but understandable.

"Yours is a nasty character, Will", Tantucci said, blushing a little. "You're as bad almost as Tertullian, who told the pagans how much he was looking forward to heaven, where he would sit in comfort, jeering at them as they roasted in hell."

"Wrong as usual", William Flete said stiffly. "Tertullian was happy at the thought of seeing his enemies in hell—I am happy because the good Sister's intervention may—I repeat, may—have saved you from the same place. That's the exact opposite of what Tertullian did. So if he had a nasty character, as no doubt he had, what does that make me?"

"A very good man", Catherine said smiling. "Which is what Father Tantucci told me you were, and that is why I wanted to meet you."

"Don't you believe it", Tantucci said. "She'll find out your faults and vices in no time at all, and you'll have to change your life accordingly."

"*My* only luxury is the trees here", William Flete said, showing his long, yellow teeth in a smile. "Even Sister Catherine won't ask me to cut them down."

"You have no oaks in England?" Catherine asked.

He gave her a withering look. "Oaks, my dear Sister, are English trees. These must have been imported."

"I see."

"But in England I can't sit under them for longer than a few weeks every year, not unless I want to become an invalid. Rain, my good Sister, rain and fog. I would catch rheumatism in no time. Here I can spend practically the whole year out of doors. I usually say Mass in the little cave over there, with only the birds as my congregation. No coughing, no sneezing, no shuffling, no clicking of beads. Just the Blessed Lord and I."

"And the birds", Tantucci said.

"Birds don't sneeze", the hermit said. "They don't shuffle and they don't—"

"I thought you were an Augustinian monk", Catherine interrupted him, surprised.

Tantucci laughed. "So he is. And his prior has asked him many a time to say his Mass up there at the monastery, but he won't leave his trees."

"Perhaps", Catherine said, "one ought to cut them down after all."

"Prior, Prior", William Flete murmured. "Fra Antonio of Nice. He doesn't understand trees; that's all it is. They are a consolation given by God. Can't pray . . . I mean, really pray . . . anywhere else."

"Oh, yes, you can", Catherine told him firmly. "And you shouldn't keep all the consolation for yourself."

"I'm a hermit", William Flete said stubbornly.

"A hermit too must love his neighbor", Catherine said. "There was a time when I lived as you do, although my cell was much smaller than your forest. But our Lord opened the door and ordered me to go out and meet people. So that's what I did."

"He hasn't ordered *me* to do that", William Flete said morosely.

"Yes, he has. First through your Prior and then through me. Now."

He stared at her. He said nothing.

"We need holy men, a whole brigade of them", she went on. "There is another Englishman in Italy, and his very name means terror and anguish and bloodshed. The Knight Aguto . . . "

"Hawkwood", William Flete murmured. "Sir John Hawkwood."

"I can't pronounce the name of this foreigner as you do."

"Foreigner?" William Flete opened his eyes wide. "My dear Sister, the man's an Englishman."

"I know. Can't you see that your task is to atone for the great evil he does?"

He eyed her thoughtfully. "That would keep me busy for the rest of my life", he said. "Slowly, Sister, slowly. I gave you one good man for your brigade: Matteo Cenni."

"*You* did?"

"I put him on the road, yes, and if God wants me to, I may send you others. No reason for me to rush things as you do."

"By all that is good," Catherine said, "I believe when you go to heaven, you will demand of our Lord that he give you a forest of trees and keep away all trespassers!"

"It is a good idea", William Flete said gravely. "That is, if the trees are holm oaks and if there is a lake nearby, like this one."

"Which means", Catherine said sternly, "that you want your heaven here on earth as well; and you want God to comply with your will, instead of doing what he wants. Do what he wants, and I tell you in the name of Jesus, you won't lose the Grace of God because you lose your consolation; on the contrary, you will find it, for doing his Will."

"I'm not sure whether God is quite as impatient as you are, Sister Catherine", the hermit said placidly.

She replied without a moment's hesitation. "By choosing One who is impatient of all delay to tell you his Will, he shows that there is no time for patience."

"Tantucci," William Flete said, "why don't you take her to Cambridge? She'd talk down all the masters as well as the students."

"She has never been outside of Siena so far", Master Tantucci told him. "In fact, this visit to you here in Lecceto is the first time she has left the city walls behind her, and that's less than three miles."

"I went with my mother to Vignone when I was fifteen", Catherine said.

"Cambridge for you", William Flete insisted. "*And* Oxford, although they don't deserve such a treat. They're a decadent lot, senile, really. Still, it might be very good for them, unless they're beyond help."

"What is he talking about?" Catherine asked, bewildered.

Master Tantucci laughed. "That I've asked myself often and never found an answer. There is only one William Flete, at least here in Italy. There are many more like him in the learned country of fog and rain."

"He may be strange," Catherine said, "but I think he loves our Lord, though in his own way, and that is what matters."

They spent the whole day in Lecceto. When they left for Siena Catherine said, "Think over what I told you and stop being a spiritual egoist, or I'll come and visit you again."

"You are a great nuisance, Sister Catherine," William Flete said gravely, "but I will take that risk. Come and disturb me again any time you want."

"Heavens above," Master Tantucci exclaimed, "I have never heard him say anything half as complimentary to anybody."

When they stopped at Saint Dominic's, Fra Bartolomeo de'Domenici came up to them. "Have you heard the news?" he asked eagerly.

"No, we've been away all day", Master Tantucci replied. "What has happened?"

"The Pope died. . . . "

"I knew it," Catherine exclaimed. "Oh, I knew it. He could not possibly . . . " She broke off. It was not permissible, she felt, to say what she knew, not here and not at this moment. But the Pope had deserted his holy city, and the punishment for desertion was death.

" . . . and we have a new Pope", Fra Bartolomeo went on. "Travellers from France arrived with both pieces of news at the same time. He must have been elected very quickly."

"A Frenchman, of course", Master Tantucci said.

"Yes. Cardinal Pierre Roger de Beaufort. He will be known as Pope Gregory XI."

"A very young man", Master Tantucci said. "He can't be much more than forty. Forty-two, perhaps, or forty-three."

"When will he go to Rome?" Catherine blurted out.

The two friars looked at each other.

"I have heard nothing about that yet", Fra Bartolomeo said.

"Yesterday is better than today", Catherine said. "And today is better than tomorrow."

The Prioress, Nera di Gano, was summoned to appear at the town hall, a most unusual occurrence. As soon as she returned, she sent for Sister Catherine Benincasa. "I have had to hear today what I have never heard before", she said tonelessly. "And I pray to God that I shall never hear the like of it again. It all concerns you, Sister Catherine, and it is my duty to ask you a number of most painful questions."

Catherine said nothing.

"I prefer to do so without witnesses, for the time being," the Prioress went on, "although I have been advised to make an official enquiry immediately. I may still have to arrange for a House Council. I must warn you: a great many things have been reported to me from many sources, including members of our order as well as others. The life of a Mantellata is far more open to observation and criticism than that of a regular nun, because we live in the world. We have no conventual life in the strict sense of the word." The Prioress was pale, and her fingers toying with her heavy Rosary trembled a little. "The life you are leading invites gossip and scandal . . . no, do not interrupt me now, Sister Catherine; you will have full opportunity to answer. You receive whole groups of people in your cell, people of either sex. You affirm stories spread about you in regard to abnormal fastings, and there are countless stories about you matching your wits against those of learned men of the Church. Your behavior in church, especially during Holy Communion, has given cause to a great deal of talk. Is all this true or not?"

"It is true, Reverend Mother, but—"

"It is true also that so far I have exercised the greatest restraint in regard to all these . . . goings on", the Prioress said. "And I have done so although there have been those who assured me that the source of your alleged visions and cures was not what you apparently believe it to be." With a bitter little smile she added, "My own experience does not permit me to judge the nature of *these* matters. I am well aware that there are a number of priests of our order who feel convinced that your . . . mystical life is a very exceptional one. But there are others who feel no such conviction, and there have once again been much talk and much dissension. I have had many sleepless nights on your behalf, Sister Catherine. Many a time I've wanted to call you here and ask you what was really going on in your heart and soul. But how could I hope to find out the truth, when you could get the better of so many learned and experienced men? I decided to wait and see." She took a deep breath. "Now I can no longer do so", she continued. "The accusations against you are such that I cannot overlook them."

"Who are my accusers?" Catherine asked.

The Prioress frowned. "You have a right to know, I suppose", she said with some reluctance. "There is Sister Andrea . . . "

"Poor Andrea."

"I know you have been nursing her for many weeks. She ought to be grateful to you, and she assured me that she is. But she says that she still regards it as her duty to open my eyes to your dangerous activities. She puts her duty toward the order first, and for that I cannot blame her. Then there is Sister Palmerina, one of our oldest and most respected members. There is Sister Angelina. There is Fra Marco Tivanello of the Order of the Friars Minor, and many others, Sister Catherine, many others. Too many."

Catherine nodded. "Our Blessed Lord warned us that there would be those who will hate us", she said. "But what am I accused of, Reverend Mother?"

"The frequent visits you receive from Friars of Saint Dominic's have led to the worst possible interpretation", the Prioress said stonily. "I have been told that activities take place in your cell, as well as elsewhere, which are a flagrant breach of our Rule as well as gross sin against purity."

Catherine fell on her knees. "By the most precious blood of our Lord Jesus Christ," she cried out, "there is no truth in this at all!"

The Prioress was silent for a while. This sudden outburst, she felt, had the ring of truth. But she was responsible for the reputation of the order in Siena. She had to make sure, as sure as she could, that she was not being taken in by a cunning little nun.

"It is my duty, Sister Catherine Benincasa, to ask you in the most solemn way, in the Name of our Blessed Lord: Are you still a virgin?"

"I am, Reverend Mother."

"You may rise," Nera di Gano said, "but I must inform you that the matter cannot be regarded as closed. I was called to the town hall today. There one of the defenders, Ser Bruno di Dorsano, told me that the accusations against you and the rumors about you are so grave and so numerous that it should be brought to the attention of high ecclesiastic authority. I replied that such authority could be only the Master General of the Order of Preachers, Fra Elias of Toulouse, and asked him to send me what material he had for study. I would then pass it on to the Master General. Ser Bruno di Dorsano . . . " Nera di Gano's fingers clenched around the pearls of her Rosary. "Ser Bruno di Dorsano thought fit to say, 'You may take too long studying it, and you may feel inclined to hush it up. I shall send the material direct to the Master General. You will receive a copy.' And that was the end of that most unpleasant . . . meeting." The Prioress drew herself up. "The matter is out of my hands, as you see," she said, "and you must expect to be called before the Master General's court."

Book Three

Chapter Fifteen

THE PENTECOSTAL CHAPTER of the Dominican Order was to be held in the Church and Monastery of Santa Maria Novella in Florence, and the provincials, the masters of theology, the bachelors, priors, lectors visitors, preachers general, and friars of the great order were arriving daily from all the countries of Christendom.

Master General Elias of Toulouse was sitting at his desk, listening carefully to the report of an Italian friar. He was a man in his early fifties. The red of his hair was greying, but his face with the strong, aquiline nose and the thin mouth was still almost free of wrinkles.

Fra Anselmo Marotti had never met him before, but he knew that he was a man of exceptional erudition and of great courage, and that he was the kind of man who would make himself obeyed even where obedience was not his due.

"The Spaniards arrived this morning", Fra Anselmo reported. "Twenty-eight friars in all."

"Good. I shall visit them this afternoon."

"The French friars are complaining that they are taking up too much room."

"The Spaniards always like to remind us that Saint Dominic was not French", Elias of Toulouse smiled dryly. "And Frenchmen always like to complain. I should know; I'm a Frenchman myself. We shall see what can be done when I have met the Spanish Brothers."

"The Capella degli Spagnuoli has been set in order for the beginning of the Chapter."

"But of course. I gave the orders for that. Anything else?"

"That Mantellata from Siena has arrived, Sister Catherine . . . Catherine Benincasa", Fra Anselmo read from his list.

"I dislike that kind of case", the Master General said. "But it doesn't matter what I like or dislike."

"There are three other Mantellate with her", Fra Anselmo went on. "Sister Lisa Colombini, Sister Francesca Gori, Sister Alessia Saracini. And two Dominican friars: Fra Tommaso della Fonte and Fra Bartolomeo de'Domenici."

"A Mantellata travelling with a retinue", the Master General said coldly. "Where are the documents of the case?"

"I have them here with me, Father General."

"Leave them on my desk. You have read them?"

"I have, yes."

"What exactly is the accusation?"

"There is no formal accusation at all. It's rather a series of complaints from various sources, with a covering letter from a member of the Sienese government."

"What are the complaints, then?"

"Life unbecoming a Sister of Penance. Excess, or pretension of excess, of fasting; permitting herself to be given homage as if she were a person of great importance. Some hints that she may be dabbling in witchcraft . . ."

"Of course," the Master General said. "When a Sister is not like everybody else she must be a witch. We had eighteen such cases, one after the other, last year and all of them rubbish. Nevertheless . . . well, we'll see. Anything else?"

"She has collected a circle of people around her who seem to regard her as a saint and obey her blindly. Some allegations of unchastity, all rather vague . . . I don't think there is much in that."

"What makes you think so?" Fra Elias asked sharply.

"There is a letter from her Prioress. She confirms a number of points, but not that one. In fact she seems to think that there is nothing to it. But lately Sister Catherine Benincasa seems to have taken an active interest in political affairs."

"What on earth do you mean? Sienese politics?"

"Nothing as minor as that." Fra Anselmo tried to keep up a straight face. "For one: she has written to the Duke of Milan, exhorting him to make peace with the Holy Father."

"The Duke will be most impressed, I suppose", the Master General said.

"She has also written several times and at great length to the papal legate and to the Pope's nephew, Abbot Marmoutier."

The Master General laughed. "She'll be writing to the Pope himself next. What does she write about?"

"There are copies of her letters in the dossier", Fra Anselmo said. "Fra Tommaso della Fonte has given them to me."

"Why does he tolerate this kind of nonsense?" the Master General said angrily. "He should know better if she doesn't."

"She exhorts both the legate and the abbot to be virtuous." Fra Anselmo was grinning openly now.

"Rather a strange thing to do, for a witch", the Master General remarked. "Very well. Leave all that stuff on my desk. I suppose I shall have to read it." He sighed. "In the meantime ask one of the Brothers to keep an eye on the woman. We don't want any mischief during her stay in Florence. An experienced man, Fra Anselmo. Send for Dom Giovanni delle Celle, too. He knows a good deal about witchcraft. Let him meet her and put out a feeler."

"He will hate that, Father General. It's long since he dabbled in it himself, and he doesn't like to be reminded of it."

"I told you that it matters little what I like or dislike", the Master General said quietly. "And that applies to Dom Giovanni delle Celle as well, although he is not under my jurisdiction."

"Yes, Father General."

A nod gave Fra Anselmo permission to leave.

Fra Elias of Toulouse looked at the pile of documents. A hundred and one important issues must be debated, thought out, and organized, and he had to study this pile of nonsense about a young Mantellata and her vanities. Ridiculous. He decided to give the dossier a cursory glance and to pass it on to someone else.

Two hours later, when he had finished reading the dossier for the second time, he rang the bell and asked for Fra Tommaso della Fonte and Fra Bartolomeo de'Domenici.

"*Eh! bien,*" he said, when the two friars stood before him, "perhaps you can explain to me why one-half of your town seems to believe that Sister Catherine Benincasa is a saint and the other half that she is the spouse of the devil. You first, Fra Tommaso."

When they had finished, he dismissed them with a curt, "Thank you for your opinion." Neither of them could make out whether he agreed with them or not.

When they had gone, the Master General rang his bell again and asked for Fra Raymond of Capua to be sent to him at once.

Fra Raymond was forty-four years of age. He had been Prior of the great monastery of Santa Maria sopra Minerva in Rome, and Fra Elias knew him well, although he had not seen him for some time. He did not seem to have changed much. The Master General studied him for a while. The forehead of a thinker, both high and broad. The eyes of a dreamer. Nose and mouth finely chiselled; they would have graced the face of a woman, and a beautiful one at that. But the chin was firm enough. In the world he had been Raymond della Vigna, of the same great family as the famous chancellor of Emperor Frederick II of Hohenstaufen, poor della Vigna who had spun intrigues against his imperial master, was caught, and preferred to commit suicide by running against the prison wall with such force that he smashed his skull rather than submit to the unspeakable tortures the Emperor's Saracene executioners had in store for him. It was safe to assume that Fra Raymond's fate would be different for many reasons. There were petty tyrants enough trying to ape Frederick of Hohenstaufen, but Fra Raymond was not likely to serve any of them. He was highly intelligent, but he was no intriguer. On the other hand he was not a man to be easily deceived. . . .

"Fra Raymond, do you know a Mantellata named Catherine Benincasa?"

"No, Father General, but I have heard of her."

"Was what you heard good or bad?"

"Both. The reports seem to be most contradictory."

"So they are", Fra Elias of Toulouse said grimly. "What is your impression?"

"Not having met her, it is difficult to say. I could not help wondering whether ours may not be the age of the third beast, and that we are in the sign of the Leopard, which stands for hypocrisy."

"Perhaps," the Master General said evenly, "and perhaps not. There is something behind this, and I must know what it is. I want you to find out. She is being accused of all kinds of things, and her case will have to be tried in the Chapter. But we cannot afford to make a mistake." The Master General paused. After a while he said with some emphasis, "Four years ago when we were in Rome together, I sent you to the nuns of Montepulciano to ask for their prayers. Do you remember?"

Raymond gave a slow smile. "I'm not likely to forget. It isn't every day that a Master General of the Order of Preachers is accused of theft and threatened with excommunication."

Fra Elias nodded. "Moreover, it was the Pope himself who called me a thief, for having stolen the most priceless of relics: the body of Saint Thomas Aquinas. I replied, 'Holy Father, he was our own flesh and blood and our brother. One cannot steal one's own possession.' That calmed him down a little. It didn't calm down the monks of Fossa Nuova. Saint Thomas had died in their monastery, and they had been guarding his body ever since. . . . "

"He died exactly a hundred years ago", Fra Raymond said, wondering why the Master General should rehearse the old story. However exciting it had been, what possible bearing could it have on this new task he was given? Or was the Master General merely indulging in old memories, as most elderly people liked to do? It was most improbable. There was nothing elderly about Fra Elias of Toulouse.

"The good monks were beside themselves with rage", the Master General went on. "I think they would cheerfully have murdered me, if they could have caught me . . . and I feel pretty sure they wouldn't have preserved *my* poor body. Ah well. They got themselves the best lawyer available, and they and he did everything possible to convince the Pope that the relic must be given back to them. They were Benedictines . . .

and, as it happened, Pope Urban V belonged to that order. Perhaps they would have won the day, if the Pope had not fallen ill. He went first to Viterbo and then to Montefiascone to recover. The Benedictines were kind enough to leave him alone there. I wasn't. I had only one idea: to win this relic of all relics for our order. So I went to Montefiascone and pestered the chamberlain until I obtained an audience. I reminded the Holy Father that Saint Thomas had acquired some merit with his predecessor in name, Urban IV, for whom he wrote the liturgy of the Corpus Christi Feast . . . "

"And the commentary to the four Gospels as well."

"That's right. And because of these facts, I humbly asked that he be given the honor of reposing among his brothers who would glorify him. The Pope replied that his own order, the Benedictines, were far more powerful and that it would be far more appropriate were he to rest again with the monks of Fossa Nuova."

"I remember all that very well, Father General", Fra Raymond said.

Fra Elias smiled. "Bear with me, Fra Raymond. You will soon see why I am reminding you of it. I said to the Holy Father, 'There is no doubt that the great Order of Saint Benedict is much more powerful than we are; indeed, we are like a grain of sand by comparison. And exactly for that reason I plead with you to let us keep this relic. For the Order of Saint Benedict has countless saints, but we have only two, apart from Saint Thomas Aquinas: Saint Dominic himself and Saint Albert of Regensburg.' And the Pope thought it over and then pronounced most solemnly, by the authority of our Blessed Lord, of the apostles Peter and Paul and of his own, that he accorded to us the body of our great saint."

The Master General leaned forward. "Now listen well, Fra Raymond: this Sister Catherine Benincasa may well be a she-leopard, a hypocrite, and a sham. But there is just a possibility, a chance, that she may prove to be that rarest of all treasures, a saint. I have done my utmost, risking condemnation as a criminal, risking excommunication, for the sake of the body of

Saint Thomas. It shall not be said of me that I failed to do everything possible to ascertain whether or not it is our great good fortune to have a living saint in our midst today."

"You really think this woman might be . . . "

"I don't know", Fra Elias said brusquely. "And it may well be that we shan't know for a long time yet. First I must discover how much truth, if any, there is in the accusations launched against her."

"But surely that is what her trial is about . . . to find out whether she is guilty or not."

"The trial will take place at the end of the Chapter. By then we should know a great deal more about her . . . through you. Some of the accusations could be serious, so much so that we may have to get rid of her. But I too was accused of grave transgressions, only four years ago. Now it will be my duty to preside at that young woman's trial. Find out the truth for me, Fra Raymond. And I entreat you . . . I order you . . . be severe, be sincere, be honest. You must scrupulously avoid giving way to your own wishes in the matter. This woman must have a very strong personality, and she has ways . . . oh, not as a woman, nothing so crude as that . . . as a person, a spiritual person, of winning the souls of both men and women. And there are learned men among them, masters of theology, Augustinians, and Franciscans as well as Dominicans. You have a great deal of experience with nuns, as spiritual director at Montepulciano. You know the types, the illnesses, the dangers. Be incorruptible . . . no, I shouldn't have said that; I know you are incorruptible. But even you must be on your guard. Go, my son."

Fra Raymond genuflected and withdrew.

At High Mass on the feast of Saint John the Baptist Fra Tommaso della Fonte was the celebrant and Fra Bartolomeo de'Domenici the deacon. Subdeacon was a middle-aged priest whom Catherine had never seen before. When Fra Tommaso joined her after Mass she asked him at once who the priest was.

"Fra Raymond of Capua. Why?"

"I have been looking for him such a long time", she said. "Now at least I know his name, and I know where he is. I must meet him."

"That will be easy, *mamma*. He wants to meet you, too. He told me so."

They met a few minutes later in the sacristy. "You have been promised to me", Catherine told him point blank. "It's just as well. I am much in need of your advice and guidance."

Fra Raymond murmured a few courteous words, but his thoughts were racing. Neither of the two Dominican priests with her knew anything about his task. Had she guessed or sensed it right from the start? Or was this her usual way of winning a man over by flattery? And what did she mean when she said that he had been promised to her?

Fra Tommaso introduced the other Mantellate to him, and he liked them: good faces, cheerful faces, no fanaticism, no affectation. He also liked the two friars from what little he had seen of them. They seemed sensible enough, intelligent, and sincere but neither erudite nor strong enough to cope with an exceptional personality. And that Sister Catherine was, no doubt. Perhaps she really did need "advice and guidance". They all seemed to flit around her like bees around the honey pot, and she took it very much for granted.

"We must go and see Ser Niccolò", she said suddenly, and there was neither assent nor dissent: the whole group started off at once. For a moment or two Fra Raymond stood undecided, but Sister Catherine promptly turned and asked him to accompany them, and he accepted.

To his surprise Ser Niccolò turned out to be Niccolò Soderini, a very important member of the Florentine government. He had a number of guests. Fra Raymond recognized some of them, men well known in politics and in business, all of whom received the pale little Mantellata with a curious mixture of respect and curiosity. Everybody was enjoying the excellent wine, and the little tidbits the servants were offering. From the corner of his eye Fra Raymond watched her refusing both with a polite little gesture. Then he turned to Soderini, whom he knew quite well. "You have known Sister Catherine Benincasa for some time, I suppose, Ser Niccolò?"

"I met her only a few days ago, but we have been in correspondence for quite some time."

"About religion?"

"That", Soderini said smiling, "is inevitable with her. One might say she is trying to spiritualize Florentine politics. I can only hope she will succeed. It would be a most pleasant innovation."

"So Florence is trying to learn from Siena?"

"Soderini is trying to learn from Sister Catherine", the elegant Florentine replied. "But if she were a man and a Florentine, she would be one of the leading figures in the government in no time at all."

"Do you mean that?"

"No, I don't, but only because she wouldn't want it. Is it true that the order is displeased with her for some reason?"

"Did she say that?" Fra Raymond asked quietly.

"Oh, no, no, no, but there is a rumor in town that there will be some kind of trial."

Fra Raymond preferred to make no comment. Instead he listened intently to the animated conversation going on nearby.

"It's no good, Sister Catherine", a florid-faced young noble said. "One must demand of one's priests a certain standard of life . . ."

"Don't be proud, Messer Amato," Catherine said, "it will coarsen your understanding."

"Well said", someone murmured.

"Serves you right, Amato", a rather effeminate-looking man chimed in.

"We must *all* start with self-knowledge", Catherine said pointedly. "If we do, we shall soon stop judging others. And a priest may be bad; he may be a downright evil man; yet it is still he whose hands give us the Body and Blood of our Lord, and for that we must honor him."

"That's one of her basic themes", Soderini explained. "She is very upset about the anticlerical attitude of some of my fellow citizens."

The debate was swinging over to purely political issues, and Fra Raymond listened with open interest. Sister Catherine seemed to know the extremely complex political structure of Florence as if she had had a hand in it for years past; she not only knew about the rivalry of the two most ancient parties, the Guelphs and the Ghibellines, but also about the discord between the various lower classes, including the *Ciómpi,* who had more than once threatened the Signoría with rebellion. She knew about the law of "official admonition", about the growing power of Ser Giovanni Dini. . . .

"How I wish you could take an active hand in politics, Sister Catherine", an elderly man said. "It is a pity they won't allow you to do anything but pray."

"Prayer is action, Messer Buonaccorso", she answered at once. After a pause she added, "A good man *is* a prayer", and the elderly man's eyes lit up and he smiled happily.

A quarter of an hour later she suddenly rose. "We must go", she said, and Fra Raymond saw a flicker of sadness go over all the faces. Yet no one dared plead with her to stay.

Outside the Palazzo Soderini Sister Catherine said, "We must go and see Pippino", and again they all seemed to take it as a kind of order.

This time their goal was a humble little house near the corn market. Francesco Pippino turned out to be a tailor, and he and his pretty wife Agnese received the group of visitors with such warmth that Fra Raymond felt touched.

There was no talk of politics this time. But in the adjacent room some thirty people were waiting to hear what Sister Catherine would tell them — artisans mostly, and their women-folk, and she talked to them very simply about the love of God. "We cannot measure it, and there is only one way to get a glimpse of its greatness: the suffering of our Blessed Lord on the Cross. And that is why the great and glorious Saint Thomas Aquinas said to a friend of his that he had learned more at the foot of the Crucifix than in books . . . he, who had read so many."

"I wish I had thought of that myself", Fra Raymond told her when they were on the way home.

"You will now", she replied merrily.

He stopped in his tracks. "Sister Catherine, you know that very soon your case will be before the Chapter of our order. Are you not worried about the outcome?"

"How could I be?" she asked. "If I am acquitted, all is well. If I am condemned, it can only be because my Lord wants it so, and his Will is all that matters to me. So, how can there be any room for worry?"

Fra Raymond remained silent for the rest of the way. This was enough, he felt, for the first day.

Chapter Sixteen

"Y<small>OU ARE VERY LATE</small>", the Master General said rather sharply, when Dom Giovanni delle Celle came lumbering in. "The case of Sister Catherine Benincasa will be heard in Chapter in a few moments."

"I am sorry, Father General," the large man with the leonine head replied phlegmatically, "but your messenger only reached me two days ago and I had to meet the good Sister and be with her for a while to be able to tell you what you want to know. These things are not exactly written on a person's forehead. They take some probing."

"Well, what is your opinion?"

Dom Giovanni delle Celle said grimly, "She knows more about Satan and his ways than I ever did."

The Master General's eyes narrowed to slits. "You mean . . . she is . . . "

"I mean she knows him so well that she is entirely without curiosity about him." The hermit grinned wryly. "I wish I could say the same thing about myself."

"Speak clearly, Dom Giovanni", the Master General snapped. "What are you trying to tell me?"

"He has no part in her", the hermit said.

The Master General gave a little sigh of relief. But then his face reddened. "You spoke to me in a misleading manner, deliberately."

"I didn't like the task you gave me", the hermit said sullenly. "I want to banish these things from my mind. There was a time when I wallowed in them, but God has forgiven me. She told me that."

"She did?" The Master General gave an angry little laugh. "I sent you to her to probe her soul and instead she seems to have probed yours."

"She didn't have to probe it. She read it."

For a while the Master General sat in silence. Then he asked tersely, "How do you know that Satan has no part in her?"

The hermit clenched two very large fists. "I tell you I know about these things. I know more about them than all your inquisitors put together, more likely than not. You too must think so, or you wouldn't have called me in. Am I right? After all, I've been through it all and they haven't. At least I hope so!"

"A hermit has to forget many things", the Master General said coldly. "But he need not forget good manners."

Dom Giovanni delle Celle gave a little bow. "Tell them," he said, "tell your inquisitors that those who are in league with the Evil One are fascinated by him, God forgive them. It is a kind of lust, but a lust of mind and soul. They love evil. Sister Catherine hates it. She hates it so much she would give her life to free a man from it. She has been attacked, not once but many times, and she will be attacked again and again, probably up to her last hour on earth. But I doubt very much whether the enemy will be able to gain a foothold. She is strong, that one, because she knows how to tap the source of all strength through union. She is not a witch; she is the opposite of a witch. Do you know what I mean?"

"Yes."

"What are you going to do about her?"

"That is up to the Chapter to decide", the Master General said stonily.

"Aren't you going to tell them the result of my examination?"

"No. They must form their judgment independently."

Dom Giovanni gave an angry little laugh. "Then why ask me to examine her? I tell you, she is . . . " He broke off as Fra Anselmo entered.

"The Chapter has assembled", the Master General said, rising. "I am much indebted to you, Dom Giovanni. Is there anything I can do for you in exchange?"

"You owe me nothing, Father General. On the contrary, I

owe to you the great good fortune of having met Sister Catherine Benincasa", the hermit said. "Nevertheless, there is something you can do for me. Leave me in peace in my seclusion in Vallombrosa."

Sister Catherine Benincasa stood in the center of the Cappella degli Spagnuoli. She saw nothing of its beauty, the beauty made by men. The picture before her was of a large crescent of black-and-white robes, topped by heads, hundreds of heads. But behind them was the altar with the tabernacle, and he was in it and saw and heard everything. He had delegated certain power to the men in black and white, and of that power they would judge her, and whatever their judgment might be, he would know about it. He had known about it before the Sister of Penance Catherine Benincasa was conceived and indeed before time itself began its course with the rest of creation. Meanwhile every one of these men was a priest and as such had a claim on her obedience and reverence, even the one who was speaking now and describing her as what her enemies made her out to be, a proud, vain, self-glorifying woman, out to dominate the minds of people by a great show of piety, a woman of whom it was said that she had performed miracles with the help of unclean spirits while pretending they were worked with the help and by the grace of God; a woman who had acquired a bad reputation with many, associating with men and women at all hours of the day and night and thus surely neglecting the Rule of the order in respect to prayers and devotions; a woman who was talked about constantly and who had become a scandal to many. The Chapter was to decide whether such a woman could be allowed to keep her status as a Sister of Penance or whether, as a first step, she ought to be deprived of a robe to which she had brought disgrace, with a most careful investigation about the origin of her alleged miracles to follow in due course.

Then another man spoke, white haired and with a face that seemed to be made from very old leather, Fra Francesco Adimari. He refuted the accusations, point by point. After that came the questioning.

Had she performed any miracles?

"Only God can perform miracles."

Did she not know that God sometimes let his power work through other beings, through the Blessed Virgin, through angels, or through saints?

"Indeed I do know that."

Did she not know that sometimes Satan and his angels also performed very wondrous deeds?

"Only if God permits it."

Had she cured anybody or performed any miraculous deed with the help of satanic forces?

"Never."

Why did she allow people to render homage to her, kneel before her and kiss her hands, as if she were a person of importance?

"I never paid any attention to what they did."

Nevertheless, she did not rebuke them. Surely this was a sign of great vanity?

"I cannot understand how anybody who is conscious of being only a creature can be given to vanity."

Perhaps the voice she allegedly heard and which she seemed to believe was the voice of our Blessed Lord had told her that, although a creature, she was even so a person of importance?

"On the contrary. He Who Is told me that I was she who is not."

So the Lord had spoken to her?

"Yes, he has."

"Often?"

"Very often."

How could he? Was she not aware that God was pure Spirit and therefore had neither mouth nor tongue?

"He has spoken to me through the Word who is our Blessed Lord, and he indeed has a mouth and tongue, having ascended to heaven in his resurrected Body."

How did she know that the voice speaking to her was the Lord's voice? Could it not have been the voice of Satan?

"I know it was the Lord's voice because all he told me was

true and he is the Truth; and because all he asked me to do was good and he is Goodness. Also I saw him, but of that I will say nothing."

Was she not afraid of being deceived by the devil?

"Oh, yes, I am, constantly, for the devil has not relinquished his intelligence. But I trust in the mercy of God and distrust myself altogether. I know I can put no faith at all in myself. But if I suffer myself in love and humility to be nailed to the Cross with Christ Crucified, the devil cannot harm me."

Did she associate with anyone in a way forbidden by the law of God, of the Church, or of her order?

"No."

The questions droned on and were answered, one by one, without a moment's hesitation. Many were traps which she destroyed with cool, unhurried simplicity. Many were straight accusations, made to provoke her to anger so that she would forget caution. She answered with such kindness that the accuser seemed boorish.

"I've always thought that heaping fiery coals on a man's head was far more painful for him than to be clubbed over it", Fra Anselmo whispered to the Master of Theology on his left. The Master of Theology looked pained but said nothing.

After three hours, the Master General spoke up for the first time. "Sister Catherine, is there anything you wish to tell us of your own volition, anything you want us to consider before we pass judgment?" His tone was cold and impersonal.

"No, Father General."

"In that case you may retire, so that the Chapter can consider the case."

She bowed to him and to the crescent of black-and-white robes and withdrew, a tiny figure, stepping out quietly and in a businesslike manner.

The rustle of a sigh went across the assembly.

"Master Livio Darelli will speak for the prosecution", the Master General announced.

The Friar rose very slowly. "Father General," he said in a husky voice, "I beg to be excused from my speech. The friars here have had enough opportunity to hear the accused. There is nothing I can add or take away."

There was a great silence.

"Fra Francesco Admirari," the Master General said, "will you speak for the defense?"

The old friar smiled. "I feel exactly like Master Livio", he said. "I also cannot think of anything to add, and God forbid that I should take away anything, unless it be the insults we have inflicted on this good handmaid of the Lord."

"In that case," the Master General said impassively, "I will call on Fra Raymond of Capua, who on my request has been in the company of Sister Catherine frequently in the last days and has reported to me at some length. There is no need to repeat everything you told me in your report," he added quickly, "but you may give us your personal opinion."

Fra Raymond rose. "It is my conviction that there is no substance to the accusations", he said soberly.

A grizzled theologian rose.

"Master Lodovico?" the Master General inquired.

The old friar cleared his throat. "Even if we accept Fra Raymond's verdict," he said, "the fact remains that Sister Catherine has antagonized a great many people."

"So did our Blessed Lord himself", Fra Francesco Admirari cried.

" . . . and she may do so again", Master Lodovico went on. "Would it not be wise to put some restraint on the activities of the good Sister?"

"Restrain a waterfall," a friar exclaimed, "and you will destroy its beauty and cause an inundation."

"Fra Raymond", the Master General said.

"I would like to remind Master Lodovico of the words of the wisest member of the Sanhedrin of old, the great Gamaliel", Fra Raymond said. " 'Men of Israel . . . if this is man's design or man's undertaking it will be overthrown; if it is God's, you will have no power to overthrow it. You would not willingly be found fighting against God.' "

There was a general murmur of assent.

"I take it then that the accused Sister Catherine Benincasa is to be acquitted and that no blame will be attached to her name", the Master General said stolidly, and again there was a murmur of assent. "However," he went on, "I cannot dismiss lightly the warning of a man as learned and wise as Master Lodovico of Verona. The situation does require a remedy. A priest of experience and of exemplary repute should be put in charge of the matter. Fra Raymond of Capua, you will be posted to Siena as Lector at Saint Dominic's. And I appoint you to be the spiritual director of Sister Catherine."

Chapter Seventeen

THE GROUP OF TRAVELLERS was making its way down the slopes of Mount Celso. With Catherine were the friars Raymond of Capua, Tommaso della Fonte, and Bartolomeo de'Domenici, the Mantellate Alessia, Lisa, and Francesca Gori, and Catherine's brother Bartolomeo Benincasa, who had decided to return to his hometown. He could not adapt himself easily to new surroundings, and Florence had proved too much for him. Stefano also had left, but he was going to Rome. The brothers had not gotten on too well with each other.

Siena came in sight. In the soft glow of the evening, it looked like a fairy town.

"This is what I call coming home in triumph", Fra Tommaso della Fonte said, beaming. "And I am such a bad Christian, I glory at the idea of how disappointed certain people will be at the outcome of their machinations."

"I have been asking for forgiveness for exactly the same trend of thought, or rather for liking it", Bartolomeo de' Domenici confessed.

"And I wonder whether I shall be able to keep a straight face when meeting certain people", Alessia said cheerfully.

"It isn't exactly a triumphal homecoming for me", Bartolomeo Benincasa said sullenly, and Catherine gave him a look of compassion. "All I wonder about is whether there will be anything left of our father's business", he added.

"There will be no triumph for anybody", Catherine said, staring straight ahead. "And there will be sorrow for many."

Fra Raymond glanced at her but as usual abstained from asking her what she meant. "At least, Siena is a very lovely and a very peaceful sight", he remarked.

"There is no peace and little loveliness", Catherine said in a strained voice. There were tears in her eyes.

"What is it, *mamma?*" Alessia asked anxiously, but she would give no answer, and they walked on in silence.

As they approached the Porta Camollia, it swung open, and Fra Tommaso, trying to dispel the sudden change of mood Catherine's strange ways had caused, said jocularly, "There you are. We're being received in state after all."

A cart came out, rumbling and rattling, driven by two horses and laden with what seemed to be a number of heavy sacks. The driver had a companion beside him. Both were wearing dark robes and their faces . . . one could not see their faces. Their hoods had slits for the eyes only.

Sister Francesca Gori stopped as if she had been gripped by invisible hands. The others stared, dumfounded. There was a faint, sweetish smell in the air that they knew. It was the smell of death. Then they saw a leg protruding from the sacking on the cart, a human leg, quivering and shaking with every movement of the vehicle, a naked human leg, covered with dark patches, bluish, almost black.

Sister Francesca Gori screamed. Fra Tommaso asked bewildered, "What is it, Cecca?" and then instinctively looked at Catherine. She looked like death herself, grey and rigid. Only her lips moved.

"The plague", Sister Francesca screamed. "The plague is back in Siena!" The dreadful word, banned for so long, sounded like blasphemy.

Fra Tommaso della Fonte stood aghast. Francesca was the only one of them who could vividly recall the epidemic twenty-seven years before, which had made him an orphan. She had lost her husband then. Fra Tommaso had been too small to remember it clearly, and Catherine only one year old.

The huge, heavy horses clattered by tossing their heads, their nostrils wrinkled, their lips drawn back baring yellow teeth, their eyes wide as if they too were in a state of stark terror. Flecks of foam dripped from their mouths. The cart was full of bodies, piled on top of one another and covered by only a single layer of sacking. The stench of rottenness was over-powering. Bartolomeo Benincasa turned away and was sick.

"Siena will die", Sister Francesca wailed. "O Holy Mother of God, Siena will die . . . "

Catherine came back to life. "Quiet, Cecca", she said softly. Sister Francesca's screams stopped.

"Come with me, all of you", Catherine said. "There is work to be done."

They followed her in silence.

Rector Matteo Cenni breathed with relief. "Thank God you're home again," he said, "you and your brigade. This afternoon I thought I was going stark raving mad. Eight of my men are dead, and five more will die before tomorrow, and fresh cases keep coming in. Come along . . . " He hurried with the four Mantellate toward the first ward. Sweaty, tousled, tired around the eyes, he was still full of strength. "How is your mother, *mamma?* Still all right? Good. Your sons, Cecca? Well, that's something to be thankful for. Your father, Sister Alessia?"

"Two nieces and a nephew of mine died", Catherine said.

"Children! That's the worst of it. At least we've had a taste of life, but they . . . no, don't say it, I know it isn't up to us to choose who's to go and who isn't. What did they do to you in Florence, *mamma . . .* or perhaps I should ask what you did to them?" He laughed. "I almost wish you were a witch as some asses have claimed. Then your magic could cure the poor devils here. It's worse, if anything, than it was in forty-seven. It's so quick. Some are gone a few hours after the first symptoms. Some last a day or two, scarcely any more than that. Three of our carts taking the bodies out didn't come back. The drivers had caught it and died on their own carts. We had to fetch them back to town . . . the carts, I mean. We needed them badly."

The ward was full of patients. "No plague in here yet", Matteo Cenni said in a low voice. "Go to work, Sisters. You stay with me for a moment, *mamma.* Just to look at you gives me fresh strength. Ward Two is full of plague cases. It'll get in here too, soon enough. It's almost inevitable. The thing is in the air. I wish I knew how it spreads. I wish I knew what causes it."

"What remedy are you using?"

"None. There isn't any. And, *mamma,* I forbid you to go into Ward Two except with a blanket all over your body and a hood over your face, all drenched in vinegar. That seems to keep off the worst—sometimes."

"What can one do for the patients?"

"Very little. Segregate them from the others. A purge with cassia—Marchesano says it cleans the blood. Maybe he's right. Some try bloodletting. I don't believe in it much. Blood is strength, and God knows one needs that. Besides, they usually die before you can do much about it. The headache, the fever, the swelling in the groin and under the armpits. Then the vomiting. Black. Stinks to high heaven. Convulsions. Death."

A man in a white robe with a hood over his face came in. He pushed the hood back. "I'm from the Scala hospital", he said. "Master Piero has sent me to ask whether you could possibly spare one of your physicians?"

"As easily as I can spare my own head", Matteo Cenni said. "Lord, man, there are only three of us left."

"Galgano di Lolo died", the man said. His eyes were tragic.

They all crossed themselves. Galgano di Lolo was the Rector of the Scala, a great and good man, an indispensable man at a time like this.

"That is a terrible loss", Matteo Cenni said. "But we all may have to go before long." He was staring at the man curiously. "Another two weeks of it and this place will be finished. I myself haven't had any sleep for I don't know how long. Before God, I cannot spare a physician for you."

The man nodded sadly and turned to go. But after a few steps he made a strange, wobbly movement, broke into what looked like a clumsy little dance, gave a sudden shriek, and fell.

"Molino", Cenni shouted. "Pasello!" Then to Catherine, very sharply, "Don't touch him."

Two hooded men came running. Matteo Cenni pointed to

the stricken man, and they bent down, lifted him up, and carried him out.

"He'll be dead in a few hours", Cenni said. "That's one of those lightning cases I told you about. They drop as if they'd been poleaxed." He sighed.

"What happened to Sister Andrea, Matteo?"

"She died a week ago."

"God rest her."

"You'll have to repeat that many times over, *mamma*. They die so quickly, we can't list them any more. Two of our Lords and Masters have died so far: Ser Roberto Valentini and Ser Bruno de'Dorsano. The plague is no respecter of persons, it seems. Some of our richest and most influential people have gone: three members of the Salimbeni family, two of the Tolomei, two Piccolominis, Ser Ascanio Robaldi and his wife Giulia . . . poor thing, she was one of the most beautiful women in Siena. . . . "

But Catherine no longer listened. Walking to a corner of the ward where the sheets and hoods were piled up, she put on the uniform of the plague and marched straight into Ward Two.

The weeks that followed were one long nightmare. Death stalked through the streets of the gay and luxurious city, clawing men and women from their beds, from the banquet table, the offices and shops.

One of the first to go was Bartolomeo Benincasa. Francesca Gori lost her three sons, all of them Dominican friars. Catherine lost four more nieces and nephews, all small children, and she buried them with her own hands.

She and her "brigade" went through street after street, looking for fresh cases or for people deserted by their relatives and servants. The Mantellate nursed them. The friars heard their confessions and gave them the last sacrament. In this work none of them used the special clothing Matteo Cenni prescribed, yet none caught the disease. To Raymond of Capua, a man of letters and of quiet, contemplative work, this kind of activity was entirely new and more frightening than to any of the others. Sometimes it was difficult for him to believe that it was he who was tramping through the streets, carrying men and women on his shoulders to the hospital whispering words of comfort to people who seemed to be putrefying alive, with dark patches on their bodies and black vomit covering their chins, instead of sitting in his clean cell in Florence, preparing a paper for students, preparing a thesis, or giving spiritual advice. But he stuck to the task grimly, working in continuous exposure, day and night until at dawn he heard with the others the terrible, hoarse cry of the cart drivers: "Bring out your dead!" But he and the others had to sleep some of the time, if only for a few hours. Catherine alone did not seem to need any sleep at all. When the others dropped off, she went on alone, armed with a bottle of smelling salts and a small torch, to look for more stricken people.

When on the morning of the seventeenth day of the plague Raymond went to the Misericordia as usual, he found the staff in a state verging on despair. "The Rector is ill."

Raymond's heart sank. Matteo Cenni! The cheerful giant was the heart and soul of the place, the only man with medical knowledge who could also organize. No one else could run the Misericordia, and his very appearance, huge and comforting in its strength, the tone of his voice, his merry laughter, did more to invigorate the others than any dozen conscientious helpers could have done. He was indefatigable, and his courage was that of a lion.

Raymond raced up to the Rector's private room. Marchesano, the chief physician, was with him and a number of members of the staff, all in tears. The huge body on the bed was motionless, and for a moment Raymond thought that the Rector had died in one of those lightning attacks to which people succumbed within a few hours. But Matteo Cenni's eyes were open, and now Raymond could see that the broad chest was heaving very slightly.

"It's got me at last", Matteo Cenni gasped. "Swelling . . . in the groin and . . . armpit . . . headache. There will be . . . patches soon . . . "

Horrified, Raymond saw what Matteo Cenni had not yet discovered: the first patches were erupting, one near the throat, two others on the chest.

"No vomiting as yet", Marchesano murmured. "But the patient's water shows that the liver is greatly inflamed. If only we had some cassia to purge his blood. We're entirely out of it."

"I'll get some if I have to comb the whole town for it", Raymond said.

"Go and look . . . after the patients . . . " Matteo Cenni murmured. "Don't worry . . . about . . . me. I'm done for." He closed his eyes. That also was a characteristic symptom, the depression from the beginning which paralyzed the will to live.

"You're not done for", Raymond cried. "Wait . . . I . . . I'll get cassia for you." He ran. On his long walks through Siena he had seen a number of shops where the medicine might still be found, though how much it would help was quite another thing. Catherine had got some only a few days ago in a shop in the Via Santo Martino. Catherine! If only she were here. But God alone knew where she was. Burying another relative, nursing some poor fellow deserted by everybody else. . . .

As it happened, Catherine came to the hospital only a few minutes later, together with Alessia Saracini. The two had fought and vanquished death in a tiny room, where the shoemaker's widow with her three children lay stricken. They had nursed them until the crisis had passed, and now they had a good chance to live, especially as Alessia had been able to find someone to look after them from now on, a young woman who was one of the first to have the disease and could move about again, although she was still rather weak. The plague did not seem able to touch again those who had recovered.

Old Brother Onofrio opened the heavy door of the Misericordia to the two Mantellate, pale and red-eyed. "Better go up and bid farewell to the Rector", he told them gloomily.

"He is ill? He is dying?" Alessia asked in a trembling voice.

Catherine did not wait for the answer. She bounded up the stairs, taking two steps at a time, and tore into the Rector's room. "Get up!" she shouted at the inert figure on the bed. "This is no time for you to be lazy. Get up at once!"

There was in her neither anger nor impatience, neither fear nor worry. She did what she had to do under the coercion of her love, calling up a fallen brother to rise and fight and go on fighting.

Marchesano and the sobbing little crowd of assistants and helpers stared at her, dumfounded. Great Lord in heaven, Marchesano thought, she looks like the Angel of Life. For years afterward he could not make out what made him think of just that, when he ought to have been angry with her for shouting at a dying man and calling him lazy.

"Get up!" Catherine commanded again.

Matteo Cenni opened his eyes. His huge body stirred. He sat up with a jerk and gaped at the small figure in the door, with his mouth half open.

Catherine smiled.

Matteo Cenni smiled too.

She laughed, gaily and aloud.

Matteo Cenni took a deep breath, rose, and stood firmly on sturdy legs. The group around him gasped.

It isn't true, Marchesano thought. It can't be true. I'm dreaming this. Before his very eyes the dreaded patches of the plague on Matteo Cenni's throat and chest paled. I'm imagining it, Marchesano thought wildly. It's because I want him so much to get well. It's impossible.

The patches vanished.

Trembling all over, Marchesano crossed himself.

"There you are", Catherine said merrily, in exactly the tone a mother might employ when her child had got up again after a clumsy fall that left it unhurt but frightened.

Matteo Cenni's hand went up to his armpit. "It's gone", he said. "Great Mother of God, it's gone." He laughed nervously.

"It's a miracle", one of the Brothers shouted.

"Sister Catherine has worked a miracle."

"She's a saint! A saint!"

"Now go back to work, all of you", Catherine said. When two of the Brothers knelt and tried to kiss the hem of her robe, she withdrew it with a jerk. "Don't do that", she snapped. "And anyway, it's dirty." She turned and went down the stairs, past a beaming Alessia, who had come up behind her and seen and heard everything. On the ground floor she asked Brother Onofrio where she was most needed, and he pointed to Ward One. "They could do with some help in there", he grunted, and she sailed in and began to work as usual.

Soon two of the Brothers who had been in Matteo Cenni's room came in too. They did not dare to talk to her, but she felt their eyes watching her, and there was a good deal of whispering.

As soon as she could manage she left the ward. "I'm going to look for fresh cases", she told Brother Onofrio.

Just then Fra Raymond came in, hot and perspiring, with a parcel under his arm. "Oh, here you are, Sister Catherine. I've found some cassia, thank God."

"They'll be glad of it in the plague ward."

"I'm taking it up to Matteo Cenni. You know that he's ill, of course."

She said nothing.

He looked at her doubtfully. "Why don't you help him?" he asked. "He's a great friend of yours, isn't he?"

"Yes."

"Well? Surely . . . "

"What is it you want me to do?" she asked blandly.

He looked rather embarrassed. "Fra Tommaso della Fonte says you can help him", he stammered. "And Fra Bartolomeo de'Domenici too. Why don't you, then?"

She smiled.

"Really, I don't understand you." Fra Raymond felt exasperated. "He is a great friend of yours. He is doing so much good. He is desperately needed to save the lives of many. How can you let him die?"

"Do *you* believe I could help him?" she asked gently, and he bit his lip. So she knew that he still doubted her.

"Everybody tells me that your prayers can achieve what is impossible to others", he said uneasily.

She smiled again. "I must go now", she said and walked past him into the street.

Shaking his head, he went up to the Rector's room with his cassia. He entered and stopped abruptly, speechless at the sight.

Matteo Cenni was sitting at his table, with a steaming dish before him, and he was eating with great gusto. Meat, carrots, and onions. Raw onions.

The battle against the plague went on as fiercely as ever. Two weeks after Matteo Cenni's recovery, Fra Raymond woke up in his cell at Saint Dominic's, feeling ill. His head ached as if it had been split into four parts, and his blood was singing in his veins. Did he imagine it, or was there really a slight pain in his groin? A quarter of an hour later he knew that the pain was certainly there, and he could feel the beginning of a swelling. Outside it was dark . . . dawn was still several hours away. And the fever was mounting.

He woke up one of the friars. "Take me to Sister Catherine Benincasa", he said woodenly.

"You are ill . . . I will call the physician."

"Sister Catherine Benincasa", Fra Raymond repeated with some difficulty. "No one . . . else." He felt weak and giddy. The friar helped him to get to the house in the Via dei Tintori, where she went every day at least once to see how her mother and her relatives were. But she was not there now.

"To the Misericordia, then", Fra Raymond murmured. But already he was too weak to walk any further. The friar had to leave him crumpled up on a bench and raced off to find the Sister at the hospital.

The swelling was growing and the fever rising still further. The world was spinning crazily around him, in a thick, red mist.

Once or twice he thought he heard voices whispering, but perhaps it was only the fever.

Then she came. He knew it because he could feel the cool

pressure of her hand on his forehead. His eyelids were so heavy he could scarcely raise them. She was kneeling beside him, her hand still on his forehead. He felt a strange pulling force, as if something were being dragged out of his limbs, as if he were being stripped of heavy and ill-fitting clothing. Perhaps it meant that he was dying, that his soul was getting rid of a body it could no longer inhabit. Perhaps he had died. The pains in his head and groin were there no longer, and there was a new feeling of freshness and strength.

She was still with him, still on her knees. Her eyes were withdrawn; only the white was visible. She was here, and as long as she was here he was safe; even if he had died he would be safe. She would not let him go to the pit. Strength and freshness mounted in him like a celestial fever; he felt happy and serene; he felt like singing.

With a long sigh she awoke and withdrew her hand. Without looking at him she said, "Rest a while. I'll be back soon."

The world was all blessed tranquility. And she would be back soon. He smiled happily.

When she came, she brought food and wine. He was ravenously hungry. He finished everything to the last morsel, the last drop.

She looked at him gravely. "Go out again for the salvation of souls," she said, "and thank God who has saved you from this danger."

"God and you", Fra Raymond said, rising on wobbly legs. "And I will never doubt you again."

News came that Stefano Benincasa had died in Rome . . . of the plague, and at the same time Mona Lapa lost another grandchild. For the eighth time since the outbreak of the plague Catherine carried the little body of a relative to its burial, with her mother walking beside her. When it was all over, Mona Lapa said, "You can't cure them all. Even I can understand that."

"I can't cure anybody, Mother."

"You know what I mean."

"Yes, Mother."

"There was a time when I would have bitterly quarrelled with God", Mona Lapa said. "So many young people . . . so many children. She was a sweet one, little Elena. And I . . . I am left here."

"I prayed for that once, Mother . . . hard."

"Yes, because I wasn't ready. I know. Maybe you prayed a little too hard. Now the good Lord seems to have wedged my soul into my body crosswise, so it can't get out at all."

Catherine smiled and put her arm around her mother's shoulder.

"But if he wants me to go on living, it should mean that there is still something I can do", Mona Lapa went on gruffly. "So I went to that Prioress of yours again this morning and asked her would she accept me."

"Mother!"

"She did, too", Mona Lapa said and she raised her chin.

"You, a Mantellata?"

"And why not?" Mona Lapa asked belligerently. "She took me at once. No need for me to get chicken pox so that I could be accepted. And I can do a bit of nursing too, if it comes to it. You should know."

A few days later Mona Lapa was taken into the order, in the same chapel at Saint Dominic's where Catherine had been invested eleven years ago. But she did not have to do much nursing. The plague's onslaught was coming to an end. It had spent its force. Over one-third of the people of Siena had gone with it.

Chapter Eighteen

IN THE YEAR 1375 all Italy was astir with unrest. Those in high places felt it, but few could interpret the signs. For the great Mediterranean peninsula was split up into so many spheres of power that there was little contact between them unless they were immediate neighbors.

The papal legates should have been able to see more clearly, but they too were seldom in touch with each other, and in their reports to the Pope in Avignon they preferred to describe things in rosy colors, knowing only too well that the sender of bad news was never popular.

There was discontent in the kingdom of Naples, ruled by a dissolute queen and her notoriously immoral court; in the powerful duchy of Milan, ruled by Bernabò Visconti; in the great seafaring republics of Venice and Genoa, archenemies and fierce rivals in trade; and in the many city-states which had shaken off feudal rule to replace it with citizen governments elected today and thrown out of office tomorrow.

Only on one issue did there seem to be unity of thought: everybody hated the papal legates, because they were greedy for power, wealth, and luxury, because they were corrupt, and above all because they were Frenchmen.

A great man might have recognized the first signs of an all-pervading urge for national unity and might have tried to coordinate the disjointed powers. But there seemed to be no such man in Italy. Only a woman, a girl of twenty-eight, saw the danger signals, and from her cell in the Via dei Tintori in Siena a stream of letters went out to both rulers and papal legates, exhorting them to fulfill not their own will but the Will of God.

The Archbishop of Pisa, a very old man, felt that religious life in his diocese was at a low ebb. He wanted a preacher for Lent, a man with enthusiasm enough to breathe fresh fire into souls, and his secretary, a young Father Marcello, suggested Sister Catherine of Siena, of the Sisters of Penance.

"A woman?" the Archbishop exclaimed. "A Mantellata? You must be out of your mind."

Father Marcello began to talk with some eloquence of the astonishing number of conversions the good Sister had brought about in her city; how she had been accused and tried and most honorably acquitted before the entire Dominican Chapter in Florence; of the miracles she was supposed to have worked, especially during the plague.

"Miracles?" the Archbishop asked sharply.

Father Marcello gave a little shrug. "Mother Church could not canonize her as yet, Your Grace, but the people have done so. Everybody here in Pisa seems to believe that she is a saint."

The old Archbishop leaned back. "Perhaps you're right after all", he said thoughtfully. "This seems to be a time when ordinary ways and means are no longer effective. But Siena! Ser Piero Gambacorti is not on the best of terms with the Sienese government. We shall have to ask our worthy ruler for permission or risk having his soldiers refuse to let her enter the city, saint or no saint. We shall have to ask permission of the Sienese government too—*and* Sister Catherine's Prioress, of course."

To the Archbishop's surprise Ser Piero Gambacorti agreed at once.

Two weeks later the Sienese government, now no longer called Consuls but "Defenders", and the Reverend Mother Nera di Gano also gave their consent, and in the first week of Lent Sister Catherine arrived in Pisa with three other Mantellate, Father Tantucci, and three Dominican friars. They were given quarters at the Palazzo Buonconti.

On Laetare Sunday the Archbishop paid a visit to the ruler of Pisa, and from a window they watched the huge crowd on the piazza, milling around the little Mantellata and her escort.

Dark-eyed, blue-jawed, stoutish Piero Gambacorti grinned. "No miracles have been reported to me yet, Your Grace, but you were right to let Sister Catherine come here. From what I hear there is something like a religious revival. That's what you wanted, isn't it?"

"I was a little sceptical about her at first," the Archbishop admitted, "but I have come to admire her. She is indefatigable. Visits to the poor, visits to the sick, speaking to this group of people and that . . . "

"To say nothing of her correspondence", Ser Piero added. "When she arrived I was surprised by her retinue. Seven people, I thought, were rather a large number for one very small Mantellata. But she needs them. They're all her secretaries, and she often dictates three or four letters at a time, like Julius Caesar. Her output is enormous, and, what is more, the content of her letters is most interesting."

"If you will forgive my curiosity," the Archbishop said, "how is it that you know so much about that?"

"My dear Archbishop, can you imagine anybody ruling Pisa without knowing what is going on within its walls? It's my business to know the content of letters sent from here to rulers and other influential people and I have ways and means to get hold of them."

"Including my own letters?" the Archbishop enquired dryly.

Gambacorti smiled beatifically. "My interest in theology and pastoral messages is limited, Your Grace. But Sister Catherine is dealing with topics of great political interest. She is strongly advocating the idea of a crusade against the infidels, for instance."

"That is one of the plans particularly dear to the Holy Father."

"Yes, but he isn't doing anything about it. Sister Catherine is. She is trying to win over practically every ruler in Italy to the idea. At the same time she gives our dear papal legates a piece of her mind. I have copies of her letters, in case you're interested. You are? Yes, I thought you might be. There is, for instance, a letter to the pious Abbot of Marmoutier . . . now, don't look down your nose, my dear Archbishop, he is after all a very powerful man and the Pope's nephew. . . . "

"His way of life—"

"Oh, I know *that* and who doesn't. Sister Catherine certainly does. I'll prove it to you." He rummaged in the papers on his magnificent desk, produced a letter, and read, " 'I think it would be well, if our dear Christ on earth' . . . she means the Holy Father, of course . . . 'would set himself free from two things which cause the misery of the Bride of Christ' . . . here I thought at first she meant herself, but she doesn't, she means the Church. 'The first is his far too tender clinging to his kinsfolk and his far too great care for them.' That's a nice slap for the Pope's nephew, don't you think? 'The second is that he is far too good-natured and merciful. Therefore do Christ's members decay, because there is no one to chastise them! There are three vices which Christ hates more than any others. They are the unchastity, the miserliness, and the puffed-up pride prevailing among priests and prelates, who think of nothing but pleasures and feasts and amassing wealth. They see devils dragging the souls of their subordinates to hell and care nothing for it, for they are ravening wolves themselves and traffic in the Divine Grace.' Pretty strong, from a little nun to a great abbot, isn't it?"

"I cannot blame her", the Archbishop said sadly. "She is telling the truth. But she does use very strong language . . . "

Gambacorti laughed. "It gets stronger toward the end, Your Grace. Listen to this: 'That which Christ earned on the wood of the Cross is now wasted on harlots. Though it may cost you your life, I bid you say to the Holy Father that he must make an end of so great shame. When the time comes that he must appoint cardinals and other shepherds of the Church, then beg him not to let himself be led by flattery or do it for money or out of simony, and to take no thought whether those concerned are nobles or commoners, for virtue and a good name ennoble a man before God.' " He put the letter down.

"It is insolence," the Archbishop said, "but holy insolence."

"I've read only a few passages to you", Gambacorti said. "You should hear what she tells Bernabò Visconti, the most powerful man in Italy. He *must* come to terms with the Pope, she says. Practically speaking that means the papal legate, of course, and Guillaume Noellet is not exactly an easy man either . . . the Cardinal of Sant'Angelo, I should have said." The ruler sighed. "D'Estaing, Noellet, Marmoutier . . . one would think Italy a French province."

"The Holy Father has repeatedly expressed his intention to return to Rome."

"That won't make him an Italian. Besides, he is a great one for expressing intentions. I shall believe it when he has arrived. No, when he has stayed in Rome for some years, not like his predecessor who came, saw, and returned to Avignon."

"Peace between the Holy See and Bernabò Visconti", the Archbishop said thoughtfully. "I have been praying for that for years." He gave the ruler a quick, searching glance. "You who know so much about Sister Catherine's letters, do you know also what answers she receives?"

"I thought you might come to that point", Gambacorti grinned. "One would think they'd laugh and throw the little nun's letters away, wouldn't one? But no, they read them very carefully and take great trouble over their answers. And that includes Bernabò—and his wife, too."

"I wonder why", the Archbishop mused.

"I can tell you, I think. That little woman is a mixture unheard of so far. She is a holy statesman, which is almost a contradiction in terms. She *is* a statesman, Your Grace. The idea of uniting Italy by giving all the rulers a common goal, that great crusade of hers, is a statesmanlike idea. And Bernabò, rough as he is, is statesman enough himself to recognize it."

"You seem to think that she is using the idea of a crusade in order to get peace in Italy."

"Indeed I do."

"If I know anything about Sister Catherine, she is preaching the crusade because she believes in it, because she feels the necessity to free the holy places so that Christians can go and pray there. . . . "

"That is the difference between us, Your Grace. You are a

priest; I am a politician. That little nun, however, is both. Mind you, she won't succeed. Not unless there are ten thousand people like her to form the backbone of such a gigantic venture. Maybe she can perform a miracle, but such a miracle would be too much for any single saint." He went back to the window. "She has just finished speaking", he said. "They are kissing her hand and touching her robe. Your Grace . . . it's my conviction that no one can sort out the political problems of our time. But for sheer courage of trying, really trying, I mean, and not just toying with the idea, there is more strength and considerably more goodwill in her than in anyone else, and that certainly includes His Holiness in Avignon."

"It isn't easy for the Holy Father . . . "

"Easy? In his exalted position one cannot expect things to be easy. That's exactly what is wrong with him, and, begging your pardon, with most high ecclesiastics in our time. I am not being personal, Your Grace, but can you dispute it? *She* doesn't. She says so herself. By the Truth of God, if there were more women like her, the world might do well to pass over the government to her sex."

"Matriarchy", the Archbishop said dryly, "exists only among some obscure savage tribes in Africa, and possibly in Cathay, though it's difficult to believe the reports from there. But it is interesting to see how carefully the ruler of Pisa attends to the political excursions of a nun. You insist on seeing her as a political factor. I must think of her as of a little Sister of Penance who is in dire danger spiritually. For she is raising herself beyond her station, if not beyond her strength, and the adulation of the people is not conducive to humility, the most important quality one must look for in a religious."

"Humility?" Gambacorti asked, with a blank face. "That's the virtue of which Saint Francis of Assisi grabbed so much that there's been none left for anybody else ever since."

The Archbishop laughed. "You're a rogue, Messer Piero," he said indulgently, "but a witty one. As for Sister Catherine, I had no idea of the extension of her political activities, and I admit they worry me. You called yourself a realist just now.

Let me follow you into your realm. Sister Catherine's activities, dynamic as they may be, will not lead to any result. You say so yourself. Then what is the use of embarking on them? Let her give the example of a truly good life to the people, that's all I ask for."

"In other words, you want her to be an ordinary nun and yet have the influence over the people she has precisely because she is not ordinary. You're asking for the impossible, Your Grace. Ah, well, as I said . . . as we both said . . . *she* won't decide the course of events in Italy."

"And what will, in your opinion?" the Archbishop asked curiously.

"Money", Gambacorti replied.

"As crude as that . . . "

"Yes, as crude as that. For with money one can buy Ser Giovanni Aguto and his White Company."

"The Englishman . . . "

"Yes. No one is able to get the better of him in battle. And he sells himself and his men to the highest bidder. Therefore there are only two ways open to a statesman. Either you hire him and let him beat your enemies. Or you may try and buy him off, so that he will invade your neighbor's territory rather than yours. He always keeps his bargains, I will say that for him. At present he is still in the pay of the papal state. But if the Cardinal of Sant'Angelo forgets to pay him . . . and the cardinals have been known to run out of money . . . then anything may be possible. And that is why I wonder whether there will be peace between the Pope and Bernabò Visconti, for that would set Aguto free to rove about, seeking whom he may devour."

A bell began to toll, then a second and a third.

"I must go", the Archbishop said. "There is Pontifical High Mass at the cathedral."

Gambacorti nodded. "Laetare Sunday", he said. "A ray of joy in the middle of Lent. The men who compiled the liturgy knew something about human nature. I shall be there myself, and so, I suppose, will Sister Catherine."

"That is one place where she cannot exercise any political influence", the Archbishop said, smiling.

"Mulier taceat in ecclesia", Gambacorti grinned. "The apostle Paul too knew something about human nature. I never said she wasn't a devout person, Your Grace. But her activity here in Pisa is political all the way through, you can rely on that."

All the bells of the town were ringing now, shouting and clanging and giving tongue joyfully. The whole sky was full of gusty blasts of clamor.

Ser Piero Gambacorti courteously accompanied his guest to the door and then walked through large, glittering rooms to find his daughter.

"Coming to church with me, Maria?"

She rose and curtsied. "Certainly, *babbo mio.*" She was a radiantly beautiful girl. Hair like spun silk, her father thought proudly. Her mother's eyes and her mother's charm as well. There could be no higher praise. Four times so far she had said No to dazzling suitors, one of them a prince, and Ser Piero had let her have her own way, although at least two of the marriages would have brought him considerable political advantage.

"But you should have put on one of your new dresses", he said. "And the sapphire necklace."

"I would rather remain as I am, Father, if you will permit it."

"You're lovely enough as you are," he said, "but why not wear the nice things I give you?"

She smiled. "I'd better get accustomed to dressing simply."

"Why? What do you mean?"

She looked down. "You once told me that you wanted me to be very careful and cautious, when it came to . . . marrying."

"I did. Nothing but the very best is good enough for my daughter."

"I have chosen the very best, Father."

"What? Who is it? Not the Duke of Spoleto? No, it couldn't be. Who is it, Maria?"

"I have chosen to become a Bride of Christ, Father."

He paled. "You're not serious. You can't be." But already he knew that she was, and his hands trembled a little. "My daughter . . . a nun. This is madness. You're made to make a man happy, to rule at his side, to have children, to live the life of a princess. . . . "

"I don't want all that, Father. And I have made up my mind. Nothing and no one can alter it. Not even you."

He saw his own determination, his own stubbornness in the girl's beautiful face, and he groaned. "Who has put this into your mind?" he stormed. "But of course, I know who it was. The Archbishop! That's his doing. Behind my back he—"

"His Grace has nothing to do with it, Father. He does not even know anything about it. So far the only one who knows is the one who has shown me so clearly where happiness lies. Sister Catherine Benincasa."

"The devil", he exclaimed. "And I permitted that woman to come to Pisa!"

"If you hadn't, I would have gone to Siena to meet her, Father."

"Never mind", Gambacorti said. "I am your father, and my will counts in Pisa. You will not pursue this absurd idea any further. I forbid it. You will never see that woman again, either. But I shall. And I shall tell your precious Sister Catherine a few things she won't forget easily."

"Do, Father", Maria said sweetly.

Sister Catherine did not go to the cathedral that day. She went to the church of Santa Cristina, where Fra Raymond celebrated High Mass. She was weary of crowds, and she knew there would not be many people here, not with Pontifical High Mass going on in the cathedral.

"*Laetare, Jerusalem*", Raymond prayed. "Rejoice, oh, Jerusalem, and come together all you that love her."

Joy was the keynote of the day, the foretaste of the joy of Easter. Jerusalem . . . that meant both the Church on earth and the City of God in heaven. And how much cause was there for joy over the Church on earth? With Christian murdering Christian in senseless, stupid wars, with foreign priests lording it over Italian towns, with foreign soldiers looting and killing, and the supreme shepherd far away and unaware of most of what they were doing in his name! Joy enough, Lord, all the same, enough and brimming over, as long as Christ himself was there to give himself to the people; as long as there was hope that peace would follow war, that the priesthood would be reformed and the whole of Christendom united again to expand and conquer, to set the holy places free, where he walked and thought and suffered and died.

Bless all the souls you have given into my care, sweet Lord; my mother who is now also my sister and my daughter. My Sisters in the order, those kneeling at my side and those in Siena; Neri and Malavolti, Master Tantucci and the friars who are with me, Tommaso della Fonte, Bartolomeo de'Domenici, and Fra Raymond, my spiritual father and yet also my son; young Maria Gambacorti and all the many others . . . keep them close to your heart, dear Lord. . . .

" . . . grant that by the mystery of this water and wine we may be made partakers of his Divinity, who was pleased to become partaker of our humanity. . . . "

But what hope could there be of sharing his glory unless one was ready to share his suffering, too? Whenever she had prayed to be allowed to carry the pain for the sins of this person or that, what was it but an attempt to soften the burden of the One who was carrying them all, the pain of millions and millions throughout the millennia. Such a puny effort, and yet he was grateful for the slightest bit of it, he whom Fra Raymond's hand lifted up high under the form of bread and wine. If only one could carry more of it, much more of it, hang on the Cross with him, bleeding as he was bleeding. . . .

The four Mantellate received Holy Communion in a row, together with a handful of other people, and others returned to their seats. Catherine alone did not. But then she often prayed on at the altar rails, and no one paid much attention to the tiny figure, all crumpled up in a heap, a little bundle of prayer.

After a while the priests came out for their thanksgiving, and Fra Raymond looked sharply at her, once or twice. She did not move.

A few more minutes, and suddenly she knelt upright and flung out her arms. Sister Alessia made a move, and Fra Raymond at once stopped her with an abrupt gesture. He rose and moved forward until he could see Catherine's face, flushed and shining. She held out her arms stiffly, minute after minute. How long could she stand it? It was almost as if something were holding her up. It was inhuman; it was impossible to keep up this position so long.

Suddenly a paroxysm of pain shot through her. Her arms still remained outstretched as before, but her fingers moved, clawing the air wildly. Then she recoiled as if she had been hit by an invisible missile and collapsed.

Fra Raymond beckoned, and Fra Tommaso della Fonte and Fra Bartolomeo rushed up and raised her to her feet. She hung in their arms, lifeless and limp. They carried her back to the Palazzo Buonconti and put her on her bed, which she had stripped of anything but its wooden boards. There she lay, moaning. Twice Fra Raymond heard her say, "Don't let it be seen . . . please, don't let it be seen. . . . " and he nodded gravely. Fra Tommaso gave him a questioning look, but received no answer. She was obviously in great pain, writhing, twisting her fingers.

"No use calling a physician, I suppose", Fra Tommaso asked.

This time Fra Raymond replied. "I doubt whether this would be within his realm of knowledge. We must wait a while." He sat down on a foot stool beside her bed. But almost three hours went by before she opened her eyes. She looked around, saw that only Fra Raymond was in the room, and gave a faint nod. Her lips began to move. "Can you . . . see . . . anything . . . on my . . . hands?"

"No, *mamma.*"

She smiled gratefully. "Thank God", she said. "Oh, thank God. I . . . begged him . . . so much . . . " Once more she lost consciousness. When she came to again, after half an hour, she whispered, " . . . by the Grace of the Lord . . . Jesus Christ . . . I bear his wounds . . . upon my body."

Fra Raymond nodded. "I suspected that from your movements. Tell me how it happened."

"He came down . . . from the Crucifix . . . ", she whispered, " . . . in a great light . . . so I rose to meet him. Rays . . . " She had to stop. "Rays . . . five red rays," she began again after a little while, "going out from his holy wounds . . . they went straight . . . to my hands and feet . . . and to my heart . . . and I knew what was coming. I cried, 'O Lord, my God, I implore you . . . let not your wounds be visible . . . upon my body . . . it is enough that I have them within me . . . and while I was still speaking and before the rays reached me the red turned to gold and then to pure light. . . . "

"Are you in pain now?"

"Pain . . . so great that I shall die . . . unless . . . the Lord grants a new wonder. . . . Most of all . . . about the heart."

That night she hovered on the threshold of death. There and nowhere else could she have seen what was shown to her . . . to her soul only, for her body lay still and bereft of its senses on the wooden boards. It was very terrible, and she could not have borne it, if he had not been there all the time and if it had not been he who wanted her to see it, if it could be called seeing. So this was to come, this thing so dreadful, so fearful there was nothing that could be compared with it. The Lord's Bride, the Church, was ill, and but for him she would die and putrefy. Long, poisonous thorns were piercing the Bride's body in a thousand places and must be extracted one by one. Thieves had broken into her house and made it their den, and they must be driven out with a scourge of cords, unclean, covetous, miserly, and proud thieves, buying and selling the gifts of the Holy Spirit. But then the thorns vanished and the thieves fled wailing and the Christian people as well as many infidels entered by the sacred wound into the Lord's heart. . . . Saint Dominic did and Saint Thomas and Fra Raymond and all her spiritual children. And the Lord laid his Cross on her shoulders and placed an olive branch in her hand, just as she desired it to happen, and he told her to go out to the people with the tidings of great joy. . . . And there was more, infinitely more of God's mysteries, but she knew she would never be allowed to talk about it to anyone because that was not part of her mission but a free gift to her alone. Her own task was clearly marked within a plan so great that she could see only a tiny part of it, and that stretched across the centuries and the destinies of hosts of men and women. There were saints and popes and bishops, monks and nuns and kings and others, and often the greatest warriors were very simple people, children and cripples and very young girls, people enduring rather than acting. . . .

Slowly she returned to health. A week later, on Passion Sunday, she was well enough to go to church. On the next day she wrote once more to Bernabò Visconti, Duke of Milan, and to the papal legate.

Ser Piero Gambacorti came to see her, fuming and fretting about the delay caused by her illness. After a discussion lasting two hours he left and returned to his palace. He seemed unusually quiet and rather absentminded. The next day an official of the treasury who wanted his signature for a new tax to raise the funds necessary for his favorite plan, the building of a lovely castle on the seashore, came out of the ruler's study, all bewildered. "He won't sign. Says the people are taxed too high as it is. When has one heard him say that before? Or any ruler I can think of?" At Easter he proclaimed an amnesty, reducing the sentences of all criminals by half, and a week later the whole town knew that Maria Gambacorti had entered the Dominican Order as a postulant.

On June the sixth a despatch rider arrived with a message from Bologna. Bernabò Visconti, Duke of Milan, and Guillaume Noellet, Cardinal of Sant'Angelo and papal legate, had met there two days earlier and concluded a truce. Peace negotiations were to follow.

Chapter Nineteen

A LARGE, FLORID-LOOKING MAN, no longer young but beautifully dressed, came slowly across the clearing of the forest of Lecceto. "Greetings, holiest of hermits", he said. "Doing nothing, as usual, eh?"

"You again", said William Flete, looking up from his book. "What is it this time, Messer Nanni di Vanni Savini? Made any more enemies lately?"

"Don't make me out worse than I am", Ser Nanni said, seating himself comfortably on a fairly smooth piece of rock.

"That's what the devil would say when meeting an angel", William Flete growled. "I wonder why you insist on disturbing me. Have you no other place to go to?"

"You don't own this forest, do you, Brother William?"

"I own nothing, thank God. And that's more than you can say about yourself."

"Less, I should think", Ser Nanni replied cheerfully. "I have the good fortune to own many things, including the rock I am sitting on."

William Flete sat up with a jerk. "You are a nasty devil, Messer Nanni", he said amiably. "A callous, scheming trickster in the grand style, a man who glories in his misdeeds. But at least up to now I have not found you to be a liar. How dare you say you own this rock? It belongs to the monastery like the forest itself."

"I don't dispute the forest", Ser Nanni declared. "I do dispute the rock. It did not grow here. It came down from the height of the mountain of Belcaro and was once part of the castle wall. And the castle of Belcaro, walls and all, belongs to me. It's half ruined and I wouldn't live there for anything. All the same it's mine, and therefore also is this rock. So I'm sitting on my own soil, and you can't do anything about it."

"Argued like a cutthroat," William Flete said, "and therefore true to the style of Ser Nanni di Vanni and so on. Very well. You may take the rock and carry it back to your castle, where it belongs. Do you a lot of good, too. It weighs just about as much as you do, but it will weigh more when you have got back to your castle, because by then you'll weigh less. You're getting fat on your ill-gotten gains."

"You are a poisonous monk", Ser Nanni said, quite unruffled.

"I must be," William Flete said thoughtfully, "or else why should you take such an interest in coming to see me."

"You do amuse me, I admit", Ser Nanni said. "I really don't know how they get on without you in Oxford—"

"Cambridge!"

"What's the difference? In any case—"

"I could tell you the difference. Oxford—"

Please don't. I am not a university man, just a simple merchant."

"Merchant you may be, but the simple are those who think they can do business with you."

"You misjudge me greatly", Ser Nanni said. "I never take pleasure in fleecing simpletons. I like a deal with a man worthy of my steel. And so, in your own way, do you. You would take no pleasure in vanquishing a poor student in a debate, would you?"

William Flete closed his book. "The trouble with you", he said, "is that you wallow in feuds. You would enjoy nothing more than the ruin of an enemy."

"Oh, yes, I would", Ser Nanni protested.

"Really? And what would you enjoy more?"

"The ruin of *all* my enemies", Ser Nanni said gaily. "And what's more, the day is fairly near when that will happen."

"You'll be a juicy morsel for the horned one, one not too distant day", William Flete told him. "Why are you always coming to tell *me* about your wicked schemes? You spoil the air here. The place will stink of sulphur and brimstone for days."

196

Ser Nanni crossed his fleshy legs. "I come to you, my holy hermit and lazybones, because I've got to talk to somebody", he said. "And you are a man who won't repeat what I say to others. Besides, if you did, no one would believe you. They'd think you've gone out of your mind as most hermits do."

"Do they?" William Flete asked. "I'm sure I would . . . if I had on my conscience a tenth of what you must have."

"My conscience is in perfect order", Ser Nanni said placidly. "At least I think it is. I haven't had time to look."

"God forgive you", William Flete said. "I wish you'd go and see Sister Catherine."

"Who? Oh, that nun you've been raving about."

"You said you were going to see her one day."

"Did I? Well, why not? Maybe I will, one day. I didn't say what day, did I? And I don't much like being beseeched and entreated by some pious female. Besides, she's in Pisa, I'm told."

"She's back in Siena", William Flete declared. "Go and see her."

"Really, my holy hermit, what's the good of it? She wouldn't be half as amusing as you are, I'm sure."

"She's much more amusing than you are", William Flete retorted. "And unlike you she's not a cat-livered coward."

Ser Nanni jumped to his feet. "No one's ever called me that", he roared.

"Well, I'm calling you that now", the hermit said coolly. "Why else should you be so evasive when I mention her? You can trick people into ruin, oh, yes. But face that little nun, that's a different thing. It takes courage."

"She's probably nothing but a prickly-tongued fury." Ser Nanni tried to regain his placidity.

"She's nothing of the kind. But it's obvious that you don't dare go anywhere near her."

"All right", Ser Nanni said, this time in a cold rage. "I'll go and see your confounded nun, if only for the pleasure of telling you what I shall tell her. Good-bye, holy hermit. And I'm sorry Oxford let you loose on our beautiful Tuscany."

"Cambridge. And I didn't ask you to come here."

Ser Nanni di Vanni Savini realized soon enough that the Englishman had tricked him into giving his promise to see that nun. But one of the things he was proud of—there were many—was that he never broke his word. There was scarcely a shady deal in Siena in which he did not have a finger or two, and for that he had to ally himself with all kinds of scoundrels. He had always got the better of them one way or the other, but never by breaking a promise. There were many other ways, and a brilliant mind would always be able to find one. He would get out of this ridiculous agreement too. He dispatched half a dozen servants to find out the exact mode of life of a certain Mantellata. When did she leave the house? Where did she go? When did she return? Within two days he had all the information he needed, and he went to the house in the Via dei Tintori early in the afternoon, when he could be quite certain that Sister Catherine would be either at the Misericordia or at the Scala hospital.

But William Flete was a wily opponent. He had sent a message to Catherine. "I am sending you Ser Nanni di Vanni Savini, the worst man in the whole of Siena and a friend of mine. If you can deal with him, you can deal with old Lucifer himself, which incidentally I do not doubt for a moment. But he is as slippery as an eel. Ser Nanni, I mean, not Lucifer. Catch him and hold him tight so that he cannot escape you."

Catherine showed the letter to Fra Raymond, and whenever she had to go out, he held the fort. When Ser Nanni arrived, he welcomed him most cordially and told him he hoped Sister Catherine would soon be back. He managed to send a boy over to the Misericordia, where she was, and in the meantime he tried hard to keep the visitor interested. He knew about him . . . everybody did, in Siena. Ser Nanni was the man who had ruined the Piccardis, father and son, and their banking business. He had bought up the debts of the Rinaldi family and had Piero Rinaldi put in jail. He had pretended to make peace between the Tolomei and the Maconi families and then used his role as intermediary to pour oil instead of water on the flames, with the result that both these rich and noble families bought consignments of arms, on which he made a large profit. He was bold enough to make enemies in the highest places and adroit enough to play them off against each other. There had been no greater rascal in Siena for generations.

Raymond knew that this type of man would never be interested in what he could tell him. The only way to delay him was to make him talk, and to Ser Nanni talk meant boasting about his achievements.

Was it true, then, that Piero Rinaldi would have to stay in jail for years to come?

"If there is any justice in the world, he ought to rot there", Ser Nanni replied and proceeded to paint the picture of his enemy in the darkest colors. But after a few minutes he suddenly broke off and said he would have to go. "I promised Friar William Flete to come and see Sister Catherine, but as she is away and I have a great deal of pressing work please make my excuses to her and tell her how sorry I am not to find her at home. Perhaps I shall be able to come back at some other time." Desperate, Fra Raymond went on another tack. "It is not often that a mere friar has the opportunity to talk to a great financier." How the friar in charge of the monastery's economy would envy him for it! And how happy he would be to know Ser Nanni's views on the prices of land and estate. Would they rise or fall in the near future?

Ser Nanni knew that the nun would not be back before sunset. There was no reason to be rude to the good friar. Benevolently he expounded his views on price development. Now that a truce was established between Milan and the papal state. . . . He was still at it when a small woman, still quite young, in the black-and-white robe of the Mantellate came in.

"Oh, here you are, Sister Catherine", Fra Raymond said, suppressing a sigh of relief. "This is Ser Nanni di Vanni Savini, the great financier."

"I know about you, Messer Nanni", Catherine said. "You

have been trying to mediate in the feud between the Tolomei and Maconi families."

"Yes, indeed", Ser Nanni said with ponderous dignity. "Unfortunately my endeavors were not crowned with success. It seems to be impossible to eradicate such ancient enmities."

"Selling arms to both parties is not likely to help much in that respect", Catherine said calmly. "But you need worry no longer, Messer Nanni. Peace is now established."

"Impossible!"

"Like all sin," Catherine said, "the matter was extremely stupid. Neither party could see farther than their noses. I talked to young Stefano Maconi, and with the Grace of God succeeded in widening his outlook a little. He soon saw that he was like a little child, playing with toys. So he sent a message to the Tolomei that he and his family and I would meet them at the Church of San Cristofano, and they came and made peace." She smiled. "Perhaps you could do good business with them again, buying your arms back cheaply", she said sweetly. "They won't have much use for them now."

"And I knew nothing about all this", Ser Nanni exclaimed, outraged.

"Why should you?" Catherine asked innocently. "It only happened last night."

Ser Nanni bit his lip. "I have underrated you a little, it seems, Sister Catherine."

"Underrating others is one of your most frequent errors", she replied at once. "And the reason for it is that you have too good an opinion of yourself."

But by now he had caught hold of himself again. "I'm a bit of a rascal, I suppose", he said gaily. "But how else could one like you shine by her goodness? Dark hues are needed to bring out the clear ones."

" 'It must needs be that scandals come, but woe to the man through whom scandal does come' ", Catherine said. "There is enmity no longer between the Tolomei and the Maconi. It is time for you to rid yourself of your other enmities."

"That I shall certainly try," Ser Nanni said, his small eyes glittering, "but I shall try it in my own way."

"God's way is better than yours. You want to destroy them. He wants you and them to live in peace. How long will you go on kicking against the goad?"

"Until I have defeated my enemies decisively, good Sister." Ser Nanni was enjoying himself now. This could still turn out to be a good story to tell the English hermit. There was really nothing very formidable about the good nun. But how on earth had she managed to get the Maconi and the Tolomei together? And why was she looking at him like that?

"Come now, Messer Nanni", Catherine said very gently. "What is the good of telling yourself that you are a great man, when all you can do is create little squabbles between people?"

"Little squabbles!"

"Siena is a beautiful town, but not the largest in Italy", Catherine said. "How can you be so impressed by your wretched little victories? The devil just laughs at your efforts . . . so unnecessary and so childish. You are no better than young Stefano Maconi was, who thought the world consisted only of the Maconi and the Tolomei and that it was of the greatest importance that the Maconi should win and the Tolomei lose. Such views may be excusable in a man not yet thirty, but what is God to think of you, a mature man of great experience? Suppose you were to die tonight. . . ."

Ser Nanni winced a little and crossed his fingers. "There is no reason to suppose that I shall", he said.

"There is no reason to suppose that you won't", Catherine said evenly. "None of us knows the appointed hour. Suppose you *do* die tonight. Do you think the omniscient Judge is going to be much impressed with your victories? And if you should live on for some little time . . . " Again Ser Nanni winced. " . . . and you succeed in ruining those enemies of yours: Will that make your final fate better or worse? Think bigger, Messer Nanni, not just in terms of weeks or months. Think ahead, as truly great men do and as all men should."

Ser Nanni drew himself up. "Enough of this", he said

ferociously. "I won't lie to you and the good friar here. So I will tell you quite frankly: my peace shall be made and sealed in the blood of my enemies. This is my resolve, and I will not be moved by anything you say. So be silent and stop troubling me."

Sister Catherine was silent. But her lips moved and her eyes seemed to look right through Ser Nanni into space, fixed on something that was not he at all, something to which he was not even an obstacle.

"Don't go", Fra Raymond said anxiously. "Please, don't go."

Ser Nanni smiled. Why, the good friar was positively pleading. He had won the battle. He could afford to be magnanimous. "Very well," he said, "it shall not be said of me that I am so hard and uncharitable that I will not relent in anything. I have four main enemies. One of them I will give up."

Fra Raymond's face shone.

"His name is Romano Terchia of the *Contrada dell'Onda*", Ser Nanni went on. "You can make my peace with him for me, Sister Catherine. Anything you decide about the matter I will accept. Now then . . . I must leave."

Catherine's gaze came back from space. She looked at him again, smiling.

"You are satisfied now, I hope", he said, and he too smiled and turned to go. She looked so happy, it made him feel quite elated. In fact he felt a joy and warmth surging up in him, the like of which he had never felt before. He felt stronger, younger, as if he had got rid of some tedious burden. Why should that be? Romano Terchia was the least important of the four men. And why should he care about Sister Catherine's happiness? It was *he* who felt joyful, as if giving up that wretched Terchia were a victory. That's what the priests were always cackling about, renunciation and all that rot. Nevertheless, there was no getting away from it, hell and damnation and a million devils, he felt happy. He looked back at Sister Catherine. Might as well tell the little woman. She was still smiling at him.

"You know how I feel?" he asked. She nodded. One should really give her another one. Renato Brucci . . . or Tebaldo Coracini . . . or better still . . . "It seems I can't go away", he said lamely. "Or maybe I don't want to. You . . . you want everything, don't you?"

She nodded silently.

Suddenly he knew that she was looking at him with love. Yet it was not he whom she loved, but something in him, something that was akin with her in some mysterious way.

"I can't refuse you anything", he said. "It is quite absurd." It was still more absurd that tears should well up in his eyes and that he go down on his knees before her. I must be out of my mind, he thought. But if that is so, it is wonderful. He raised his hands. "I don't know what is happening to me", he said. "You tell me . . . tell me what to do. I'll do anything. . . . "

A week later Fra Raymond was again eagerly awaiting Catherine's return. He looked so worried, she knew at once that he had bad news. "Ser Nanni has been arrested", he said. "He's in jail."

Catherine frowned. "He has made peace with all his enemies", she said. "Why should this happen to him?"

"It has nothing to do with his enemies. It's the government. He has never been on very good terms with some of the Defenders, and now they have clamped down on him. They did the same thing to him four years ago. He was fined very heavily then, just because Francesco di Naddi had been at his house once or twice."

"The conspirator?"

"Yes. Di Naddi was beheaded, although his guilt was never quite clearly established. The merest hint of a conspiracy seems to make our rulers act with terrible ruthlessness. But how unfortunate that this should happen to Ser Nanni just after his conversion. I wonder why God allowed it. I pray the poor man won't fall into despair. His faith, after all, is newly found and may not be strong enough to withstand such an attack."

"I have an idea God can judge that better than we can", Catherine said with gentle irony. "What did you expect? It is in heaven that the rueful sinner will cause more joy than ninety-nine just men, not on earth. If it were different, people would never have to overcome their worst enemy, the self. They would love their neighbor because they would be sure to get their love back at once and with interest. Love would be reduced to a good bargain, with God under the obligation to reward every good action immediately in the form of worldly advantages."

"True enough," Fra Raymond admitted, "but what will be the effect on Ser Nanni?"

"Visit him in prison", she said. "Tell him from me that this misfortune shows that God has pardoned the sins of the past by letting him undergo temporal pains instead of everlasting ones. He won't despair. God has already delivered him from a worse dungeon than the one he is in now."

Only a few days later Fra Raymond came to tell her that Ser Nanni had been released. "But he was made to pay a fine of two thousand gold florins."

"Excellent", Catherine said merrily. "Our Lord has taken away at least some of the poison that endangered him."

"You were right; he did not despair", Fra Raymond went on. "In fact, he was quite cheerful about it all. What is more, he asked me to give you this." He produced a sealed document.

"What is it?"

"A title deed, conferring on you the castle of Belcaro, just above Lecceto, where Friar William Flete lives, and quite a piece of land with it."

"I can't accept that", she exclaimed impulsively.

"Oh, yes, you can, wholeheartedly", Fra Raymond told her, smiling. "You wouldn't use it for your personal benefit, would you? Why, even Saint Francis of Assisi once accepted the gift of Mount Alverno, and it was there that he came closest to our Lord. However, we shall have to petition the government. Belcaro, although half ruined, is still a castle, a fortress, and no fortress may be either built or destroyed without the government's permission."

"I begin to understand", she said in a low voice. "This is a great gift, and I will accept it most gratefully. We shall make a convent of Belcaro, a convent of Dominican nuns. And I shall call it Santa Maria degli Angeli."

"We shall have to petition for that also", Fra Raymond told her, smiling. "No convent may be built without the permission of the Pope."

"He'll give it to us."

"It is very likely," Fra Raymond admitted, "although he is going to be occupied with matters of a very different nature. For here my good news ends and the bad begins."

"What has happened?"

"No one seems to know for certain, but there is word that the papal legate has dismissed General Aguto and his English mercenaries."

"Why should that be bad news?"

"One can dismiss a tiger from one's service, but what is the tiger going to do?"

There was a pause. "Well?" Catherine asked. "What is the tiger doing?"

"Every town north of Rome is asking that question, *mamma.* I had a long letter from Pisa about it."

"From Ser Piero?"

"No, from the Archbishop's secretary, Father Marcello. They want you back there very badly."

"Why?"

"He's not too lucid about that. In fact, I had the impression that he is afraid his letter might fall into the wrong hands. Apparently, great things are in the offing. The papal legate has told the Florentine government that he can take no further responsibility for the actions of General Aguto and that he has no more money to pay him and his troops. The Florentines are suspicious. They seem to think that the Legate has simply given the Englishman a free hand for an invasion of Tuscany. When it succeeds, they think, Aguto will present the entire province to the papal state—Florence, Pisa, Lucca, Bologna, Siena, everything. There is some talk about a new Florentine government, bent on open war with the papal state. They have sent ambassadors to Milan. Father Marcello thinks they will conclude an alliance and then declare war on the Holy Father."

"The end of the truce we've been working for so hard", Catherine exclaimed. "They want to start bloodshed all over again."

"And this time it would be much worse than before", Fra Raymond said. "Milan alone is bad enough. But Milan and Florence, that's a deadly combination."

"They are moved by the devil, and they don't see it. What does Ser Piero Gambacorti say? He has a good mind."

"Father Marcello doesn't know, or if he knows, he doesn't say. I suppose he has to be cautious."

"If I leave Siena again so quickly, they will start talking, as they did before", Catherine said bitterly. "Unless the Archbishop himself asks me to come, I cannot leave here. But you must go at once. Get me as clear a picture of how things are as you possibly can, and as quickly as you can. Dear Lord, what a beautiful world it would be, if we weren't always trying to spoil it. How can we have a crusade, when Christian is fighting Christian all the time? Hurry, Raymond, hurry."

Fra Raymond left for Pisa the same day.

Chapter Twenty

I NEED YOUR HELP, *mamma*", said Fra Tommaso Caffarini. His boyish face was pale and despondent.

Catherine's thoughts came back from Florence, Pisa, and Rome. "What is it, Fra Tommaso?"

"They discovered another conspiracy", the young friar said sadly. "At least they think so."

"Here in Siena?"

"Yes. Allegedly it has something to do with Perugia. The Abbot of Marmoutier is the papal legate there, and the Defenders seem to think that he intends to undermine the government and bring about a revolution. Then that Englishman, Aguto, would march in and take the town over for the Pope."

"Always the same nonsense."

"One never knows for sure, with the Abbot of Marmoutier, does one?" Fra Tommaso Caffarini was a good Sienese.

Catherine bit her lip. "Who told you all this?" she asked. "It's not a mere rumor, is it?"

"The consequences are no rumor. I've just been at the town hall. They called for me, or rather they asked for a friar and I was sent. I wish it had been someone else."

"Why? What did they want of you?"

"They caught a Perugian spy. Or so they say. They interrogated him yesterday in great secrecy. This morning he was put on trial and sentenced to death. So they asked for a friar to come and hear his confession and dispense the last sacrament."

"Poor man."

"Yes", Fra Tommaso said tonelessly. "Poor man. He . . . "

"Well? Why don't you go on?"

"I failed him", the friar said unhappily.

"What do you mean?"

"He refused my help. I tried every bit of persuasion I know, but it was all in vain. He ranted, he shouted abuse, he refused to listen. He told me to leave him, and when I pleaded with him, he . . . "

"He attacked you?"

"Well, yes, he did. It wasn't bad. But the things he said against God were."

Catherine nodded.

"He thinks he is innocent", Fra Tommaso went on. "He really does. I spoke to Ser Alberto Varuzzi, one of the Defenders, and he gave me his solemn word that the man's guilt had been quite clearly established. He is a Perugian by birth."

"What do you intend to do?"

"What can I do, *mamma*? Nothing. Tomorrow morning at dawn he is to be beheaded."

"He may repent in his last hour."

Fra Tommaso shook his head. "That's just it", he said. "He won't. Not this man. He's the worst of all human mules I've ever encountered. He will not repent. He will not go to confession. He will refuse the sacrament. And even if he does die innocent of the crime for which he has been condemned, he told me—shouted at me, rather—he had never been to confession and Communion in his life, and he was not going to start now. All his sins since baptism are upon him, and he repents of nothing."

Fra Tommaso Caffarini was a good man, a man of heart as well as of intelligence. But perhaps his approach had not been right, or the prisoner had taken a dislike to him for some unfathomable reason. Perhaps another priest ought to try. Catherine was still formulating her thought so that it would not offend one of her dearest children, when Fra Tommaso said, "I couldn't bear the idea, so I went to see the Defender again and suggested that he should send another priest to the prisoner, as I could do nothing with him." A smile rewarded him, but he made a deprecating little gesture. "Ser Alberto said to me, '*You* are the other priest. Father Pallini tried before you, and he got nowhere. Set your mind at rest. We've done everything we could to force that scoundrel to make his peace with God. If he wants to go to hell, we can't stop him.'"

"'Set your mind at rest'", Catherine repeated bitterly. "How can one, when one's neighbor is in the greatest of all dangers."

"That's what I thought", Fra Tommaso said. "And that's why I came to you. Perhaps if you pray for him, the way you prayed for those criminals who were executed some years ago . . . "

"They knew they had done wrong", Catherine said. "This man thinks he is innocent. I must go and see him."

"You?" Fra Tommaso exclaimed, horrified. "That's out of the question."

"It is necessary."

"It is utterly impossible. He is like a madman. He would kill you."

"Perhaps. But it isn't likely."

"They won't permit a woman to enter his cell. It's against all the rules."

"They will have to make an exception."

Fra Tommaso shook his head. "If only Fra Raymond were here", he groaned.

"What is more, I must see him alone. And it will take some time. Several hours, I think."

"This is absolute madness", Fra Tommaso was beside himself. "Think, *mamma,* I beg of you! Think of the gossip it will cause, the tongues that'll wag about a Mantellata going into the cell of a condemned man and staying alone with him for hours. . . . "

"It isn't the slightest use trying to frighten me with the obvious", Catherine said. "The execution will be tomorrow morning, you said. There is no time to lose. Lead me at once to Ser Alberto. And leave all the rest to me."

Ser Alberto Varuzzi, like everyone else in Siena, knew about Sister Catherine Benincasa. Some people, in fact quite a number of people, thought that she was a saint, some others that she was a madwoman. And indeed, only a saint or a madwoman could make this kind of suggestion. "You don't know what you are asking, Sister Catherine", he said indulgently. "This man is desperate. He has nothing to lose. I myself would not enter his cell, except armed and with at least two guards."

"I must see him alone."

"My dear Sister Catherine, I regret, but I cannot permit it. Why, the High Council of Defenders would put me on trial if you came to grief."

"Fra Tommaso Caffarini here is your witness that I insisted on it and would not be deflected from my purpose", Catherine said. "This has nothing to do with the Council, except—" she leaned forward—"except, if you could see your way to change the verdict to imprisonment."

"Quite impossible", Ser Alberto Varuzzi said coldly. "The verdict of Their Magnificences, the Lord-Father-Defenders of the people of Siena, was unanimous. Nothing and no one can change it."

"Then it is a matter of the prisoner's soul and beyond worldly jurisdiction", Catherine said firmly. "You too have a soul, Messer Alberto, and you must guard it even more diligently than the doors of your prison cells. If you do not permit me to try to prepare this unfortunate man for his death, you will be responsible for it in eternity."

Ser Alberto frowned. "Are you threatening me?"

"God is threatening you", Catherine said stonily.

Ser Alberto rose and turned away. "Very well", he said after a while. "It is senseless. It is hopeless. But you shall have your wish. You are my witness, Fra Tommaso Caffarini, that I tried to dissuade Sister Catherine as best I could."

"Yes, Messer Alberto", Fra Tommaso said unhappily.

The Defender sat down at his desk, scribbled a short note, and tugged at the broad, silken bell string beside him. An official of the municipal police entered.

"Lead Sister Catherine to the cells", Ser Alberto ordered. "She has permission to enter cell seven. Tell the sergeant-at-arms to watch carefully—"

"But outside", Catherine interposed.

Ser Alberto sighed. "Outside", he repeated. "Perhaps you will keep him company, Fra Tommaso Caffarini."

"Yes, Messer Alberto."

"And thank you, Messer Alberto", Sister Catherine said very gravely. "Now at least you can be at rest about this matter . . . if your verdict was just." She gave him a little bow and left, followed by Fra Tommaso and the bewildered official. "I almost forgot", she said, as they were descending the marble stairs. "What is the prisoner's name?"

"Niccolò di Toldo", the official replied. After a while he added, "It's not my business to question His Magnificence's orders, Sister, but I must ask you to be very cautious. We never had a more dangerous man."

Catherine said nothing. The marble stairs ended on the ground floor. The steep stairs leading down to the cells were of ordinary stone, and the air soon became dank and musty, all sweetness drained from it.

"His hands and feet are chained, and he is chained to the wall as well", the official said. "Nevertheless he can move about very quickly within a space of about four feet. Remember always to keep out of his reach. If he tries anything, shout at once." The corridor was lit by an old oil lamp. A huge shadow appeared, followed by a dumpy little man with the face of a fat rodent. Beside a dagger and a short stick hung a bunch of keys on his belt. When he saw Catherine he grinned incredulously.

"Gorro," the official said, "the good Sister will visit number seven. Open the cell for her."

The turnkey's grin widened, showing the stumps of a few teeth. "Number seven ought to be very pleased", he said.

"Keep a civil tongue in your head", the official snapped. Still grinning, the turnkey selected the right key and opened number seven. Catherine crossed herself and entered. Behind her the door closed, without haste but with a decisive thud. The cell was so dark that it took her a while to adjust her eyes. The only light came from a single candle stump, placed high up in a niche. The prisoner was sitting on a stool, his head buried in his hands.

211

"I am Sister Catherine Benincasa", she said. "And I have come to ask you for a favor."

The man raised his head, and she saw that he was very young, little more than twenty years of age. She was deeply shocked. Somehow she had expected him to be a much older man, hardened by bitter experience. This was a mere youth, years younger than she was herself. His eyes were little points of green light, set in deep caverns, like the eyes of a wolf.

"A woman", he said. "What do you want of me? I have nothing to give anybody." He spoke the soft dialect of Perugia, and his voice was that of a man of culture.

"It is true", she said. "None of us has anything of his own. We are stewards, not owners." He gazed at her, then looked away. "Even so," she went on, "you have a great treasure."

"Either I am already mad or you are", he said. "A woman in this cell! I have nothing. The only thing left to me is my life, and that they're going to rob me of. I am dreaming. You are a dream woman. Go away. But if you are real, you ought to be ashamed of yourself for coming here." The little green lights flickered. "A nun, too", he said. "Hell and damnation, I'm awake. They could do nothing with their priests so they sent me a nun. Go home and pray, you fool. I don't want you here, or anybody else." He moved and the chains on his hands and feet clanked. "Go, I say", he shouted. "Miserable woman, if you want to stare at a man who is about to die, why don't you wait until tomorrow? Then you can see. The whole world can. Tomorrow morning they'll kill me. Tomorrow morning . . . " His voice trailed off. "A curse upon them all", he whispered. "A thousand curses, for being cowardly brutes." The whisper was like hissing. "Hell take them all, the cold-blooded murderers, and their wives and children and their whole town." The chains were shaking with his rage.

"You are innocent of the crime for which they condemned you?"

"I am", he shouted. "I am. I am. I told them so a hundred times, and what did they do? They just smiled. Their Magnificences just smiled, the devil rot their guts. They want me to be guilty, so I'm guilty. They want my blood. They'll stand there watching; they'll all stand there watching, when . . . when it happens."

"You still have a friend."

"What are you talking about? Go away."

"You still have a friend."

"I had a hundred friends, good and faithful and loving friends. 'I'd do anything for you, Niccolò. You can rely on me, Niccolò. Without fail, Niccolò.' Women, too, such charming creatures. 'Oh, Niccolò, how handsome you are! Oh, Niccolò, you kiss like a god.' 'Oh, Niccolò, how handsome you are! Oh, Niccolò, you're wonderful.' Beautiful women. But when they arrested me, did anybody come forward, man or woman, to speak out for me? Not one."

"You still have a friend. God is your friend."

The prisoner raised his head so high, she could see the dark roots of hair on his jaw. He began to laugh, a sick, toneless laugh. "God", he said. "Don't you dare talk to me about God. He's supposed to be just, isn't he? Rewarding the good and punishing the evil? Look at me! I'm twenty-three. I've only just begun to live. And he allows them to kill me for something I never did. Where's your justice? Where? Why, if there is some sort of a being, some God, then he is a devil, a cruel, repulsive beast. Perhaps the pagans were right and the gods are jealous and vicious, smiling at some and hating others, showering one with their presents and destroying another, as the whim takes them. That may well be. But don't talk to me about a loving Father in heaven as those priests did. And don't talk to me about a friend. If God exists, he is the worst of my enemies, and if he is all-powerful, as they prattle, then he's the most unjust of them all."

"My poor Niccolò . . ."

"Be silent, nun. I know everything you could tell me. Whom God loves, he punishes, eh? My answer is: For what, in the name of damnation? What have I done? No better and no worse than any other young man I know. Yet they are allowed to live; they can still walk across a field with a pretty girl; they

213

can hunt and play and eat and drink. They can ride a lovely horse and vie with each other for a beautiful lady's favor. They can hear music and golden poetry. They can see the sun rise and set and sleep blissfully into a new day. And I? The injustice of it cries to heaven. But from heaven there is no answer. Do you know why? I'll tell you. Because heaven is empty."

"Heaven always answers, Son."

"Don't call me that, nun. I had a mother once. She was the loveliest lady of Perugia. She is dead, and it's just as well."

"She prayed for you. And it is in her name and in the name of the most glorious Mother of all mothers, of Mary, Mother of God, that I am talking to you now."

He laughed. "Aren't you presuming a great deal, nun?"

"You be the judge of that, when you have heard me", Catherine said. "What do you think the Mother of God felt, when she was standing at the foot of the Cross? She did not pass away before her Son died; his death was not spared to her. She was there and saw it. He was as innocent as a lamb, but they led him to slaughter. Him, of whom God said that he was his only begotten Son in whom he was pleased. What is your innocence, compared to his? He too was sent to trial by his enemies, and they twisted everything he said to please their own hateful aims. Are you entirely free of sin, my Son? None of us is, but he was. Yet he took upon himself your sins and mine, and he prayed just as you have been praying too. . . . "

"I did not pray", Niccolò di Toldo said. "I can't pray."

"Of course you prayed. I heard you do so. All your raving and ranting was one prayer, and it said, My God, my God, why hast thou forsaken me?"

The prisoner gasped.

"When our Lord cried out in those words," Catherine said, "he was carrying the sins of all men, and by his bruises we are healed. But he did not cry in despair. For these words are far older in time than he was as a human being. He had first put them into the mouth of David, the King, whom he had chosen as his ancestor. It was to become the beginning of a psalm, heralding his own fate on earth. And mark my words, Son . . .

that psalm ends in triumph. As you will end in triumph, if you will do as I tell you."

"You are a strange woman", the prisoner said, and his voice was shaking a little. "How can there be ... triumph ... for me? I'm as good as dead."

"You are as good as alive within the Life of Christ", Catherine said. "And oh, how I could envy you for that, miserable as I am. I must wait still, until it pleases my Lord to call me, too. I must see sin and fight it and all kinds of evil; I must raise my voice against those who will not listen. I still have to carry my burden. You will be permitted to shed it and enter into the peace and happiness of God, to find the Mother of God waiting for you, together with your own mother."

"You believe that?" he asked hoarsely. "You really believe that, upon your oath?"

"I believe it with all my heart and all my mind and all my strength. Don't you see now why our Blessed Lord chose to die the way he did? Ever since he did ... how can we raise ourselves against God and speak of injustice? He let his own innocent Son shed his precious blood for us. Can you understand now how the martyrs felt, when they were allowed to shed their blood for the Faith? As they did so, they became one with him, and what could be more glorious?"

"Almost ... I could believe you."

"You said heaven gave you no answer. Can you still say so? Do you not feel in your heart that the answer has been given to you, through me?"

"I ... I do feel ... something. Yes, I do."

"Then I will speak now to your innermost self. I will speak to the will behind your will, and that is the treasure which you still have. Will you submit your will to the Will of God?"

"I ... I will, if I have the strength."

"God will give you the strength, if you do as I tell you."

"What ... am I to do?"

"The priest who spoke to you before me is a good and holy man. I will send him to you, and you must confess the sins of your whole life to him. Do not worry about not remembering them. He is there to help you. Then you will go to Mass and receive the whole Christ into you."

"Will you . . . go with me?"

"I will."

"They won't let me go."

"They will. I shall ask it of them myself."

"Then they will. But they said . . . they told me that I shall be . . . that it will happen very early in the morning. . . . "

"Before that I shall come and fetch you to go to Mass with me, and I shall kneel at the communion rail beside you."

The prisoner looked at the nun. She was smiling. "And then?" he asked. "When they come and take me away . . . " He jumped up and fell on his knees before her. "I'll do it", he shouted. "I'll do it all. But don't leave me alone . . . out there. Be with me when . . . when it happens. I . . . I can't face it alone. For the love of God . . . be with me."

Three heartbeats passed. Then she said, "So be it." She was still smiling.

"You . . . promise?"

"I promise", she said, and she pressed both his outstretched hands. He kissed her hands fervently. "I shall see you again in the morning", she said. "Now do away with everything that is between yourself and God." She turned, walked to the door, and gave it a gentle knock. It was opened at once. "Come in, Fra Tommaso", she said. "My brother Niccolò is waiting for you."

She spent that night on her knees in her own cell, no bigger than that of the prisoner. Long before the bell of the Mangia tower gave the sign permitting the citizens to leave their houses, she slipped out, with her little lantern, the same she had used to go from house to house at the time of the plague. At the door of the jail she waited until the great bell struck. Then she entered. This time there was no questioning and no warning. Official, guards, and turnkey received her with a kind of apprehensive reverence. Cell number seven was opened to her at once. It was pitch dark, but her little lantern was still burning. As she entered, the prisoner gave a stifled exclamation.

He tried to rise and fell back, exhausted with the effort. "You have come", he whispered. "Oh, thank God . . . thank God . . . "

"I promised", she said.

He gave a sobbing little laugh. "I told myself again and again you would come. But so many things could have happened. They might have forbidden it . . . or . . . or . . . "

"I am here," she said, "and we shall go to Mass together. They have a chapel here. Fra Tommaso will say the Mass."

"You were right", the prisoner said. "He is a good and holy man. You were right about everything. There is only one thing . . . oh, Sister Catherine, Sister Catherine, I am so afraid."

"There is no shame in that", she said. "Even our Lord was afraid, in Gethsemane. He tasted fear as he tasted torture and death. But come now. I shall lead you where strength is waiting for you, and Love. And no one will be in the chapel but Fra Tommaso, the acolyte, and you and I, until our Lord joins us."

"I . . . can't get up."

She put her arm around him as she had done to hundreds of sick people and led him out and up the stairs. But behind them came the heavy steps of four guards. The chapel had no windows, so they could afford to wait outside. Four more were placed in the sacristy. Their Magnificences, the Lord-Father-Defenders of the people of Siena, were not taking any chances.

Little more than half an hour later Catherine and Niccolò di Toldo emerged. He walked without her help, holding himself erect. "All will be well", he whispered to her. "I shall die content." But when he saw the guards, he faltered a little. Seizing Catherine's hands he laid his head on her breast, like a child. Catherine stood immobile. The blood that was going to be poured out was not hers, and yet it was. He was going to die, and she felt the beginning of her own death in her own blood, and it filled her with a deep joy. Come, death, she thought. Come soon. She was ready. Then, from the soft trembling of his face she knew that the boy was not. Over his head she saw an official entering with more guards.

"Don't leave me", the boy murmured. "I'll be good. But don't leave me."

"Courage, sweet brother", she murmured. "Soon now we shall go to the marriage feast. You will go to it, cleansed in the blood of the Son of God, with the name of Jesus constantly in your mind. And I shall wait for you at the place of execution."

He looked up to her, and she saw that his eyes were shining. "How can it be", he said, "that such abundant Grace is given to me ... that the joy of my soul will wait for me at the holy place of execution!"

The holy place of execution, she thought in exultation. He had understood, then, in his last hour of his young life. He had grown above himself, beyond all recognition, like the good thief on the Cross. "I will go now", he said smiling. "I am full of joy and strength because I know you will be there. How I shall miss you on the way there! It will be like waiting for a thousand years till I see you again. You are my sister and my mother and my great, beloved saint!"

The official approached. "It is time to take him to the courtyard", he said politely. "The cart is waiting."

Sister Catherine had a long way to go. Siena's place of execution was outside the town, and she stepped out briskly, listening from time to time whether she could hear the drums or the sound of the cart. But they were taking their time. They wanted the prisoner to be seen by all the people; this was what happened to conspirators against the government, so be careful, all of you. The prisoner's feelings did not matter to them. They would not hurry. But she wanted to make quite sure to be there first. She had to be there when he looked for her. Out by the Porta Romana; past peasants in the fields, past carts, drawn by long-horned oxen, carrying vegetables and fish to the marketplace; past San Mamiliano and San Lazzaro, the leper quarters; she could see the ruin of Belcaro castle, where one day, please God, the Pope and the Sienese government, the Convent of Santa Maria degli Angeli would be. Here was the Coroncina, the little inn they called the Rosary, because the executioner and his aides would start saying the Rosary when they passed it. The distance from here to the hill of execution was just right for the Credo, the Pater, the three Aves, and the five decades of the sorrowful mysteries. And here was the hill, the Pecorile.

There was no scaffold. They had merely put a few crude boards together, to prevent the executioner's foot from slipping, and set the block, on which the prisoner put his head.

No one was here as yet, and therefore the birds were singing to their hearts' content. Larks there were and blackbirds and even a few nightingales. Flowers were growing all around the wooden boards. Golgotha was still at peace, and she knelt and prayed, and as so often before she soon knew herself no longer alone. Saint Catherine was there, the fearless girl from Alexandria, virgin and martyr and her patron saint. And she was there, who had stood at the foot of the Cross, when the world was redeemed from the top of a small hill like this one . . . as far from the nearest gate of Jerusalem, perhaps, as the Pecorile was from the Porta Romana. Whatever the guilt he may have incurred in this young life of his, it was forgiven when Fra Tommaso gave him absolution by the power of your Son, my Lady and my Mother. And whatever punishment he must take in expiation of his guilt . . . would not the manner of his death be sufficient? Your Son, great Lady and my Mother, told the good thief that he would be in paradise with him that selfsame day. Ask him to do no less for the soul of Niccolò di Toldo, ask him for my sake, and if there is any measure of pain left, let me carry it for him, for he is my neighbor and my brother and my son, and I love him with a licit love. . . .

But the birds around her rose with a whirr of wings and were gone, and she saw a long stream of people coming up the road. She heard the sound of drums, too, and far behind the people she saw the cart, flanked by guards, and the points of their pikes shimmered in the early light of the sun.

Quickly she walked to the block and knelt again and put her head on it, as soon he would have to do. "Hear me, I beseech you, my Lady and my Mother," she said, with an awful determination, "give him the grace of light and peace not only when he has come home, but now, in his last hour on earth. Hear me, hear me, you must hear me." She was doing violence to heaven, and she wanted to. The whole of her will was compressed into a tight ball of spiritual energy, and she thrust it upward as she pronounced the one word "Mary!"

The answer came in a flash, filling her soul so completely that for a while it was cut off from the rest of her being and she could neither hear nor see nor feel anything. When slowly the interaction of body and soul began again, she rose and saw that the cart had come to a halt at the foot of the hill, and there he was, descending from it without help and looking at her and smiling. Big, burly men seized his arms and marched him up the hill, and he was still smiling, as if he could see no one and nothing but her.

A dozen guards followed them and now the official in charge of the execution approached her. "You ought to leave the hill now, Sister."

Instead, she walked up to the prisoner.

"Make the sign of the Cross over me", he pleaded. "For if you do, it will stay."

She did. "Up to the marriage, my dear brother", she said. "Soon you will begin life everlasting." The lean boy's face before her was radiant.

The official turned away with a shrug, but a thickset little man came up with a large basket which he placed behind the block, carefully measuring the right distance. A look of sudden revulsion came into Niccolò di Toldo's eyes as he realized the purpose of the thing.

"There is no need for that", Catherine told the thickset man sternly, and he gaped at her. She turned to the two aides. "Take your hands off him", she said and they obeyed, stupefied.

She took the boy's arm herself and led him toward the block. "Kneel, my brother", she said. "And I will hold your dear head." The executioner muttered something, but neither of them listened, so he looked questioningly at the official in charge. The official tugged at his chin. He had ordered her off, but she would not go. One could not treat a Mantellata like one of the oafs who came here to enjoy the spectacle. She might well be a relative of the man. She had called him brother, if he had heard right. She must have some high connections, too, or they would not have let her visit him in his cell and go to Mass with him. And she seemed to keep the prisoner quiet. Even so, she could not possibly remain where she was now. She probably did not realize what was going to happen when the axe came down. God, the fellow knelt like a lamb, and she was placing his head right and baring his neck and all as gently as a mother making her child ready for sleep. . . .

The executioner looked at his aides. "She's doing your work for you", he wanted to say, and then did not say it when he saw their vacant stare. Once more he looked at the official, and this time he received an impatient gesture as an answer. He took up his axe. The drums began to roll.

"Think of the blood of the Lamb", Catherine whispered into the boy's ear.

"Jesus", he stammered, "Jesus . . . Catherine . . . "

The great axe flashed through the air. She closed her eyes. "I *will*", she said aloud. She did not hear the crashing, crunching sound, nor did she feel the terrible impact that shook the block and the boards. She saw the God-Man, bright as the sun, and Niccolò's soul entering his heart.

Then she was back and someone was taking the head out of her hands and her white habit was white no longer. She made no move. All around her there were voices and sounds. They were taking away things. They were leaving. No one spoke to her, or if anyone did, she did not hear. She was alone in a great ecstasy of joy. For now she knew that man may be saved not by any merit of his but by Mercy alone. The goodness of God was boundless.

How long must she wait for it herself? How long, O Lord, how long?

Chapter Twenty-One

W E HAD TO HAVE YOU back in Pisa, Sister Catherine",
the Archbishop said. "Both Ser Piero Gambacorti and I
agreed on that. I fully understand your susceptibilities, or
rather those of the government of Siena and of your Prioress,
and I am glad they both gave their consent. The issue at stake is
too great—"

"—and brooks no delay", Ser Piero interposed. "Let's go *in
medias res,* Your Grace, if you'll permit." He rose, went on
tiptoe to the door of his study, and opened it with a jerk.
There was no one in sight, except a sentry, patrolling at some
distance. The ruler closed the door again. "There are agents all
over the city", he said. "Things are becoming rather dangerous.
That's why I had to stop Fra Raymond from writing to you
too openly, Sister Catherine. The letter might have fallen into
the wrong hands." Fra Raymond looked down. The Archbishop raised his brows a little. Neither of them spoke.

"A red flag is flying over Florence", Ser Piero said. "And if
things go on the way they're going now, it will fly over the
whole of Italy."

"A red flag?" Catherine enquired.

"Yes. The Florentines have chosen it as the banner of rebellion.
It's as red as blood. There's no coat of arms on it. Just the one
word *Libertas* in large white letters."

"Freedom", Catherine said. "There is only one freedom for a
Christian: to do the Will of God. And not to rebel against his
supreme representative on earth."

"They have also chosen a new government," Ser Piero went
on, "most suitably called the Eight of War."

Catherine groaned.

"Their first measure", Ser Piero said, "was to impose a new

tax . . . a heavy one . . . on all ecclesiastics and on all Church property."

"Only the Holy Father can—"

"I know, Sister Catherine. So, as you may imagine, does His Grace here. Nevertheless, that's what they did, and the people of course were delighted because for once *they* didn't have to pay. The money thus gained will be used for defense purposes."

"In other words," the Archbishop said grimly, "they want to fight the Holy Father with the money of the Church."

"Florence", Ser Piero continued, "is about the worst enemy the Holy Father could have. They have sent out emissaries and agitators to all cities and towns in Tuscany, inciting them to join what they call the Tuscan League—their best speakers, including the famous Donato Barbadori, who could convince a saint that the devil is as innocent as a snowflake."

"They say he is the greatest orator since Demosthenes and Cicero", Fra Raymond added.

"Meanwhile the red flag of the Tuscan League is making progress everywhere," Ser Piero resumed, "and evil things happen wherever it appears. In Florence itself two prelates were murdered. In Prato they discovered a conspiracy . . . or thought they did or said they did."

"It was a pack of lies, nothing else", the Archbishop said.

"Most likely. A priest was accused of trying to deliver the town to the Pope. It's much the same story in other towns, too. The mob flayed the priest in Prato alive and threw his flesh to the dogs before his eyes. For he was still alive when they started on that horror. I'm sorry to have to tell you such things, Sister Catherine. . . . "

"Tell me all you know", she said stonily.

"Dozens of towns have followed Florence's lead", Ser Piero went on. "The rebellion is growing like wildfire. Three days ago an emissary came to me."

Catherine drew in her breath sharply.

"This thing does not suit me", the ruler went on quietly. "But I knew that on a flat No, Florentine agents would become extremely busy here, and within a few weeks I would probably have my throat cut. So I pretended to vacillate and spoke of potential neutrality."

"There is no neutrality between God and the devil", Catherine said.

"I suppose not", Ser Piero said slowly. "But the papal legates are not God, and those who resent at least some of their actions are not all devils."

"That is true," Catherine said sadly, "and it is the worst part of it. But what matters is the cause of our Lord and of his Mystical Body the Church, not the wickedness and corruption of some legates and governors; that is what the rebels forget."

"And that is why we have asked you to come again, Sister Catherine", the Archbishop said. "You know how to remind people of the cause. Loyalty to our Lord and to his Church."

Ser Piero Gambacorti sighed. "You won't find it easy just now, Sister Catherine. People are afraid. And there are many who believe what the Florentine emissaries tell them in the inns and at the port and a hundred other places. Besides, there is still another danger . . . but in that you can't help us, I'm afraid."

"What do you mean, Messer Piero?" Catherine asked.

The ruler shook his head. "Trouble of a very different kind has arisen, and the ruler of this city must deal with it . . . if he can."

"Tell me", Catherine insisted.

Ser Piero shrugged his shoulders. "You have heard of Ser Aguto, I suppose", he said with some reluctance.

"A brave man, a great leader of men, but cruel", she said curtly.

"Well, yes. He and his troops have made camp less than three miles away. Florence has bought him off. It cost them a hundred and thirty thousand florins. Now he wants us to buy him off as well, but we can't afford his price. And if we don't pay he will attack. I am keeping the walls manned day and night while negotiations are going on. This morning I made my final offer to him. Thirty thousand florins. It is all we can afford, but less than half of what he demands. He will probably refuse."

"And then?"

"Then", Ser Piero said tonelessly, "he will attack."

"And he has never yet lost a battle", the Archbishop added wearily. "The Florentine agents are making capital out of this, of course. They never tire of telling our people here that Aguto is secretly still in the pay of the Holy Father and that it is really the Pope who is holding them up for ransom."

"Pisa is in danger", Ser Piero said. "No use denying it."

"I wouldn't have asked you to come to us just now, if I had known all this", the Archbishop said. "Nor would Ser Piero. It all happened very suddenly."

"I shall go and see Ser Aguto", Catherine declared calmly. The Archbishop looked at her with incredulous eyes. Ser Piero, after a moment of stupefaction, began to laugh. "What an idea", he gasped. "Good Lord, what an idea!"

"I have been thinking about that man for some time." Catherine was quite unruffled. "I thought of writing him. He would be a very good man for the crusade."

"No doubt he would be", Ser Piero said dryly. "But he won't see any reason why he should go and fight Saracenes, Turks, and Arabs, when he can get any amount of money from Italian cities just by appearing before their walls. And money is the only thing he wants. As for going to see him . . . forgive me, Sister Catherine, but that is sheer madness. He is not the kind of man to respect your habit, and even if he were, his men certainly aren't."

"I am not afraid", Catherine said tranquilly.

The Archbishop spoke up sharply. "Sister Catherine, as long as you are in Pisa, you are under my jurisdiction, and I forbid you to go into Aguto's camp." When he saw her bitter disappointment he added more gently, "Surely you must realize that you could not possibly go into a soldiers' camp alone. You would have to take other Mantellate with you. If they suffered indignities or worse from the hands of those wild soldiers . . . could you take the responsibility for it?"

She hung her head. "I could go with the friars", she murmured.

"No", the Archbishop said. "The soldiers might kill the friars . . . they probably would. You do not realize what has happened in towns conquered by Aguto's men. By your vow of obedience, Sister Catherine, you will not go."

"Your Grace," Fra Raymond said wryly, "thank you for speaking to Sister Catherine with authority. I could never have held her back."

This time Catherine and her companions were staying at a hostel. The great house of the Buonconti was closed. The family with all the staff had gone to a castle near Montefiascone. As soon as she had returned from the ruler's palace, she asked Sister Alessia Saracini to write a letter for her. An hour later she called in Fra Raymond. "Holy Obedience forbids me to go and talk to the Englishman Aguto", she said. "Yet talk to him I must, if bloodshed is to be avoided. So I have written to him, and you will take him my letter."

Fra Raymond paled a little. "In that case you will have to look for a new adviser and confessor, *mamma,* for he will have me killed."

"I doubt it", Catherine said with a sincerity that made the good friar wince. "But if he does not get my letter, he may well kill us all." She sighed. "I would much prefer to go myself", she said. "Perhaps if you talked to the Archbishop once more . . ."

Fra Raymond too sighed. "No," he said, "I will go. But for the sake of God, pray for me."

"You should not go alone", Catherine told him. "Take Fra Bartolomeo with you."

"May I read what you have dictated?"

"Certainly. You must know what to tell him when he asks you questions about it."

Fra Raymond read, "In the name of Jesus Christ Crucified and of our Lady. Beloved and dearest brothers in Christ Jesus! I, Catherine, servant and handmaid of Jesus Christ, am writing to you in his precious Blood. I would like to see in you true sons and knights of Jesus Christ, so that you would be ready, when necessary, to shed your blood a thousand times in his service, which would be no more than an atonement for the many offences against our Savior." The address then switched to Aguto himself. "Most beloved, best brother in Jesus Christ! Would it really be such a great difficulty to do some heart searching and to consider how many troubles and hardships you have undergone in the service and pay of the devil? My soul desires that you should turn away from him and enter the service of Christ Crucified, you and all your companions and mercenaries and thus become a company of Christ, going to war against the infidel dogs in the Holy Land, where once the Divine Truth was living and suffered and died for us. I entreat you therefore—for God wills it and so does the Holy Father—to march against the infidels. If war and fighting mean so much to you, then I beg of you, stop indulging in it here and go to the unbelievers! Thus you may prove that you are a man and a true knight. This letter is brought to you by my father and son, Fra Raymond. Have confidence in what he says. He will not counsel you anything that is not to the glory of God and to the salvation and glory of your soul. I entreat you, dearest brother, do not forget how quickly time flies! I will say no more. I beg of you, think of the brevity of your life. Remain in the holy Love of God."

"Go at once", Catherine said. "Every hour counts."

"Y-yes, *mamma.*" Fra Raymond hunched up his shoulders and sent to find Fra Bartolomeo de'Domenici. The plump little friar was aghast when he heard their mission. He too read the letter and wagged his head. "This might work on a prelate, but not on Aguto the Terrible", he said. "Fra Raymond . . . how fortunate we are to have made the vow of poverty."

"What do you mean?"

"If we hadn't, we would have to make our last will and testament."

"We couldn't", Fra Raymond said with a wry smile. "*Mamma* wants us to go straight away. Every hour counts, she says."

"All right, then", Fra Bartolomeo said resignedly. "One can

die only once. But she might have chosen Master Tantucci as your companion, instead of me."

"Why?"

"Well, he's an Augustinian."

"So?"

"As it is, Saint Dominic will be deprived of two of his sons at a time. It doesn't seem fair."

"We're not dead yet", Fra Raymond said bravely, but his voice was not quite firm.

At the gate of the town a grim-faced guard made them wait, and for a few moments they both hoped that they might be forbidden to leave. But the man came back from the guard-room and opened the gate for them. Out they went. "We had to visit people stricken by the plague", Fra Raymond said. "I wonder why this seems worse to me."

"Because human malice and brutality are worse. That's a campfire over there, isn't it?"

"I don't feel well", Fra Raymond said.

"Neither do I."

"You do look rather green."

"Of course. It *is* a campfire, so let's keep left."

A few minutes later they were stopped by an outpost.

"A message for your general", Fra Raymond said.

"How many are you?"

Atrocious Italian. "Just the two of us."

"Advance slowly and keep your hands out of your sleeves."

They obeyed. The leader of the outpost came up and looked them over. "A couple of tonsured magpies", he said. "Has the town of Pisa no nobles left? All right. Geoffrey . . . Martin . . . Hubert . . . and you, Will, take these two over to the general's tent. Better blindfold them first. Don't worry, magpies, you're not going to be eaten . . . yet. Geoffrey, you're in charge. Off with you."

For what seemed an eternity they stumbled through the darkness. Around them a hubbub of English voices started. The strains of bawdy songs swirled past them, much cursing and clanking of armor.

"Stop now", one of the guards said. "Wait here."

"I hope *mamma* is praying", Fra Bartolomeo murmured. "I don't find it very easy to become a martyr."

More voices, more curses, and a sharp order.

"Forward", somebody said in Italian. They obeyed, and the musty smell of sackcloth and leather told them that they were entering a tent. A moment later the bandages were taken off their eyes. The tent was huge and furnished with a broad bed, an Oriental carpet, a table, and a single chair. The man who occupied it was a giant. Between eyes of icy blue, a beak of a nose. A mouth like a trap, thin lipped, merely the frontier between the nose and a jutting chin. There was no need to guess the man's identity. Mothers all over Italy had come to frighten their children into obedience by mentioning his name. Dukes and princes paled when they heard it. His cruelty was proverbial. It was said of him that he caught, in a conquered town, two of his soldiers fighting over an unfortunate nun, whom both of them regarded as their rightful share of the loot. The nun was on her knees, praying for deliverance. General Aguto solved the problem for all three of them. He drew his long sword and with one stroke cut the nun right through. "One half for each of you", he decided. It was this second and unholy Solomon the two friars were facing now.

"May the good Lord give you peace", Fra Raymond said, trying hard to keep his voice steady.

"And may the good Lord take away all alms ever given to you", Aguto bellowed. "The devil thank you for wishing me peace. D'ye want me to starve? I live on war as you do on alms."

Fra Bartolomeo managed to laugh at what he thought was a joke of the grim soldier. Aguto stared at him, and the poor friar's laughter broke off.

"I have a letter for you, great Commander", Fra Raymond said.

"So I'm told. And I hope your little ruler is bettering his offer. Because otherwise . . . "

"The letter", Fra Raymond said, "is not from Ser Piero

Gambacorti. It is from . . . it is from Sister Catherine Benincasa of the Order of the Sisters of Penance."

There was a pause. The huge Englishman's face was blank. Pray, *mamma,* Fra Bartolomeo thought ardently, or we'll be dead before we can make a decent act of contrition.

"Sister Catherine Benincasa", Aguto repeated, frowning heavily.

"Yes, great Commander. Here is the letter." He put it courteously on the table. The Englishman seized it as a man will seize a club. He is going to throw it in our faces, Fra Bartolomeo thought.

"Thornbury", Aguto roared. The flap of the tent flew up, and an apple-cheeked little man came in.

"Sir John?"

"Read this to me."

Thornbury took the letter, wedged it under his arm, produced from a large pocket in his doublet a pair of iron-rimmed spectacles, breathed on them, wiped them on his sleeve, put them on his round reddish nose, drew the letter from his armpit, opened it, and looked at it. "That's no letter to Sir John Hawkwood", he said. "It's meant for all of us, it seems. Ah! The main part is for you after all, Sir John."

"Don't babble at me . . . read, man, blast and damn you."

"Yes, Sir John." The little man read and Aguto listened, his face entirely devoid of expression. When Thornbury came to an end, there was a long silence.

"Sister Catherine Benincasa", Aguto said slowly. "Is that the woman who held a man's head while he was being executed?"

"Y-yes, Commander", Fra Raymond said, amazed. "It was in Siena."

The Englishman nodded. "That woman is the only real man in Siena . . . and a few other places as well."

"She is more than that", Fra Raymond said.

The Englishman gave him a keen look. "She speaks well of you. And from her that ought to mean something. What have you got to tell me?"

Fra Raymond took a deep breath. "Pisa hopes you will

content yourself with the offer you were given", he said. "I heard Ser Piero Gambacorti say that it was the utmost the town could afford."

"Is Pisa going to join the rebels against the Pope?" Aguto asked.

"Ser Piero does not want to, and he and the Archbishop have called on Sister Catherine to keep the citizens loyal", Fra Raymond replied.

The Englishman nodded. "I've taken a hundred and thirty thousand from Florence. Damn rebels. Pisa's offer of thirty thousand is pretty shabby, but I'll take it. Tell that to Sister Catherine, and let *her* tell it to Piero Gambacorti. And tell her this, too. . . . " He rose, and his head almost touched the tent's ceiling. "Tell her I like her", he said. He began to march up and down, and the soil seemed to tremble. No wonder they say he has to change his horse every two hours, Fra Raymond thought. All of a sudden Aguto stopped. "I've been a soldier all my life," he said, "and she too is a soldier. So she understands me and I understand her. Tell her I will go and fight the infidels for the holy places as soon as I have the chance. For this we shall need a larger army than my merry band of men. When that gets together, I won't fail her. That's all. You may go, good friars. Hey, Thornbury, have them taken back to the nearest gate. No need to blindfold them again."

The rebellion made progress. Within two weeks eighty towns were flying the red flag with the word *Libertas* on it. The Eight of War had a genius for winning allies and were aided and abetted by the hatred of all Italians for the French legates of the Pope.

Ser Piero was jubilant at the message of Aguto. Catherine was not. "I am glad he saw reason about the ransom money. I am glad he will not fight for the rebels. But I don't want him here in Italy at all. I want peace in Italy."

They told her that the Pope was planning a new consistory to be held in Avignon.

"New cardinals are badly needed", she said. "But please God

the Holy Father will choose the right men ... and not only Frenchmen and members of his own family."

She went to Lucca to fortify that town in its decision not to join the rebels, and she succeeded. Florence sent the famous orator Donato Barbadori there, and to Pisa as well, but Catherine's influence prevailed. However, Città di Castello fell to the rebels and so did Gubbio, Forli, Todi, Viterbo, and finally Perugia. Alessia, Francesca Gori, and Lisa Colombini were in tears; the friars hung their heads.

Catherine said somberly, "Milk and honey."

They stared at her.

"This is milk and honey", she repeated, "in comparison to what is still to come."

Sensitive as he was, Fra Raymond felt that this was not merely pessimism. There was more behind it. She *knew.* He shivered. "What could be worse than this?" he asked in a low voice.

She looked past him into the void. "This is the rebellion of laymen", she said. "But the time will come when the clergy will rebel. And the Church will be divided." Thunderstruck, they remained silent.

The next day they returned to Siena. From the Mangia tower a great flag was fluttering in the wind. It was blood red, and on it was written in large white letters the word *Libertas.*

The list of new cardinals was out. Fra Tommaso Caffarini brought the news to Sister Catherine, and when she saw his expression her heart sank.

"How many?" she asked.

"Nine."

"How many Italians?"

"One."

"Dear God. Dear God."

"And one Spaniard", Fra Tommaso went on. "All the others are Frenchmen. Three of them are relatives of the Pope. And one of the three is the Abbot of Marmoutier."

"Now Pisa will fall", Catherine said. "And Lucca, too. All Italy." She drew herself up. "Fra Tommaso, write a letter for me, please."

The friar sat down and took parchment and pen.

"To His Holiness Pope Gregory XI," she said, "in Avignon."

Book Four

Chapter Twenty-Two

I WOULD LIKE TO SEE in you a fruit tree full of sweet and ripened fruit'", Prelate Malherbes read aloud and with some gusto, " 'planted in the fertile soil of self-knowledge.' "

The Pope smiled affably, and affability suited the well-favored, rather delicate face. From the corner of the room, where Madame Elyse de Beaufort-Turenne was playing chess with Cardinal Robert of Geneva, came a duet of laughter. "My dearest uncle," Madame pleaded, "tell us, who is the author of this charming address?"

Prelate Malherbes' eyes asked for permission to answer the question, and when Gregory XI gave it with a little shrug, he said, "It is the beginning of a very long letter from a Sister Catherine Benincasa of the Sisters of Penance in Siena."

"A nun!" Madame exclaimed. "And she wants the Holy Father to be a fruit tree? It's forbidden fruit to her in any case." The Cardinal threw back his head, laughing.

"I have heard a good deal about this woman", the Pope said. "Many people seem to think that she is a saint."

"Saints", Madame said roguishly, "should keep away from fruit trees."

"My nephew Gerard de Puy has been in correspondence with her for a while", Gregory XI went on. "He seemed to be rather amused by her letters, poor boy."

"Why 'poor boy'?" Cardinal Robert of Geneva enquired. "You've just given him the red hat. A nice promotion for the Abbot of Marmoutier."

"Yes, and I hope it will do him some good. He has had so many disappointments lately. He was in real danger, too. They almost killed him in Perugia. They did kill four of his priests."

"Italy is under a curse", the Cardinal said. "I wish you'd let me carry out the plan I told you about yesterday, Your Holiness."

"What plan?" Madame enquired.

"Politics, dear niece", the Pope said. "A very dangerous and very boring business. What does the good Sister want of us, Malherbes?"

"She starts off with something very much like a sermon, Your Holiness. Self-knowledge as a necessity, inducing hatred of the self. Such hatred a necessity because self-love kills the fruit of the tree. He who is enamored with himself can only do evil. He is like a woman bringing forth still-born children."

"What a dreary person", Madame said.

"Why write that kind of thing to the Pope?" the Cardinal asked.

"Never mind", Gregory XI said. "Go on, Malherbes, read the next sentences in the original, or rather, translate them into French as literally as you can. My niece's Italian is not too fluent, and I have forgotten much of my own."

"When such a man is set over others, he will do evil", Malherbes translated. "For because of his self-love and the fear of men to which he is given because of his selfishness, holy justice is dead in him. He sees his subjects commit sins, yet he does not reproach them and pretends not to see anything. Or if he reproaches them he does it with so much tepidity and indifference that there is no result, and in the end vice sticks to them only more firmly than before. He is always trying to avoid shocking anyone and raising contradiction. And why? Because he is seeking only himself. . . . If one does not cauterize the wound with fire and iron, but only puts on an ointment, one does not cure it but poisons everything and often enough causes death."

"That's not bad at all", the Cardinal interposed with meaning. "Just what I told you, Your Holiness."

"Yes, but whom does she mean?" Gregory said. "Judging by what she wrote to my nephew, she doesn't mean the rebels, but my legates and governors."

"In that case you ought to apply her own prescriptions to her and have her put in a very strict convent, Your Holiness", the Cardinal said dryly. "One where nuns are not allowed to write letters."

"What else does she say, Malherbes?"

"She tells Your Holiness to stop using ointments", the prelate said, cocking a humorous eyebrow. "She calls you a blind shepherd who ought to be a physician but cares only for his own comfort...."

"What impudence!" Madame said.

" ...and who will not use either the knife of justice or the fire of ardent love. She compares you with the hireling who does not think of saving the sheep entrusted to him but leaves them to the wolf or even eats them himself. She says—just a moment—here it is: 'I wish you were that good and true shepherd who would give his life to the honor of God and the salvation of the creatures in his trust.' "

"She ought to be publicly whipped", Elyse de Beaufort-Turenne said in a fury.

"She tells Your Holiness to avert your love from the self and from creatures without consideration of friends and relatives and worldly possessions...."

"What insolence!" Madame cried. "Of course it's very easy for her to talk like that. She has no possessions to lose."

"She invokes the Savior", Prelate Malherbes continued. "She cries woe over the bishops and shepherds who are blind and proud and pleasure seeking. She evokes Pope Gregory the Great as the example for those who carry his name...."

"So she really means you personally, Your Holiness", the Cardinal said. "It's unbelievable."

"She admonishes Your Holiness to do as she tells you," the prelate went on, "and not to let yourself be intimidated but to act like a man in this present storm that has been raised by those corrupt members of the Church, the rebels."

"Ah", Gregory said, and he sat bolt upright. "So she is not on the side of the rebels after all."

"She wouldn't dare say so, of course", Madame said scornfully.

"She has dared more than that, I think", the Cardinal said.

"What else does she say?" the Pope asked calmly.

"She tells Your Holiness again to be courageous and to go on the holy and much-desired voyage back to Rome", the prelate said, studying the letter. "To raise the banner of the Holy Cross that alone leads to peace."

"A slap in the face to the rebels with their red flag", Gregory said intently. "Go on."

"To ask the rebels to keep a holy truce", the prelate went on, "and to carry the war to the infidels instead. There follows a rather eloquent plea to come and comfort Your Holiness' unhappy children who are awaiting you with so much longing and love. Then another plea for Your Holiness to write to the towns of Lucca and Pisa who have not yet succumbed to the constant threats of the Tuscan League. . . . "

"Who's that?" Madame asked.

"Florence and its allies", the Cardinal explained.

"And there is one other passage here, about Your Holiness' consistory. She says, 'As I hear you have created cardinals. I believe it would be more to the honor of God and better for you, too, if you would always see to it they are worthy men. If not, it would be a great crime against God and pernicious to Holy Church. Then you can no longer be surprised when God punishes and scourges us. It would only be just. I implore you, do bravely what you must do, in the fear of God.' There is one more passage promising further letters and asking for Your Holiness' blessing."

"Apparently the good Sister doesn't approve of your choice of cardinals", Robert of Geneva said. "I must say I fully agree with my charming partner at chess. This nun is the most impudent person I ever heard of."

"The Archbishop of Pisa writes that he regards her as a woman of holy insolence", the Pope said.

"I don't know about the holiness," the Cardinal retorted, "but I vouch for the rest."

"I wonder what she really is", Gregory XI said slowly.

"A fanatic", Madame said contemptuously. "And a religious busybody."

"There are certain tales about curing people", Gregory said. "Including some who were stricken with the plague."

"I don't believe a word of it", Madame said. "Miracles may

have happened in the past, but in our time they are hopelessly out of date. Anyway, who *wants* miracles?"

"Apparently you do in chess, gracious lady", the Cardinal said. "How else can I explain the fact that your black knight is suddenly in a position to threaten my queen?"

Madame gave a silvery laugh. "I did so hope you wouldn't see the little change I made, Your Eminence."

"I shall do what Sister — what's her name? — condemns so strongly and pretend not to see it", the Cardinal said. "But I shall move my castle like this. Check."

"Oh . . . "

"What is your opinion of her, Malherbes?" the Pope asked.

"Your Holiness asked me to read the letter to you", the prelate said. "I would have been quite content to put it in the wastepaper basket. Why, the poor Sister writes letters in that vein to almost everybody. One should perhaps draw the attention of her superiors to the fact that she will scarcely be able to fulfill her spiritual duties if she goes on writing so many letters. . . . "

The Pope made a gesture of impatience. "There is something about this woman that interests me", he said. "Reform of the clergy . . . return to Rome . . . and a crusade. These three things were on my mind when I was elected to my office. That is what I wanted to do. So much has happened to make it impossible . . . yet here she comes to remind me of them. She . . . she may be my own conscience. She may be the conscience of the Christian world."

"Your Holiness is extremely gentle toward one who has so many harsh words for you", Malherbes said with some acerbity. "Sister Catherine Benincasa seems to believe that God has only one faithful servant: Sister Catherine Benincasa."

"In any case it's madness to think of a crusade when things are as they are in Italy", the Cardinal said, looking up from his chessboard. The pretty Elyse was still not checkmated; she had wriggled out of the danger for the time being. "When your own castle is burning, you have no business to think of conquering your neighbor's."

"A real reform is hopeless at present", the Pope said. "So is the idea of returning to Rome. But I shall write to Pisa and Lucca today, as Sister Catherine suggests."

"Pisa! Lucca!" The Cardinal shrugged his shoulders. "Florence is the author of the rebellion. Florence is what matters. Think of what I suggested yesterday, Your Holiness. The earlier you give me your permission the better. We are losing precious time. Let me start the necessary preparations at least."

"The case of Florence will come to trial next week", the Pope said. "Wouldn't you rather be present?"

"Yes", the Cardinal growled. "If only to prevent your gentle advisers from counselling Christian clemency and forbearance. On *that* point I'm all for your Sister Catherine. No more ointments for the rebels. Fire and iron . . . didn't she say so?"

"Sister Catherine did not suggest war against the rebels", Gregory said. "It may come to that. But there are other weapons too."

"None as effective. Not against those bandits. They must be crushed without delay."

"Check, Your Eminence", said Elyse de Beaufort-Turenne. She leaned back voluptuously. "And mate", she added with a charming smile.

On February the eleventh the Consistory decided to send Florence an ultimatum. All the leaders of the rebellion, fifty-nine in number, were summoned to appear before the Pope in Avignon, no later than the end of March. If they failed to obey, under whatever pretext, the Pope would proclaim the Interdict.

Chapter Twenty-Three

THE EXCITEMENT IN THE FULL SESSION of the Signoría in Florence was tremendous.

"The Pope's demand is an insult to Florence", Ser Benvenuto Minuccio cried.

"Exactly!"

"He has shown once more what we have known all along: that the Church is no longer a valid factor in public life", Minuccio went on.

"He's hammering on the table in front of him as if it were the pate of a French prelate", Buonaccorso di Lapo whispered.

Niccolò Soderini groaned. "I've had a letter from Sister Catherine Benincasa", he murmured. "I only wish I knew how to answer it."

"What does she say?"

"The gist of it is that we must be obedient to the Pope."

"Poor woman. All she can think of is peace, which no one wants but herself."

"And a few others, surely", Soderini said. "Must I remind you, Messer Buonaccorso, that you yourself—"

"Shshsh . . . it won't do any good to repeat that here. *He's* looking." They fell silent, as most people did when Ser Giovanni di Dini's pale eyes were on them. The First Member of the Eight of War was not famous for his patience.

"It is indeed an insult", di Dini said. His voice was surprisingly high and reedy for a man of such commanding personality. "It seems that those scarlet men around the Pope still don't realize that the voice of Florence is the voice of Italy." Applause thundered across the hall. Only the pictures of the great men of Florence on the wall remained unmoved. "And the voice of Italy", di Dini went on, "is the true voice of Christianity."

Applause again, but this time a shade weaker, and the speaker was well aware of it. "My first reaction", he said, "to this letter from a schoolmaster to recalcitrant boys was to accept the invitation . . . "

"No!"

"Never!"

" . . . to accept the invitation in the same way a great prince once did. He replied that he would come with twelve thousand foot and eight thousand horse. Whereupon the Holy Father—not this one, but one of his more recent predecessors— very quickly cancelled the invitation." Storms of laughter. "But we have no intention of going to war", cried Giovanni di Dini. "All we want to do is to set our Italian house in order, and no one and nothing will stop us from doing that."

"Tinkling cymbals", Buonaccorso di Lapo whispered. "When is he going to *say* something?"

"This is no time for weak hearts," di Dini went on, "nor for turncoats and priest worshippers. It is a time for *men.* We Florentines are proud to have rallied not only Tuscany but almost the whole of Italy around the flag of Liberty." The applause was deafening. "We are responsible statesmen", di Dini continued in a calmer voice. "However much we resent the arrogant message His Holiness has thought fit to send us, we shall not answer in the same vein." No applause this time. "Instead the Eight of War will hold council and see what can be done to set things right. But this answer we can give to Avignon here and now: the town of Lucca has declared for us. The town of Pisa will follow, and after that Bologna. The more threats from Avignon, the more allies in Italy! Perhaps they'll learn something from that, even at this late hour." Final applause. The great Signoría began to disperse.

"In half an hour it will be all over Florence that the Pope has threatened to proclaim the Interdict", Soderini said. "What will the people say?"

"They will howl with di Dini and manhandle or kill some more priests, as they did last week." Di Lapo looked over his shoulder. "The Eight of War have retired", he said. "Let's be on our way too, friend. I am longing for a little sunshine. I usually feel like that when I'm leaving this building, beautiful as it is."

"It isn't the building's fault."

"I agree. God knows what they're going to decide. I fear the worst."

"What? That we shall send an army to Avignon?"

"No, no, Niccolò. Even di Dini knows that he can't afford a war with France, and that's what it would mean. He isn't as foolish as all that. In fact, he isn't a fool at all. Your feelings sometimes carry you too far."

"Really?" Soderini's eyes narrowed. "You could acquire merit with him quite easily, of course ... if you were to repeat certain things to him."

Buonaccorso di Lapo shook his head. "You shouldn't say such a thing, Niccolò. Not to me."

Soderini bit his lip. "I apologize, old friend", he said. "But the air in Florence these days—"

"And what is wrong with the air of Florence?" asked a smooth voice. They both swung round.

"Fra Raymond of Capua", Soderini exclaimed. "Thank God it's you. I thought—"

"Never mind, never mind, I understand", Fra Raymond said quickly.

"Has Sister Catherine sent you?"

"Yes. She is extremely worried, as you may imagine. We have written to the Holy Father three times in the last weeks."

"She is a great woman, but I'm afraid even she won't be able to stave off the worst. Things are as bad as they can possibly be. The Pope demands that all leaders of the rebellion, as he puts it, must present themselves in Avignon by the end of March. If they do not, he threatens us with the Interdict."

For one wild moment Fra Raymond saw the consequences: no Mass could be said, no Holy Communion given, no marriages ... good God, a great city without the sacraments. ...

"Not that", he stammered. "O God, don't let it happen. ..."

"They're quite beside themselves here", Buonaccorso di Lapo

said. "The defection of all those cities and towns makes them think that they can do almost anything."

Fra Raymond nodded. "It isn't very different in Siena. You two are Sister Catherine's hope. What are you going to do?"

"We are only members of the Signoría", Soderini told him. "Not of the Eight of War. They alone have the power to make decisions. And they are holding council this very hour."

"Messer Niccolò Soderini . . . Messer Buonaccorso di Lapo!" The head usher of the Signoría bowed to them. "The Council requires your immediate presence, if you please."

The two Florentines looked at each other. The official cleared his throat. "It is most urgent", he murmured.

"Until later then, Fra Raymond", Soderini said. "At least . . . I hope so. If you will kindly excuse us now. . . . " They hurried back.

Giovanni di Dini and his seven colleagues were conferring in a small room with thickly padded doors. "Welcome, Messer Niccolò", he said amiably. "Welcome, Messer Buonaccorso . . . have some wine with us, and thus fortified you may be able to render service to Florence."

"I am always ready for that, Messer Giovanni", di Lapo said with dignity, and Soderini nodded agreement. "There is no need for wine."

"As you wish. Did I just see you conversing with a Dominican friar?" Giovanni di Dini pointed to the open window overlooking the piazza.

"Fra Raymond of Capua has come to see me on behalf of Sister Catherine of Siena", Soderini said. "She is a very remarkable woman, and I—"

"Oh, but we know all about her", Giovanni di Dini interposed. "I thought that was Fra Raymond. A very good and eloquent man, is he not?"

"Indeed he is, Messer Giovanni."

"Florence has need of such men in times like these. I know I can count on *your* support. After all, the message of His Holiness affects us all equally. You will find both your names on the list of the fifty-nine men whom the Pope has summoned to appear before him. If you will take the trouble to look at the original letter . . . here it is."

Soderini took it. Di Lapo looked over his shoulder. It was true. They too were regarded as rebel leaders.

"What better proof could there possibly be of your loyalty to Florence *and* to its government", Ser Giovanni di Dini said with a maddening smile. "Well, Messers, let's be frank with each other. Neither you nor I are likely to enjoy that journey much, so let's try to find a different way. It is obvious that His Holiness has been gravely misinformed. There is no other explanation for the . . . severity of his message. Therefore we should first of all send a man who sees the issue in an impartial manner. Not as an official ambassador, of course, but shall we say as a forerunner of an embassy? Do you think Fra Raymond of Capua would undertake such a task for us?"

"I am sure of it," Soderini replied, much relieved, "though Sister Catherine herself would be better still."

"I think we would be satisfied with Fra Raymond", Giovanni di Dini said. "Will you inform him, Messer Niccolò? Will you too try and persuade him, Messer Buonaccorso?"

"We shall do our best", Soderini said.

"Excellent. I shall have to talk to him, of course. Tell him I expect him tomorrow afternoon at three o'clock."

"Without fail, Messer Giovanni."

When Soderini and di Lapo had left, Ser Giovanni di Dini turned to his colleagues. "March the thirty-first is not too far away," he said, "but far enough to give us a little time for gathering information. The Cardinal of Geneva has left Avignon for an unknown destination. I don't like that very much. He is more of a general than a priest, and the 'unknown' destination has turned out to be Brittany, the very region from which the best French mercenaries are culled. We shall see. By all means let's go on kindling the indignation of the people, but in the meantime we must persuade the Holy Father to believe in our goodwill toward him."

"Are you really going to send this friar to Avignon?" Ser Alessandro dell'Antella asked, rubbing his sharp, pointed nose.

"Of course, Messer Alessandro. It's the best way to let the peace-at-any-price people here think that we're trying our best to avoid trouble. It will give us time, and that's all we need. As soon as Bologna has joined us, we can speak far more frankly to Avignon."

"When do you expect that to be?"

"In two or three weeks, Messer Alessandro. Perhaps less."

Fra Raymond beamed when Soderini made his offer. "I was going to Avignon anyway", he said. "Sister Catherine is sending me there, with another letter to the Holy Father. She must have *known* that I was going to be asked the same thing here in Florence. It's just like her." He had to request his order's permission first. The Provincial gave it to him with joy and many good wishes from trembling old lips. Ser Giovanni di Dini received him with great courtesy. Fra Raymond asked, "Is it understood that I am going to Avignon not to negotiate . . . "

"You have no power to negotiate."

" . . . nor to represent Florence, but only to awaken the Holy Father's fuller understanding of the situation here in Tuscany and to prepare the ground for negotiations to follow?"

"That is what we ask you to do, Fra Raymond. That and no more."

"In that case I accept." He reported in a long letter to Sister Catherine and set out. Five days after his departure Bologna declared itself for the rebellion and unfurled the red flag on the town hall.

As soon as that news arrived in Florence, Ser Giovanni di Dini had Niccolò Soderini, Buonaccorso di Lapo, and a number of other members of the Signoría arrested and put in jail. "For two excellent reasons", he explained to his colleagues. "First: this will be the end of the peace-at-any-price party of which they were the leaders. Thus there will be no interference from within. Secondly: we now can truthfully inform His Holiness that his request is impossible to fulfill. We can't very well let prisoners out of jail to have them travel to Avignon, can we?"

"Nicely thought out", Alessandro dell'Antella admitted. "But what are we going to do now? You don't expect that friar to be successful, do you?"

"Of course not. Besides, he has no powers. No . . . now we shall send a real embassy. You, Messer Alessandro . . . Ser Domenico di Silvestro . . . and as your speaker the best man we have for the part, the man who can really tell the Pope what Florence stands for: Donato Barbadori. Give him one hour, give him half an hour with the Pope and the cardinals, and then they'll be ripe for negotiations on *our* terms."

"And if he doesn't succeed?" dell'Antella asked.

An ugly red mounted in di Dini's fleshy face. "We are called the Eight of War", he said. "We shall fight anyone who bars our way, be he pope or devil or both." When they remained silent, he glared at them. "You still don't understand, do you? This is the kind of chance fate grants only once. What I told those fools in the Signoría the other day was quite true. If all goes well, Italy will be ruled from Florence."

Chapter Twenty-Four

S ER DONATO BARBADORI was not only the greatest orator
Florence had ever had; he was also a very handsome and
elegant man. There was a saying among Florentine ladies:
"You may resist Adonis; you may turn up your nose at Apollo;
but if you wish to remain virtuous, close your eyes when
Donato Barbadori passes by." He had conquered dozens of
towns by his eloquence and, unlike his two companions, he felt
no doubt at all that he would fulfill his mission in Avignon
too. Sharp-nosed Alessandro dell'Antella was worried but
managed not to show it. Barbadori was always at his best when
he felt assured of victory. It would be unwise to pour cold
water on his enthusiasm. Domenico di Silvestro showed neither worry nor self-assurance. He was a placid man, and his air
of superciliousness was mainly due to the fact that his features
provided it quite naturally. He was neither a good speaker nor
a particularly intelligent man, but he came from a very good
family. When the three set out for Avignon, the saying went
round Florence: we have sent the Pope the best we have . . . a
peacock, a fox, and a camel. But Ser Giovanni di Dini had his
own version. No one could present the case as well as Barbadori.
No one was a more wily tactician than dell'Antella. And no
one could be relied upon to report the truth as conscientiously
as Domenico di Silvestro.

The trio stood in the great hall of the huge brown papal
palace at Avignon, waiting for their audience, di Silvestro as
stiff as a board, dell'Antella nosing about, and Barbadori tugging at the sleeves of his magnificent coat of black velvet
decorated with silver tassels and trimmed with fur. He was a
little nervous, as always before a performance. They had not
seen much of the city, nothing really, except the accumulation

of ships on the Rhone River, galleys, a great many more than one would expect in peacetime. And small groups of soldiers were marching through the streets almost continuously, Breton foot. There seemed to be a large camp north of the town. Troops and galleys. Dell'Antella had made some mental notes. So had di Silvestro.

The huge doors were flung open, and a chamberlain appeared with his gold-tipped staff. "The ambassadors of the Republic of Florence", he said in a low voice.

Barbadori drew himself up and marched forward. Dell' Antella and di Silvestro followed. Before them in the great Gothic hall was the throne of the Pope, flanked by sixteen lower thrones for the cardinals, eight on each side. Through dell'Antella's brain flashed the idea that it might have been better to get in touch with some of the few, the very few, Italians among them, before bursting into a full session like this. But Giovanni di Dini had insisted on a last-minute arrival. "It is symbolical. It will make the Pope think. Nothing could be worse than to give him the impression that we are in a hurry. He who is in a hurry is worried. We are *not* worried, not in the least." Today was the last day of March. . . .

Barbadori was going through the elaborate ceremony of presenting the embassy's credentials. The Pope's face seemed gentle enough, but some of the cardinals looked grim and forbidding. Only two or three seemed to be uneasy and possibly embarrassed . . . the Italians, more likely than not.

"Three envoys", the Pope said. "We sent you a list of the persons whose presence is required here. It contained fifty-nine names. Where are the others?"

"Your Holiness must excuse their absence", Barbadori said. "A number of the persons mentioned on that list are active members of the government who could not possibly leave Florence for a single day, let alone for the long journey to Avignon and back."

"There might have been no need for them to go back", snapped Cardinal Robert of Geneva.

Barbadori was wise enough to take no notice of the remark. "A number of others, I regret to say, are in prison", he went on.

"That's where all of you belong", Cardinal Gilles Aycelin de Montaigu muttered fairly audibly.

The wind was cold, but Barbadori was accustomed to that kind of weather ... at the beginning. "If the great republic of Florence has sent only three men," he said, "no disrespect was meant toward the wishes of Your Holiness. And we feel that we can plead our case sufficiently well to clear up the entire issue at stake. We have been asked to come here under duress. A great threat has been pronounced against us, as if we were accused of dire crimes, as if we were fugitives from justice, trying to escape from deserved punishment. I most solemnly assure Your Holiness ... and indeed also Your Eminences ... that such treatment has greatly aggrieved our government, and not only our government: it was felt as undeserved by every single citizen of Florence. Far from being the villains in the case, it is we who have reason, and abundant reason, to raise our voice in accusation and to complain with all vigor against the treatment meted out to us by Your Holiness' legates, governors, and envoys."

"Rank insolence", the Cardinal of Geneva snapped, but the Pope raised his hand and Barbadori went on. The picture he now unrolled was a lurid one. He described at length a great many misdeeds, real and alleged, that the papal administration had committed. As the Pope had given a sign not to interrupt the speaker, he felt safe and made the most of his opportunity. He was an orator who lived his part, and he plunged into it with ever-growing ardor. From misdeeds he passed on to crimes and from crimes to vice. He exaggerated. He multiplied. Before an audience turned to stone he described papal governors as vicious brigands of heathen cruelty and the clergy in general as ignorant, vain, and grasping.

Most of the cardinals were looking at the Pope. How long would he permit such insults? But the gentle face of Gregory XI only looked sad. He knew that a great deal of what the man in black velvet said was true. Sister Catherine of Siena had told him in no less than four letters. The last one had come with the Dominican friar Raymond of Capua, who had begged him on his knees to grant the wishes of that extraordinary woman. Reform of the clergy was always the first point she made. Then the return to Rome. Then the proclamation of a new crusade. She hammered her three points in, time and again. It was dreadful to have to listen to all these accusations, knowing that many of them were true.

At this moment Cardinal Robert of Geneva felt the strong, the almost irresistible urge to get up, push the poor weakling from his throne, sit on it, and excommunicate that impudent playactor from Florence, his companions, and his whole town, before he could mouth more of his blasphemous nonsense. The Cardinal's hands were clenched into fists. Two thousand more horses would arrive tonight. In a very few weeks he could set out with an excellent army and reduce Florence to rubble. They would draw in their blood-red flags soon enough in all those other towns, after that.

Barbadori went on. He was far too experienced a speaker not to sense that indignation and fury were mounting, but he was past caring. This was his supreme moment, the crowning glory of years of work. All that he had told the assemblies in Pisa and Lucca, in Montefiascone and Viterbo, in Forli and Bologna and a hundred other places he could now throw in the face of the Pope and the cardinals in Avignon, the source of all woe, the birthplace of all trouble in Italy. He felt his eloquence rise like a great white charger, and he rode on. Several times Alessandro dell'Antella tugged at his coat . . . he had been watching the faces of the men in scarlet and he knew that Barbadori was going too far, much too far. But the speaker took no notice of the warning. The white charger was running wild, and no one and nothing could stop it. "Such are the men you sent us, Holy Father", Barbadori thundered. "And such is what they have done to us. Can you be surprised when the martyred people of Tuscany rise, oh, not against the Faith which they hold as dear as ever, but against those most unworthy men? Withdraw them and punish them as they deserve it, Your Holiness! That is what the republic of Florence demands. Do not, we beseech you, require the unconditional surrender of the innocent, but rather punish the guilty men who ill use the great office of prelate and priest." Bowing, Donato Barbadori made a step back.

There was no sound. The Cardinal of Geneva stared at the Pope. Still no indignation, no rage, not even the slightest sign of anger. It was too much. He rose. "Your Holiness," he said, "may I suggest that any decision be deferred. I have good reasons."

Gregory XI looked down. "We have heard sad things," he said in a low voice, "things that almost break our heart. Where grievances are justified, redress must certainly be made." The few Italian cardinals murmured their assent. "We shall consider the case the ambassadors of Florence have put before us in the light of the information we possess," the Pope went on, "and we shall give our decision later."

The Florentine envoys withdrew with stiff courtesy. Outside, Donato Barbadori whispered the old, old question of all actors: "How was I?"

"Magnificent", Alessandro dell'Antella said dryly. "I only hope you haven't ruined us."

"What do you mean?" Barbadori asked, startled. "I said everything I was asked to say, didn't I?"

"Oh, quite. You practically excommunicated the Pope and the entire cardinalate."

"I softened him up, didn't I? He was almost crying at the end. In fact, I think he *was* crying."

"Maybe so", di Silvestro said woodenly. "But the French cardinals weren't."

"Never mind them", Barbadori said. "Nothing could convince *them.* They're all of a kind. The Pope was what I was out for, and I got him, believe me."

"I wish I could", dell'Antella said. Di Silvestro said nothing, but he was breathing heavily.

In the audience room Cardinal Robert of Geneva said, "Holy Father, we have had to listen to the most impudent speech ever delivered in this palace. The criminal, far from beating his breast, pretends to be the accuser and the judge. Much as I admire Your Holiness' charity, I must appeal to Your Holiness' conscience."

"We have some bad servants, it seems, Your Eminence."

"That is something Your Holiness will no doubt examine and, where necessary, put right. Meanwhile we are dealing with a group of rebels who have topped their rebellion with open disobedience to your summons. . . . "

"May I draw Your Holiness' attention to the most important fact of all", Cardinal de Luna interposed. "The remarkable Florentine never for one moment denied the accusations made against Florence. Prelates and priests murdered! Churches looted! Not a word about those grave and terrible crimes. They are not nullified by counteraccusations."

The French cardinals jumped to their feet to felicitate their Spanish colleague. The Italian cardinals looked glum. The Pope sighed.

"Your Holiness," Cardinal d'Estaing said, "I know Italy. I have been there long enough as your legate, and my conscience does not prick me unduly. It is my duty to say this: if we do not act now with the utmost severity, they will take it as a sure sign of weakness."

"Yesterday they have killed some prelates and priests. Tomorrow they will kill them all", stormed Cardinal Aycelin de Montaigu. "And history will say that such things happened because the Pope was too weak to take action when it was necessary to do so."

Nothing stings the weak more sharply than to be accused of weakness. The Pope frowned. "I have not given my decision yet", he said testily. "I must ask Your Eminence not to take it for granted."

"My apologies, Your Holiness."

"Nevertheless it is a terrible decision to make", Gregory said. "So much suffering . . . " The letters of the little Sister of Penance came back to his tortured mind, the pleas of the Dominican friar she had sent to him. He closed his eyes in anguish.

"I don't think we shall have to worry too much, Your Eminences", Cardinal d'Estaing said aloud. "The Holy Father is well aware of the position. He won't let the honor of the Church be dragged through the mud by a handful of Florentine rabble-rousers and their minions."

"My army will be ready very shortly", Cardinal Robert of Geneva said. "And I have assembled it with the explicit permission of the Holy Father, exactly because he foresaw the development we are facing now."

"The honor of Holy Church is at stake", cried the Cardinal of Lyons, looking fixedly at the Pope, who after all was a Frenchman and a de Beaufort. The quiet figure on the throne stirred.

Cardinal Brossano leaned over to Cardinal Corsini. "Poor Florence", he whispered. Cardinal Corsini shrugged his shoulders.

In the afternoon the Florentine envoys were asked to return to the audience hall. Barbadori was no longer quite so sure of himself. "At the very best, I think, we are at the beginning of negotiations", was dell'Antella's verdict. Di Silvestro preferred not to express any opinion at all.

The sight of the cold and severe-looking assembly gave them an ominous feeling. The Pope himself looked pale and resentful. "We shall now give our decision", he said. Cardinal Robert of Geneva rose, walked to the throne, knelt, and handed the Pope a document. Gregory XI began to read it. The Florentine envoys listened with growing consternation. " . . . and as the aforesaid republic through its accredited envoys so much as tried with one word to refute the most grave accusations raised against it, to viz.: the murder by execution of a Carthusian prior, the massacre of several priests and monks, the wholesale confiscations of ecclesiastic property and other crimes and offenses; and refused to comply with the order to send the leaders of the rebellion here to appear before us, we, Gregory XI, Vicar of Jesus Christ on earth, Successor Saint Peter, Pontifex Maximus . . . "

"No," Barbadori stammered, "no, it can't be . . . "

" . . . pronounce the city of Florence and all Florentine territory to be under Interdict as from the fourteenth day of May of the year of our Lord one thousand three hundred and seventy-six. Given at our place in Avignon on the thirty-first day of March of the year of our Lord one thousand three hundred and seventy-six, and duly signed and sealed."

"No!" Barbadori shouted. Looking about in despair, he saw the large crucifix hanging at the wall on his left. He ran toward it, flung himself down, and cried, "Great God: we delegates of the Florentines appeal to you and to your justice from the unjust sentence of your Vicar. O you who can never err, whose anger is ever tempered with mercy, you whose Will it is that the people of the earth shall be free and not slaves, you who abhor tyrants, be today the help and shield of the people of Florence who in your name will strive for their rights and liberties!"

"Unheard-of impudence", thundered the Cardinal of Geneva.

"Crazy rascal", shouted Cardinal Aycelin de Montaigu.

"Presumptuous fellow!"

"Playacting buffoon!"

Barbadori jumped to his feet. With eyes rolling he began to speak again, but his words remained inaudible in the general uproar. Cardinal d'Estaing, pale with rage, beckoned the papal court marshal, who in turn snapped out an order. Six men of the guard came clanking up to the delegates, who found themselves pushed back despite their protests. A few moments later they were again in the anteroom. The court marshal strode after them. "The envoys of Florence are excused from a visit of leave-taking", he said icily.

Chapter Twenty-Five

I THOUGHT I SENT capable men to Avignon", Ser Giovanni di Dini said. "It turns out I sent a market crier and two mutes."

"I told the Pope only what you asked me to tell him", Barbadori defended himself.

"Imbecile", di Dini snarled. "Did I ask you to address him and those red devils of his as if they were a bunch of country yokels? Did I ask you to make one great, big, disastrous speech and then to disappear? Is that your idea of negotiations? And you, dell'Antella . . . I didn't ask di Silvestro to speak. I'm well aware of *his* limitations . . . but you!"

"Two men can't talk at the same time", dell'Antella said quietly. "And no one has a chance of saying anything, with Barbadori present."

"The Pope had, apparently", di Dini retorted venomously. "And what's more, he said a great deal. Of course I wanted you to present our side of the case. But what we needed were negotiations, prolonged negotiations, endless negotiations . . . until we are firmly in the saddle everywhere in Italy. Then, and only then, we could afford a break. This may well cost us the leadership I established with so many pains. And more! Here . . . " He crashed his fist on a pile of letters on the table before him. "Protests", he roared. "Protests from Florentine citizens everywhere. No one is paying any debts to a Florentine. No one is giving any credit to a Florentine. All agreements, pacts, and business deals with foreign firms are cancelled. In Naples! In Rome! Everywhere in France. There are more than a hundred Florentine merchants in Avignon alone. They'll be ruined in a few months. Many are already ruined."

"I thought that might happen," dell'Antella said, "but you can't make an omelet without breaking some eggs."

"God in heaven give me patience", di Dini swore. "We still have a few weeks before that hellish thing is in force on May the fourteenth. But then ... then you'll see what will happen. There'll be demonstrations. There'll be riots. What do you think our good citizens will say, when no Mass is said, when the church bells are mute, when there are no sacraments? What about marriages, with no priest permitted to bless the couple? And every other town will know that helping us in whatever way will bring the same curse upon them as well! I sent you out to plead the case of the finest city in Italy and you come back with a result that makes us outcasts, lepers!"

"Very well, then", di Silvestro said woodenly. "What do we do now?"

" 'What do we do now?' " di Dini aped his tone ferociously. "We must try to rid ourselves of the curse, of course."

"Give in to the Pope?" Barbadori asked, wide eyed.

"Like most stupid people you can see things only in alternatives", di Dini told him contemptuously. "Must things be either black or white? Can't they be red or blue or any of a hundred shades of green? The Eight of War will convene this afternoon. By then I shall have a number of measures ready to save us all from ruin."

That same day Niccolò Soderini and Buonaccorso di Lapo were released from prison. Three days later Soderini was summoned to the Signoría, and di Dini had a long and private talk with him. "It was my zeal for Florence that made me act against you and your friends, Messer Niccolò," he concluded, "and I know now that I did you an injustice. The best I can say is that by my very action I gave you a better standing with the Pope than the rest of us have. Now the time has come for us to work together. Will you agree to that?"

Pale and haggard, Soderini agreed to help as much as he could. "I love Florence no less than you do, Messer Giovanni."

"The rest of your friends will be freed today. Get in touch with them. Tell them to calm the citizens. Tell them we shall do everything in our power to get the Interdict removed."

"What can you do?" Soderini asked point blank.

"We must reopen negotiations."

"How? From what you told me about the fate of the delegation, the Pope will refuse to receive us. Of course, if there were a complete change of government . . . "

Giovanni di Dini's face darkened. "There'll be nothing of the sort", he rapped out.

"In that case we shall need an intermediary", Soderini said.

"I suppose so", di Dini admitted. "But whom? Bernabò Visconti of Milan is not exactly popular in Avignon either. And if we left it up to Bologna, they'd probably betray us."

"None of the cities under the red flag will be able to do anything", Soderini said. "It must be a personality whom both the Pope and we can trust."

Di Dini laughed. "Aren't you asking for the impossible?"

"No," Soderini said. "There is one and only one possibility. Sister Catherine Benincasa."

"That nun", di Dini exclaimed. "What makes you think that she can do anything?"

"The fact that I have the good fortune to know her", Soderini replied stiffly, "and the fact that she has written me, offering just what I suggested."

"Interesting", di Dini said. "But a nun . . . a woman! Is Florence to hide behind a woman's cloak?"

"I can't think of better fortune for anybody than to hide behind the cloak of the Madonna", Soderini said. "So why should it be disgraceful to hide behind the cloak of a lesser saint?"

"Yes, yes, quite so." Di Dini cleared his throat. "But as a nun she isn't likely to be impartial, is she?"

"The letter I received", Soderini said, "is accompanied by a second one, addressed to the Signoría as a whole. Sister Catherine did not know that I was in prison. She thought I was still a member of the government."

"Do you have the letter with you?"

"Here it is."

Di Dini scanned it. " . . . I would like to see in you true sons and not rebels against your father . . . " He grunted. " . . . For God has so instituted things that through his hands must come to us the blood of Christ and all the sacraments of the Church. There is no other way . . . what we do to him we do to Christ in heaven, be it reverence or infamy. You see that by your faithlessness and your persecution of the Church. . . . " How long would she go on preaching? " . . . When God is at war with you because of the wrong you have done to his Vicar, your father, you are powerless, for you will not have his help. Even if many of you may think that they do not offend God and may even render him service . . . for when they persecute the Church and its shepherds, they defend themselves by pointing out their malice and wickedness . . . even then I say to you it is God's Will that even if they were devils incarnate we must submit, not for their sake, but for God's sake. For Christ wants us to obey his Vicar. . . . " With some difficulty di Dini managed to read on. "My sons, I beseech you with tears . . . reconciliation . . . no war . . . don't wait until the anger of God comes upon you . . . do no longer remain blind and obdurate! Run into the arms of your father, and he will receive you with kindness . . . and you will find peace and quiet for soul and body, you and all Tuscany. Then the banner of the Holy Cross will be raised, and the war will go to the infidels. . . . Do not think God is asleep. He is awake. And do not let us deceive ourselves when we think to be successful! For under the success the scourge of God's all-powerful hand is hidden. Yet he is ready to give you his pardon. So do not remain obdurate any longer, my brothers . . . he who humbles himself shall be exalted, Christ says, and he who exalts himself shall be humbled. . . . " Angrily di Dini put the letter down.

"You haven't read the end", Soderini said evenly. "Read it."

With a shrug di Dini took up the letter again. More preaching. "Forgive my presumption . . . I would rather tell you all this personally, instead of writing to you. If I can contribute anything to the honor of God and your reunion with Holy Church, I shall be ready to give my life for it, if needs be. Remain in the holy Love of God . . . " and so on. Giovanni di

Dini's face was quite expressionless, as always when he was thinking hard. Soderini was right. Here was an offer to mediate.

"What makes you think that the Pope will listen to her?" he asked casually.

"Fra Raymond of Capua told me in his last letter that the Holy Father has high regard for her."

"Well, *he* wasn't much good to us."

"She has sent two more of her friends to Avignon", Soderini said. "Ser Neri di Landoccio dei Pagliaresi . . . "

"The poet?"

"Yes. And Master Giovanni Terzo Tantucci of the Augustinian Order."

Giovanni di Dini grinned ruefully. "A Dominican friar," he said, "three members of the government, a poet, and an Augustinian monk. Why not a nun for a change?"

"Shall I tell her to come, then?" Soderini asked eagerly.

"By all means, Messer Niccolò, by all means. Tell her to come at once."

"I'm glad", Soderini said. "I was afraid you might be put off by some of what she said. . . . "

"But my dear Messer Niccolò, how can I expect a nun to speak against the Pope? She seems to have a heart for us, though. Most unusual for a Sienese, but then no doubt she is a very unusual person. And the very fact that she pleads for us cannot but make a good impression on the Pope."

"I intended to read the letter to the Signoría in session. . . . "

"No need for that, Messer Niccolò. Leave it with me. I shall show it to my colleagues. You just go and write to her in all our names, and tell her to come as soon as she possibly can."

"I will", Soderini said. "At last we are on the right way. Now I can forget those weeks in prison." When he had gone, Ser Giovanni di Dini sat fingering the letter in front of him and smiling. After a while he began to laugh.

The elders of the trade guilds were awaiting her at the gate, white-haired men, many of them, and with them Niccolò Soderini and Buonaccorso di Lapo as representatives of the government. Had it really been only two years since she had come here to defend herself against the accusations raised against her in Siena, an unknown little Mantellata of doubtful repute? Now they were greeting her as if she were the envoy of the Blessed Savior himself. Most of the men had tears in their eyes.

"The Interdict went into force last week", Soderini said in an unsteady voice. She nodded. She could not speak. Silently they walked together into the stricken city. As always, she went into the first church on her way. It was full of people praying, and she joined them. There was no service, of course. And worst of all, she knew that the tabernacle on the altar was empty. Christ was in the hearts of the people, no doubt, but he was not there in the flesh. The church was terribly quiet. All one could hear was an occasional whisper or a sob. She left soon, to take up residence, not at the Palazzo Soderini, but at Francesco Pippino's home.

"The great lords have got us into a horrible mess", the tailor said bitterly. "D'you think you can get us out of it, *mamma*?"

"I'll try hard."

"Good thing that it hits them too", the tailor said. "And where it hurts them most. Their moneybags. They say the government is desperate about the financial situation. Is it true that the Interdict means that any Christian prince may wage war on us?"

"Yes, Francesco."

"And that no one is allowed to help us in any way?"

"Yes, Francesco."

"Well, we deserved it", the tailor said grimly. "Are you going to see the Eight of War?"

"Yes."

"Don't trust them too much, *mamma*. They're wily and cunning, and the very word intrigue was born here in Florence." The little tailor sighed deeply. "Why is it that we are ruled by such men? Why does God permit them to lead us into such terrible situations?"

"Many a Christian in Rome at the time of the apostles must have asked the same question", Catherine said. "And the blood of the martyrs answered it. How many men and women in Florence would be ready to die for their Faith?"

There was singing in the street.

"A hymn", Catherine said. "What is going on?"

"Another procession, I suppose", the tailor told her. "There have been some every day, ever since the curse came upon us. And the churches are full. I've heard of some new religious confraternities too, among both the nobles and the common people."

"When we break an arm or a leg," Catherine said, "that is when we suddenly realize how important it was to us, whole. Here is the answer to your question, Francesco. They are beginning to long again for something they had come to take for granted. We learn through suffering because we refuse to learn in any other way."

A whole week passed before she was received by the Eight of War in a small room of the government building. Soderini came with her to make the introductions.

"Florence is grateful for your readiness to help us, Sister Catherine", Ser Giovanni di Dini said courteously. "My colleagues and I have studied your letter most carefully. We only wish we could share your conviction about the paternal feelings of His Holiness toward us."

"I have no doubt of them at all."

"Unfortunately," di Dini said gravely, "we have had definite reports about the imminent departure from Avignon of a strong papal army under the command of Cardinal Robert of Geneva. The soldiers are talking quite openly about the conquest of Florence and indeed of all Tuscany. If we are attacked, we shall have to defend ourselves."

"I shall write to the Holy Father about that this very day and send the letter by the quickest messenger I can find", Catherine said. "I want to tell him also that you are sending another embassy to him."

Di Dini looked at his colleagues as if to ask for their opinion.

Then he said slowly, "You may say that, Sister Catherine. It will arrive either at the same time you do or immediately afterward."

"They will keep in touch with me?"

"Of course."

For a while she sat silent. Then she said, "There is one thing that matters first and foremost. You must be repentant of the faults you committed. You must humble yourselves and beg mercy from the Holy Father." There was complete silence. "There is no other way", she said passionately. "Not between a father and his sons."

Di Dini gulped. "We are ready to be humble", he said.

Catherine looked around, from one face to the other. "Think, my lords," she said, "if you really intend to submit yourselves in word *and deed;* if I can present you to the Holy Father like sons who are dead and whom he is to raise again and take to his heart . . . then I will do my utmost for you. *But under any other conditions I will not go."*

Again there was a pause. Then di Dini said, "We accept." He stared at the others and they nodded obediently.

Catherine rose. "I shall go." They murmured their gratitude and Soderini led her out. When the door closed behind her, di Dini leaned against it, facing his colleagues. He smiled with great satisfaction. "Nothing official", he said triumphantly. "Nothing in writing."

An hour later Catherine was dictating to Alessia Saracini another letter to the Pope. "It seems that God in his goodness is changing the great wolves into lambs. I am now coming to see you at once, to lay them humbled before you. I am certain that you will receive them like a father, although they have injured and persecuted you. . . . Keep back those soldiers you have hired to come here and do not allow them to come, for they would ruin everything rather than set things right. . . . " She added one more glowing appeal for the Pope's return to Rome. "Do not heed any opposition you may meet, but come, like a virile man who fears nothing. Take heed, as you value your life, not to come with armed men, but with the Cross in your hand. Come like a meek lamb. For only in this way you will fulfill the Will of God. Any other way would disregard it. Be glad! Be jubilant! Come . . . come . . . "

Chapter Twenty-Six

L A BELLA BRIGATA WAS SAILING up the Rhone, carrying Sister Catherine with a retinue like that of a travelling prince, except that a prince would not have travelled steerage or on the back of a humble mule on land; he would not have spent the nights in guest cells of convents or in hostels for the poor, nor, probably, would his followers have been as cheerful or as devoted to their master. With Catherine travelled Fra Bartolomeo de'Domenici; three friars from Pisa; the Mantellate Alessia Saracini, Francesca Gori, and Lisa Colombini; young Stefano Maconi, who proved to be an excellent secretary; and a number of devout Florentines—more than twenty people in all. Before them now rose the steeples of the churches of Saint Ruf and Saint Agricole, Saint Pierre and Saint Didier, the convent church of the Knights Templars, the monastery of the Augustinians, the church of Saint Catherine of Alexandria, next to the convent of the Cistercian nuns and the Cluniac church of Saint Martin. And here at long last was the great Rock of Doms. " 'And upon that rock the popes have built their palace' ", young Stefano Maconi misquoted. "It looks more like a fortress, don't you think?" They were nearing the famous bridge at one end of which a grim watchtower proclaimed that here the Pope's territory ended and France proper began.

"It is not a hallowed place", Catherine said. "No martyr's relics are resting here. It is not a fortress either, Stefano. It is a prison, and we come to set the prisoner free."

"From all I've heard it must be a very luxurious prison", Maconi said.

"So much the worse." But then Catherine's face lit up. She could see three figures standing on the shore, where the ship was going to land, and a few minutes later she was welcomed enthusiastically by her three forerunners: Fra Raymond, Neri di Landoccio, and Master Tantucci.

"Before anything else," Catherine said, "give me the state of the situation in one sentence, Father Raymond."

He knew her well enough to take her literally. "The Holy Father is easily persuaded to return to Rome, to be kind to the Florentines, and to launch a crusade, but it is quite impossible to make him persevere in any of these things, particularly the return to Rome."

She nodded. Now she knew where she was. "Lead us to where we are going to stay", she said.

"It is what they call a *livrée,*" Fra Raymond said, "a house for special guests. It used to belong to a cardinal; I've forgotten his name, but he died long ago. There will be room for all of you. And there is a lovely little chapel on the first floor."

"That is where I am going now."

The Cardinal's house too looked like a fortress. It had the form of a very large tower.

"I wonder, *mamma*", Stefano Maconi said in low voice.

"What about?"

"Whether we are going to free the Holy Father, or whether we're going to imprison ourselves."

The high dignitaries of the papal court were slowly assembling in the audience hall. "*She'*ll be here any moment now", one of the chamberlains whispered to the Bishop of Lens.

"Who?"

"Sister Catherine Benincasa, if that means anything to you, my lord."

"Not that nun from Siena? I've heard she has written the most extraordinary letters to the Holy Father . . . as if she were instructed from on high."

"That is quite true, my lord. Master Tommaso di Petra, who is in charge of the Holy Father's private correspondence, says she is definitely impertinent."

"Really? How very amusing. I'm looking forward to this."

The chamberlain smiled maliciously. "Now Your Lordship can find out whether or not she can read men's hearts, as people say."

"Oh, I'm not so curious by nature", the elegant prelate said. "Besides, it may be better for her if she doesn't read mine too closely. She might find it upsetting, and I wouldn't like to upset a good nun. If she is a good nun, that is. Is she?"

"The Holy Father seems to think so."

"Ah. Yes, most likely he does. But *he* is not one to read people's hearts, is he? Which is just as well. We've had one pope named Gregory who was a saint; it's better not to have another. I do so hate confusions."

"Yet Your Lordship is not entirely free of confusion yourself", the chamberlain said with a mocking smile.

"I? What do you mean?"

"Well, we've had the pleasure and honor of your presence in Avignon for more than six months now, and we have come to the conclusion that you regard it as your diocese instead of Lens."

"My dear friend," the bishop said with a shrug, "obviously you've never been in Lens. No life! Nothing but routine business. No intrigues, unless I start a few myself. No gossip. Above all, no ladies, or none to speak of. Can you be surprised if we unfortunate rustics long for the city of elegance? However, if I am no longer *persona grata* . . . "

"Oh, oh . . . I was only joking. Except that the Holy Father made a remark the other day about bishops staying away too long from their dioceses."

"Did he really? Never mind. But what is the idea of receiving that nun in state? We don't do that sort of thing even for a Mother General. Of course, if she *is* a saint . . . "

"She is coming as the ambassador extraordinary of Florence."

"Extraordinary", the bishop said, "is the word. Dear me, how scarce men must be in Florence. Well, so much better for our beloved and militant Cardinal Robert of Geneva and his iron men."

Cardinal d'Estaing and Cardinal Aycelin de Montaigu entered

the hall together, and the chief chamberlain led them to their seats. When he was out of earshot Aycelin de Montaigu asked, "Have you ever met her?"

"No," Cardinal d'Estaing answered, "but she wrote me, some time ago, when I was in Italy. Amazing woman."

"Amazing or not, the very fact that she is coming here to speak for those rebels shows that she cannot be trusted."

"She may be no more than a pawn in their game", d'Estaing said. "Or else the real reason for her visit is a different one altogether. She's been advocating the return of the Holy Father to Rome for years on end."

"Oh, oh." Cardinal de Marsac leaned over from his seat. "Is she the one to whom we owe that . . . that plan? The Holy Father has spoken about it to me no less than three times."

"I am in no doubt about Your Eminence's reaction", Aycelin de Montaigu growled. "The Holy Father asked me about it too . . . only once, though. He had enough of me, after that, I think. He asked you too, didn't he, d'Estaing?"

"Oh, yes. I told him I'd rather go without meat for the rest of my life than spend another six months in Italy, and that I was too fond of him to wish him that disagreeable fate."

"What we would have to go without, if we'd go back to Italy, is decent wine", Cardinal de Marsac said. "It doesn't bear thinking of. Horrible. Horrible."

"We would have to live like Saint John the Baptist in the desert."

" 'Locusts and wild honey' ", quoted Cardinal de Marsac. "At least we'd get those if that nun persists in another favorite idea of hers, a crusade."

"Crusades are no longer the fashion, my niece says", Cardinal d'Estaing smiled. "She thinks Sister Catherine is hopelessly behind the times."

"And how is the most beautiful lady in Avignon?" de Marsac enquired.

"Miramonde will be much flattered when I tell her what Your Eminence called her", d'Estaing said with a chuckle.

"But I'm afraid she is not as beautiful as Madame de Beaufort-Turenne."

"A mere difference of style, Your Eminence. The Holy Father's niece is a very imperious lady. Phidias would have sculptured her as the hunters' goddess, Artemis", said Cardinal Aycelin de Montaigu.

"Artemis," Cardinal d'Estaing said blandly, "was a virgin goddess, I believe."

The chief chamberlain crashed his staff on the floor. "His Holiness", he announced. All talking ceased abruptly. The Pope came in slowly, exchanging a word with this prelate and that. When his eye fell on the Bishop of Lens he frowned. "How is it that you are not in your diocese, my lord?" he asked.

The Bishop knelt, kissed the fisher ring, and still on his knees asked very softly, "Holy Father, how is it that you are not in yours?"

A tinge of red rose in the pallid cheeks of the Pontiff. He turned away sharply and walked on. Only those standing very near had heard the Bishop's retort. To the others he seemed to have replied with some respectful excuse. The Pope sat down on his throne.

"Sister Catherine Benincasa of Siena, of the Order of the Sisters of Penance", the chamberlain announced. "Fra Raymond of Capua of the Order of Preachers." Many people in the huge Gothic hall had heard of the nun from Siena, and most of them felt rather disappointed when they saw the small figure walking in, with a Dominican friar at her side. Just a little nun, like so many others, was the general verdict.

Sister Catherine crossed the hall as if she were in a hurry, knelt before Gregory XI, kissed the ring, and, at a gesture from the Pope, rose again. He welcomed her in French and she answered in Italian. "Tuscan, rather", Archbishop Prignano whispered to Cardinal Corsini. "But *they* wouldn't know the difference."

Fra Raymond began to translate Catherine's words into Latin. It gave the Pope time to study the pale, small face with the large, deep-set eyes, curiously slanting and surrounded by rings of a pale violet color. That and her thinness made him ask a question he had kept in reserve for a later opportunity. In a voice so low that it was almost a whisper, he said, "My daughter, is it true that you do not take any food except the Holy Eucharist?"

"Yes, Holy Father."

"If I ordered you to eat something," the Pope asked, "would you obey me?"

She answered at once, and the Pope saw Fra Raymond suppress a smile.

"Translate her words literally", the Pope ordered suspiciously. "Keep your voice low."

"Yes, Holy Father. Sister Catherine says, 'I would obey most assuredly, Holy Father, but I could not obey you if you ordered me to keep it down.'"

The Pope, too, smiled. There was a robust sincerity about her answer, strangely incongruous with the frailty of her appearance. The thought came to him that the mind and soul of this woman were far too strong for her body; that their power had whittled down her body to a mere shell, a very thin shell; and that she was not likely to live long. Was *he* going to live long? He banished the thought. Sitting back a little, he said aloud, "You may now state the case of those who sent you."

Catherine began to speak. After each sentence she had to pause to give Fra Raymond time to translate. Nothing much of what she said was new to the Pope, but it was new to most of the others. The Florentines were ready to humble themselves before the Holy Father. Another embassy would arrive shortly, in fact, any day now. In Florence the hunger for religion, for the sacraments, was growing daily. Processions passed constantly through the streets, and the churches were filled with people praying for peace with God and the Vicar of Jesus Christ on earth. Even the most warlike men in the government had agreed that she should mediate for them. They had their grievances, which were real and serious, but they knew now—however much they felt that they had been treated unjustly by papal envoys, legates, and governors — they had no right to rebel as they had.

Gregory XI had read it all before in her letters. He was watching her rather than listening to Fra Raymond's translation. If this woman were a liar, all truth had flown to heaven. He understood now what Fra Raymond had told him about her . . . the conversions of all kinds of people, of libertines, criminals, lapsed friars, and that man condemned to death . . . the story of her trial before the Master General and the Chapter . . . the story of her work in Siena during the plague. He thought of Innocent III, listening to Saint Francis of Assisi. But above and beyond all that he felt something almost like envy for so much strength. She was still quite young, but she looked so thin and frail and she was so small, yet the strength of her will created a zone of power around her. The Florentines never gave in of their own accord, the Pope thought. She had done it. She had subdued them. And behind that thought came another, quick-footed and suspicious: Would their newly found humility endure? Or would they wake up and be their old selves again, now that Sister Catherine was no longer among them? He shook it off. If she must be disappointed, let the guilty be the Florentines and not he. At once another secret thought whispered agreement: by all means let the burden be on the conscience of the enemy. Meanwhile he must act quickly, before there could be any interference on the part of the cardinals, especially the hotheads among them.

She had come to an end. He had to make a reply, and he was ready. "So that you may see my desire for peace and concord," he said, "I will put the matter into your hands."

She understood at once, before Fra Raymond translated it to her, and her eyes were shining. But there was utter amazement in the faces of many cardinals, the kind of amazement that precedes anger.

"But," the Pope went on quickly, "you must never forget the honor and dignity of the Church." At once he rose and left the hall. His last words had taken the wind out of the sails of the most alert among the cardinals. There was silence.

To Catherine the words of the Vicar of Christ were quite clear and decisive, and as he had gone, there was no reason for her to stay. What she wanted now was to spend some time in the chapel in thanksgiving and then to dictate her first report to the Florentine government. She gave Fra Raymond an energetic nod and began to march out, with her usual hurried little steps.

As soon as she had disappeared the huge hall began to hum with muffled discussions, twenty, thirty at a time. "Most extraordinary", Cardinal d'Estaing said. "So now she's supposed to handle business of state!"

"Did you see the way she stared at the Holy Father? Do you think she's got the evil eye?"

"There's no such thing as the evil eye, but there are evil people. She doesn't look evil, I will admit, but we know that the devil and his demons can disguise themselves as angels of light."

Said Cardinal Aycelin de Montaigu, "It may be worth while to find out a little more about this woman."

"A witch, believe me, no doubt whatsoever", whispered the court marshal. "How else could she have such composure, such self-assurance in front of an assembly like this?"

"Oh, oh, my dear Count," said the Bishop of Lens, "do you mean she felt so sure of herself because she thought we are birds of a feather?"

"Your Lordship's wit is misplaced", an older prelate said acidly. "If Sister Catherine enjoys the confidence of the Florentine government, she may be able to render an invaluable service to the Church."

"On the other hand she may soon enjoy the confidence of the Holy Father, too", Cardinal Aycelin de Montaigu murmured. "In fact, I very much fear that is already the case. And God alone knows what kind of dance she will lead us all."

Cardinal d'Estaing nodded. "The least we can do is to find out more about her. It would be like that man, Giovanni di Dini, to send us—"

"A spawn of Satan, disguised as a peace-loving nun", Aycelin de Montaigu completed the sentence for him.

"Not necessarily. But a member of some mystic sect, perhaps, like the Fraticelli."

"Leave it to me, d'Estaing . . . I know exactly whom to send to her."

"Your Eminence arouses my curiosity."

"There's nothing secret about it. I shall send three of our most learned men to examine her, theologians of the first order, men with brains as sharp as a razor."

"Inquisitors?"

"Exactly. And if they should trip her up on anything . . . well, the Holy Father can't very well accept the mediation of a heretic."

Chapter Twenty-Seven

MANY VISITORS WERE CONTINUALLY COMING to see the nun from Siena who was a saint or a witch, an ambassador or a spy, the adviser of the Holy Father or a heretic. Stories galore were told, believed in part or in full and in either case spread all over the town. She had sworn to make the Pope lift the Interdict against Florence; she had told him he would die within a year, unless he returned to Rome; she was preaching a crusade and had offered to lead it in person. . . .

Most of the visitors were received kindly, and at least some of them tried to impart a true picture to those who asked them what impression they had of the mysterious nun. But Miramonde de Paucelles, niece of Cardinal d'Estaing, and other ladies found themselves treated with a certain coldness, and Elyse de Beaufort-Turenne decided to find out for herself. She arrived at Sister Catherine's *livrée* in a magnificent carriage, together with her cousin, Blanchefleur de Massy, a poor relation who served as her *dame de compagnie* and had to keep four little dogs on the leash. Fra Raymond, who had met the imperious beauty at the Pope's palace more than once, made the introductions. To his acute embarrassment Catherine was stiff and monosyllabic, excused herself curtly after the first few words and hurried away to the chapel. Madame de Beaufort-Turenne, extremely displeased, withdrew in a huff, dutifully followed by Blanchefleur de Massy and the four little dogs. As soon as Catherine reappeared Fra Raymond said reproachfully, "You have made yourself an enemy, *mamma,* and a dangerous one. I told you the lady was a relative of the Holy Father."

"I'm sorry, Father, I couldn't help it."

"But why did you do it? You scarcely spoke to her at all. . . . "

"It's the stench, Father, the horrible stench. . . . "

He shook his head. "I know she always uses a rather heavy perfume, but—"

"No perfume in the world can cover up the stench of her sins. It was bad enough with the women who came yesterday, but this one . . . " Catherine shivered. "I don't want to see her again", she said.

Madame Elyse de Beaufort-Turenne gave her cousin Blanchefleur a piece of her mind, which she repeated with some embellishments to Miramonde de Paucelles, Estephanie de Vaurigard and Enemonde de Montarlier. "The woman is no better than a peasant, *mes amies.* She has no looks, no conversation, and, above all, no manners."

"Apparently she failed to show you proper respect, *ma mie*", Miramonde said sweetly.

"She told me bluntly she didn't like all those ladies who appeared before her, dressed like overgrown peacocks", Elyse lied with a charming smile.

Miramonde made a *moue.* "We can't all be nuns."

"You certainly couldn't, Miramonde dear", Estephanie de Vaurigard said. "Why, they'd cut off all your lovely hair."

Enemonde de Montarlier laughed. Like nearly everyone else she knew that Miramonde wore a wig because she had lost most of her hair when she had been ill with typhoid. But Elyse de Beaufort-Turenne had no interest in baiting Miramonde. She was after a more important prey. "That nun insults us all," she said, "and what is more, she's doing it deliberately and for a purpose. She knows we are not in favor of her insane scheme to make the Holy Father go back to Rome."

"But I'm told your dear uncle is quite taken with her", Miramonde said. "Why, there are people who say she's cast a spell over him."

"There's no need for that", Elyse said. "My poor, dear uncle is so easily influenced. Fortunately nothing lasts very long with him . . . not even spells, I think."

"Well, you've seen her, Elyse, and you too, Blanchefleur", Estephanie said. "I haven't. What is your *real* opinion of her?"

"I couldn't form any", Blanchefleur said truthfully. "We only saw her for a few moments." She gave her cousin an anxious look. It did not pay to contradict her.

"There are many who think she's a saint", Estephanie mused.

"What nonsense", Elyse exclaimed. "Why should she be? You don't believe those miracle stories, do you? Only rustics do."

"One never knows for sure", Miramonde shrugged. "And if she is a saint, or worse yet, if she's a witch, I don't want her to cast a spell on me."

"Surely saints do not cast spells", Blanchefleur murmured. It seemed a safe remark to make.

"She's no more a saint than I am", Elyse declared hotly.

"In that case there wouldn't be much danger", Miramonde said in a sweet voice.

Enemonde laughed, but Estephanie shook her head. "I don't know," she said, "and I don't like it. I've heard some strange stories about her from people no one could call rustics. The Bishop of Lens told me he has seen her in church and she had a rapture, as he calls it. He was rather impressed."

"The Bishop of Lens?" Enemonde cried. "*He* is not the man to be easily influenced, and he certainly isn't a rustic. If he says so . . . "

"What *is* a rapture?" Blanchefleur inquired.

"Some kind of trance or ecstasy", Miramonde explained. "They only have it when they're holy or something like that."

"Yes, and she's supposed to have it every day", Estephanie went on. "Always at the altar, when she's receiving Holy Communion."

Elyse gave a snort. "That's an easy one", she said. "All you have to do is to go rigid all over and turn up your eyes . . . like this."

"Well, I suppose I better own up", Enemonde blurted out to her friends' surprise. "I saw her in that state only yesterday, in the Dominican convent church. She's there every morning. She did go all rigid, and they had to carry her out. They say she sees and hears and feels nothing, when she's like that." She shivered a little. "If that was playacting, it was awfully well done", she added.

"Very well," Elyse said grimly, "I'll prove to you that she's no more than a playacting hypocrite. We'll all go to that church tomorrow morning."

"How can you possibly prove it?" Miramonde asked, wide eyed.

"Leave that to me and be there. You'll see."

The first private audience Catherine had with the two-hundred-and-first successor of Saint Peter proved to her that Fra Raymond's judgment was only too true. It was easy enough to influence Gregory XI, but it was extremely difficult to make him persevere. He wanted to reform the clergy, but he could not harden himself for the task. He wanted to return to Rome, but he was afraid of meeting the resistance not only of his cardinals but also of the Romans themselves. Besides, there was still no embassy from Florence, and that gave the Pope an argument difficult to counter: if Catherine was wrong about the embassy, she might also be wrong in her other ideas. "They tricked and deceived you", he told her. "They'll trick and deceive everybody for sheer love of trickery and deceit. One of my predecessors, Boniface VIII, used to say there are five elements: earth, water, fire, air, and Florentines. No one can foresee what they will do next. And things have now reached such a pitch that either the Church will destroy Florence, or Florence will destroy the Church."

"Not all the elements combined could do that", Catherine replied. "Not even the gates of hell." But when the Pope told her about trustworthy reports that Florence, far from being humble, had increased the tax on priests and Church property, she wrote to the Eight of War. "I wish to see you as real sons, humble and obedient toward your father; that you would not fall again, but persevere in your pain of having insulted him. When the offender shows himself impenitent he is not worthy of forgiveness. I invite you to true humility of the heart. Do not turn away; go forth and fulfill your sacred proposal! If you want to be received in the arms of your father, come as dead sons and ask for life! I hope, by the goodness of God, you will receive it, if only you submit and acknowledge your faults. But I must complain about you bitterly, if it is true what is said here: that you have taxed the clergy. If that is true, it is a great wrong. Firstly, you offend God, for you cannot do this with a good conscience. But it seems you want to ruin conscience and every good thing and that you care for nothing but material and temporal goods. Yet we do not see that we must die and do not know when! What a great stupidity to rob oneself of the life of Grace and to give death to oneself! I don't want you to go on like that! You know, surely, that not the beginning is worthy of eternal bliss, but perseverance to the end! Not in this way will you have peace, but by constant humility. Stop persecuting the servants and priests of the Church of God.

"Your action is noxious and evil for a second reason. You are frustrating your own peace efforts."

Maconi wrote what she dictated with furious speed. She ended by saying that in the circumstances no one could believe that they wanted peace. That the Holy Father had received her kindly and was full of joy because of their repentance. "At the end he said he was ready to receive you again as sons and to do what seemed good to me. He was of the opinion that he need not give another answer, as your ambassadors had not arrived. I am surprised they have not! As soon as they come, I shall go with them to the Holy Father. Then I shall write to you about the situation. But the way you are behaving you are spoiling what I am sowing. Stop, for the love of the Crucified *and* for the sake of your own advantage. I will say no more. . . . "

"Given at Avignon", Maconi concluded, "on the twenty-eighth day of June, 1376. Oh, *mamma,* if it would only help! But we Sienese know only too well that you can't trust one Florentine, and there are eight in the Eight of War. May I go to Mass with you?"

"Yes. And tonight you had better pray for all those whose word cannot be trusted. . . . "

"In Florence? That means all the citizens!"

283

" . . . in Siena. There are enough of them there as well."

At Mass in the morning Maconi was kneeling just a few steps behind her, when she went to the communion rail. Suddenly a waft of heavy perfume assailed his nostrils, as a flurry of elegant ladies pressed their way forward. He recognized some of their visitors, including the Pope's niece. Could it be that *mamma* had won them over after all? They were huddling together so closely, they seemed to form one multicolored, silken, bejewelled creature of elegant femininity.

The priest came down with the Blessed Sacrament, and Maconi bowed his head, praying.

"Now", Enemonde de Montarlier murmured, "look at her, Elyse. Just look at her."

Elyse de Beaufort-Turenne saw the little face, as white as its veil. She saw the body gone rigid. The priest swept on. Those at the rail rose and left to make room for others. Catherine stayed.

"Now watch her jump", Elyse whispered. From a belt encrusted with rubies she drew a long needle. She bent down, as if in prayer, and with a steady movement stuck the needle deep into Catherine's foot.

Catherine made no move at all.

Elyse pressed her lips together. She paled a little under her heavy makeup. Wrinkling her nose, she withdrew the needle and hid it again in her belt. Then she rose abruptly, turned, and walked away. Enemonde, Estephanie, Blanchefleur, and Miramonde followed hastily. Outside their carriages were waiting.

"Oh, Elyse", Blanchefleur wailed. "What have you done! She didn't flinch! She—"

"Shut up, you goose", her beautiful cousin snapped. "I thought she was only playacting. Well, she wasn't. She's a witch. That's why she didn't feel anything."

"A witch going to Holy Communion?" Miramonde asked. "Don't be absurd, Elyse. I . . . I wish I hadn't come with you." She entered her carriage. "Home, quickly", she told the coachman.

Enemonde and Estephanie had already departed.

Elyse raised her eyebrows. "Saints, witches, or geese", she declared. "I'm sick of women." Then she too entered her carriage, and Blanchefleur followed, trembling from head to foot.

Inside the church Maconi saw Catherine stir. The people had gone by now, as usual, before she came to. She rose, uttered a moan, and fell back on her knees. At once he was at her side.

"My foot," she murmured, "my left foot . . . "

He saw the wound. There was very little blood, but it was deep. Somebody had . . . those women, of course, one of those women!

"Lean on me as heavily as you can, *mamma*", he said, his voice shaking with anger. "I shall get you home somehow."

And still no embassy from Florence. Instead three sharp-eyed, solemn-faced visitors appeared, an archbishop of the Franciscan Order and two prelates. Maconi opened the door for them. They had come, they said, to pay their respects to Sister Catherine, of whom they had heard so much. Maconi called her out of the chapel and she came, together with Master Tantucci.

The Archbishop stared at her. "We are here with the full knowledge of the Holy Father", he declared. "Is it really true that the Florentine government has sent you here? And if so, how is it that they could not find some eminent man, worthy of such a mission, but instead had to send us a wretched female? And if they did not send you, how dare you pretend they did and talk to the Holy Father about issues of such importance?"

Master Tantucci drew in his breath sharply. Maconi, crimson in the face, gripped his leather belt as if it were an enemy.

"I am well aware of my unworthiness, my lords," Catherine said, "yet they did send me." She remained standing, although her left foot still hurt her and she was forced to keep her weight on the right one. Maconi knew that. Yet somehow she looked to him like a solid little block of black and white. For one mad moment he thought that the three prelates together, strong and large as they were, would not be able to move her one inch, if she did not want it.

Now they began to fling questions at her in quick succession. About her fasting. About her ecstasies. About certain theological points, abstract matters whose meaning completely eluded Maconi's mind. She answered each time in a very few words, and Maconi was shrewd enough to observe that when she did, the prelate interrogating her never asked any further question on the same subject, but passed on to another, or let one of his colleagues do so. This went on for quite a while, and Maconi would have been bored if he had not been sensitive enough to feel that a battle was raging in the small room. Three men against one very small woman, he thought, and began to maltreat his leather belt again. What right had they to ask her such things? And why didn't Master Tantucci come to her aid?

A few minutes later Master Tantucci did just that. The good Augustinian was furious, and unlike Maconi he knew that Catherine was being asked questions many learned theologians would not have been able to answer at once, if they could have answered them at all. And when Catherine did, the inquisitors' faces remained expressionless, showing neither approval nor disapproval. Suddenly, he could bear it no longer and blurted out the answer before she could speak. The Archbishop turned on him with lightning speed. A few sharp, incisive questions and Master Tantucci began to stammer and to shrug.

"You ought to be ashamed", one of the prelates said. "And you a master of theology! Let her speak for herself; she has given us better answers than you have."

"Oh!" Maconi exclaimed beaming, and then, horrified, put his hand over his mouth.

The Archbishop gave him a cold stare and then shot another question at Catherine. This time her answer was a little longer in coming than usual, and the Archbishop waded in, pressing his point. It was terrible, devastating. He seemed determined to crush the little black-and-white bundle before him. His questions were now like so many hammer blows, now like so many kicks. And still she answered, calmly, demurely, and without raising her voice.

Once again the Archbishop attacked. But the same prelate who had rebuked Master Tantucci interrupted him. "Stop it", he said. "The Sister *has* answered that one. What more do you want of her?"

The Archbishop answered angrily, and for a few minutes both Master Tantucci and Maconi had the rare pleasure of watching the two learned men quarrelling with each other in vehement Latin. The third prelate chimed in suddenly. "The Canon is quite right", he said. "There is no object in going on. She has answered better than any man in my college would have done . . . or in yours, Your Grace."

For a moment the Archbishop stood speechless. Then the long thick vein in his forehead deflated, his eyes became sober, and he said, "Perhaps you're right. But I was enjoying this. One doesn't often . . . well, never mind. Sister Catherine, we thank you." A casual nod to Master Tantucci, a half-nod to Maconi, and the large, heavy man sailed out, with the two prelates in his wake.

"May God have mercy on his proud servants", Master Tantucci said, his voice shaken by anger.

"But who were they?" Maconi asked. "Do you think it's true they came from the Holy Father, *mamma?*"

"The Holy Father may have known that they would come to see me," Catherine replied quietly, "but I doubt whether he sent them. He knows me too well by now to make me go through this."

"I never thought I'd feel like murdering an archbishop", Maconi muttered.

"What did you say, Stefano?"

"Nothing, *mamma.* Just muttering to myself."

"I shall tell the Holy Father about it", Catherine said. "In case he doesn't know." She did, at her next audience, two days later. As before, Fra Raymond served as her interpreter. The

Pope said gravely, "They did ask me for permission to see you. They did not say they intended to put you through such an ordeal."

"It is not important", Catherine said.

"You are underestimating these men", Gregory XI told her. "They are the most learned theologians in the Church and of great influence with some of my cardinals."

"It is not important", she repeated. "What matters is Rome. When you are there, Holy Father, everything will come right."

"Nothing seems to have come right so far", Gregory XI said wearily. "But I have news for you. The Duke of Anjou, brother of the King of France, is on his way here. He wants to meet you."

She nodded cheerfully. "He wants to tell me that you should stay here, of course."

The Pope smiled thinly. "What makes you think so?"

"It is obvious, Holy Father. What a loss for France, when you leave! But it can't be helped. Rome is where Saint Peter died, and Rome is where the Pope should live. The King of France wouldn't like it if he had to live in Italy, and no one would have the right to stop him from returning to France."

Gregory gave her a candid look of admiration. Not only had she guessed why the Duke of Anjou was coming, she also knew his own fear that France might obstruct his departure, and she gave him a good argument against it. He might well use it, if the Duke came out in the open. She was probably a saint. She certainly was a gifted diplomat and she had finesse. The daughter of a dyer! She was a theologian, too; she must be, or she would never have escaped the clutches of her three inquisitors. It was infamous that they dared to start such an examination behind his back. De Marsac was behind that, and Aycelin de Montaigu; perhaps a few others as well. Trying to trick her so that they could discredit her. The Pope could not take the advice of a nun who might have heretical beliefs, could he? He saw it all, and it made him very angry. "If those prelates should come to see you again," he said with sudden sharpness, "I want you to have the door closed in their faces."

Fra Raymond translated his words with intense pleasure. It was unnecessary, as in many cases before. Catherine had come to understand the Pope's gestures and facial expression, and she could guess more often than not what he said before Fra Raymond had begun his translation. The Pope, too, often grasped the meaning of her Tuscan Italian.

On the way back to the *livrée* Fra Raymond said, "The Holy Father likes you . . . but I can't help feeling that he is a little afraid of you."

"Of course he is."

"But why should he be?"

"Because I say aloud what his conscience says to him in a whisper."

True enough, Fra Raymond thought. But he knew that was not the whole truth. The Pope must know by now that she was a saint. And saints were uncomfortable people. They had a way of inspiring fear in those who had not yet reached perfection. . . .

Chapter Twenty-Eight

MACONI CAME IN with a rush. "They've arrived", he shouted. "They're here."

There was no need to ask whom he meant. "Have you seen them?" Catherine asked eagerly.

"Yes . . . " The young man was almost out of breath. "Three ambassadors . . . a retinue . . . of fifty. They've been given the Palais de Morin as a *livrée.*"

"Do you know their names?"

"Yes, *mamma*. The leader is Alessandro dell'Antella. The others are Michele Castelloni and Pazzino Strozzi."

"Two of them are new men," Catherine said, frowning. "I haven't heard their names before."

"You're right, *mamma*. There have been some changes in the government. But Giovanni di Dini is still the head of the Eight of War."

She gave a little sigh. "We must wait until they call me." Wait . . . To her, nothing was more difficult. She waited all day and nothing happened. The next day she sent Fra Raymond, Master Tantucci, and Neri di Landoccio to the Palais de Morin to welcome the embassy and ask for a meeting before they went together to see the Holy Father.

Her envoys came back after less than an hour, pale and dismayed.

"Prepare yourself for bad news", Fra Raymond said. "Very bad news."

"I am always prepared", Catherine said.

"They disown you", Neri burst out. "They say they have no authority to get in touch with you at all."

She said nothing.

"It is as Neri says," Fra Raymond said bitterly, "and it is even worse than that."

"Did you speak to the ambassadors themselves?" Catherine asked. Her face was rigid.

"To Castelloni, yes", Fra Raymond told her. "Dell'Antella would not even speak to *me,* and he drew Strozzi away with him. And Castelloni . . . oh, I can't repeat it."

"You must", Catherine said curtly.

He took a deep breath. "Castelloni had the effrontery to say, 'We shall have to save the situation. Your precious Sister Catherine has done us no good at all.' "

"What can he mean by that?" Catherine asked in a low voice.

"I found out what he meant", Neri said grimly. "They have asked for an audience, just the three of them, and when the chief chamberlain suggested that surely you too would be present, they insisted that they and they alone were the ambassadors of Florence."

"Oh, *mamma,*" Maconi wailed, "so much splendid effort . . . and now all is lost."

"Nothing good is ever lost", Catherine said. She walked away to return to the chapel, and as she did, Fra Raymond had an experience so strange and unexpected that he stood staring after her in dumb incredulity. She seemed to be growing all the time, growing to an immensity no longer permissible, no longer tolerable. The small stairs seemed to groan and bend under her foot and the tower to expand to contain her. And still she grew. So immense was the height of the woman in black and white that he knew his voice could no longer reach her. But just then young Maconi laid a hand on his shoulder and Raymond came back as from a dream. "W-what is it?" he asked. He felt numb and confused.

"I said she's a great woman the way she takes it", Maconi told him. "Anybody else would have broken down and cried. You know, there are moments when I'm afraid of her."

"You are not the only one", Fra Raymond said.

"What? You too? Even you?"

"Yes", Fra Raymond said slowly. "Yes. But it's no ordinary

fear. Nor is it awe. I fear her ... sometimes ... as a dwarf may fear a giant."

"Fire", Maconi blurted out. "She said it to me herself, once. 'Fire is my nature.'"

"It is."

"You cannot sit still; you cannot relax when she is present, burning wildly. You must go and do things all the time. A man may want to rest, but he can't, not when she is present. He doesn't really want to, either. Oh, the force she is ..."

"But would you be without her?" Fra Raymond asked softly.

"Never", Maconi cried. "It's unthinkable. I couldn't. Neither could Neri, nor Alessia, nor Tantucci ..."

"Nor I", Fra Raymond said.

The next day Catherine was summoned to an audience with the Pope. Gregory XI was alone. "You know, I suppose, that the Florentine ambassadors have disowned you."

"Yes, Holy Father."

"I have refused to receive them", the Pope said, almost proudly. "I have asked Cardinal d'Estaing and Cardinal Aycelin de Montaigu to deal with them."

Catherine said nothing.

"I told you before that they are the most treacherous people", Gregory went on kindly. "They have been deceiving both you and me all the way. The new ambassadors are as arrogant as the first ones. There is not a trace of humility in any of them. They do not plead; they demand. Nothing will come of these negotiations, however long they may drag out."

"I have written to Florence again," Catherine said, "and very frankly."

"The army under Cardinal Robert of Geneva has been successful on Bolognese territory", the Pope said. "No, do not say anything, Sister Catherine. I know quite well how you feel about it, but it was too late to recall them. Armies are not as easily dismissed as mere messengers."

Catherine sighed. "I warned you in vain, Holy Father."

"I wanted to tell you all these things myself", Gregory said.

"But in future we must not meet too often, or the Florentines will accuse you of working against them, because they would not work with you."

"They practically said so as soon as they arrived, Holy Father."

"I shall keep you informed, of course", the Pope said. "Either through Fra Raymond or through my notary, Tommaso di Petra. Whatever either of these two tells you, you can trust. But perhaps you will want to return to Siena now?"

"No", Catherine said firmly. "Not before you, Holy Father."

It was his turn to sigh. "I have spoken again to my cardinals", he said wearily. "Do you know that some of them were in tears when I told them I would have to go to Rome?"

"I do not doubt it, Holy Father."

He could not help smiling at her scornful expression. "You are so sure of yourself", he said. "It never fails to amaze me."

"I am sure only where God's Will is concerned," she replied, "but never of myself. How can one be sure of no-thing?"

"Rome is a hotbed of intrigue", the Pope said. "Anything can happen there. And I have no one to rely on."

She could hear the very inflection of Cardinal d'Estaing's voice in his words. "You have our Blessed Lord", she said. "You have Saint Peter and Saint Paul. What more do you want, Holy Father?"

Again he sighed. "Yesterday, in one single morning, three of my advisers told me separately that going to Rome would be my certain death", he said with a deprecating smile.

"Death comes to all of us," Catherine said dryly, "and it will not come to you any faster in Rome than elsewhere. They are trying to influence you, because *they* do not want to go."

"I will go", he assured her. "Do not worry. I will go." He sighed for the third time, and she knew that the battle was far from won.

"He is like a man who is told to leave his comfortable life and go on a dangerous venture in the lands of savages", she told Fra Raymond. "And everything that seems to make the venture unnecessary or impossible is welcome to him."

For several days she heard nothing. Then she was invited to be presented to the Duke of Anjou, brother of the King of France. She was determined not to let him stand in her way and promptly won him over. He invited her to Villeneuve, one of his castles, to meet the Duchess, and instead of trying to convince her that the Pope's presence in Avignon was a necessity for France and indeed the whole of Europe, the two charming and excitable aristocrats sat at her feet and asked for her advice. She gave it. "Tell the King to end that quarrel with England and join us all, fighting for the Cross." The Duke promised to put her counsel before the King, but by now she knew him for the volatile, overenthusiastic man he was and did not expect much from him.

When she returned from Villeneuve to Avignon, the Florentine embassy was still there and still getting nowhere at all. There had been no answer to her letter to Florence, and, worst of all, there was no word from the Pope.

"A bad sign", Fra Raymond said. "They must have won him back. I wonder . . . "

"What about?"

"Whether that invitation on the part of the Duke of Anjou was not instigated by his cardinal friends to get you out of the way so that they could have a free hand with the Holy Father."

"I don't think so," Catherine said, "but I think they made full use of my absence. And after what the Holy Father told me last time it's useless to ask for an audience. Once again we must wait, wait, wait."

About a week later Tommaso di Petra came to see her. The Pope's notary was a small, birdlike man, dressed in black. "The Holy Father regrets to tell you that the Florentine ambassadors are not changing their attitude", he said. "There is no doubt now that the negotiations will end entirely negatively."

She nodded impatiently. She had given them up the very day they refused to work with her. "When is the Holy Father going to leave for Rome?" she asked bluntly.

Tommaso di Petra looked down his long, pointed nose. "We have had rather nasty reports", he said. "While these ambassadors were negotiating with us, their government has sent embassies to Emperor Charles, to the King of Hungary, and the Doges of Venice and Genoa, with a view of forming a grand alliance against us."

Catherine closed her eyes. "Nothing will come of all that", she said after a while. "Not one thing. But now it is even more important that the Holy Father's return should no longer be delayed."

"I'm afraid the news has shaken His Holiness' confidence", Tommaso di Petra went on in his grey little voice. "Besides, he has received a letter from a very saintly friar in Spain, warning him not to leave Avignon, as he will surely be killed on the journey."

Without a moment's hesitation Catherine said, "Write down what I tell you, Master Tommaso."

He looked up sharply. He wanted to tell her that he was the notary of His Holiness and not hers, but when she repeated, "Write at once", he produced his pencase and paper, and she dictated a letter to Gregory XI: " . . . I desire to see you delivered from all slavish fear . . . "

Tommaso di Petra stopped, aghast, but she went on, and he found he had to go on too. " . . . so that only holy fear may remain . . . do not listen to the voice of those incarnate devils who would frighten you and hinder your journey by saying that it will be your death. Be a man, Father, arise! I say to you that you have nothing to fear. But if you do not do your duty, then indeed you may have cause for fear. You *ought* to come to Rome, therefore *come* . . . and if there are some who would hinder you, say to them what Christ said to Saint Peter who in mistaken goodness would have held him back, 'Get thee behind me, Satan; thou art a scandal unto me; because thou savorest not the things that are of God, but the things that are of men' . . . Say to all others: though I lose my life a hundred times, yet will I do the will of my Father. . . . "

"Sister Catherine . . . " Tommaso di Petra was sweating profusely. "Are you really quite certain . . . absolutely certain . . .

they won't kill the Holy Father? He wants you to find out about it in prayer."

She did not answer. A shiver went through her body, and Tommaso di Petra saw her change into a statue. There was not the slightest movement. She even seemed to have stopped breathing. He had watched her before, several times, when this kind of thing happened to her, but that had been in church. To find her changing over to this strange state right in front of him and seemingly at will was far more frightening . . . like finding oneself quite suddenly on the brink of another world.

But Tommaso di Petra overcame his feelings. He prided himself on not being taken in by anybody or anything. Of all the men at the papal court he was the most sceptical, and natural caution and legal training had brought that innate quality to a fine point. He sat back, watching her quietly. After a while she began to murmur some words, at first almost inaudibly, then more clearly. Coolly, the notary proceeded to jot down what she said.

What she said was a prayer. She asked for mercy for herself and for her sins. She asked Christ to open the eyes of his Vicar on earth, so that he would love him, but not for his own sake . . . that he would not love himself for his own sake, but Christ for Christ's sake . . . she offered her body for punishment for her sins . . . she was ready to die in torment, if only she was heard and Christ's Vicar would do the Will of Christ. "Grant him a new heart", she prayed with a tremendous intensity. "Grant him a new heart. . . . "

Tommaso di Petra's pen raced to follow the flow of her words. When she ended, she still remained rigid as before. He spoke to her, but she would not or could not answer. Worried, he looked around and called for Fra Raymond.

The Dominican came in, took one look, and shouted for Maconi to run and fetch some holy water. After less than a minute Maconi came in with it, and Fra Raymond poured it over her face. Then he took her by both shoulders and shook her with all his strength. "In the Name of Jesus, come back", he ordered in a loud voice.

Her eyes returned to their normal position. "Praised be God", she said. She looked at Tommaso di Petra. "The Holy Father will not die on his way to Rome", she said quietly.

The notary rose, bowed, and left. Half an hour later he was sitting before Gregory XI. "Genuine, Your Holiness", he said. "Beyond all doubt genuine." He reported the whole of the discussion he had had with Catherine. He read what he had written down.

At the words "Grant him a new heart", the Pope stirred. His noble, weak face was very pale. "It is well", he said slowly. "Thank you. You may go."

The notary withdrew. At the door he could not help looking back. Gregory XI was sitting stiffly upright. His shadow on the wall was huge, a second Pope, many times larger than the one of flesh and blood. Silently Tommaso di Petra slunk out of the room.

The Pope rang the bell for Prelate Malherbes.

The elegant dignitary came in, all smiles. "Holy Father, His Eminence Cardinal de Marsac humbly asks to be received in audience."

"I will not receive him", the Pope said, and at the tone of his voice Malherbes looked up in shocked surprise.

"Holy Father, I believe it is rather important . . . "

" . . . to the Cardinal, no doubt. He will have to write to me. Now listen: All the letters to Rome are ready?"

"Oh yes, Holy Father, they have been ready for months, but not dated, of course."

"Exactly. You will fill in the date. Today's date. We shall leave here one week from today."

The prelate stared at him. "But, Holy Father . . . "

"You heard what I said. Send orders to the Grand Master of the Order of Saint John, Jean Ferdinand d'Hérédia. The ships at Marseilles are to be ready on October the first."

"Y-yes, Holy Father."

"Tell the marshal of the court, if any one of my cardinals wants an audience before our departure for Rome, he is to be informed that I will have no further discussion about the departure itself. I know all the arguments, and I will not listen to them again."

"Yes, Holy Father." Malherbes departed in a flurry. For days he told everybody that he had never seen the Pope like this before. "He is a changed man. I don't know what has come over him."

"Has that nun from Siena been with him again?" Cardinal de Marsac enquired acidly.

"No, Your Eminence. She has not had an audience for weeks now."

"Then I don't understand it", de Marsac said. "Even so . . . he hasn't gone yet."

"The Florentine ambassadors have left", Fra Raymond reported. "Like the first embassy, they were excused from a visit of leave-taking."

"And nothing has come of it."

"Nothing. At the papal palace they are extremely busy with preparations for the journey. For the first time there seems to be no doubt that the Pope is leaving."

For a while Catherine was silent. Then she frowned. "I must have one more audience", she said. "It is necessary."

"I shall try my best, *mamma,* but they say the Holy Father is very difficult these days."

"Not to me", Catherine said softly.

She was received the next day.

"I shall miss this room, you know", Gregory XI said with a rueful smile, looking around him. "Here my spirit has always found repose in study and contemplating the lovely things."

She was not going to let him indulge in this kind of mood. "You shall abandon all these beautiful things and take the road to Rome, where perils, malaria, and discomfort await you. The delights of Avignon will soon be no more than a vain recollection. Remember, our Lord too left the security of Nazareth to go on his mission."

"To be crucified in the end", Gregory said gravely. "A letter reached me from a source that has always proved to be trustworthy. It says I am going to be poisoned in Rome."

"There is as much poison in Avignon as in Rome", Catherine said phlegmatically. "That kind of thing can be bought any-where."

"I suppose so", he admitted lamely.

She smiled at him. "Don't be a timid boy, *babbo mio dolce*", she said. "Be a man. Open your mouth and take the bitter with the sweet."

The homely analogy made the Pope smile against his will. "I'm going this time", he said.

"And you won't let anybody dissuade you again, Holy Father? You promise?"

"No one of flesh and blood will be able to dissuade me."

She gave a happy sigh. "The Bride awaits the Bridegroom on the seven hills", she said. "Once you are there, all other things will take their proper place."

"What about you?" the Pope asked. "Will you travel with us and enter Rome at our side?"

"Heaven forbid, Holy Father. I shall go back to Siena, where I belong as you belong in Rome."

Fra Raymond, interpreting as usual, could not read the Pope's expression. Was it regret? Was it relief? Perhaps it was neither . . . or a mixture of both.

"Is there nothing we can do for you, then, my daughter?" Gregory XI asked kindly enough.

"Only to remember what I said . . . and to remember me in your prayers."

"You forget the convent of Santa Maria degli Angeli", Fra Raymond said quickly.

"Ah, yes. And the portable altar . . . "

Permission to found the convent on the hill of Belcaro was granted at once, and Fra Raymond was adroit enough to get a few minor matters settled as well, not only to take a portable altar with them on their journeys, but also special permission for himself, Master Tantucci, and one other priest to hear confessions in all dioceses. Both matters made them independent of the local clergy. Then Sister Catherine and Fra Raymond kissed the fisher ring and left the Presence.

When they came back to the *livrée,* Catherine seemed very tired. It was as if she had left all her strength with the man on the throne of Saint Peter and that a mere shadow of herself would return to Siena and oblivion, just a little Mantellata like so many others.

Yet even now the French cardinals had not given up hope that the Pope would change his mind. As the preparations for the great journey proceeded, they sent letters of growing urgency, full of warnings and ample quotations from Scripture to underline them. To their dismay Gregory XI seemed to take no notice at all. The fleet in Marseilles assembled. Chests and bags by the dozen, by the hundred, were sent there by mule trains. The Vicomte de Turenne was appointed Governor of the city and Province of Avignon. Six cardinals received permission to remain in France. Their less fortunate colleagues were miserable. As a last resort they mobilized the Pope's aged parents and two of his sisters, and the entire family appeared at the palace, imploring Gregory to change his mind. Everybody knew how much the Pope cared for family ties. His mother and sisters wept. His father, old Count Guillaume de Beaufort, entreated him not to desert his country for the sake of a few old tombs. "Here you are a Frenchman among Frenchmen. There you will be a hated foreigner in the midst of Italian intriguers, mountebanks, and cutthroats."

The Pope, astonishingly, remained unmoved.

In despair, the old count prostrated himself on the threshold. "I will not let you pass", he shouted. "The body that gave life to you shall serve as a wall."

For some moments Gregory XI stood motionless. As from afar he heard once more the words Tommaso di Petra had read out to him: "If there be some who hinder you, then say to them what Christ said to Saint Peter who in mistaken goodness would hold him back, 'Get thee behind me, Satan . . . ' " but it was Catherine's voice he heard, not the notary's.

To the incredulous horror of his family and of the cardinals present, he stepped over his father's body, words of exorcism on his lips. "We shall leave at once", he told the officials outside. "Get the carriage ready."

Within minutes the palace resembled an antheap, stirred up by a strong man's foot. Despite all previous preparations the sudden order came as a shock. The marshal of the court, the chief chamberlain, the master of ceremonies, and other high officials tried to obtain a breathing space of at least a few hours. The Pope would not hear of it. If they were not ready, they would have to follow him as quickly as they could. He was leaving now. And he did. Only five other carriages went with his; all others and most of the luggage were to follow later. Prelate Malherbes and Notary Tommaso di Petra were allowed to share the Pope's carriage. Neither of them, nor indeed the Pope himself, saw the little group of people around a very small Mantellata, watching them pass.

"At last", Catherine said calmly. "Now, my children, we can go home, too."

Chapter Twenty-Nine

THE WAY HOME was long. Their first stop was at Toulouse, where the news of their arrival spread quickly. Half the town came to gaze at the woman who was either a saint or a witch, but more likely a saint, as it was known that the Pope did everything she asked of him. From Toulon they travelled by ship, but a storm drove them into the port of Saint Tropez, and they took the road along the glorious winding coast of red rocks and pine trees. Daily the country became more and more like Italy. On the third of October they reached Varazze, on the fourth Genoa. There Mona Orietta Scotti gave them shelter in her palace in the Via del Canneto, near the harbor. It was just as well. They were at the end of their strength, especially Neri and Maconi, who had both been ill. Worst of all . . . there was no news of the Pope's arrival. Heavy gales were raging all over the Ligurian Sea. Perhaps they had delayed the papal ships.

The gales played havoc with the papal fleet. Again and again it took enforced refuge in harbors all along the coast, from Port Miou and Saint Nazaire to Saint Tropez, Nice, and Villefranche. Off Monaco the papal galley only just escaped being wrecked. The whole voyage was full of mishaps from the very start. A full sixteen days after the departure from Marseilles the badly battered fleet reached Genoa. Everybody from the Pope to the least member of the crew was exhausted. The reception on the part of the Doge and the municipal authorities was polite enough, but not exactly warm. The palace put at the Pope's disposal was a huge, rambling building with long, dark corridors and a musty atmosphere. The kitchen was so far away from the dining rooms that all meals arrived stone cold, which did not add to the physical well-being at least of the older men, and especially of the cardinals, who had only just recovered from recurrent attacks of seasickness. It took the marshal of the court and the chief chamberlain five days to get the most essential things organized, and by then a stream of reports poured in about the events of the last three weeks during which they had been cut off from all affairs of state.

The news was shocking. In the north as well as in the east papal troops had been beaten by Florentine levies. In Rome itself there was daily rioting. Courier after courier came in with reports of fresh upheavals. The only reliable ally of the papal cause seemed to be, of all people, Queen Joanna of Naples, but her troops, ill equipped and badly led, were beaten wherever they appeared in the field.

The cardinals vociferously clamored for a consistory to be held, and Gregory XI, tired, weary, and discouraged, gave in to their demand.

"We can see now clearly where this ill-starred return to Rome is going to lead us", Cardinal Aycelin de Montaigu declared. "Many a time we have been reproached for thinking of our own comfort first and foremost, that we preferred the amenities of our life in France to the hardships awaiting us in Italy. And I for one admit that I do prefer a good bed to a bad one, and a decent meal to a few cold scraps, which I would not offer to the least of my servants, even to a dog. But these things, disagreeable as they are, are no more than symbols of the really important issues. Your Holiness! Your Eminences! It should be clear to every one of us by now that this expedition is a failure. We have no one to rely on . . . we are surrounded by enemies. . . . "

"Too true", Cardinal d'Estaing interposed. "I'm not sure even of the city of Genoa. The Doge has been most careful not to treat us as either friends or enemies. There's no knowing what he will do, if the Florentines exert more pressure or make a good enough offer . . . "

"We are not safe in Genoa", Cardinal d'Herbeville chimed in. "But this is safety itself in comparison to Rome . . . if we ever get there, that is."

"We have no army with us", Cardinal de Marsac said. "All along the way to Rome we shall be just treasure trove for anybody in command of a couple of thousand cutthroats. It's useless to complain about the hardships we have suffered so far. The first part of our journey has been the easiest and safest."

"Let us dismiss any thought of our own safety", Cardinal Aycelin de Montaigu said gravely. "Let us forget even that the sacred person of the Holy Father himself is in danger. There are moments when a priest, like a soldier, must be ready to risk his life."

For the first time the Pope looked up. But he said nothing.

"The question is", the Cardinal went on, "whether this is such a moment. And let me say at once: the answer is decidedly No. Those wretched city-states are like so many devils, going about roaring and seeking whom they may devour. Hercules himself would be unable to clean the monstrous stable of Augeas that is Italy. The whole country is in turmoil. The voice of wisdom is drowned by the clamor of power-mad factions and equally power-mad governments. All we can expect is to be murdered, all of us, and the Holy Father first and foremost. They have killed popes before, these Romans. Why, they killed Saint Peter himself! But even the blood of martyrs would no longer be a fertile seed, as in the past, not with those hyenas in human form."

"They will bow only to power", exclaimed Cardinal du Puy.

"Exactly! So what are we doing? We are delivering ourselves into their hands. Your Holiness! Your Eminences! The time has come to reconsider this misguided adventure. We still have the time and the opportunity to save the situation. There is a fleet waiting for us in the harbor. Let us board our galleys and return to Marseilles and Avignon at once."

"There we can lay our plans in safety", Cardinal d'Estaing said.

"There the King of France guarantees our position", cried Cardinal du Puy with an accusing look at his uncle. "We should never have left France."

"Back in Avignon we have a chance to unravel the unholy knot of affairs here in Italy", Cardinal Aycelin de Montaigu concluded. "Whoever heard of unravelling a knot by putting one's head into it! Now it has become a noose around our necks and may be drawn tight at any moment. This voyage has been a debacle from the very start. The quicker we put an end to it, the better."

Cardinal de Marsac looked steadily at the Pope. "The Holy Father will remember the advice our Lord himself gave to his apostles: 'And whoever shall not receive you nor hear you, go forth from thence, shake off the dust from your feet for a witness against them.'"

"Yes," Cardinal du Puys agreed, "and he said also, 'And when they shall persecute you in one city, flee to another.'"

Cardinal d'Estaing rose. "Holy Father, let us put the return to Avignon to the vote."

"No", Catherine said. "I will not leave Genoa."

"But *mamma,* why not?" Fra Raymond enquired. "We have no more business here. Mona Oreitta has been more than kind to us, but don't you feel we are imposing on her kindness by staying overlong? Besides, you yourself are sick and weary of the constant visits you have from people with all kinds of problems you are supposed to solve for them. You said so last week, and yet we're still here."

"So is the Pope", she said.

"He arrived long after us. Any day now he will depart for Rome. You have achieved your aim, and it may prove to be a far more important thing than even the peace with Florence. So why are we waiting?"

"I don't know", she said tonelessly. "I wish I did. But I can't leave. Let all those leave who want to, Father. Leave yourself, if you wish. I must stay."

"If you stay, we shall all stay, of course, *mamma.* You know your children."

She smiled and promptly sank back into what seemed to be a dark reverie, and he left her.

Visitors came as usual, nuns, theologians, nobles, and simple people, some with problems, some out of sheer curiosity. "You never belong to yourself, *mamma*", Alessia Saracini said compassionately.

"I don't, anyway", Catherine answered.

"I am tired", Gregory XI said, as he entered his bedroom. "I will have no one read to me tonight. You may go, Fabrot."

"What about the lamp, Your Holiness?" the old valet asked.

"Leave it burning. I shall read my breviary for a little while."

The valet bowed deeply and withdrew.

Sitting up in bed the Pope opened his breviary, read a few lines, and put it away. He looked up at the ceiling. Frescoes, showing phases of Genoese history. Ships, a grand array of ships. Bold men with swords and flowing capes, obviously winning a victory . . . their enemies were fleeing before them. Perhaps the Florentines would have such frescoes painted on the walls or the ceiling of some new palace, showing the Pope fleeing before their might. Well, what if they did? Victory . . . what was victory? Vanity, no more. The only true victory was won by a Man hanging from a Cross, at the very moment when his enemies triumphed because they thought they had made an end of him and all he stood for. Yes, but he allowed himself to be crucified, Sister Catherine would say. And Christ did not flee. He walked straight into danger, torture, and death.

The Pope groaned. They were right; he should never have come into this strange, foreign land, full of enmity and treachery. The very walls of the building were hostile. Shabby, too . . . the paint was peeling off the ceiling in many places. "O Lord, help thy servant to do the right thing." Perhaps he should never have accepted the election that made him a successor of Saint Peter. De Marsac, d'Estaing, or La Grange or Aycelin de Montaigu . . . what kind of a pope would any one of them have made? Futile question. God alone knew about that and about all the worlds that might have been. He was the Pope. The decision was his; he could not avoid it, and doing nothing at all was a kind of decision too! Ultimately, as always, conscience had to decide, poor conscience, harassed and cajoled, threatened and implored by so many conflicting voices. One could envy those simple men who were always so sure of themselves, because they could never see more than one side of any problem . . . their own. Conscience . . . was it not conscience that made him make the decision in Avignon? That made him deaf to his mother's tears and step across his father's body?

The bell of some church was striking. . . . He did not know its name or what it looked like. In Avignon he had known the sound of every bell, although there were so many that they called it the city of bells.

He was in a strange land and utterly alone, and he could not bear it. The idea came back to him, begging for his judgment, the idea that had flashed through his mind when the cardinals were voting . . . voting so eagerly, so quickly. The idea sat at the foot end of his bed like a bird, staring at him with beady eyes. It was a madness, of course. But . . . was it?

Eleven. The clock had struck eleven, and the twelfth hour was beginning. The stillness after the last stroke was like a foreboding, heavy and oppressive. Something was expected of him. No use letting all those facts pass through his mind again; he knew them all and yet could not form a synthesis.

The idea was madness, but he would have to try it. Something stirred in his blood, something young and hot and adventurous. It was a risk, a hundred risks bundled together, and he would take it. He swung out of bed and walked over to the small adjacent room, where Fabrot had stored his clothes. Cupboards full of clothes, robes, vestments, gloves, caps, shoes. It was dark, though. He had to go back and fetch the lamp. Nothing of all these. Nothing red, or scarlet or purple. Nothing with fur. A dark habit, the one he put on when he confessed his sins to Father Duchesne, the habit of a simple priest. Black shoes. And, of course, no pectoral cross. Only his ring he kept, the fisher ring. Death alone would part him from that, and then it would be destroyed like his body. There, he was ready.

He carried the lamp back, put it on the table, and extinguished it. Then, on tiptoe, he went to the door leading to the anteroom and opened it softly. There was Fabrot, fast asleep, on his chair. Dear Fabrot. How old he was getting. Sleep on, Fabrot, and dream of Avignon or, better still, of heaven.

The Pope passed by him, crossed the room, opened another door. The guards saw him, but he put his finger on his lips and they stood like statues and let him pass. An officer would inspect them at midnight, but by then he would be far away. Down the staircase with its thick carpet. Two more guards at the door to the courtyard, two more at the gate. They did not seem to recognize him in the bleak light of the lantern, hung high up over their heads: just another priest; there were so many of them here. Just another priest.

And here were the street and the start of the real adventure. He had not been out in the street alone for decades past, not since early youth. It was the strangest feeling to walk without being stared at, without a retinue making room for him. He must take a left turn now, he remembered that clearly. That would lead him to that square with the statue of another Genoese conqueror on horseback; he had forgotten what the man's name was. And from there . . . There was a noise, a clattering, thunderous noise. Looking up, alarmed, he saw the carriage coming straight at him. He jumped aside only just in time and promptly stumbled and almost fell. As he walked on his legs felt as if they had no bones in them.

"Look at him", a woman's voice behind him said. "He's drunk." She giggled stupidly.

"And a priest, too", a man added derisively.

He felt his face burn as the blood welled up in it. For a moment or two he thought of turning and going back to the palace, but he did not want to pass the couple. He did not really want to go back either. He marched on, angrily. His legs had bones again.

Four sailors came up in a row, their arms around each other's shoulders and singing lustily. They *are* drunk, the Pope thought, and he crossed the road to avoid them. They shouted some coarse jokes and staggered on.

Left turn again. Women with thickly painted faces hovering in doorways. Women scurrying across the street.

Ah, this was the Cathedral of San Lorenzo, and the proud building down there was the palace of the Companía di San Giorgio, both banking house and seat of the government. It could not be far from here, not from what he had heard Tommaso di Petra say to Malherbes the day before yesterday, when they talked about her and all those people who went to see her. They did not know that he could hear what they said.

A patrol of armed men. He could ask them. "Of your kindness, Messer Commandante, where do I find the Via del Canneto?"

The tall young officer looked down on him. "Walk on for another two minutes, Father, and you'll find it on your right."

"Thank you, Messer Commandante." As he walked on, he could hear the man say, "Another of those Frenchies. The town is full of 'em these days."

He reached the Via del Canneto. The first few houses did not look right, but at least there was no doubt now that he would find the place. This one? There was a coat of arms at the gate, thistles . . . was that not the flower of Scotland? The Scotti family came from there, though they had been living in Italy for generations. This was it, it had to be. It was a strange feeling, and not altogether disagreeable, to be deciding such things himself, instead of leaving it to underlings. He tugged at the bell string.

The valet, opening the door, looked sleepy and suspicious.

"Is this the Palazzo Scotti?"

"Yes, Father. But . . . "

"Sister Catherine of Siena is still staying here?"

"Yes, Father, but she must be resting by now."

"So should I be . . . and you, too. As it is, you must announce me to her."

"At this time of night? Impossible, Father. Come back tomorrow."

Gregory XI bit his lip. Was this to be the end of the adventure . . . refused entry by a mere valet? It was on his tongue to tell the fellow his true identity. But how could the man possibly believe him? He would laugh and close the door in his face. It was hopeless to invoke one's own authority. He would have to invoke a higher one. Softly the Pope said, "My need is great. I must see Sister Catherine. Let me come in, in the name of Jesus Christ."

"Ah", the valet said noncommittally. Abruptly, he opened the door. "I'll tell her", he said grumpily. "What is your name, Father?"

"Tell her . . . tell her Father de Beaufort from Avignon must speak to her at once."

When the priest from Avignon entered, Catherine gave him one look, closed the door behind him, and fell on her knees to kiss the fisher ring. "And how have I deserved that the Father of all Christians on earth should come to me?" she murmured.

"Alas," the Pope said, "what you will hear from me is no Magnificat."

Her room, as always, was stripped of almost all furniture, but there was a visitor's chair, and Gregory XI sat down heavily. His face was ashen.

"You are not ill, Holy Father?" she asked anxiously.

"No, I don't think so. But it was . . . difficult for me to come."

The enormity of the thing began to dawn on her. "You mean . . . they don't know that you are here?"

"No one knows." He smiled wryly. "I had to pass the guards. It made me feel like an intruder trying to sneak out again. But the streets were the worst."

She nodded. She could well imagine how he must have felt. "It was an act of great courage, Holy Father."

"It was a necessity. I had to come. And if they had known, they would have found ways and means to make it impossible.

At least I wouldn't have been able to talk to you alone and undisturbed. Sister Catherine ... I ..." He clutched at his throat.

"Take time, Holy Father", she said gently. "You are safe here, and there is no hurry now."

After a while he said, "There has been a consistory. The overwhelming majority of the cardinals voted for an immediate return to Avignon."

There was a pause. "And you, Holy Father?" Catherine asked slowly.

"I said ... I would think it over."

"I see."

"My daughter ... the situation has changed terribly since I last saw you. Even if I tried, I might not be able to get to Rome. Do you want me to become the prisoner of the Florentines, or of some little prince or duke in league with them? And if I did get there ... Rome is in a state of revolution. The mob would probably kill me and everyone with me. And if they didn't, I would still be powerless. I could never restore the situation. I ... I'm afraid I'm not big enough a man for such an undertaking."

"No one is", Catherine said. "But, Holy Father, who ever said that you should do all these things with your own strength and by your own power? Do I have to tell the Father of all Christians what Faith is?"

He nodded. "I thought you would say that. But you should have heard my cardinals. De Marsac reminded me of our Lord's order to his apostles, when they were neither received nor heard, to shake off the dust from their feet and leave. And Cardinal du Puys quoted, too: 'When they persecute you in one city, flee to another.'"

"Let us see how it goes on", Catherine said. She took a well-thumbed book from the table. "Saint Matthew, tenth chapter, verse twenty-four", she said. "But the very next verse says, 'No disciple is above his teacher, nor is the servant above his master.' And one later goes, 'Therefore do not be afraid of them ...'" She looked up with her luminous smile and then read on, " ' . . . For there is nothing concealed that will not be disclosed and nothing hidden that will not be made known. What I tell you in darkness, speak it in the light, and what you hear whispered, preach it on the housetops. And do not be afraid of those who kill the body but cannot kill the soul. But rather be afraid of him who is able to destroy both soul and body in hell.' And here, at the end, 'He who finds his life will lose it, and he who loses his life for my sake will find it.' "

"A good lesson in Sacred Scripture for Their Eminences", the Pope said. "If you were a man, Sister Catherine, what a cardinal you would be."

"The Lord", Catherine said, "has chosen me to speak to you because I am only a lowly born, weak woman. He told me so."

"I believe you", Gregory said. "I do believe in you. What could prove it better than this visit?"

"I know little about the many problems and dangers awaiting you," Catherine said, "but it is clear to me that they should never be judged from the viewpoint of success. Success, like blessedness, is with God alone. Therefore it matters little whether you win or lose, but much that you should do the Will of God. To die doing the Will of God is a thousand times better than to live doing your own will."

"That is the source of your strength", Gregory said. "You look at everything *sub specie aeternitatis.*"

"What other way can there be for you and me?" Catherine asked. "You are not merely a worldly ruler! And surely you would not regard the worldly power God gave you as the Vicar of Christ on earth as more important than that of which it is no more than a symbol, and a poor one at that? I am not talking to the ruler of Pisa or the Doge of Genoa. I am talking to the successor of Saint Peter. He too, it is said, wanted to flee from Rome, because those around him begged him to save his life, but when our Lord appeared to him, he turned and went back to the city whose glory he is today and forever."

"He turned and went back," Gregory repeated, "and then he was killed most cruelly. I won't be killed . . . you told me that much. But I don't think I shall live very long." He looked at her searchingly. She said nothing, but he understood and nodded. "I won't live long", he repeated. "And yet you may be right."

"I know I am right", Catherine said. "They begged me to leave for Siena, but I would not go. I didn't myself know why. Now the Lord has shown me."

"Sister Catherine," Gregory said, "by the love you bear our Lord, I adjure you: Are you certain it is the Will of our Lord that I should go to Rome?"

"Quite certain, Holy Father."

He rose. "I wish you weren't", he murmured. "But why should the servant expect a better fate than his Master? The chalice did not pass him by, and I too must drink from it." Once again he saw the luminous smile that seemed to enter one's body like a stream of strength and joy.

"When Abraham was ready to sacrifice his only begotten son, Isaac, the Lord sent an angel to tell him that he accepted a ram in the boy's place", she said. "I will ask God that of his infinite goodness he will allow me to be the ram. Shall we pray together, Holy Father?"

"God may not accept your sacrifice. But let us pray that his Will be done."

When Gregory left to return to the palace, the city was shining silvery in the first light of dawn. With his permission, Catherine sent Fra Raymond, Master Tantucci, and two of Mona Orietta's servants with him. They left him at the palace gate and waited until the spare, dark, lonely figure disappeared.

Chapter Thirty

THE FOLLOWING DAY Pope Gregory XI proclaimed to his cardinals that notwithstanding their conviction and feelings in the matter, it was his inexorable intention to go to Rome. They received the news first with protests, then in glum silence. A few days later the Pope sailed first for Livorno, then for Corneto, where he set foot on his own soil, for the town belonged to the papal states. And here, at long last, he was received with enthusiasm. The people came out with olive branches and flowers. For the first time Gregory had the feeling of homecoming, instead of that of an intruder. He decided to stay till after Christmas.

Reports, however, continued to be bad. The Florentines had routed the troops of Queen Joanna of Naples again and decisively, it seemed. The Tuscan League had conquered Ascoli, and Bolsena had joined in the rebellion. The cardinals feared the worst and said so.

Then, on the twenty-first of December, Prelate Malherbes and Tommaso di Petra rushed into the Pope's study. Such was their excitement that neither of them was able to speak. Their faces were flushed, their hands trembling.

"In the Name of God," Gregory cried, aghast, "what has happened now?"

"Rome . . . " Malherbes gasped, "Rome is . . . Rome has . . . "

"Deputation," Tommaso di Petra managed to say, " . . . with the keys . . . of the city."

"Rome surrenders to the Holy Father", Malherbes blurted out. Gregory XI crossed himself. He wanted to rise from his chair and could not. "Are you . . . certain?" he asked.

"Quite certain, Holy Father." Tommaso di Petra had recovered his breath. "The deputation is waiting downstairs: Prince Orsini, the Count of Fondi, and the municipal authorities."

"Call the cardinals, Malherbes." Gregory XI tried hard to keep his voice steady. "I want them to be present." The prelate ran.

"So you were right after all, Holy Father", Tommaso di Petra said, beaming.

"*She* was right", Gregory XI replied.

At that moment Catherine was kneeling in the church of Saint Dominic's in Siena, with all the Mantellate. Mona Lapa was on her right, Alessia Saracini on her left, and both of them saw large tears running down her cheeks, yet at the same time she was smiling happily. Neither of them asked a question. They were accustomed to her ways.

The papal fleet had passed Ostia and was sailing up the Tiber, as countless Roman ships had done in the course of two thousand years. At nightfall they arrived, greeted by thousands of Romans carrying burning torches. The landing took place near San Giovanni Laterano, but the Pope and his court remained on board. The Lateran Palace, burned down seventy years before, was still in the process of being rebuilt and not yet habitable. The next day at dawn Gregory XI disembarked. He and the cardinals mounted white mules. Escorted by knights in full armor, Roman troops, and a multitude of cheering people, he entered the city through the gate of Saint Paul. Slowly he rode through the streets, gay with flags and banners, with flowers strewn on his way and people crowding the procession right and left, leaning from the windows and the rooftops, shouting, "*Viva il Papa*" and "*Viva Gregorio*". Even the cardinals had to admit that the reception was overwhelming.

At the stairs of Saint Peter's the Pope dismounted and entered the great church for thanksgiving.

The papacy had returned to Rome.

Book Five

Chapter Thirty-One

THE BUILDING OF THE CONVENT of Santa Maria degli Angeli took time. Catherine, meanwhile, had gone to Rocca d'Orcia, the lonely castle of Angiolino Salimbeni, at the foot of Mount Amiata. The Salimbeni family had called her there to mediate one of their malicious, vindictive, and often downright idiotic internecine feuds, a feud that threatened to cause bloodshed all over the countryside.

Rocca d'Orcia was a wild and desolate place. The people, nobles and commoners alike, were hard, egoistic, and vicious. Their own problems were all that mattered to them; the outside world did not really exist for them.

To deal with them was as laborious and difficult and demanded as much patience and effort as dealing with the Pope and his cardinals and with the theologians and the women of Avignon.

Avignon! It was as far away from here as Cathay. And so were Rome and the Vatican, where the Pope now resided in all the majesty of his office. By now he had probably forgotten the little Mantellata who had pestered him until he gave in to the Will of God. Please God he had not forgotten the most important, the most immediate task: the reform of the clergy....

Catherine wrote to him about it.

There was no answer.

She told herself that this was only natural. The Holy Father had so many things to deal with, now that he was back where he belonged. He had no time to answer. Besides, that did not matter. What mattered was for him to take action.

But a few weeks later she wrote him again.

Again there was no answer. This time she began to worry seriously. Fra Raymond tried in vain to put her mind at ease. "Something is wrong", she insisted. "I can feel it. I can't leave

Rocca d'Orcia—these madmen will be at each other's throats within a day. So you must go to Rome for me, Father. I shall give you another letter for the Holy Father, and I charge you to put it into his own hands and no one else's."

"Very well, *mamma.*"

She sighed deeply. "Come back with his answer as soon as you can."

The very next day Fra Raymond set out for Rome.

A week passed, and another. Half a dozen times a day she asked the guard on the watchtower if he could see Fra Raymond returning. At long last the man called down, "I can see him!"

"Oh, thank God. Are you sure, Mauro?"

"He's wearing the black-and-white habit. But he's riding a different mule."

She flew up the stairs of the tower to see for herself, and her heart sank. It was not Fra Raymond; it was a Dominican friar she had never seen before.

A few minutes later he arrived in the courtyard. He was a lay brother, Fra Onofrio, and he had a letter for her, "From the Prior of the monastery of Santa Maria sopra Minerva", he said.

A strange foreboding assailed her. It was Fra Raymond's handwriting. She thanked the man, saw to it that the Salimbeni servants looked after him, and fled to her room.

The very first lines of the letter confirmed what she had feared. The Master General, Friar Elias of Toulouse, was in Rome. On the explicit wish of the Pope he had appointed Fra Raymond Prior of Santa Maria sopra Minerva. He could not return to her.

There was worse to follow. He had given her letter to the Holy Father, but there would be no answer. The Pope was very unhappy in Rome; he felt that he was surrounded by people he could not trust; the attitude and behavior of the municipal authorities and of the citizens were incomprehensible, and no one seemed to have any respect for his authority. He complained about meeting gross insubordination everywhere and was convinced that his return had been a ghastly mistake. . . .

Fra Raymond was too kind to say so directly, but it was clear enough that the Pope was angry with her, so angry that he did not have even a single word for her.

The double blow stunned her. "Suffering", she murmured. "Now there is nothing left for me but suffering."

She wrote back to Fra Raymond, but halfway through the letter she addressed herself to the Pope . . . perhaps he would have the courage to read the passage to him. "To whom shall I turn, if you abandon me?" she pleaded. "Pardon me, Most Holy Father, for all my ignorance and for the offense I must have committed against God and against Your Holiness. Let the Truth excuse me and set me free. . . . I humbly ask your blessing."

For once all the strength had gone out of her.

Lightning struck. It was a single stroke, but it shook Italy from top to toe. The Pope reeled under its force and sank into a somber silence. Bernabò Visconti, the terrible despot of Milan, was said to have exclaimed in horror, "That, at least, they will not be able to say of me."

Cardinal Robert of Geneva, soldier, intriguer, and priest, had let his troops take up their winter quarters in Cesena, a fairly large town in the Romagna. Cesena was loyal to the Pope. Steadfastly it had resisted all temptations and all pressure to join the Tuscan League. But the Cardinal's Breton soldiers treated it like a conquered town. They looted. They brutalized the men and behaved with open license toward the women. Incidents multiplied to such an extent that in the end the outraged citizens rose and killed every soldier they could lay their hands on, several hundreds of them.

Cardinal Robert of Geneva had taken Sir John Hawkwood, the dreaded Aguto, into his pay. Secretly at night, he let him enter Cesena with his men, and what followed was an orgy of murder and destruction. More than four thousand citizens were slain that night, women and virgins violated, houses burned, palaces destroyed, works of art ruined, handicrafts laid waste; that which could not be carried away was burned, made unfit for use, spilt on the ground.

Thousands of men, women, and children tried to flee to the nearest towns, but most of them died, from cold, hunger, and exhaustion, on the way. February, in the Romagna, can be a hard month.

The crime cried out to heaven. And a cardinal had given the order!

"That is what Italy can expect from the Pope and his henchmen!" the Eight of War in Florence were quick to proclaim through their agents everywhere. In Florence itself a systematic priest hunt resulted. Many were killed, others wounded. A new and exorbitant tax was levied on all Church property. To top it all, the government issued orders that in the future the Interdict was no longer to be kept. Priests would be forced to exercise their functions. Poor Bishop Ricasoli was not strong enough to resist.

Thus Mass was said again in all the churches by priests too weak for martyrdom, their consciences laden with guilt, and Holy Communion received by people who probably knew that they were trying to make the Lord come to them.

The rebellion was no longer only political and military. It was spiritual as well and thereby total.

Catherine, still on Rocca d'Orcia, broke down and sobbed her heart out. But then she went into action. If she was allowed to do nothing in the large world outside, then she would concentrate on the region where she was. She fought the pride and egoism of the warring Salimbeni family, mastered them, and settled their troubles. Fresh fervor began to fill the people in the country. They came down the wild, craggy mountains in droves, sometimes more than a thousand at a time, as though summoned by invisible trumpets, among them men who had not been to confession for decades. They brought possessed people to her and she cured them.

Yet at night, when the others were asleep, she would stand on the *sprone,* the boldly projecting terrace of the castle, looking down into the hills and the valley, a little figure in white, her veil torn and fluttering in the wind, and many a time people would take her for a ghost.

Never in all her life had she been so lonely.

"Rome is bad enough", Gregory XI said. "It is a pit of snakes. It is everything I was told in Avignon. But Florence will be my death."

Fra Raymond said nothing. He was accustomed by now to such outbursts of petulant anger.

"When I was in Genoa," the Pope went on, "I thought the situation could not possibly become worse; it *had* to become better. How wrong I was! Florence will be my death. I feel it. The venom of that city has poisoned me through and through. And yet there are certain reports that the Guelph party is on the move again. They ought to be reliable, but then what is reliable about Florence? Have you heard anything, my son?"

"Yes, Your Holiness. I had another letter from your humble servant, Sister Catherine of Siena."

"I wish I had never seen any of them", Gregory XI said bitterly. "I wish I had never met her. Though she is right about one thing she said in one of her letters to me: that it looks as if the world were ruled by devils. Peace, she cries all the time, peace, make peace, Holy Father. How can I, when my enemies insist on waging war? They have broken the Interdict. There seem to be no crime and no sin that they have not committed, but give them a little more time and they'll invent another one." He sighed. "What does Sister Catherine want this time?" he asked with a shrug.

Fra Raymond had waited patiently. "Ser Niccolò Soderini has secretly come to see her", he reported. "Your Holiness will remember his name, perhaps. He is a very important political figure in Florence, but not a member of the government. And he swears that the time is ripe for a complete change there. The Guelphs are ready to take over. And the citizens are longing for peace. No more than half a dozen men in Florence want to go on with the war, Soderini says."

The Pope looked up sharply. "Do you believe that?" he asked.

"I know Ser Niccolò as a man of intelligence and integrity, Your Holiness. He says the people have been told a tissue of lies by the Eight of War. Unfortunately what happened at Cesena seemed to justify them. But now, he says, all that is needed is a gesture, but one that really reaches the man in the street. A capable emissary to convince them that they can really have peace and that their spiritual exile will end."

The Pope asked softly, "Will you go, Fra Raymond?"

The Dominican shivered a little, but he said, "I will, if the Holy Father commands it."

"No", the Pope decided. "I will not have you go. They'd ill-treat you. They'd kill you. They've killed enough of my priests. But Sister Catherine may go."

Fra Raymond gasped. "But surely, Holy Father . . . she too would be in danger. . . . "

"I don't think so", Gregory XI said. "They are not likely to harm a woman. And they have always had a feeling of reverence for her. Tell her to go." He gave a wry little smile. "She came to me as the envoy of Florence", he said. "Now let her be my envoy to Florence. Come back tomorrow morning for her credentials. You will *send* them to her by messenger. I don't want you to leave here. And make it clear to her that she must not take any priest with her this time. I will not send a single one into that nest of Satan."

"But you don't mind sending her", Fra Raymond thought. "And what's more, *mamma* will go there and *hope* they'll kill her." He said, "She is most unhappy about having incurred your displeasure, Holy Father. A kind word . . . "

"I will write to her", Gregory XI said. "She has put me into the most awkward, the most disagreeable position, but I will write to her."

Armed with papal documents, Catherine came swooping down from the castle of Rocca d'Orcia like an eagle. Faithful to the Pope's command she allowed none of her priest friends to come with her, and her retinue consisted only of Alessia Saracini, Francesca Gori, one other Mantellata, Neri di Landoccio, and

Stefano Maconi. She stayed at the Palazzo Soderini, and Ser Niccolò and Ser Buonaccorso di Lapo took her around to the houses of influential friends and to meetings of the Guelph party, some open, others secret. When she spoke, she did not mince her words. "You must have been mad, all of you", she told them. "Do you think you can make war on God and win it?"

"The Pope isn't God, Sister Catherine."

"And the cardinals are no angels."

"The Pope is Christ's lawful representative on earth, and however badly his prelates behaved, you had no right to disobey them. How many times must I tell you that? Those taxes of yours are sinful, your arrogance was more sinful, and now you have gone so far as to rebel against him openly by not keeping the Interdict. The very first sin mankind committed was the sin of disobedience. Do you think you can regain a lost paradise by more disobedience?"

"But what are we to do?"

"The first thing you must do is to keep the Interdict again until the Holy Father lifts it, and I hope that will be soon."

The Guelph leaders were ready to obey. They knew very well that Sister Catherine was an asset for them. A rumor went through Florence that the Guelphs together with the saint from Siena would set all things right. The Guelphs certainly began to show boldness in the Signoría, and the Eight of War took notice, sensing trouble.

"I can see no reason why the Guelphs should have sole rights to Sister Catherine", di Dini declared in secret session.

"You will find it difficult to get her into our camp", they warned him. "After all, we did disown her in Avignon."

"And very clumsily, too. If you ask me, she has come to avenge herself on us. On us, not on Florence. And if we let her go on much longer, she may well succeed", di Dini said quietly.

"Then we must act quickly", Pietro Corradino declared hotly. He was the youngest member of the Eight.

Di Dini grinned. "What do you want to do, cut a saint's throat?"

"How do we know she is a saint?" Alessandro dell'Antella asked. "And even if she is ... "

"Careful now", di Dini warned. "There are things that should never be said. By the way, I'm told she is here officially."

"What?"

"Yes. Documents from Rome."

"Then why hasn't she been in touch with us?"

"Because she's a much better statesman than you are, Corradino. She is biding her time until she has the feel of everything. She may even hope that there will be a change of government."

"She is an official ambassador of the Pope? Incredible."

"At least as official as she was when we sent her to Avignon", di Dini said. "In other words, as official as we want her to be. And I think we want it. Very much."

"Why, in the name of all the devils ... ?" Corradino asked.

"Because, my shortsighted young friend, there is peace in the air. I can sense it. And I'd much prefer that the peace should be concluded with this government than with a bunch of Guelphs. That's why. Besides, there is just one more small thing. ... "

They all knew him well enough to realize that the main thing was coming now. They listened with bated breath.

"Just one more small thing", di Dini repeated slowly. "I've had a letter from Milan — from Bernabò Visconti. Sister Catherine has been in touch with him, too. Apparently the Pope wants a conference of all the great powers in Italy, on the highest level."

"A peace conference ... "

"Exactly. Oh, we can say No, of course. But I don't think it would be wise, not with Bernabò willing to oblige and that ... that little saint undermining our city under our noses. So I shall send out an invitation to her at once. We shall receive her in the Signoría, full assembly, all the honors due to a papal envoy. And if the conditions are tolerable ... maybe there will be peace. Under this government, friends ... that is the thing to keep in mind."

A week later Catherine wrote a letter of thanks to Bernabò

Visconti. She wrote to the nuns on Mount Belcaro and to her own Prioress in Siena, to pray for peace. She wrote to her old friend in Lecceto, William Flete, once of Cambridge, "Let us hope that God will have mercy upon the world and upon his sweet Bride, the Church, and will disperse the darkness from the minds of men. And it seems to me that the dawn is coming. . . . " The Palazzo Soderini was flooded with people to see her. The Eight of War had given her a magnificent reception; the assembly at the Signoría had cheered her.

Within weeks the conference was agreed upon. It was to take place in Sarzana. Bernabò Visconti came from Milan to preside in person. The Pope sent three French cardinals, Florence five envoys, and the Queen of Naples her new husband, handsome Otto of Brunswick. Both France and Venice sent ambassadors.

Everything went smoothly. Florence agreed to pay an indemnity and did not seem to be unduly upset by the figure demanded by the cardinals. Another day or two and the Peace of Sarzana would go into the annals of history.

Catherine was praying in the private chapel of the Palazzo Soderini when she saw a shadow fall across the altar. Turning, she saw Ser Niccolò standing at the door. His face was grey. She finished her prayer, crossed herself, rose, and walked toward him. "Bad news?" she enquired.

"The worst."

"The conference?"

" . . . has dispersed."

"But why? Why?"

"God does not seem to think us worthy of peace yet", Soderini said sadly. "Pope Gregory has died."

Chapter Thirty-Two

S HE WOULD NOT LEAVE. "The Holy Father has sent me on a mission," she declared, "and it is to make peace between the Church and Florence. I shall stay until I have accomplished it, even if it should cost me my life." Gregory XI had died, after a short and sudden illness, but there had been a conclave, and it was said that the new Pope was an Italian—Cardinal Tebaldeschi. Then word came that that was an error. It was not Cardinal Tebaldeschi, but another Italian: Bartolomeo Prignano, Archbishop of Bari, not a member of the College of Cardinals. Catherine remembered having seen him in Avignon, a dark-eyed man with bushy eyebrows, sturdy and rather brusque of manner. Perhaps he was the kind of man who could do what Gregory would never have been able to do: reform the priesthood, unite the whole of Christendom, and weld it into one tremendous power under God . . . perhaps . . .

Meanwhile she had to cope with Florence, the head of the Tuscan League. All her friends told her that the di Dini government would have to go. Especially di Dini himself and dell'Antella di Corradino were no longer acceptable. The notorious Florentine law about so-called admonitions appeared to be the best way of dealing with them. For a Florentine politician to be officially "admonished" was tantamount to receiving a vote of no confidence and immediately excluded him from office. Until recently no one in his senses would have dared to try that kind of thing on any of the members of the formidable Eight of War. But now the Guelph party gave out that the saint of Siena herself had insisted on it and on more admonitions to come. When Catherine found out about it, she protested vehemently. "I suppose our men have been a little impulsive," Buonaccorso di Lapo admitted, "but it's too late now. Di Dini *has* been admonished today in the Signoría. Don't be upset, Sister Catherine. Believe me, it's all to the good. That man was a devil of an intriguer, and one could never be sure what he was going to do next."

"I am here to make you all do the Will of God," she stormed, "not to meddle in your party politics." But the Guelph party was jubilant. A new Signoría was elected and promptly went on admonishing the men of the former regime. The Guelphs not only got rid of dell'Antella and Corradino; they also threw out their enemies by the dozen and more often than not under the flimsiest of pretexts. And still they used Catherine's name to persuade the people that it was she, a saint, who was purging Florence of all those who were trying to ruin the city. Soon the fight was no longer political. They were indulging in personal vendettas. When Catherine spoke openly against these machinations, she found to her horror and anguish that people would not believe her. Some even shouted insults and threats. She warned Soderini. She warned di Lapo. But the two men could no longer control the evil flood of ambition, malice, and vindictiveness around them, and the situation went from bad to worse. Only one Guelph leader foresaw the disaster of total disintegration: the new *Gonfalonière della Giustizia,* Salvestro di Medici. At first he tried to put an end to the terrible system of "admonishing". When that proved impossible, he chose the most effective, but also the most dangerous, remedy. He went straight to the people. In wild mass assemblies he stirred them up against his own party, and he succeeded only too well. A mass demonstration of all the guilds took place on the Piazza Signoría. Every man there was armed. There were wild, rabble-rousing speeches against the Guelphs. Then the huge mass of men began to move, simultaneously, in all directions at once. Hundreds attacked the Palazzo Albizzi at San Pietro Maggiore. Others invaded the Palazzo Strozzi at the Porta Rossa, and others crossed the Ponte Vecchio. "Down with the admonishers! Long live the people!" "Down with di Lapo! Down with Soderini! Down with Canigiani!" The jails of the city were surrounded, broken open, and the prisoners set free, irrespective of whether their crimes were political or not. Murderers, thieves, and robbers were soon on the rampage. Horrified, Salvestro di Medici tried to stem the tide. It was too late. The forces he had conjured up swept him aside.

A monastery was looted as soon as it became known that a number of frightened citizens had fled there with their most prized possessions. Two lay brothers, trying to keep the mob back, were killed. Fires started in half a dozen places at once. It was the hour of all malcontents, all extremists, and all criminals.

Niccolò Soderini hastily sent Catherine and her small retinue away. "Go to the place of the Canigiani . . . not their townhouse, mind you, the one with the large garden, on the outskirts. Ser Cristofano here, my notary, knows it well. He'll be your guide. But for the love of God, be quick about it, or they'll kill you."

"What about yourself?" Catherine asked.

"I must try to get to the soldiers' barracks. They're our only hope. The whole city is stark raving mad."

Twice on the way to the Canigiani house they had to hide from swarms of ruffians, brandishing axes and knives.

On the outskirts of the city things looked fairly quiet. Young Barduccio Canigiani received them with warm affection. "I only hope they won't come here," he said. "So far they haven't. Let's sit in the garden, shall we? The house is hot and stuffy."

The garden was a lovely thing, glowing and brilliant with flowers, a little world by itself, an oasis of beauty and peace. But at a far distance they could see columns of smoke rising in a dozen places.

"If the wind changes, half the town will go up in flames", Neri said. Plump little Ser Cristofano nodded. "There's a new fire starting", he said. "It's near the river, not far from . . . my God, it's the Palazzo Soderini!"

Catherine nodded silently. The three Mantellate were sobbing. "There's a curse on these people", Neri exclaimed. "Each time *mamma* sets things right, they must go and spoil it all."

"I never thought I'd live to see the Palazzo Soderini burning", Ser Cristofano said, outraged. "Listen . . . what's that noise?"

"We should know by now", Neri said, turning white. "Running feet and foul language . . . they're coming here."

"Search the house", an angry voice roared. "Search the garden, too. Angelo says he's seen the witch enter, so she must be here. Get those torches ready."

Neri swung around, wild eyed. "Run, *mamma*", he gasped. "I can see them. There are at least fifty of them."

Catherine said, "I will not move one step."

"But, *mamma* . . . "

From behind a cluster of acacias a man appeared, a grimy fellow in shabby clothes. He grinned broadly, his eyes lighting up like a wolf's. "Here she is", he screamed. "Here, everybody. I got her."

There was a tumult of voices, and in an instant six, ten, twenty wild figures appeared, armed with pikes, axes, and swords, and some of them carrying burning torches.

"Where?" a deep voice roared from somewhere farther back. "Wait . . . I must have a look." The speaker broke through the ranks of his men, a burly fellow, bearded, a naked sword in his hand.

"Here she is, Manella . . . one of those black-and-white church mice here must be the Catherine woman. They're probably all witches."

Catherine stepped forward. The hour had come at last. She was not merely glad; she was jubilant. She freed her *mantella* from Alessia's anxious fingers and waved Neri aside, who bravely tried to draw his silly little sword. The blessing of God was upon her, and she would never be able to repay fully the great Grace she was about to receive. She was innocent of any of the things for which they hated her so much. Everything she had done, she had done in the Lord's service, and now he permitted her to die the most glorious death of a martyr, and her blood would bring about what she had not been able to bring about alive, peace between the Holy Father and his sons. As she approached the men—still more of them were pouring into the garden—she was walking on air and breathing bliss.

"That's her", a man shouted. "That's the witch. I've seen her before. Run her through, Manella. She's the ruin of Florence."

Fingering his sword, Manella barked at her, "Are you Sister Catherine of Siena?"

"I am", she said slowly and clearly. "If you seek me, take me, but let these go their way."

Manella blinked. Somewhere in the recesses of his mind a memory stirred. He had heard those words before. Armed men storming into a garden and one solitary figure saying calmly what this little woman said. He had heard the story read out from the pulpit. But there were sixty men behind him, and they expected him to act. He looked about him and saw them staring at her. And she smiled. Good God in heaven, she smiled as happily as a child.

"Go away", he said between his teeth. "Go away . . . quickly."

"I am very well where I am", she replied serenely. "Where should I go? I am ready and willing to suffer for God and the Church. I wish for nothing better."

The man's face contorted and suffused with red. He looked as if he were in acute pain. Abruptly he turned on his heel and walked away. For a few moments more the others stood, goggling at the tiny woman. Then they too walked off, slowly and with an air of indifference. A minute later everything was as quiet as before their arrival. Only a few crushed flowerbeds remained to prove it had not all been a bad dream.

"Glory be to God", Ser Cristofano ejaculated, and there was a hubbub of praise and admiration.

"You have put sixty men to flight!" Neri exclaimed. "There is no one like you."

"Did you see that man's face?" Cecca Gori asked. "He looked as if *mamma* had pierced him with a dagger."

Neri, the serious, grave-faced Neri, began to behave like a child. He danced about, crowing with delight. "How they all slunk away", he shouted. "Like wild animals who wanted to devour her and then found that she wasn't edible." He broke into nervous laughter, but stopped at once when he saw that Catherine was crying. No wonder, he thought. That experience would have been too much for anybody.

"We should leave quickly", Ser Cristofano warned. "Those men may lose their fear and come back. And they are sure to tell others where Sister Catherine can be found."

"But where can we go?" Alessia Saracini asked.

"It would be best to leave the city altogether, at least until this storm has blown over", Ser Cristofano said.

Catherine wiped her eyes. "I will not leave Florence", she said. "Not before my mission is accomplished. Apart from that I don't care where I go." Neither Neri nor the Mantellate understood the real reason of her sadness, and she knew it. Only Fra Raymond would have understood how much she longed for the triumphant death that had been so near, only to be withdrawn again.

"Let's go to Francesco Pippino's place", Alessia suggested. "He's a great friend of *mamma's.*"

"He's a tailor," Cecca Gori said, "and he lives in a little house near the corn market, not in a palazzo. Perhaps that will be safer."

"An excellent idea", Ser Cristofano agreed. "Near the corn market, you said? We can get there without having to cross the main streets. And no one is likely to look for you there. But we must wait until it's dark. It won't be long, fortunately."

Francesco and Agnese Pippino received them with open arms. The tailor just laughed when Catherine pointed out to him that her presence might endanger him. "What if it does?" he asked. "I'd die once and in a good cause. If I didn't give you shelter, my conscience would murder me every day anew. But have no fear on my account. This thing will blow over very soon, and the worst is over even now. The government has sent troops into the city, and my neighbor told me an hour ago that they had a number of rioters hanged publicly, five of them in every district. By tomorrow all will be quiet again, I think."

That night Catherine wrote her first long letter to the new Pope, Urban VI. Never before was her plea for peace so intense and so moving. She managed to write another letter to Fra Raymond, telling him about the day's incident. It started with the words: "My eternal Spouse played a great joke on me. . . ."

Pope Urban VI was in Tivoli. He had just finished his noonday meal when Fra Raymond came in with Catherine's letter. The new Pope had taken a fancy to the Dominican. "You read it to me, Son", he said. He listened quietly and without any of the impatient interjections he usually made. At the end he said gruffly, "The woman's right. There's been far too much delay. The conditions for peace were as good as fixed when my predecessor died. No reason why we should not act at once. Get that lazy good-for-nothing secretary of mine here, Son."

Fra Raymond raced to fetch the unfortunate man. The Vatican officials found the new Pope increasingly difficult to deal with. His temper was very easily roused, and when it was, he could say the most terrible things, to a secretary or to a cardinal. Was that why only the four Italian cardinals had gone to Tivoli with him, while the French preferred to spend the hot months in Anagni? Or was there some other, political reason? Fra Raymond had seen and heard a good many things in these last months. Sooner or later he would have to inform Catherine.

The herald came to Florence on Sunday afternoon, July the eighteenth, 1378, a young man on a magnificent white horse with the papal coat of arms on its purple caparison. He was unarmed and carried a large olive branch. The guards at the gate cheered him, and the cheers were taken up by the people in the streets. He rode straight to the Signoría, dismounted, and went in, and within a few minutes the Piazza was black with people. Then the great bell began to toll from the Palazzo Vecchio. Four members of the government strode out on the balcony, and one held up a large document for all to see and then read it out in a high and strident voice. The Holy Father agreed to the terms discussed at Sarzana. A treaty would be signed in ten days, and in due course the city and territory of Florence would be freed of the Interdict and the ban of excommunication. The olive branch was fastened on the balcony, a message to all those who would come later to enquire whether it was really true.

Francesco Pippino, the tailor, heard the news at the headquarters of his guild and came racing home to tell Catherine. But by then the bells were ringing all over town and she knew. Overwhelmed with joy she wrote to her "children" in Siena: "Oh, dearest children, the lame walk, the deaf hear, the blind see, and the mute speak and shout with a loud voice: peace, peace, peace. Rejoice! . . . " A minor official of the Signoría, an elderly man, brought her three leaves of the olive branch. He had plucked them off secretly for that purpose. She thanked him and put one of the leaves into her letter. Those three leaves were the only recognition she received. They were extremely busy at the Signoría preparing the final draft of the peace treaty; they had no time for her. Niccolò Soderini was out of town. He had lost his magnificent palace and could talk of nothing else. Other Guelphs avoided her quite ostentatiously, and some were heard to say that the revolt of the guilds was due to her mistakes, though no one seemed to know quite clearly what these mistakes had been. Young Barduccio Canigiani was furious. So was Neri. And it was just as well, perhaps, that Catherine had sent Stefano Maconi back to Siena, or he might well have done something rash.

"They are singing, dancing, and feasting," Neri said bitterly, "as if they had brought about their own salvation."

But the moods of Florence were unpredictable. After two days of rejoicing another revolt shook the city to the core. This time the *Ciómpi* started it, the unskilled artisans who had no political rights, aided and abetted by the many criminals who were still at large. They burned, looted, pillaged, and killed, until a wool carder, Michele di Lando, restored some sort of order. A new government was the inevitable consequence, the third within a few weeks and no better than any of the others. Poor Soderini was sent into exile for the alleged misuse of his powers. The Canigiani family was heavily fined. All was quiet again by the end of July.

On the last day of the month Pippino came into Catherine's

336

room. "They are feasting again," he said, "and again they have not invited you."

"It does not matter, Francesco. The peace matters."

"There is no peace for you in Florence, Sister Catherine", the little tailor said gravely. "More and more people say that all these revolutions are your fault, that you have the evil eye, that you are a witch, and that you should be driven out of town."

She smiled sadly. She said nothing.

"I've heard it not once but several times today", Pippino said. "And I've heard that those behind it are members of the Signoría. They want to take all the credit to themselves, so your name and your work must be ruined." The little man almost cried with rage. "I'm ashamed of my city", he said in a trembling voice.

"We shall leave for Siena tomorrow", Catherine said simply. She was human enough to feel bitter in the face of so much ingratitude. She wrote a farewell letter to the government: "I did not expect to have to write to you, for I thought by word of mouth and face to face to say these things to you and to rejoice with you at the holy peace for which I have labored so long and with all my strength. Now it seems that the demon has set hearts so unjustly against me that I must fear still more injustice. I have gone away consoled, for that is accomplished which I set before my heart when I entered this city: never to leave it until I saw you reconciled with your father, even if it should cost me my life. And I have gone away with grief and sorrow for the city's bitterness."

When the new masters of the Signoría read her words, she had left, never to return.

Chapter Thirty-Three

APPROACHING SIENA, Catherine was filled with a strange premonition of impending disaster. She had felt it before, many years ago, also on her way back from Florence, and then found the plague raging in Siena. It was exactly the same feeling, but stronger, as if the plague had come down not only on Siena but on all the world. Yet no cart laden with bloated corpses came rattling out of the gate, the streets were full of merry life, all was well with her loved ones, and Alessia said smiling: "Thank God, for once you were wrong, *mamma.*"

But Catherine's eyes were fastened on a letter, waiting for her on a table. A letter from Rome. From Fra Raymond. She opened it and read. It was the longest letter he had ever written her, and the things it spoke of were such that she was set to swaying to and fro, moaning as if she were racked with pain beyond endurance. He had kept these things from her deliberately. She had a task to fulfill in Florence, and it would have been senseless to put more burdens on her mind and soul. Now he could no longer remain silent. She must know what had happened, and she must know it as it really was, not as rumors and hearsay would have it.

The Florentines were not the only ones who could behave like madmen. The Romans could too. Poor, gentle Gregory XI had not yet died when the Banderesi, municipal high officials of Rome, practically forced their entry into the room where he lay. They wanted to make quite certain that his illness was indeed fatal and a papal election therefore imminent. Satisfied that it was so, they then proceeded to spread the word among the Roman population that only a Roman was acceptable as the next pope. This was acclaimed enthusiastically. Excitement mounted. When, eleven days after Gregory's death, the conclave assembled, huge crowds on Saint Peter's square shouted in chorus, *"Romano lo volemo!"* That same night the mob broke into the Vatican cellars and looted them.

The cardinals agreed, thirteen votes to three, to elect Bartolomeo Prignano, Archbishop of Bari, a Neapolitan by birth. But with the mob howling outside for a Roman and only a Roman, they were afraid for their lives. So they dressed up poor Cardinal Tebaldeschi, who was born in Rome, in papal vestments, the old man protesting in vain—and presented him to the people, who shouted acclaim and dispersed. Whereupon the cardinals left Rome in a hurry. The next day the city was informed of the true outcome of the conclave, but as the chosen man was at least an Italian and not a Frenchman, the people did not object and some even laughed at the way they had been tricked.

Ten days later, on Easter Day, the new Pope, Urban VI, was solemnly crowned in Saint Peter's.

Soon the cardinals became aware that they had chosen a hard taskmaster for themselves and, above all, a man of fiery, almost ungovernable temperament. They began first to fret, then to intrigue. Letters were sent to the French cardinals who had remained in Avignon. The strongest personality among them, Cardinal Jean la Grange, came to Italy. The intrigue thickened and became a conspiracy. The heat of the summer provided a welcome excuse for leaving Rome, and no fewer than thirteen cardinals went to Anagni. Only four stayed with Urban VI, who preferred Tivoli, all of them Italians: Old Tebaldeschi, Orsini, Brossano, and Corsini.

At long last Pope Urban sensed that something was brewing. He promptly did the worst thing he could do: he sent three of his cardinals to Anagni to reason with their French colleagues, keeping only Tebaldeschi with him. The three Italians did not return. And in August, the French cardinals sent the Pope a letter, addressing him as "Bishop of Bari" and declaring that he had been elected only under duress and therefore invalidly. On August the ninth they excommunicated him as an "unlawful" pope. But by then they had secured the help and protection of the powerful Count of Fondi, whose feelings Urban had ruffled in one of his rages, and they began to hire mercenaries by the thousand.

Any day now, Fra Raymond wrote, the French cardinals would assemble in conclave and elect another pope. "Do you remember that day in Pisa, *mamma,* when you told us that all that had happened so far was like milk and honey in comparison to things that would happen: that the clergy itself would rebel and the Church be divided? I fear the time has come when your prophecy will be proved true. Any moment now it may happen. . . . "

But neither Catherine nor Fra Raymond could foresee how bad it would be. On the eighteenth of September Urban VI at last created twenty-three new cardinals. Six others refused to accept. It was too late. On September the twentieth the cardinals in Anagni went into conclave and elected, of all people, Cardinal Robert of Geneva, the butcher of Cesena. He was, after all, a relative of the King of France. And he intended to reside in Avignon. . . .

With unconscious irony he chose the name of Clement VII, and he was crowned in the Cathedral of Fondi.

The election of an antipope divided all Europe into two camps. To many people it seemed that the Church was doomed.

Catherine threw herself into the fight at once. She wrote fierce letters of encouragement to Urban VI. She entreated—in vain—Cardinal Pedro de Luna, the Spaniard, to remain faithful to the Pope for whom he had given his vote at the Roman conclave. Then the report came that even the three Italian cardinals, Orsini, Brossano, and Corsini, had refused to come to Urban's aid and preferred to stay "neutral". That was too much for her, and a letter like a thunderbolt went out to these princes of the Church.

"What proves to me that you are ungrateful, crude, and mercenary? The way in which you and the others persecute the Church at the very moment when you should be shielding her from blows. You know well the truth that Urban VI is the valid Pope, the Sovereign Pontiff, chosen in orderly election and not influenced by fear, elected by divine inspiration rather than by your human cunning. So you have proclaimed to us yourselves, and it is the truth. Now you have turned your backs on him like cowardly and miserable knights, afraid of your own shadow. What is the cause of it? Self-love which poisons the world! That is what has made you, who should be pillars, weaker than straw. . . . Instead of being angels in human form, you have taken on the office of demons. This is not the blindness of ignorance. No: you know the truth; it was you who announced it to us, not we to you. Oh, what madmen you are! You give us the truth and taste a lie yourselves. Now you want to deny this truth and make us believe the opposite, saying that you elected Pope Urban out of fear. It is not so; whoever says so is a liar. (I am speaking to you without reverence, for you have deprived yourselves of reverence.) It is quite clear to anyone who really wants to know that the one whom you pretended to elect out of fear was Cardinal Tebaldeschi! You may say to me: Why do you not believe us? We who elected him know the truth better than you do. But I answer you that you yourselves have shown me how you depart from truth. When I turn to your past lives, I do not find them so good and holy as to convince me that you would retract a lie for your conscience's sake. How do I know that the Lord Bartolomeo, Archbishop of Bari, was elected canonically and is today Pope Urban VI in very truth? The solemnity of his coronation has proved this to me. And I know it was carried out in good faith by the homage you paid him and the favors you begged and received from him and which you made full use of. You cannot deny this truth except by lying!

"Fools that you are, worthy of death a thousand times over! You are so blind that you do not even see your own shame. If what you say is true (as true as it really is false), did you not lie then when you announced Urban VI as the lawful Pope? Did you not commit simony when you asked for and received favors from one whose authority you deny? Yes, indeed. But the truth is that you could not endure to be corrected . . . a sharp word of reprimand made you lift up your heads in rebellion. . . . Your crime is even greater than that of the foreign cardinals, for the Holy Father is an Italian, and you are Italians too . . . so you were not even urged by patriotism like those from beyond the Alps. Therefore I see no other reason for your action than self-love."

She wrote to Joanna of Naples. She wrote to the Count of Fondi. And once more she wrote to the lawful Pope, "I wish for no more words; I want to find myself on the battlefield, enduring pain and fighting beside you for the truth unto death, for the glory and praise of the Name of God, and for the reforming of Holy Church. . . . I have heard that those demons in human form have elected an anti-Christ against you. Now, forward, most Holy Father! Go into this battle without fear. I and all those whom God gave me to cherish with special love and to care for their salvation are ready to give our lives for the truth; we are ready to obey Your Holiness and endure unto death. . . . I shall never rest in peace until I am in your presence . . . because I wish, unworthy as I am, to shed my blood and give my life and distill the very marrow of my bones for Holy Church. . . . Tell me your will that I may obey in everything until God shall send me the grace to die."

Her spirit was flowing over; all the strength that was left in her demanded action. She knew she must go to Rome. Perhaps she knew also that she would never leave it alive. In any case, like any knight soon to depart for the battlefield, she wanted to set her house in order. There was time for that, for she was not going to Rome until the Pope asked her to. She could not. The government of Siena was watching her with more than a hint of suspiciousness. After all, she had been a political emissary to Florence. She was linked up in some way with the Salimbeni family. Perhaps she was using the cloak of sanctity to shield and cover all kinds of political machinations. Was she a saint at all? Many people doubted it now. Did not Christ say, "From their fruit ye shall know them"? What fruit had her endless, her feverish activities brought forth, but strife and discord and catastrophe? If she had never persuaded Gregory XI to return to Rome, there would not have been this terrible schism. Better, a thousand times better, a pope in Avignon than two popes warring against each other and dividing the loyalties of all Christendom. And what about her famous crusade against the infidels? She had never generated unity. All she produced was division, and was not division the typical work of Satan? At best, the woman was a failure, a hysterical female babbling about visions and fasting herself to death—unless, of course, she was secretly having good, filling meals at night when no one was around to watch! But perhaps she really was what she had so often been suspected of being—a witch, a spawn of the devil, sent to play merry hell with popes, cardinals, and people, and all under the mask of sanctity. Surely it was clear now that her touch meant destruction, that war came whenever she preached peace, that every counsel of hers led to disaster.

"Do not listen to them, *mamma*", Stefano Maconi said with burning anger. "They are the kind of people who wagged their heads and spoke of failure when our Lord was hanging on the Cross."

He spoke for all her loved ones. None of them doubted her. They had seen and experienced too much in all the years with her. But she suffered, and she felt that her hands were tied until the Pope and the Pope himself asked her to come to him.

She set her house in order. First she settled the affairs of the convent of Belcaro, for which she was responsible. Then, in the course of five days and five nights, she wrote her last will and testament. It was a book, a book the size of a missal, so long she must dictate it to three men. Stefano Maconi, Barduccio Canigiani, and Neri di Landoccio wrote it down in rotation. She gave it to them, now on her knees, now wandering about her cell, now standing stiffly upright like a statue, and all the time in a trance.

The book was a dialogue between God and a human soul. And it had the God-made order and beauty so baffling to man in his discoveries, the order and beauty of a crystal or of a solar system. The imagery was bold in the extreme. Thus God held the world as a whole in his hand, saying, "I will that thou shalt know that none can be taken from me. Whether they are under my justice or under my mercy, they are all mine. . . . And because they are all gone out from me I love them unutterably, and for my servant's sake I will have mercy upon them. . . . "

Her love, mounting to heights known to few human beings, made her grieve and rejoice at the same time, and still it soared up and up, until she could see the bridge that stretched from earth to high heaven and it was the only bridge that was and all must ascend it. And the bridge was alive and was a man, the God-Man.

The way was slow and went in many stages, and at every stage some men were lost. Not all of them knew that it was a living bridge, luminous and clear as it was, and not all of them knew that the waters flowing under it were the waters of death. And she dived deeply into the souls of those ascending, describing their state, from the grosser sins to the subtle and treacherous ones of those who thought of themselves as good, yet retained self-love, ready to serve God only as long as it gave them a personal joy and withdrawing at once when it did not; and that last sin of them all, when a man refused to look at his neighbor's ills because it might disturb his serenity and peace of mind. . . .

Again and again she intoned the great *leitmotif* of Love and self-love, the first pearl of wisdom the Lord had taught her when she was little more than a child and a recluse in her parents' house. Of discretion she spoke and of prayer, of the Providence of God and of tears, of obedience and of the Resurrection. Ultimately, the whole book was one great promise of Divine Mercy; for all, through the charity of God's Providence; for the Church, when priests repented and lived as they should live; for the world to which God gave Christ, the bridge, and for herself, too, if she persevered in her struggle. The very end of the book was praise and thanksgiving in the language of love: "O eternal Father, O fire and abyss of Love, O eternal Beauty, eternal Wisdom, eternal Goodness, O Hope, O Refuge of sinners, O immeasurable generosity, O eternal infinite Good, O foolishness of Love! Do you then need your creature?

Indeed, it would seem as if you could not live without it! You, Life itself, from whom everything else has life . . . why are you so foolish? Because you are in love with your creature. . . . You are as one drunk with the desire for its salvation. It flees you . . . and you go seeking it. . . . "

Five days and five nights, and the book was finished.

The answer came from Rome in the very form she had requested: a command to come.

She set out at once. With her went Fra Bartolomeo de' Domenici and Master Tantucci, Neri di Landoccio and his friend Gabriele Piccolomini, Barduccio Canigiani, and her faithful Mantellate, Alessia Saracini, Francesca Gori, Lisa Colombini, and Giovanna di Capo. Mona Lapa and Stefano Maconi, who had to look after his ailing mother, would follow later.

She did not look back to see the Mangia tower disappear behind the hills. She rode on, a crusader and a leader of crusaders, though not against the infidels but in that most terrible contingency—civil war. She arrived on the twenty-eighth of November and was at once summoned to an audience.

Pope Urban VI received her in the midst of all the cardinals in Rome—only those he had created himself.

This time there was no need for an interpreter. Her address was short. She had come to give battle to the enemies of the Church. She would fight wherever the Holy Father would want her to fight.

The dark-eyed, sturdy man on the throne looked around. "This little woman puts us all to shame", he said. "She is calm and fearless where we are afraid." He looked back at her, and the fire that was in her sparked his own. "What should the Vicar of Christ fear?" he said aloud. "Even if the whole world were against him . . . Christ Omnipotent is stronger than the world. He will never forsake his Church."

Chapter Thirty-Four

YET CHRIST SEEMED to have forsaken his Church. With papal authority divided, two bishops would claim the same see, two priests the same parish, and before the horrified eyes of the faithful the great and solid ship of Saint Peter ran aground, tossed about by gales of such force that it seemed to be doomed. In the countries of Europe the rulers in their palaces and castles sat weighing chances very carefully: not whether Urban VI or Clement VII was the real pope but on whose side they were likely to find the greater advantage for themselves. That was the real problem not only for the great crowned monarchs on the thrones of England and France, of Aragon and Castile, of Hungary and Poland, but for every duke and prince, for every city-state, and ultimately for every man.

The ruler first and foremost on Pope Urban's mind was, naturally enough for a Neapolitan, Queen Joanna of Naples. But he had done everything to drive her into the enemy's camp. At a state dinner he had insulted her husband, Otto of Brunswick, and her Chancellor Spinelli. For good measure, he had insulted her personally as well by referring in drastic terms to her way of life in the hearing of many people, including her ambassador.

Now he wanted to win her back, and Catherine was to go to Naples for that purpose, together with Princess Karin of Sweden, the daughter of the saintly Birgitta. But the Princess refused point blank. She had been at the Queen's court six years ago, with her mother and her brother Charles, when they were on their way to the Holy Land. Charles was married, and so was the Queen. But, true to her nature, the Queen had developed a wild passion for the handsome, blond Swede, and although she was in her fifties, her charms were still potent. The two even wanted to go through some kind of marriage ceremony. The Swedish princesses prayed for hours on end for God's intervention. It came like a thunderbolt. Charles fell ill and died. The very thought of returning to that horrible Queen and her equally horrible court was too much for Karin. Besides, the Queen was quite capable of avenging her dead lover on his pious sister.

Catherine could not understand that way of thinking. To her the journey to Naples was simply part of the war she was waging. There was always danger in war; as for personal memories, how could they possibly count for anything, when the cause of the Church was at stake? She was indignant when Fra Raymond too opposed the plan, just as he had opposed her when she wanted to visit Sir John Hawkwood at the gates of Pisa. Fra Raymond's argument was practically the same, too: What if the vindictive Queen had Catherine and the princess subjected to indignities worse than any cruelty? She was quite capable of it.

The Pope quickly agreed with Fra Raymond, and the journey was cancelled. He would not send her to France either. Instead he sent . . . Fra Raymond.

It was a bitter blow for Catherine. He was the only one who really understood her, the greatest and most loved of all her friends. She had only just found him again. Now he was whisked away.

That day she began to understand that God deliberately took away from her not only all earthly ties, however pure and innocent, but also all spiritual help she might have received from other human beings. He wanted her to fight on her own, without comfort or consolation. She knew that Fra Raymond hated going, and she knew with merciless certainty that in this life they would never meet again.

They had a last long talk. She gave him a number of letters she had written, to the King of France, to the Duke of Anjou, and to a number of French prelates and dignitaries. She walked with him to the port, watched him embark on the galley, and waited until the ship began to move. Then she knelt down, crossed herself, and wept.

There was no human being dearer to her in the world. But when she heard that he had not dared to cross the French frontier, having been warned that the Clementists had laid a trap for him at Ventimiglia, and that he had gone back to Genoa, she was as angry with him as any general with a commander who refuses to take a necessary risk. The fact that many "Urbanist" priests had been arrested, thrown into dungeons, and some of them even killed did nothing to soften her anger. "You were not yet worthy to go into battle", she wrote him. "You turned back like a boy and were glad and willing to escape. Oh, bad little Father, how happy your soul—and mine—would have been if with your blood you could have fixed a stone in the wall of the Church. . . . "

But Fra Raymond stayed in Genoa, and the Pope found work for him there.

Like a general, Catherine was now trying to concentrate her forces. She summoned all the holy men she knew to Rome to form a spiritual wall of fire around the Pope's throne. Letters like marching orders went to William Flete, to Antonio of Nice, to Fra Giovanni delle Celle in Vallombroso, to the Prior of Gorgona near Pisa, and many others. Few obeyed her call. William Flete, for one, did not. No one, not even his much loved and admired friend Catherine, could get him away from his wood at Lecceto. "Cut through your bonds; do not untie them", she wrote to him. "The martyrs of Rome are calling you." He wrote back declining. He could pray so much better in Lecceto. The tumult of Rome would only disturb him. Catherine snorted. "It seems", she replied, "that God can only be found in the woods and not in other places, where he is perhaps needed more. Besides, there are woods here too." But she could get nowhere with him. "He is too simpleminded", she declared with a shrug. For once she was wrong. The B.A. of Cambridge was a very much bigger man than she ever knew, although of a kind quite alien to her own nature. She understood nothing of the Englishman's peculiar delight in being taken for stupid.

Fra Antonio at first declined too, then changed his mind and came, and so did many others. The household in the Via dell Papa increased to thirty and even forty people, and Alessia Saracini, in charge of it, had difficulty in feeding them all. The fellowship would not accept money from the Pope for that purpose. All food must be acquired by begging.

Rome was in danger, from both within and without. The Castel Sant'Angelo was in the hands of French soldiers, installed there under Gregory XI and commanded by an excellent officer, de Rostaing. The Castel was as good as impregnable and far too close to the Vatican for safety. Urban VI had to retire to the other bank of the Tiber and resided in Santa Maria in Trastevere. From there he launched his bull of excommunication against Cardinal Robert of Geneva and his principal supporters, and from there he tried to enlist military help to bolster up the weak papal forces. It was high time to do so . . . the forces of the antipope were on the march.

That was when Catherine met Alberigo da Barbiano. The young noble, tall, slender, with the eyes of a bird of prey, was a military leader in the Pope's service. He came to see her, as so many men did, out of curiosity. She spoke to him for half an hour. "By God," he said, awestruck, "you are a much better soldier than I am." He left, his head awhirl with the ideas she had implanted, and at once got in touch with a number of friends. They began to form a new corps. Mercenaries, for they were to be paid well, but Italians, not foreigners, and men tried in war under all kinds of flags. Da Barbiano enlisted no more than fifteen the first day, another twenty-five the next, a hundred and ten in a week, and a little over four hundred two weeks later. That was the new corps, and he called it by the name Catherine suggested, the Company of Saint George, "for they are called to kill dragons". Then da Barbiano marched them slowly past Catherine's house in the Via dell Papa. They all knew who she was, and none of them would forget that tiny figure with the great, luminous eyes, standing in the doorway, her right hand raised to bless them. They were straining for battle, as if Catherine had infused her own soul into every one of them.

Their first task was to reinforce the papal troops besieging the Castel Sant'Angelo. The defenders were running short of food, and the vigorous attacks of the newly founded Company of Saint George proved too much for them. For more than seven months they had been expecting help from the outside. Now they despaired, and, after some negotiations in which Catherine herself took part, they capitulated. Catherine watched the stream of prisoners emerging, flanked by the men of the Company of Saint George. One of da Barbiano's soldiers raised his sword to her and called her "our little Lady of Victory", and the others broke into cheering.

The very next day reports came that the antipope's troops were marching on Rome. "Just when the siege is over", Alberigo da Barbiano exclaimed. "That shows who it is whom heaven favors."

The Company of Saint George left Rome secretly at night and then apparently disappeared entirely.

The regular papal troops left the city one day later. At Marino, in the Alban hills, about thirteen miles from Rome, they met the Breton mercenaries under their three leaders Montjoie and Silvestre Budes and Bernard della Salle. At the decisive moment the Company of Saint George came pouring down from its hiding place in the hills, crashed into the flank of the Bretons, and broke through. Twenty-five picked men went after each of the three enemy leaders and managed to take them prisoners. The surviving Bretons fled as fast as they could and . . . ran into the one and only cavalry detachment of the Company of Saint George, only sixty men in all, but fresh and full of fight. The Bretons who escaped fled on singly or in small groups.

The news of the victory of Marino spread like wildfire. The "little Lady of Victory" was the heroine of Rome. The Banderesi came to congratulate her as if she had led the troops herself . . . as in a way she had. Alberigo da Barbiano bent his knee before her.

She spoke to the Company. She scolded the Banderesi for not doing enough for the wounded. And she wrote at once to the Queen of Naples, King Louis of Hungary and Poland, and the King of France.

Now that the Castel Sant'Angelo was no longer in enemy hands and the enemy beaten in battle, Pope Urban could return to the Vatican, and he did so in a solemn procession of thanksgiving, marching barefoot all the way from Santa Maria in Trastevere to Saint Peter's.

The whole of Italy was astir with the news of this first triumph of Italian arms against foreign mercenaries. And such was the impression it made on the antipope that he left hurriedly, first for Gaeta and then for . . . Naples. Queen Joanna received him with all the honors due to the Pope. Not so her subjects. The Neapolitans promptly rioted, and the Queen narrowly escaped with her life. Clement VII was forced to leave again in a hurry. While all around him the Italian communes submitted to Urban VI, he hastily boarded a ship and sailed for France. He rode in state into Avignon, wearing a tiara one of the French archbishops had carried away from Rome. When the news arrived at the Royal court, the King of France said triumphantly, "Now I am Pope!"

England decided for Urban. And Brother William Flete, still in his oakwoods at Lecceto, heard about it and permitted himself a grin of satisfaction. Sister Catherine was quite right: there were woods in Rome or near Rome too. But there were also many Clementine agents there, and his letters to certain prelates and other dignitaries in England might have been intercepted. It so happened that these men had a great deal of confidence in the intellectual, moral, and political discernment of their humble friend and servant William Flete, and at least some of them had the ear of good King Richard II and knew exactly what to whisper into it. It was helpful, of course, that England's enemy, France, was pro-Clement. But that alone would not have been a decisive factor, not for King Richard. And thus, by disobeying Catherine, one had been able to keep England on the right side. It would be absurd to tell her that, of course. She did not understand Englishmen, being a foreigner. He would tell her in heaven, one day, or maybe she would know without being told, things in heaven being what they were, more likely than not. Here on earth, however, she would have to go on thinking that William Flete, B.A. of Cambridge, was a fool, a lazy fool, far too deeply in love with his oak trees. And thus for once William Flete, B.A. of Cambridge, knew Sister Catherine of Siena better than Sister Catherine knew William Flete; it might well be that he knew her better than did almost anyone else. Few people realized, in his opinion, what she was and that the Pope should regard it as an honor to be among her sons. For she was carrying the sins of the Church like a gentle mule—and as obstinately, too. And the Holy Spirit was truly in her. After which trend of thought William Flete returned to a meditation about a passage in Saint Paul's Letter to the Galatians.

King Louis the Great of Hungary and Poland also recognized Urban and was ready to come to his help. His Queen wrote charmingly to Catherine, calling her her most special friend. "Catherine's work again", Urban VI exclaimed when he heard the news. "She is our good angel on earth." He was never brusque to her as he was to everybody else when in a temper. But she also treated him quite differently from the way she used to treat Gregory XI. She begged him more than once to control his anger better, but on the whole she was very cautious with him. She seemed to know exactly how much truth he could bear.

Urban had a genius for making enemies. Old Cardinal Tebaldeschi died, and so, soon afterward, did Cardinal Orsini. But Brossano and Corsini went over to Clement. If Gregory XI was too weak and indecisive to reform the clergy, Urban was too hasty and impulsive. He wanted his prelates to live like monks and have no more than a single dish for a meal. Living very austerely himself, he judged easygoing priests with a severity bordering on cruelty.

Barduccio Canigiani told Catherine that he had heard of a conspiracy in Rome against the Pope and that his very life might be in danger.

She gave a deep sigh. "Write, my Son. To the Most Holy Father, Urban VI. . . ."

The young man obeyed. Once more she entreated the irascible man to be more gentle. "You know the nature of your Roman children, that they are led and bound more by gentleness than by force or by harsh words. . . . You know too how necessary it is for you and for Holy Church to keep these people in obedience to Your Holiness. . . . " It was not a long letter, but Barduccio saw that it was not an easy one for her. She made pauses. She gasped a few times, as if she were in physical pain. Suddenly she faltered, gave a moan, and slid to the floor.

Barduccio shouted for help, and everybody came running. A wail of anguish and horror went up. They thought she was dead, but she recovered very quickly. A few hours after the attack she was up but complained that she could feel evil all around her and that a cloud of demons was assembling over the city.

Chapter Thirty-Five

THE DEMONS STRUCK. A mob of thousands pressed through the streets toward the Vatican. They passed the Via dell Papa, and Catherine knew at once what was going on. She ran after them, half dead and in an agony of pain. A few hundred men forced the entrance of the Vatican and overwhelmed the guards.

The Pope had seen them gain entrance. Whatever his faults, he never lacked courage. The men crashing into the audience room found him sitting on his throne in full regalia, the tiara on his head and immobile as a statue. The half dozen clerics with him were trembling all over. He stared at the ruffians. "Whom do you seek?" he asked. The words of Christ when the temple guards came to arrest him in the garden of Gethsemane were spoken by a man convinced in his heart of hearts that he was Christ's representative on earth and that by insulting him these men were insulting Christ himself. The look of outraged majesty, of almost superhuman anger, proved too much for the rabble. They pressed back, turned, and fled.

Outside on the Piazza Catherine was speaking to the crowd, commanding them to disperse. Once more she seemed to have a chance of being martyred, and once more she had to see that such a death was not permitted to her. The mob saw a little wisp of a woman, a white phantom, as nearly disembodied as a human being could be and still be alive. She seemed to be kept up only by her habit. To go against this apparition might be sacrilege. The mob dispersed.

She was very ill. On the day of her attack, the thirtieth of January, 1380, she had seen her own body as if she were standing outside of it, unable to take possession of it again, but it was two weeks before she could get herself to tell about the experience in a letter to Fra Raymond, still in Genoa. Racked with pain, she still dragged herself to Saint Peter's every day to pray, as thin and frail as a white wafer to be transubstantiated into the Lord's body.

Underneath the portico of the vast church was a mosaic by Giotto, showing the *Navicella*, the bark of Saint Peter, shaken by storm, with the apostles crouching in fear and Christ walking toward them on the waves. Before that mosaic she kneeled for hours, praying that once again he would come to the help of his Church. Never before had she known such agony of body and soul. She had fought and fought ... and what had she brought about? The Pope was in Rome, yes, but an antipope was lording it on his throne in Avignon, and all Christendom was divided. Had it all been a mistake, an error, all her travelling about and persuading and threatening, all her letters? Should she have remained in her cell in silent and solitary prayer like any other Mantellata? Was God showing her that? She knew how many people thought of her as a woman who insisted on imposing her own will on others, from beggar to pope, and if she had done so for her own will's sake, and not for the sake of the Will of God, then indeed her entire life was one long chain of errors and sins. How often had she offered herself for the sins of others, for the sins of the whole Church! She, who could so shrewdly analyze the human soul and its innermost motives, had she overlooked the most colossal spectre of presumption in her own soul? And it seemed to her that Christ on the waves took up the *Navicella* with all the men and put it all on her shoulders, and she crumbled up under the weight and fell helpless on the floor.

They carried her home, Master Tanucci and Barduccio Canigiani. She was not a heavy burden. ...

Stefano Maconi paid a visit to the Misericordia hospital to chat with Ser Matteo Cenni, still in charge of it. He visited the chapel, thinking of his *mamma* and the memories this little

room would invoke in her. She had told him about the place
more than once. The time of the plague. . . . He could think no
further. He knew, suddenly, that something was wrong, very
wrong with her. He raced home, gave a few hasty instructions,
had his best horse saddled, and rode off. He was an excellent
rider. All through the night he sped on in the direction of
Rome.

He arrived, entered her room, and stared, transfixed, at a
woman so changed that he hardly recognized her. Her skin
had become as brown as bronze and hardly covered the bare
bones of her face. The mouth was a mere slit. But she opened
her eyes and recognized him, and something like the ghost of a
smile flickered across her wasted face.

She was clearly dying, and a whole world was dying with
her. The faithful Mantellate were there, so shaken that they
were beyond tears. Master Tantucci was there and the Prior of
Sant'Antimo, and Mona Lapa, who had arrived a week earlier.
But so many of her friends were missing: Fra Raymond first
and foremost; Fra Bartolomeo de'Domenici, who had had to
go back to Siena on the order of his Provincial; Fra Tommaso
della Fonte and Tommaso Caffarini. Neri, too, was away.
Catherine had sent him to Naples.

When awake and conscious, she was in terrible pain and yet
quite content and at peace. She had passed across the abyss into
knowledge of things hidden. And she knew now that all evil
would be conquered not by suffering but by virtue of Divine
Love.

Mona Lapa was sitting beside her bed of boards just as she
had done eighteen years ago, when Catherine had chicken
pox. It was scarcely believable that she had been little more
than a child, then. Mona Lapa, of course, was an old, old
woman now, but seeing mother and daughter together it was
difficult to say who looked older than the other. Yet Catherine
had only just passed her thirty-third birthday.

She asked for her mother's blessing. Mona Lapa gave it to
her with the dignity of a great lady and then knelt at the
bedside, shaking with grief.

On Sunday, the twenty-ninth of April, shortly before dawn, Alessia and Mona Lapa saw that the end was near. Catherine's breathing was becoming stertorous. Everyone in the house assembled. Master Tantucci pronounced over her the plenary indulgence the Pope had granted her for the hour of death. Catherine promptly asked that the pronouncement should be repeated, for two popes had granted that indulgence to her, and once more her will prevailed.

The Prior of Sant'Antimo anointed her.

Suddenly she showed signs of an inner struggle, raising her arms, as if to ward off blows. "Lord have mercy upon me, a sinner", she prayed, gasping for breath. A few minutes later she said quite firmly, "No, never my own glory, but the Glory of God." Then her expression became calm and serene again.

"Stefano . . ."

"Mamma . . . oh, mamma . . ."

"I want you to join the Carthusian Order, Stefano."

"I will join it, mamma."

"Give Neri my love . . . give my love . . . to all . . . my children." Her voice sank to a murmur, and from then on only God could hear her. Outside, the sun was rising.

At nine o'clock in the morning her life flame flickered and went out. Bending over her body Master Tantucci saw a strange thing. On her hands and feet dark marks appeared, as if they had been wounded, as if they had been pierced. The stigmata she had received in Pisa, never visible during her life, became visible now. The others also saw them. No one said anything. They only looked at one another. Then they closed all the windows and locked all the doors to be alone with their beloved saint.

The next day, the whole of Rome went into mourning.

Brother William Flete left his wood at Lecceto and went to Siena to preach the funeral sermon for Siena's greatest daughter at Saint Dominic's. "It is with hymns of joy, not with tears, that we should celebrate the death of Catherine", he began. Then he broke down and cried. After some time he continued, "Simon of Cyrene carried the Cross of our Lord for a little while; Catherine of Siena tried to carry it throughout her whole life...."

Epilogue

ALESSIA SARACINI DIED only a few months after Catherine.
Barduccio Canigiani too died soon afterward from consumption. Fra Raymond became Master General of the Dominican Order. It was he who wrote the first Life of Saint Catherine of Siena. Neri di Landoccio became a hermit, and his volatile friend Francesco Malavolti—after several relapses—a monk. Stefano Maconi became a Carthusian and a prior of that order. Pope Urban VI kept his throne. But he died, nine years later, friendless and mourned by no one.

The schism continued on until the Council of Konstanz ended it, thirty-five years after Catherine's death. And the bark of Saint Peter sailed on to face more storms.

But the papacy never left Rome again.